Praise

"Susan Salluce's *Out of Breath* is an extraordinary gift to bereaved parents and is an incredible resource for bereavement counselors. Readers are brought into the lives of characters touched by the sudden death of a child. Susan is a rare and talented counselor who breathes life into the story and shows how everyone grieves in their own way. *Out of Breath* reveals Salluce's considerable talent as a story teller. Readers, touched by their own loss, will take healing breaths as they turn each page. Susan Salluce's writing style is personal and informal, which makes it easy for those grieving to continue reading and find solace in the story. As a bereavement specialist, it is encouraging to see a book that addresses changed relationships, continuing the bonds, and how bereavement can become a time of personal growth where young and old alike find meaning in their loss."

—Barbara Rubel, MA, BCETS, CBS, *Keynote Speaker and Author,* But I Didn't Say Goodbye: Helping Children and Families After a Suicide *and* Death, Dying, and Bereavement: Providing Compassion During a Time of Need
www.griefworkcenter.com

"Susan Salluce's book, *Out of Breath*, is excellent, full of meticulous details, well presented characters, and swift action. From the breaking up of a marriage, to the loss of speech of one of the children, to wrongful incriminations for drug use, these plot twists will keep readers breathless."

—Phyllis Matson, author of *War Orphan in San Francisco*

"Susan Salluce, is a gifted story teller. In *Out of Breath*, she has created a compelling narrative, which is heartbreaking to read, but difficult to put down. This is an engaging story that focuses on the themes of loss, grief, and healing. Anyone who has experienced the death of a loved one can relate to the characters and the struggles they face in the wake of tragedy. A must-read for anyone who has experienced loss, it is the perfect resource for counselors and other mental health professionals to provide to their clients, as a comforting example of both the grieving and healing process."

—*Kelly Perry, Life Smarts Publishing*

"Susan Salluce writes with passion and sensitivity about issues of loss..."

—*Edward Abramson, Ph.D., author of* It's NOT just Baby Fat: 10 Steps to Help Your Child to A Healthy Weight, *Professor Emeritus at California State University, author of four previous books including* Baby Intelligence *and* Emotional Eating

"I highly recommend Susan Salluce's *Out of Breath*. It is a moving account of loss, bereavement, addiction, and redemption woven into a colorful description of the Santa Cruz surfing culture. This emotional tale will have special meaning to anyone who has experienced the loss of a loved one."

—*John Mel, Owner Freeline Design Surf Shop*

OUT OF BREATH

by
SUSAN SALLUCE

Hidden Beach Publishing

Hidden Beach Publishing

Out of Breath, Copyright © 2011 by Susan Salluce. All rights reserved. Unless otherwise noted, no part of this publication may be reproduced, stored in a retrieval system, or transmitted in any form or by any means without the consent of the author, Susan Salluce.

Cover photo by iStock, photographer Jeff Goulden

Copyright (c) 1993, by Portia Nelson from the book *There's A Hole in My Sidewalk*. Reproduced with kind permission from Beyond Words Publishing, Hillsboro, Oregon.

Distributed in U.S.A. by Hidden Beach Publishing
P.O. Box 791, Shingle Springs, CA 95682
Library of Congress Control Number: 2011941231
ISBN: 978-0-578-09092-4

Out of Breath is a work of fiction. Names, characters, and incidents are either the product of the author's imagination or are used fictitiously and any resemblance to real persons, living or dead, is completely coincidental. Although real business establishments are cited in this work, the names of employees as well as incidences have been changed.

Please visit my website at: www.sipnsharewithsusan.com
I can be reached at: susansalluce@yahoo.com

Acknowledgements

There are so many people I want to thank that my acknowledgements could be a short story. My apologies ahead of time if I forget anyone.

First and foremost, I want to thank my husband, John, and my children, Kellen and Marina, for supporting my dream to become a writer and believing in me. Thanks for tolerating my moodiness, my tears when those nasty rejection letters arrived, for your hugs, the flowers, and cards, and rejoicing with me when I won contests and celebrating when I decided to "go for it." John, thanks for reading and re-reading, your happy tears, sad tears, and tears that fell as you read my pages, and always, always having faith in me. I'll never forget, after you finished reading my book, you said, "Wow...you're a writer." I love you.

Thank you to the many readers/editors/friends who pointed out errors, glitches (e.g. she's two different ages), and told me things that made them say, "Oh...wow,": Christina (my fabulous writing partner, author of *Arrow of the Mist*, and trusted friend), Juli, Adri, Aimee, Dario, Donna, Barbara, cousin Lisa, Jackie, Jennifer, Karen, Kelly, Manuel, Pastor Kent, Vicky, Lynnee, Marianna (beloved sister-in-law and promoter in Venice, Italy), Dr. Abramson, Sherri, Susan, Wendy, Brian, and Brenda.

I must mention Catherine Underwood, MFT, who at a counseling staff meeting asked, "What would you attempt to do if you knew you could not fail?" To which I answered, "I'd write a book." My life was never the same, Catherine. Thank you!

For their expertise in marijuana drug testing, thank you to Shandon at Valley Toxicology Services, Inc., Sacramento, California. Dr. Laurence Miller, forensic psychologist in Boca Raton, Florida for his knowledge about Fit for Duty Exams and police psychology.

Steve Smith, childhood friend, peace officer, and teacher of criminal justices, you gave breadth and dimension to Greg's character. Mike Leimbach, MFT, high school friend and outstanding human being, thanks for your consultation on youth culture and drug use in surf communities. Captain John Wiegel, Diamond Springs-El Dorado Fire Protection District, my thanks to you for your friendship and crash course (no pun intended) on emergency terminology and cold water drowning. To Scott Underwood, former E.R. physician and cardiology specialist, who was kind enough to repeatedly explain probable heart conditions in layperson's terminology. A huge hug to Barbara Rubel, grief specialist and the closest friend I've never met. Through on-line chats, e-mails, and phone calls, you've taught me about suicide, writing, self-publishing, and believing in myself. One of these days we'll finally meet face-to-face.

In the surfing world, a shout out to John and Peter Mel at Freeline Surf Shop in Capitola, California. John sat down with me one Labor Day morning to explain the "ins and outs" of running a surf shop. Peter gave me the buzz words and locations of the Big Wave Surfing Tournament. I must add a personal touch that my time with you, John, after you read my book as we were tucked beneath rows of wetsuits in your shop, will forever be a sweet memory; thank you for your transparency and encouragement.

When in town, we always bring our guests to Freeline, the true original surf shop of Santa Cruz! To Ed Childers, my former neighbor, die-hard long boarder, and unbeknownst to me until I wrote this book, the builder of Freeline's factory, I thank you for your skillful description of the craft of surfboard making. Dan Gomez, neighbor in Aptos, for your thorough explanation of contemplating the perfect wave and how it can go so terribly wrong, and for giving me the word "tombstoning."

To Basil, Jr. at Upstarts Organic Seedlings in Watsonville, Ca. for his knowledge of winter gardening.

No acknowledgement page would be complete without giving proper credit to my writing community. Once again, thank you Christina Mercer for editing, re-editing, listening, crying, telling me not to give up, and being faithful. Emily Underwood, you were the first to make preliminary edits and you introduced me to Grammar Girl. You pushed me out of my comfort zone. Leslie Cretina, who stayed in my critique group a short time, but should have been paid for her critiques—she's that good. South Bay Writer's Group gave me the East of Eden Conference where I learned about queries, pitching to agents, polishing my manuscript, and the business side of writing. I almost gave up right then; I'm glad I didn't. Jordan Rosenfeld, you taught me more than any class ever could; you are an editor extraordinaire! Any errors in this book are purely my fault. Jordan is author of the writing guides, *Make a Scene*, and, with Rebecca Lawton, *Write Free*. Her work has been published in the *San Francisco Chronicle*, *Publisher's Weekly*, *St. Petersburg Times*, *The Writer*, *Writer's Digest* and more. She freelance edits and teaches through: http://www.facebook.com and www.jordanrosenfeld.net. Thanks to South West Writer's Club for the award for this novel, the opportunity to meet agents, to have the experience of a lifetime in New Mexico; I'll carry those special memories with me forever.

Bob Thomas, www.TheImageArtCompany.com, you made me feel like a super model rather than a middle-aged mom when you took my author photo. Every time I see my photo, I'll smile and remember that lovely morning.

Finally, a special word to the "real" Seths and Alyssas of the world: may your grief be soothed with time and may you find peace and comfort through others sharing their stories.

Out of Breath

Alyssa

Here's what I see: a closet, like a time capsule, holding clothes I'll never wear again. My teacher's wardrobe, blousy and in a bouquet of color, crammed up against the left side of the closet where they've remained untouched for over six years. Nothing, especially a job, would get in the way, I told myself, of being the perfect mother of my two children. What other lies have I told myself to see what I needed to see? Alongside my discarded kindergarten teaching wear is my wedding dress—not the traditional, puffy sleeves, sequins or pearls. Seth and I would have none of that. No, I strove to match his blue Hawaiian shirt with a soft, cotton white sundress and strappy sandals. I rip the dress from its hanger and feel my face flush.

My breath quickens as I sift through my maternity clothes: an oversized flowered overall get-up, cotton leggings, and thick, stretched-out wool sweaters—all of them a reminder of what they covered—you. My legs give way and I land hard on the carpet. I punch the ground as if my tantrum will somehow stomp out the fiery pain in my gut. The whole room haunts me of the life I had only two weeks ago: a framed photo of the four of us together up for a picnic on the redwood trail; a picture of Seth and me, tan, windblown, passionately in love, standing in front of our long boards on a surf trip to Costa Rica.

I call out, just as I did that night, "Where are you Nevaeh? Why, Seth?" My screams go unheard, echoing through the house.

There is nothing here for me. I shake until my teeth chatter. I've got to get out of this house. I'll have Oma pick up something black to drape over me and then I'll tear it to shreds and bury it.

Keep an eye on her. She's a busy one. Why did I trust him again? If I'd only thrown him out after the first relapse, or kept you by my side all night. You'd be here, with me. Right now, with your face pressed up against my breast and I could smell the sweet scent of your sweat. "Nevaeh!" I call out. All I hear is the pounding of my heart as it threatens to blow apart.

I'm startled by the sound of keys jiggling in the front door, but not enough to actually move.

"Alyssa, it's just Oma. Daisy's staying at Carolyn's for the evening. Thought it'd do her some good," I hear my grandmother call out in a high-pitched, nervous voice. She's my anchor, but even anchors get ripped up in storms.

"I'm in here," I say in a raspy voice. My throat is sore and parched.

She appears in the doorway, slightly askew, favoring her hip that is starting to give her trouble. It's as though Nevaeh's death has caught up to her all at once and she finally looks all of her seventy-seven years.

"I thought maybe you might need this." She pulls out a fitted, black skirt and long sleeved black blouse—my funeral dress.

"Thanks. I don't have anything," I reply, pointing to the closet. Her eyes look over toward the wedding dress that is crumpled beside me. She cocks her head and purses her lips together.

"Everything is much bleaker at night." I know she's referring to my marriage with Seth, or rather, separation from him.

Out of Breath

"Oma, it's not the night that makes it bleak. I can't see any hope. Nothing. I wish I'd died with her." I grab my knees and pull them tight against my chest. My back muscles ache from night after night of wakefulness.

Oma squats beside me, grunting on the way down, then pulls me into her warm, soft body. As a child, about the only thing that comforted me was the feel of what I called "the lumps" of my grandmother—her oversized bosom and rolls of doughy flesh are like my security blanket. I let her comfort me, wanting to crawl inside her and disappear. "Shh, now don't say such things. God needs you here for our Daisy."

Daisy. Poor Daisy. My five-year-old hasn't spoken a word since the night her little sister drowned. The last sound she made was a shrill scream.

I sob, wipe my face across my sleeve, and come up for air. "Oma, how much can a person take? I look ahead and all I see is a huge string of demands. Counseling appointments to make, court dates, social service visits..." I start to hyperventilate, "...I mean, I can't take it. My baby just died! All I want to do is curl up and—"

Oma cuts me off, "We take it a step at a time," she says, patting my hand. "Tomorrow, we go to the funeral." The sound of that word sends shards of glass through my veins. "We cry, and weep, and do that some more. You and Daisy stay with me as long as you wish. Forever if that's what it takes."

I wasn't asked to leave the home. Seth was. Daisy and I can stay here, but all I can see is my old life mocking my pain. A finger-painted picture of Nevaeh's is magnetized to the refrigerator. Her stuffed animals wait for her and Daisy to set up another tea party in their room. The stain of pink fingernail polish dots the rug in the bathroom. Just three weeks ago, Nevaeh locked herself inside to paint her toes, fingers, and half her hand and foot. She's everywhere and yet she is nowhere.

"I'm going to my daughter's funeral," I say, my voice oddly foreign. "I dreamt of proms and showers and weddings." Oma squeezes me so hard that I feel I could break, but the pressure is soothing, like being swaddled.

Untimely death, parental grief, out of sequence—all of these terms swim in my head from the night at the hospital where a social worker held my hand and handed me pamphlets that would "help me cope." What no one knows is how Nevaeh was mine. I don't just mean mine, as in my daughter and not Seth's; Daisy and she have the same father. But Daisy, she's all Seth, right down to the color of her skin to the flecks of gold in her brown eyes; to her evasive temperament that keeps people at arm's length.

Nevaeh, she's all me. Blonde, blue-eyed, dreamy, like time doesn't exist. Our idea of the perfect day is cuddling, taking a walk down on the sand and letting the waves touch our toes, then more cuddling. I feel her absence like a limb, no, more than that, like half of me is sheared off.

Oma gets up on her knees and holds out a hand as if to assist me. I grin through my tears. "I should be the one helping you up," I say as I take hold of her arms and help her right herself.

She smiles. "Thank you Alyssa. Even in your grief, you are full of light." She always sees the best in me, even at my worst. As a child, I thought when my mother went back to work all day, leaving me at Oma's full-time, often night after night, that this was the worst. As it turned out, I wasn't left at all—it was as though I'd come home. Then I thought the worst was when my mom let me know, via a letter, *a letter*, that she'd fallen in love again and was moving to Germany. I'd had 48 hours to adjust to the idea. It wasn't the worst. I threw myself into my teacher's training, vowing to be just like Oma, the most wonderful kindergarten teacher alive. I thought the worst was waking up in Seth's apartment, still fresh with the smell of our sex, and seeing him get high before the sun came up. It wasn't the worst. I grew numb. The worst is knowing that in growing numb to his behavior, my baby was sacrificed. That's where Oma is wrong—my light went out the night Nevaeh died.

We turn off the lights and lock the door behind us. Now that I've moved the bulk of Daisy's and my clothes over to Oma's, it's as if I'm closing the door to this life. Oma squeezes my hand as if reading my mind. "Gregory called earlier to say he'd be by around 9:30 to take us over to the cemetery for Nevaeh's funeral," Oma says, eyes brimming with tears, as I follow her out to my beat up Toyota beside her old Ford.

Cemetery. Nevaeh. Funeral. How can these words be in the same sentence?

Autobiography in Five Short Chapters
Chapter One

I walk down the street.
There is a deep hole in the sidewalk.
I fall in..I am lost..I am helpless.
It isn't my fault.
It takes forever to find a way out.

—Portia Nelson

Chapter 1
Two Weeks Before

Alyssa

Santa Cruz in the fall—there's nothing better. All summer, a thick blanket of fog huddled overhead, letting through only a few hours of sunlight at a time. Oma says it reminds her of the days when she and my mother lived in West Germany and the winter skies nearly drove them mad. People come in droves to northern California beaches in the summer, but only we locals know that fall begins a stream of sunny days.

I sprinkle a palm full of broccoli seeds in several holes I've dug and push my straw hat back into place. Finally I've gotten organized enough to plant a winter garden. I overturn the dirt clods that litter the yard hoping to transform it into a garden of color and sustenance. A tubful of bulbs—orange and pink tulips, yellow and white daffodils, purple irises—is perched against the fence where my one-and-a-half year old daughter, Nevaeh is content spooning shovels of dirt across her pudgy legs. I'm running close to "D" time—that's what Nevaeh says when I say her older sister is on her way back from kindergarten, 'D-time! D-time.' The bulbs will have to wait until tomorrow morning.

It's our family's fifth year of solely depending on Seth's income. It's rough. As popular as his surf shop is, it still only gives us a meager monthly salary. Most of the profits are pumped right back into the business and the huge expense of living here. I know I should be grateful. Daisy's in a school that teaches mindfulness as well as academics; the weather here allows us to be outside nearly every day; and my grandmother and a handful of friends support us. Paradise, right?

Yet I feel empty and lonely. I wrestle with the deep, familiar ache of Seth's absence. His presence in our family is intermittent at best, and not just from working long hours. My stomach sours recalling how he missed Daisy's first day at West Side Arts Academy. "The waves were incredible and I just lost track of time. Don't be mad, babe," he'd offered, as though his absence was a novelty.

Daisy will be home in just minutes. Time flies by and it looks like I've accomplished nothing all day. Inside, a mountain of dress-up clothes litters the family room. Unstrung wooden beads dot the scuffed kitchen table. Duke, our chocolate lab, continues to lap up bits of homemade Play Doh that are scattered across the kitchen's peeling, yellow linoleum. Looking around at the constant disarray, I wonder, *where am I in all of this?* I love being a mother, but at the end of the day after the girls are tucked in, I ache for more.

I organize my days around Seth's work schedule, Daisy's school hours, and Nevaeh's naps. Seth would barely see the girls at all during the week if I didn't pack up a picnic, and take the three of us down to his shop. In the last three weeks, between squeezing in surf lessons, waiting for equipment to be returned, and catching a few sets himself, he hasn't been home before 8:00; well after the girls are asleep. His high school intern is back in school and Jeff his assistant…well, Jeff is about as dependable as Oma's old Ford Pinto.

Wiping my brow, I push down these nagging thoughts. "Come on baby, let's give you a bath before Sasha drops off Daisy and Fiona," I say, surveying my baby whose blanket and body are covered with dirt. Nevaeh smiles up at me with her teeny white teeth and mop of blonde curls blowing in the breeze. All of the angst about my sense of purpose melts as I bury my nose into Nevaeh's neck, kissing her moist, baby skin. "Oh, Nevaeh, Nevaeh. You are truly the air that I breathe," I whisper as Nevaeh plants a wet kiss on my cheek.

The afternoon is a whirlwind. Daisy and her friend Fiona's boisterous laughter result in Nevaeh being awakened. She screams and is inconsolable. I rock her in the rocking chair by the fireplace, softly singing lullabies, but it's useless. Each time she drifts off, another chorus of giggles or the screech of excited little girls startles Nevaeh out of her sleep once more.

By 4:30, Fiona's been picked up, Nevaeh continues to wail, Daisy is ushering a string of demands for juice and a puppet show, and I'm plastering on Rescue Remedy like lotion. "I want you to play with me, Mommy," Daisy hollers from her bedroom.

I put Nevaeh down on the rocker telling her to sit still for a minute and march into Daisy's room. I feel my face getting hotter with every step I take. "That's it Daisy! I've had it! I might have had time for a story or puppet show right now if you hadn't woken your sister up every five minutes. Now, go sit on your bed."

Daisy's big brown eyes grow even wider and her lip quivers. Even I am startled at the volume of my voice. She races off to her room and slams the door. It just adds to the chorus pouring out of Nevaeh's mouth. Gently, I lift Nevaeh from the rocker and mutter to myself, *I love my screaming baby. Even after hours of crying. I love my screaming baby.* Laying her down on my bed, I summon all of my conscientious teacher training and patience and whisper, "Nevaeh, I need to go talk to Daisy. I hurt her feelings and made her sad. Could you please lie in Mommy's bed and get it all warm for her?"

Nevaeh inhales. Her breath is choppy from so much crying. She nods 'yes', and promptly grabs her filthy, pink blankie, pops her thumb in her mouth, and lets out a big sigh. I want to crawl in bed beside her and sleep the rest of the day. There it is, that special bond we share. I think we know the language of one another's hearts, even though she's just a baby herself. With Daisy, I pray for peaceful moments. She's not a "snuggler" or one to settle by my side with a book and lazily let the hours pass. Seth and I joke that she's his first-born son. When Seth does have a free moment, he's suiting her up in her miniature wet suit and teaching her how to paddle and stand up on small waves.

I know Seth wanted a boy. It was the way he talked about Daisy when she was in the womb: the trades he'd teach her, the way they'd hang out down by the water, go on surf trips. I told him that girls do that, too. I think the thought of a daughter scared him, like she'd be fragile, in need of protection, maybe secretly worrying that someday a guy would treat her like he treated women in the past. Luckily, Daisy came out kicking. Even a tumble onto the concrete hardly fazed her. By two-years-old, she was begging to be with Daddy out in the water.

Gently closing my bedroom door, I hear Daisy crying. It sounds like the mews of an abused alley cat. Guilt. Shame. I knock on the door. "Daisy, can I come in?"

"No! I want to talk to Daddy."

Ouch. I probably deserve that. Then again, if the tables were turned and Seth yelled at her, would she refuse to speak to him? Actually, I can't remember a time when he ever yelled at either of them. Or me. It isn't his way. Walk away and walk out, yes.

I struggle with what to say. "I'm very sorry I yelled, Daisy. When you are ready to open the door, I'd like to give you a hug."

"Go away!" she screams.

After several minutes of lying down on the couch to recollect myself, I hear her footsteps behind me. Her eyes are downcast. She wriggles her way under my arm and lets me hold her. If I could freeze time, I would. Thank you, God. As I bathe in our truce, the back door from the garage swings open. It's Seth. Daisy scrambles out of my arms and leaps into his. Any newfound relaxation drains away.

I listen to their chatter about her day and how Seth saw a pod of dolphins when he taught a lesson this morning. I wander into the kitchen, feeling out of place, and pull out a saucepan to boil some pasta. Each day after Seth arrives home, I anticipate a nibble on my neck or his hands to trace my back, trailing down past my waistline. Lately, a nod of the head is all I'll get before he grabs a beer and heads to our bathroom for a shower.

I peer over my shoulder and watch Seth pull a Heineken from the six-pack in his hand. He sits in my rocker and pulls Daisy onto his lap with one arm. His arms are muscular and brown from day after day of paddling the surf. I miss the feeling of being inside them, and yet, I want more...a soul connection.

"Tell me a story Daddy," Daisy says.

It's a ritual he keeps with Daisy whenever he's home at night. He's a master storyteller, weaving tales that could silence Huck Finn. Often he embellishes stories of his childhood in Santa Cruz, toning down the scandalous parts to make him and his friends look less like hellions and more like saints. I wonder if he's tamed all of his wild hairs or if he's just learned to comb them differently.

"So, there I was, surfing down at the Hook, when all of a sudden, something was pulling on my leash."

"It wasn't a shark, was it?" Daisy asks, nearly bouncing up and down with anticipation.

"I thought it was that horrible sea monster that they found 100 years ago. But after I looked around, I saw this amazing mermaid with long, brown hair, just like yours."

I watch Seth play with Daisy's hair. A smile slowly spreads across her face and her eyes brighten. "Really?"

"Really."

My heart grows warm. I want to be a part. I leave the water to boil and walk back into the family room to listen. I decide to move in closer, feeling forgiving of Seth's shortcomings for the moment.

As I drape my arms behind him, I draw in a deep breath when, wham, it hits me—that scent—damn it, that familiar, home-wrecking, sweet, smoky scent. Not resin, or the smell of kelp. God, it can't be. He promised that we were his top priority. I want to scream as my temples begin to pulsate.

"Seth," I interrupt, "Umm, I need to see you in the garage. Now."

Both Seth and Daisy stare up at me as though I've just told them that garbage is for dinner. "Mommy, he's not done," Daisy whines.

Seth ignores me and continues his mermaid story. No. "Seth, this can't wait." He nudges Daisy off his lap.

"Honey, go on down and play in your room for a minute. Mom and I will be there in a sec." Daisy pads down the hall as though she were just given a prison sentence.

We step out into the garage. Seth runs his hands through his hair. Bits of sand fall to the already gritty floor. "What's so important that it couldn't wait?"

I want to slap him for insulting my intelligence. "Seriously, Seth. Like I'm not going to notice. I can't believe this is happening again. When did you start getting high again?"

Seth glares at me. "You know, it feels like I'm talking to my mother rather than my wife." He turns to go back in the house. "You need to back off," he continues.

Before he can walk back in, I grab the shoulder of his sweatshirt. He turns and shoots me an angry look. "You can't walk away from this. It's too important and I can't do this by myself. I'm alone night after night. What the hell is going on that you won't even…" I struggle to find the words, "…be with me." My eyes pan the garage that is stuffed with the six years of our lives: old clothes, pictures, baby toys. "What's it going to take, Seth, something to happen to me or one of the girls to get you to wake up?"

Seth holds up a hand telling me to stop. "We'll talk about this later, Alyssa. The girls need their dinner and Daisy needs her bath."

I'm fuming. As if he ever thought about what any of us need. It's just a way to get me to shut up. We proceed with the evening—dinner, bath time, and tucks into bed. Nevaeh sleeps through it all. Seth escapes to the garage leaving me alone to sip my tea that promises calm while I wonder who will break the silence first. But then I know that's a ridiculous thought. It's always me. Our whole relationship has been punctuated by moments of silence and great passion.

I think back to the time we moved in together. We'd only known one another for three months. I was giddy, in love (or lust), and totally out of touch with the voice inside me that was tapping at the glass to get me to pay attention to Seth's erratic behavior. Looking over at Seth's empty beer bottle on the mantle, I remember this one winter morning, a week into living together. Beer bottles lined the counters from late nights with Jeff and his other buddies. Dirty laundry mounded in the corners of the bedroom and bathroom. Surf wax, invoices, and Zig Zag rolling papers cluttered the desk. I cranked up one of my retro-disco CD's, opened the windows, snapped on a pair of gloves, and started a deep clean.

I was singing along to Earth, Wind and Fire, when I heard the front door slam and saw Seth's keys skid across the freshly polished counter tops. Seth scowled, hitting the off button of the stereo, "What the hell's this?" he asked, referring to my music. "Who even listens to this crap anymore?"

A week later, I found my CD in the trash, cracked in half. When I'd asked him how it got that way, he made up some lame excuse about one of his tools bumping into it. It was the start of Seth chipping away parts of me that he found unacceptable.

If I hadn't wound up late for my next period, I wonder if I would have stayed at all. Any hesitation I had was pushed aside when Seth brought home a cradle he'd hand carved along with an armful of flowers...daisies. I was carrying our first daughter. "Let's call her Daisy," he'd whispered in bed after making love. I was reeled back in, telling myself that everything would be better after the baby.

Daisy's asleep and the house is finally quiet. I don't know how to get Seth to open up. Oma, cluing into Seth's and my distance with one another, has given me the name of a therapist she knows in town—Katherine Middlebrook. She said she specialized in grief, but did a fair amount of couple's work. Her specialty suits us fine. In college, I'd seen a therapist for nearly six months about my abandoning, erratic, mother. The counselor's revelation that was supposed to be life changing: I looked for men who abandoned me just as my mother had. I quit after that session.

I throw off the blanket that has failed to take the chill from me. Opening the garage, I stand in silence and watch my husband. He's in the early stages of crafting a custom surfboard. Saws, glue, resin, sealants, and dust masks litter the expansive table where he's working. Sweat is pearled across his nose and along his creased forehead. It's the same spots where Daisy's sweat pools when she runs non-stop on the beach or playground.

Seth is beyond good looking to me—he's breathtaking. His defined, muscular arms work back and forth in an angry, sexual way. He's completely involved in his work as though nothing else in the world matters; something that drew me to him the minute we met. I always feel that there's a quiet, brooding storm that's ready to erupt, contained in his movements and stares.

He doesn't hear my footsteps over the angry lyrics of Kurt Cobain. I slip my hands around his waist. Seth startles. He reaches over and lowers the music, takes a drag off his cigarette, and blows smoke off to the side. The garage is the one place he's allowed to smoke at home. "I thought you were pissed."

"I am," I reply. I stroke his arms and trace his tight abdominal muscles.

Seth stubs out his cigarette and his eyes squint the way they do when he's furious or turned on. He leans in and kisses me deeply on the mouth. I fall into his dirt, sweat, and the mess between us. I breathe in familiarity, exhaling forgiveness.

"Remember how I used to visit you at your shop when we were first together?" I undo the top two buttons of his Levis.

His hipbones are prominent over the lip of his waist band pointing to his sculpted abs.

"Yeah," he says.

Seth yanks off my shirt and pushes me down to the sofa. He kisses me all along my back, down to the word "dream" that I had tattooed this year for my 30th birthday. I grab his mound of brown curls and pull him into me. I taste the sweeter, simpler times when it was just the two of us. My ache is temporarily soothed. As I lay naked in his arms, I get part of what I'd come for.

"I miss this. I miss you. Where have you been?" I say, hoping he won't pull away.

Seth is very still and quiet. I fear I've pushed for answers too fast. He reaches over to his jeans that are tangled up with my clothes, and pulls out his pack of Camels. He slowly lights his cigarette, and draws a long drag as he sits up. "I don't know 'Lyss, I know I screwed up. I can't even talk about it right now." He's standing above me. His 6'2" frame towers over me. He's running a hand through his hair again. "My mom is totally messing with my head and I'm thinkin' about how I'm going to make enough to add to our inventory for the holidays. I don't even know how you put up with me. I just needed somethin' to calm me down."

Seth is split wide open, the way he was when I first met him and we'd make love until one of us would drop from exhaustion. I'll never forget the first time it happened. We'd had an afternoon of insatiable, raw, almost animalistic sex. As the rain began to ping against the window of Seth's room, I felt water drip onto my arm. I searched the ceiling for a watermark, then saw where the water had come from—Seth's eyes. "Hold me. Don't ever leave me," he'd whispered. I felt like I was comforting a child, drying his tears with my kiss.

I stand and bring him into an embrace. "We'll figure it out, Seth. We always do."

Staring intensely into my eyes, he replies, "I'm going to turn this around. I promise. After tonight, no more getting' loaded and bein' away from you and the girls—swear."

I gently take his face in my hands just like I do when I comfort my children from a bad dream, offering the same words of comfort, "It's going to be alright."

"You believe me?" he asks.

"I believe you."

Chapter 2
Two Weeks Ago

Katherine

Client cancellations afford me the freedom to slip away down to the ocean, breathe in the salt air, and clear my head from the drama of other people's lives. I watch the eucalyptus sway in the breeze on the cliffs above. Usually, this grounds me, reminding me that life isn't full of pain all of the time.

That will not be the case today. We're having an unseasonably, foggy, damp day and for the life of me, I can't imagine why my mother wants to meet me down here, unless... Her message on my voice mail said she needed to talk. Her over-enthusiastic tone used to cover up real emotions was what got my attention and led me to cancel my afternoon clients. "Just wanted to have a little talk and see if you could work me in." She was a terrible liar in her drinking days. Now that she's sober, nearly twenty years, she's worse.

Sitting on the concrete wall, overlooking the sand in Rio Del Mar, I watch a handful of mothers and their toddlers bundled up around a picnic of Goldfish crackers, juice boxes, and peanut butter and jelly sandwiches. Wasn't it just yesterday that Collin, Tory and I did the same? Aside from the family on the beach, a couple of teens smoking and texting, I am the only person within a mile. I wonder if this little talk with Mom is going to be the beginning of the end.

Within minutes, I hear the distinct sound of her Accord pull up behind me in the parking lot. She primps in the rearview mirror, checking her make-up, brushing back a wisp of grey hair that is out of place. I stand and watch her lock the door, check that it is indeed locked, and return her wave. She's limping—a lot. It's not sciatica. Damn it.

"Hi, Mom." I lean in and kiss her cheek. She smells of Merle Norman pressed powder and Youth Dew.

"Oh, Katie, it's so good to see you," she replies, as though we see one another only once a year rather than every other day. She's the only one on the planet allowed to call me Katie. Katie sounds like a nine-year-old girl with pigtails. But then, this is probably how my mother sees me despite my fifty plus years and a PhD.

I survey her limp and ask, "Shall we find a bench, or—"

"A bench would be fine," she replies almost too quickly and with the same high-pitched voice as she did on my answering machine.

We walk arm in arm, slow and silent for a good fifty yards then find a bench with a memorial plaque on it: David Whipple—father, friend, missed. It's both endearing and ominous. Immediately I feel the moisture of the bench penetrate my pants. I worry that the cold will hurt my mother's hips.

Seconds pass, feeling like hours, and the silence becomes painful. With clients, I can wait all hour if that's what they need to sort out their thoughts or feelings. Now, I'm like a fresh intern, ready to fill in the pauses and uncomfortable moments of quiet. "So, Mom, tell me what brings you out on this strange, foggy fall day?"

She smiles. The crow's feet around her eyes dig in deep. Mom didn't age well—drinking hard for thirty years never plays out well on the face. "Oh, Katie, but I guess you know?" she asks, rhetorically.

I smile back, but only to be polite. My nose tingles from the tears that are forming. Through the fog, I make out the front of the cement ship, the S.S. Palo Alto. Built in 1918, it was docked in 1929 and used as a casino and dance hall. Slowly it sank under its own weight, rendering it unsafe for entertainment, but fine as a fishing pier. Now, only the wooden pier leading up to it can be used for fishing. Across a chain-linked fence separating the boat from the pier are signs warning of its danger: Do not trespass. Dangerous. I can feel myself sinking, thinking this conversation is one I do not want to have.

"Tell me what the doctor said." I look straight ahead. All my years in Hospice and private practice as a grief counselor, and yet I can't make eye contact with my mother at this critical moment.

"It's back," she says, her voice devoid of any emotions. The words hit me like a tidal wave. "It's in my bones." Oh dear God, not bone cancer. A group of sanderlings run along the water's edge like children playing tag with the water.

Finally, my third eye kicks in and tells me to look at how aloof I am being and to reach out and comfort my mother. I don't want to comfort anyone, though. I want someone to comfort me and tell me everything is going to be fine if I am a good girl, eat my vegetables, go to church, and treat everyone as I wished to be treated. I turn and see that my mother is also off someplace else in her mind. I put my arm around her and open my mouth to say, 'I'm sorry,' but nothing comes out. I just let the tears fall and finally, she breaks, and her tears merge with mine.

BACK HOME, I survey my upcoming client list and curse. I forgot to cancel my new client at 6:00—shoot. I made special arrangements to work him in tonight because of his schedule. I've got to make adjustments in my practice now that Mom's cancer is back. I check my account balances on-line and figure I could limit my practice to fifteen clients rather than thirty. After Tory followed Collin down to UC Santa Barbara, I nearly doubled my caseload to fill the emptiness. My husband, Carl has been after me for over a year to work less. I tell him it's who I am. He says I'm the one who'll need a shrink if I don't stop listening to other people's poison all day long. How can I explain to him that when I'm with someone in the room, it isn't poison? It's an invitation into their very soul—an honor, a privilege, to bear witness to their pain, struggles and revelations. What's new is how terribly exhausted I am by the end of the day and less fresh the next morning. Chalk it up to menopause, I suppose. Sometimes cancellations are answers to prayers so I can rest or sit at the sea.

Now I need to factor in my mother's prognosis: two years at best, six months or less if it continues to metastasize. With the kids away at college, I can certainly move her in if her health rapidly declines. Carl and I can take turns with the help of a Hospice volunteer and staff. Just the word Hospice sends a jolt through me—her death is really going to happen. When I worked at our local Hospice, it was like working with saints walking the earth, but I was still removed; death was outside of me. Now I must invite the saints to live amongst us.

I push aside these thoughts as I swing open my cottage door—an in-law quarters that Carl and I remodeled and decorated for my therapy office. Even though these walls are witness to great pain, it's my place of refuge. It's altogether my space—from the Steve Hank's paintings, depicting families in various combinations down at the sea, to the floral, high backed chairs that I reupholstered. A red light flashes on my answering machine. I push the button to retrieve my messages. Jean is cancelling tomorrow at 3:00. Predictable. She isn't ready to talk about her husband's death. I sift through the mail that is stacked half a foot high. There's an invitation for me to speak this spring in Monterey. I file it in the "to do" basket.

My new client, Greg, will be here in less than ten minutes. Just enough time to fire up my new espresso machine and read over the preliminary notes from my phone interview with him. A police officer, I remind myself. Not my typical client.

Greg

Downtown Santa Cruz can comfortably fit several hundred people strolling up and down the tree-lined sidewalks. When a few thousand are packed in shoulder-to-shoulder, raising anti-war signs, the comfort level plunges. Weaving through the crowd of "Peace is patriotic" and "No blood for oil" chanters, my ears strain to hear something other than "Bush-bashing" from these liberal fanatics. I hate this kind of crap. Why people can't be civilized and write their congressmen or the White House is beyond me. It's an excuse to get together, get riled up, drink too much, and litter the streets.

My partner Bill and I have another three hours of patrolling this nonsensical event. I live for the day when I can move up the ranks and get off the streets. My mouth is parched as hell and a headache is building again at the base of my skull. As I scan the crowd, I spot a gang of tatted up and pierced punks hanging out in an alley. One of them, whose hair is blue-tipped, takes a swig of something out of a brown bag. His buddy holds up a sign with a picture (embellished, no doubt) of a U.S. soldier holding a gun at a Middle-Eastern kid's head. Across the top in red, the sign reads: Just Like Nam—Baby Killers.

I fly through the crowd like a hawk spotting its prey. I slam the sign-holding prick into the brick wall, withdraw my pistol, and point it at his forehead. "What the hell do you know about being a soldier and what's in the bag?"

"Jesus Christ, Greg," my partner whispers into my ear, attempting to block me from the crowd.

When I get no answer, I put my mouth a half an inch from his face and spit, "Are you going to answer me or am I going to have to pull this trigger?" I cock my gun for effect. Almost instantly, I feel something wet splash my ankle. I look down and see a wet spot spreading down the pant leg of the kid in front of me. He's pissing himself! I stifle a laugh. "Jesus, you're a real tough guy, huh?" I grab his sign and break it over my leg then snatch the brown bag from his friend. "Get the hell out of here!" I holler. They run down the alley and out toward the three-hour free parking lot.

"Are you out of your goddamn mind?" Bill asks as we turn to face the riled up mob in the street again.

I open the brown sack and look inside. I can't contain my laughter. "Tea. It's iced tea." I laugh and toss the contents into an overstuffed garbage can.

"You're out of your mind, Greg," Bill repeats. "You gotta get a grip or you'll have Internal Affairs in your face again."

Bill's covered for me more than once over the past year. What did I.A. expect, that I'd simply ignore it when teenage runaways and bums hocked loogies at me, spewing profanity? Sometimes people need to be taught a lesson.

The afternoon drags on without any more excitement. We finish off the day at 4:00 and head over to JJ's for a beer. I need it to calm my nerves. Seeing a shrink isn't something that is setting too well with me. It's bad enough that my doctor wants me to take these damn anti-depressants. I took 'em for a few days then chucked them in the trash.

At ten of 6:00, I'm tired of listening to my scanner. I walk down the steep driveway that leads to Dr. Katherine Middlebrook's office. I shouldn't have had that beer—my head's really pounding now. I wipe my sweat-drenched hands on my jeans—don't want her to think I'm a nut case when I shake her hand. All afternoon I've been wondering what to bring up in the first session. Should I start with how crappy my marriage is? Or how my wife accuses me of being an absentee father? I guess those would be the obvious, easy conversation starters. Or, that I can't seem to move past the one girl who chose a druggie over me? The bottom line is that I can live with all that. What I can't live with is my brother Steven's death. Almost six months now and I still wake up screaming in my sleep. I just hope to God this woman knows how to keep her mouth shut. I don't want any of this getting back to the department.

I knock and the door opens. "Good-evening, Greg. Won't you come in? I'm Katherine."

"Nice to meet you, Katherine."

She's smiles. "Have a seat wherever you'd like. Would you like some tea? Instant coffee?"

"No, I'm good." Pillows surround me as I sink into her couch. There's something vaguely familiar about Katherine, but I can't place it. The smell of lavender that fills the room brings me back to my childhood at West Side where the teachers bathed themselves in the stuff. She sits down quietly in front of me. I want to get up and walk out. What am I doing here? I don't know what to say.

"Why don't you tell me a little bit about yourself in person," she begins, as if sensing my impulse to flee. "I know from speaking with you briefly on the phone that you are having some marital issues and that you're an officer. That must be somewhat stressful, I'm sure?"

I look her over. It's probably a bad habit, sizing people up. I can't seem to help it. Katherine's probably a few years younger than my mother. I'm guessing she's fifty or so, well put together, blazer, slimming skirt, thick in the middle from years of sitting. She's never had a drug problem—clearly no rap sheet. Her face used to be prettier before so many lines of life etched away her youth.

"Uh, before I say anything, I just need you to know that no one's forcing me to be here. I still can't believe I'm sitting here… willingly." She smiles again and tilts her head, probably wondering what the hell I'm going on about. "I was in therapy once. Saw the department's shrink. They call it a Fitness for Duty evaluation."

"Ah-hah," she acknowledges.

"If we shoot someone or if we're not handling stress well on the job, those kinds of things, then we may have to go to an FFD. In my case, anyway, I was involved in a shooting. Some slime-ball foster parent pulled a gun on me after killing his thirteen year-old foster kid."

Katherine winces and nods her head, unable to hide her recognition.

"You heard about it?" I ask.

"Yes. I know the social worker who was on the case."

"It was no big deal. I got back to work in a week or so. I just want to be sure that if I ever wanted to talk to somebody, you know, about personal stuff, that it won't find its way back to my file. What's my business is my business." *Oh, my head.*

"Absolutely, and you should be concerned. What you say in here is held in confidence unless there's a disclosure of abuse or intent to hurt yourself or someone else. But, I hear your concern. What and when you decide to disclose is totally up to you. This is a process."

I feel my jaw loosen a little. We go through the rest of the session talking about how Jenny thinks I'm a terrible communicator and how she wants us to do couples therapy. That's a no. Maybe I should tell Katherine that I rarely make love to my wife, that it actually disgusts me. Surely, a shrink would love to sink her teeth into that. I want to talk about Steven, but the words get caught in my throat each time I try. I think about today and how Bill reamed me about needing to get a grip on my anger. It's nobody's business what I do at work as long as I do my job. I'll go for a run down on the sand later and shake it off. By the time I'm done talking about my two-year-old Aidan and four-year-old Jeremy, I sink into the pillows and think that maybe this won't be as painful as a root canal after all.

Chapter 3
The Day of

Seth

I step out of my pick-up and can make out the voices of at least a dozen kids running around Oma's property. Strung along the trellis that hovers over a dozen picnic tables are twinkling white lights (fairy lights, as Daisy calls them). They're up every year at this time and taken down after New Year's. Pumpkins line the path to Oma's door with small calendula candles giving off a stink to keep the lingering mosquitoes away.

    I know Alyssa and the girls have been here since 7:00 this morning to set up the prize booths and parent-run stands that sell everything from tie-dye shirts to homemade apple-butter. Alyssa thinks I hate these school activities—that I don't have an "emotional connection" because I wasn't raised at the school, hand-dying silk capes in the second grade, and weaving rosemary crowns. I may not have the same long-running ties as she does to West Side Arts, but I do wish I could be here more often…with her…with my girls. If I could've gotten out of a Saturday down at the shop, I would have. I'm making a boatload more money working as much as I can without hiring on someone other than Jeff. Come summer, I'll pick up another high school kid, but I'm cutting corners where I can. I just wish Alyssa wouldn't hound me about it.

Anyway, last night, together…finally. I don't want to be an asshole. It just seems to be a mold I can't break out of. Out in the garage, holding her, God, it makes me want to run off to some secluded island with just my girls and not have to do "life." I recognize my daughter's voice above the commotion of laughter and screams. "Daddy, Daddy! Daddy's here."

Daisy throws herself at me. I catch her and twirl her around. "Hello, my little gardener." She's dressed in overalls, a red handkerchief, and sports a child-sized trowel in her back pocket. "Get a lot of good loot today?"

"What's loot?"

"Stuff—you know, candy, treats, whatever."

She rolls her eyes at me. "Dad, we aren't allowed to have candy." She pours open her bag showing me the contents. "See, we got a ball of yarn for finger-knitting, a handful of dragon tears, some fairy dust, and," she holds out a crinkled muffin wrapper, "a berry muffin that I ate this morning."

I smile and try to contain the smirk that spreads across my face. These poor kids will become sugar addicts when they finally get their fingers on a Jolly Rancher. "Da Da. Da Da." Nevaeh's hoarse voice calls out. My mother told me I had the same voice as a toddler. I was shocked my mother remembered anything about my childhood other than all the grief she says I caused her.

"Look at you, little fairy." Nevaeh's fairy wings are askew and covered with playground dirt. Her chubby legs buckle as she trips over an oak tree root. I throw Daisy into one arm and sweep down to grab Nevaeh before her face smacks into the bark. "Whoa, slow down there, little one. You're gonna get hurt."

She plants a sloppy kiss on my cheek. I set them down and they both say 'hello' to Jeff, who is currently trying to sneak them

Out of Breath

some candy corn. I grab it out of his hand and shove it in my pocket. "What, are you trying to get me killed?" Then turning to Nevaeh and Daisy I ask, "Girls, where's Mommy?"

"Up at the house with Oma," Daisy replies.

I hoist Nevaeh on top of my shoulders and Jeff does the same with Daisy. Their giggles make me warm like the Hawaiian tides. We run up the hill, bouncing them up and down. "Let's go give Mommy kisses."

"Kiss Ma Ma," Nevaeh says.

I wander through the maze of cousins, teachers, and West Side friends who are all affectionately (or more annoyingly) referred to as aunts, uncles or cousins to the children. I'm sure Greg and his brood is here. When I see him, I'm sure to find Alyssa. "Is Uncle Gregory here?" I ask the girls.

"Mommy says he has to work tonight," Daisy answers. *Thank you Santa Cruz P.D.*

I FINALLY SPOT Alyssa. Her waist-long, blonde hair is knotted on top of her head. Strands have fallen in the back and along the side of her face. She's sexy without even trying. When I climbed up the stairs from a morning surf on the east side six years ago, there she was— like a freakin' angel. I was hooked. I sneak up behind her and pinch her rear end. Daisy spills into laughter. "Daddy, that's naughty."

I whisper into Alyssa's ear, "That's how Mommy likes it." She swats me on the arm. "What, are you feeding the whole county tonight?" I say as I look at the tables covered with plates full of food.

Alyssa tosses a green salad, tastes it, and reaches for the garlic salt. "Oh, you know Oma, just transforming seven loaves and fishes into a feast for 5,000." She hurries around to the other side of the island counter and sticks a hand-carved wooden spoon into a mound of potato salad. She covers the salads with a paper towel and hands the bowls to me. "Put these out on the patio. We'll be eating in about fifteen minutes."

"Girls have a good time today?" I ask, grabbing a slice of Oma's homegrown tomato.

"Yeah, except when it was time for Nevaeh to have her nap, I couldn't find her blanket. She was out of her mind earlier."

"I'll have a look for it back at home." Just as Alyssa's about to scurry back into the kitchen, she stops, stares, and her face crumples into a scowl. She's caught sight of Jeff who is playing a string game with Daisy.

"What?" I ask. "Come on, babe, he didn't have anywhere to go tonight. He's been working overtime without any compensation. It's one night." I put an arm around her and kiss her cheek. She pulls away.

"Seriously?" Her tone is angry. "I hate when he's around." I hear the same speech every time about how Jeff is always an accomplice to my bad behavior.

"I know. Look, we'll grab the girls, keep them out of your hair, and bring them up when we hear the dinner bell." Oma loves to ring the old-fashioned silver dinner bell mounted outside her kitchen; I think she likes to imagine she's a pioneer.

"Alright," she sighs. "Keep an eye on them; they're a handful."

We grab the girls and head over to the tire swings. The sun is setting, painting a picture of orange, pink, and lavender streaks across the sky. It's one of my favorite times of day. "You see that color on top?" I ask Nevaeh, bending down on one knee beside her. She nods. "That's orange."

"Owange," she repeats in her toddler-speak.

"And underneath that, it's red"

"Wed."

"Right," I say and kiss the top of her head.

Daisy is spinning so fast on the tire swing that even I feel nauseous. Carolyn's kids, Ricky and Trevor (our girls' "real" cousins, even if they are only second cousins), are down at the pond, having an 'I can throw the biggest rock contest.' The splashes make Nevaeh squeal with delight. She claps her hands, exclaiming, "Again!"

"I don't imagine it's kosher to smoke around here?" Jeff asks.

I raise my eyebrows. "I could use one myself." Then, I think back to the morning's events. Nevaeh could have dropped her blanket in the truck when she kissed me good-bye as she has in the past. "Crap, I need to grab somethin' out of there for Nevaeh before she gets overtired." Nevaeh's up by Daisy and is watching her spin in circles from being so dizzy on the tire swing. "Daisy, take your sister up by your mom. Jeff and I gotta grab something out of the truck."

Daisy nods and takes Nevaeh by the hand, "I'll go in a second."

Alyssa

I dread losing an hour tonight to the end of daylight savings; the darkness has always scared me. As a child, I'd lay awake in the middle of the night, begging the sun to rise faster. Most nights, I'd wind up cradled in between Oma and Opa. Even today, I sleep with a nightlight. It's so dark, that I can't see down the hill, but hear chatter, laughter, and happy squeals. Ricky and Trevor come bounding up the hill, both arguing about who has thrown a bigger stone into the pond and whose splash was bigger.

"Hi boys. Have you seen Uncle Seth, Daisy, and Nevaeh?"

"Umm," Ricky starts, "Daisy and Nevaeh were watching us throw rocks in the pond, and then Daisy said she needed to take Nevaeh up to Oma's."

"Oh, okay. Wait, what?" A bubble of anxiety surfaces. Where's Uncle Seth?"

They both shrug their shoulders. "I don't know," Ricky answers.

I start down the hill, looking for Seth's six-foot stature to stand out above the others. As I'm on my way down, Daisy runs up to me, panting. "I can't find, Nevaeh, Mommy."

I shake my head, thinking she must be confused. Seth's supposed to be watching her. "What are you talking about? Daddy's supposed to be with you and Nevaeh."

"He and Jeff said they had to go up to Daddy's truck to get something…"

"What do you mean he's not with her?" I yell, grabbing her by the shoulders.

"He told me to keep an eye on her," she starts to whimper, "and so I took her over to where Trevor and Ricky were throwing rocks, and then I went over to the tire swing one more time, and then, I don't know. I don't know, Mommy." Daisy is still talking, but it's as though I'm underwater. I can't hear anything except the quickening pace of my heart rate pounding in my ears.

I see Seth and Jeff walking toward me. They're laughing and sipping a beer. I run up and am immediately hit with the unmistakable scent of pot. "You son of a bitch!" I scream, slapping him across the face. I take off running up the hill. Seth only has to take a few steps before he catches up. "Hey," he grabs my arm and says, "What the hell was that for?"

"Where's our daughter?"

Seth looks around. "What are you talking about? I told Daisy to bring her to you about fifteen minutes ago."

"Fifteen. Fifteen minutes? Christ!"

"Alyssa, I was in my truck looking for..."

"Don't!" I hold up my hand. "Just shut up and help me find Nevaeh."

Within minutes, a search party is formed. Oma's hands tremble as she hands out lanterns and flashlights. The sliver of a moon is little help. Friends and family fan out in groups of two searching the house, the school grounds, and classrooms that are connected to Oma's property. Daisy and the rest of the children are ordered to stay with Oma at the house. The festive smell of BBQ and garlic mocks my senses as I search for my daughter.

"Nevaeh!" Her name hangs in the air, heavy with the misty fog. If she has gotten hurt, fallen or lost, she's certainly freezing by now as well. I'm sure she's hiding somewhere. Any moment, she'll pop out from behind a tree and think we were all playing a huge game of hide-and-seek. Across the five, heavily wooded acres, her name bounces back and forth, like a game of Marco-Polo.

It has been nearly thirty minutes. I'm on the verge of throwing up and tearing out my hair with worry. Ricky's words reverberate in my head: "Daisy and Nevaeh were watching us throw rocks in the pond." The pond. I point my flashlight in the opposite direction, careful not to lose my step on the wet bark. I slide down to the bank and see a pile of stones beside a pink pair of ballet slippers—Nevaeh's tiny shoes from her fairy costume. My flashlight falls into the mud. I pick up her shoes and a primal scream that even I don't recognize as my own tears into the night.

From every direction, people come running and tripping down the hill to where I stand. My Great-Uncle Fritz orders people to join hands and step across the expanse of the pond. The people in the center are up to their waist in mucky water. I stand on the edge next to Seth, willing my daughter not to be found.

"Move forward, dragging your feet," Uncle Fritz calls out. Everyone obediently steps forward. "Again." It's eerie quiet except for the sound of water sloshing around. After several minutes, that sound is interrupted by an, "Oh my God," by our friend, Dave. I see him drop the hands of friends on either side, bend down and grab hold of something. It's got to be something other than Nevaeh's body, probably just a large boulder or a tree trunk that fell down last winter. His arms break the surface of the water. I hear screams. A shriek of horror tumbles out of my mouth. Nevaeh's body is lifeless and wet in his arms.

"Someone call 9-1-1! Call 9-1-1!" he frantically shouts.

He runs through the water and lays her on the banks where my Uncle Fritz attempts CPR. Everything moves in slow motion. "Nevaeh, wake up, honey. It's going to be okay. Nevaeh, come on, sweetie, Mommy's here. Nevaeh, please!" I scream, stroking her freezing little arm.

Greg

It's just misty enough tonight to piss me off. No rain in nearly six months and it has to hit tonight. I hit my wiper blades and turn up a street above the golf course. Up ahead is an undeveloped piece of land surrounded by trees where teens hang out to drink on Friday and Saturday nights. I drive with my fog lights on and park far enough away that my car won't be recognized. Stepping out, I hear sprinkles of laughter, the clinking of bottles, and foul-sounding hip-hop music pulsating. Here's the part I like best: I pull out my flashlight and pour light onto the crowd. "Like roaches in a dirty kitchen," I say to nobody in particular. Reflections of boys zipping up near their vehicles and girls tugging at their shirts are caught in the stream of light. I'm about to walk into the frenzy of their fun when a signal on my police radio grips me.

"Zone 5 fire units respond to medical aid. Possible child drowning at Newcastle Lane."

Newcastle Lane. Only Oma and the school are up there. I jump in my vehicle, accelerate to the top of the hill, blare my horn, and swing my cruiser around. I tell myself that dozens of kids are up at Oma's. It doesn't necessarily mean it's someone I know. Situations like this are never my favorite. I feel ill equipped offering comfort to someone when there's been a death. What can I possibly say to a mother who witnesses her child's body splattered across the highway? 'I'm sorry' is so meaningless. The image of Steven's shredded body pops into my mind. *Push it away, Greg. Not now.*

Minutes later, I pull up behind the ambulance and break into a sprint toward the crowd that is huddled by the pond. Familiar faces flood my eyes: Alyssa's cousin Carolyn, our friend Dave, a teacher at West Side, Peter, a friend of the family's. A hair-quivering sound erupts from the center of the circle, a cry I recognize from my youth—a cry that ripped from her when she split her arm in two. My knees nearly buckle. *Not Daisy or Nevaeh. Please God, not one of my godchildren.*

I push my way through the crowd. It is worse than any highway bloodbath. Ahead of me is the girl who I let dress me in her mother's clothes to play house; the girl who let me practice French kissing under the guise of not knowing how to do it; the girl who remains the keeper of my heart—Alyssa. She's rocking back and forth, wailing, her hair matted from the wind and drizzle. Nevaeh is sprawled out on a stretcher as a medic delivers CPR.

"My baby, Gregory! My baby! He didn't watch her Gregory and now she's gone!"

I don't understand what she's talking about until I see Seth off to the side, covering his face with his hands. "What the hell is your problem?" I yell at him.

I feel a paramedic's hand on my shoulder. "Take it easy, Greg. Let us do our job here." In a small town, everyone's too familiar.

I don't know who I want to throttle first, the medic or Seth.

"She's not responding," the medic delivering CPR calls out. "Step aside," he says to the crowd. "We need to bring her in."

"What? Where are you taking her?" Alyssa stands, grabbing hold of Nevaeh's arm. "Where are you taking my baby?"

I pull Alyssa to my side. I've seen a cold-water drowning before; they aren't always what they appear. Sometimes the body shuts down when it's in hypothermia. We had a case of it down at the beach just last summer. After bringing the boy in, he was revived. Not quite the same boy he was, of course, but alive. "There's a chance they can revive her at the hospital Alyssa. Come on. Get in my cruiser. We'll follow the ambulance."

Before Alyssa can object, the doors of the ambulance slam shut and I'm rushing her over to my car. "But wait, what about Seth?" I watch her search the crowd. Others begin to look around. Seth isn't in sight.

"We don't have time for this. Come on. Carolyn!" I call out to Alyssa's cousin. "Tell Oma that we're on our way to Dominican." I don't give a damn where Seth is—right now anyway.

Seth

It's now frightfully quiet across the school campus as the last night of October merges into November. I'm sure everyone's at Oma's, waiting to hear something. I'm paralyzed. I tell myself, *go up to*

Oma's, call the hospital, but I can't. It's totally my fault and I don't know what the hell to do. My legs itch from the oak leaves that litter the floor of the tree house. It wasn't that long ago that I took Nevaeh up here for the first time. I let her run around with her sister, putting my body in front of the stairs to protect her. I thought I could protect her from everything.

My stomach growls from throwing up over and over. I want to throw myself over the rail and end the pain that's ripping through me. They didn't revive her. I saw her body…grey, still. I felt her body, cold, already growing hard.

A drop of blood drips from my hand. I've pounded the floor so hard that my skin has ripped open. Just as I contemplate standing up and climbing down, unsure of where to go, I hear footsteps crunching leaves below. A ray of light pans across the playground. Someone's looking for me. I feel acid spread through my stomach—I hurl again over the side. After wiping my mouth with the edge of my shirt, I peer over the railing and see a police uniform. My insides become jellyfish. My nightmare is about to continue.

Greg

I shine my flashlight up toward the tree house, where I heard movement. The hospital has left a sour, disinfectant taste in my mouth. I spit and call out, "You up there, Seth?" I hear him curse. Adrenalin pulses through my body. I bound up the stairs, grab Seth by the neck of his shirt, and shove him against the trunk of the tree. He reeks of vomit, beer, and smoke.

I drive my fist into Seth's stomach. He pukes on my feet. As he rights himself, I punch him in the face. Blood seeps from his cheek. "You were so wrecked that you couldn't even bother to watch your girls?"

"I wasn't high tonight," Seth says as he spits out blood.

I draw my knee up and ram him in the balls. He drops. "B.S. I'd like to throw you off these stairs, but you aren't worth my job."

Out of Breath

Every warning I gave Alyssa, every piece of advice I gave her after he'd sting another part of her heart— it's like all six years of my hatred toward Seth are spewing out of me. I wish I could enjoy it more. "You're like some damn high school kid, running around with your surfboard, neglecting your family, getting high. How you managed to produce two of the most beautiful girls in the world…" I can't get the words out without choking on my tears. "You threw it all away, didn't you Seth? Didn't you?" I bring an elbow down into his back.

Seth

I want to speak—to tell him where I was, what I was doing. Greg's made up his mind. His hatred pierces me like a laser. I keep waiting for the click of his gun. I wouldn't put it past him. It would end the emotional and physical pain that's shredding me. He's screaming at me again.

"You didn't even have the balls to come to the hospital and see if she made it. Or comfort your wife as the social worker held her hand, telling her Nevaeh's gone. Dead!"

Dead. I knew she was and yet it's new all over again. How can my baby be gone?

"Are you going to say something? Or do I need to smack you around some more?" Greg screams, inches from my face.

"Where's Alyssa now?" I ask. I can't imagine what I'll ever say to her, or Oma, or Daisy. Oh God, poor Daisy.

"With Oma. Where you should have gone."

I'm on my feet and about to ram my fist into his face when he grabs my arm, twists it behind my back and stands behind me, whispering, "By the way, I know you were with Jeff tonight getting high. This little scuffle we've had up here, it never happened. You and Jeff got into it. Understand? And if I hear that you try that, 'I wasn't high' crap on Alyssa, I swear to God, I'll make sure that more than THC shows up in your chem panel."

My breath stops. The reality of this situation hits me. I'm going to be arrested. It's like a long line of dominoes has been stacked before me. Greg's knocked the first one down, and I can't stop the rest.

Greg pushes me toward the ladder of the tree house. Once we're down, he shoves me onto a bench, handcuffing me as though I'm a fugitive. I've sat on this bench and held my daughters, listened to the songs they've learned. My salty tears sting the cut on my face. I can barely see out of my left eye from the swelling. Greg goes into a one-stall bathroom, leaving the door open. I can see him wash the blood from his fist and wipe the vomit from his shoes. The hatred that I feel for him competes with the grief that shakes my bones.

Once I'm inside the back of Greg's patrol car, I see Carolyn's VW heading toward us. Alyssa is in the passenger seat. I want to jump out and hold Alyssa, cry with her, hear that everything is going to be all right. But of course, everything is not all right.

"Did you find him?" I hear Alyssa ask with terror in her voice.

Greg points to the back of the cruiser. It's like watching a horror film that you know is going to haunt your dreams. Greg takes her hand in his, consoling her. Alyssa's cleaned up since I saw her last. No more mud. Her hair hangs straight down in her face. Clean. But her face—it's full of worry lines and etched with anger.

She's talking again, "Well, where was he? Why isn't he up here checking on Daisy or me?"

Greg talks to her quietly, not wanting me to hear, I'm sure. I can't make out what they're saying. I see Alyssa's eyebrows arch high on her forehead. Greg tells her that he's taking me down to the station.

"You're arresting him? It's not like he pushed her in," Alyssa says, wild eyed. I wonder, for a moment, if she's actually on my side.

Greg's eyes narrow and he shakes his head. "When are you going to stop protecting him? Huh? Look what happened to Nevaeh!"

She peers at me through the glass. Then I see Greg's arms pulling her into his body. It's like all their quiet talks and giggles on the phone or afternoons with the kids have groomed Alyssa to need him, depend on him. I want to scream, "Get your hands off my wife!" I bang my head against the window.

Alyssa startles, throws me an angry look, and turns back to Greg, whose hands are resting on her waist. "I swear to you, Gregory, if he was high tonight, he's never coming home."

Greg nods and pulls her into his arms again and holds her tight. He looks my way. I swear I see a smile creep across his lips.

Chapter 4

Katherine

I'm taking a much-needed break while Mom naps in Tory's bed. The chemo upsets her stomach; toast and crackers are the only things she can keep down. Carl and I have urged her to stay with us full-time, but she's fighting it. "Just until my strength returns then I'll get out of your hair." I want her in my hair. I want her here with me every day that I can still have her.

Carl's lit a fire to take the chill out of this crisp, fall morning. He's my anchor. After twenty-nine years of marriage, we still hold hands across the table when we're out for dinner and kiss one another after a long day of work (much to the protest of our children when they're around).

I'm momentarily lost in this month's book club pick. Of course it involves tragedy, loss, grief. I can't escape it. Nonetheless, these books bring me comfort—my own loss unites me with the souls of others. My solitude is interrupted by a grunt of disgust coming from Carl. He throws the morning paper onto the couch beside me. "Can you believe this?" he blurts.

I lay my novel down on the driftwood coffee table and read the headline: *Child Drowns in Family Pond—Possible Drug Involvement.* "Oh God, that poor family." I exhale.

Carl and I lock eyes; neither of us willing to share what memory the headline stirs inside us. I look away first. Carl snatches the paper from my hands. "Did you see where it happened?"

"Well, I might have if you hadn't ripped the paper out of my hands." He tosses the article into my lap. I comb through the article trying to tune out Carl's ranting over his misplaced day planner. The article details the drowning of a one-and-a-half year old. *The father, Seth Buchanan, tested positive for drugs on the night of the drowning. Buchanan is the grandson-in-law of well-known community figure Elsa Schultz, founder of West Side Arts Academy.*

I feel my stomach flip. "Ohhh…Carl—"

"I hope they throw his ass in jail." A bagel in one hand and his found day planner in the other, Carl leans over and brushes a hurried kiss across my cheek and squeezes my shoulder, a covert message of 'I know, Katherine, I'm thinking of her too.' "I'll be home by four. Love you."

"Love you, too." I hear the door slam.

Here's what we didn't say: that she would have been twenty-nine this year; that she never even got to see what two years old was like; that her death is the one corner of our relationship that stays privately tucked away like a diary deep in a drawer. I was twenty-one when Carl and I married after meeting in college. He was finishing his masters; I was in the middle of my B.A. studies. We married within a year of meeting. Through the first months of our pregnancy, we joked that Nicole was the souvenir from our honeymoon.

My pre-natal tests went smoothly. We painted the room a neutral green. The day I was to go home with my new baby, I never made it out to the car. She had a funny rash. Like it was yesterday, I can feel my lungs contract, grasping for air…I knew right then that something was terribly wrong. A rush of tests ensued. Carl and I were often alone, stewing with worry, not talking, in fear that saying something would make it so. A few days later, a social worker joined the doctor to tell us that our baby had leukemia and to prepare ourselves for the worst. I felt my heart shatter into a thousand piece, like a mirror dropped from a six-story building. She lived only six months.

After she died, I threw myself into my studies. Carl taught part-time at the community college and began to design high-end homes along the northern coast. We considered being a childless couple. We had more money than most of our peers and traveled a great deal during my school breaks and on weekends. It wasn't our lifestyle that held us back from considering children, I later learned, but rather our monumental fears of losing another child. I'd see a new mother cooing at her baby or a family down at the beach picnicking and I'd rush to my car, later stuffing my sorrow in fear of upsetting Carl. What a colossal mistake.

The semester before I was to begin seeing clients in the university clinic, my fellow classmates and I underwent intense sessions of peer disclosure where we practiced our newly acquired counseling skills. I'd saved up four years worth of tears, memories, and private pain that could fill a library. I sought out my own therapy throughout the rest of graduate school. My mother reentered my life during that time, finally clean, remorseful, and humble. I wish that it didn't take my child's death to awaken my mother, but I cherished the blessing of our new relationship after Collin was born.

When I became licensed, I was drawn to grief counseling, but with no intentions of treating parents who lost a young child. Lucky for me, I'd had only a few referrals for this over the years. Feeling a bit shameful, I handed the cases to other therapists, claiming my practice was full. I just knew I wouldn't be able to keep the boundary of my pain and that of my client's clear enough.

That was nearly thirty years ago, though, and now I wonder if it's time to break through my resistance. I can almost hear the phone ring with a referral from Leah for this case, given the limited number of therapists who specialize in grief. If Carl's my anchor, then Leah is the one who puts wind in my sails. We've worked together for nearly twelve years and have a friendship that has withstood the weathering of life. I told her as long as I'm able, I'll do my duty to the community and accept a couple of low-fee clients who stream through her office. It's the least I can do. If child services had intervened when I was younger, maybe my parents would have sobered up faster and my father would still be alive. Maybe.

If she refers this case, I know it's going to be all-consuming and I'm not sure the timing is right, given my mother's illness. The oncologist did reassure me that after my mother's chemo ends next month, she'll probably be strong enough to resume her normal life if all goes well. My mind, of course, holds onto his last four words: *if all goes well*. I'm not a pessimist, but rather, a realist. I know my mother's cancer is aggressive and the grim stories of widows and adult children in my Hospice bereavement groups are never far from my thoughts.

There's no sense in trying to return to my book. I check on my mother. She's still asleep. God, she looks so fragile. I dread the day her eyebrows fall out. To me, it's the first thing I notice on someone's face, the thickness of the eyebrows, their movement—they seem to say so much about a person, in this case, "I'm sick!" Just in case she wakes up and wonders where I am, I leave her a note on the dresser: Be back in ten minutes. Went down to my office. Katie.

Leah

If the stack on my desk gets any higher, I'm going to ask to be buried with it, since this job is going to be the death of me. I look at the three piles I've made: delegate to the new intern, investigate in the next thirty days, and urgent. I grab the file on top of the urgent pile and read it over before this morning's meeting. I pick out the major themes—child death, possible drug involvement, criminal charges pending. A glorious start to another day at

Children's Protective Services. This is why I don't read the daily news on-line or otherwise.

I pick a few white cat hairs off my black slacks and head off to our staff meeting. My eye catches the post-it I've stuck to the side of my cubicle: call Katherine. Katherine and I are like the odd couple. I'm a mess while she's neurotically neat. I love tofu and she thinks beef is a specialized group in the food pyramid. She's married to a man who worships her. I neither want a man nor has one ever worshiped me. But, I love her like a sister. We got to know one another from the volume of child abuse reports she had to phone in years ago. (She's sworn off kid clients since). I was the worker on Tuesday and Thursday who had the lovely privilege of listening to the detailed reports of burns, bruises, and neglect. Gaining her as my most treasured friend made it worthwhile.

I'm ten minutes late, as usual. Jamie, our program director, flips through her notes and gives me a snide look as I sneak in and take my seat. "So, as many of you heard on the news, we are involved in the case of the baby who drowned. Dad tested positive for THC that night. The arresting officer knows the family well and knew to test him based on his past. Plus, I guess he reeked. No drugs were found on him. Mom tested clean. Standard protocol even though she has no history."

I take this opportunity to check my cell phone on my hip and ensure that the ringer is turned off. I've pissed off Jamie more than my share this year by having my damn phone go off in the middle of a meeting. It doesn't help that my ring tone is, "I'm Too Sexy."

Jamie is talking again, "The whole family swears that Mom has never been involved in drugs and is a model parent. Kris, you've been out to interview both parents."

Kris nods her head, but before she can speak, I interject, "Wait a minute. How is the whole family able to back her up on anything? She lives in a commune?"

Jamie peers over her black-framed reading glasses and sighs. "Sorry to have interrupted your busy morning, Leah. Before you arrived, we discussed some of the details regarding the recent death of the Buchanan toddler. It happened off Newcastle Lane. Given its high publicity, I'd have thought you'd heard about it."

Newcastle Lane. Why is that address so familiar? Jamie's prattling on, but I keep searching my mind. I know that address from somewhere. Suddenly, I have a vision of Tory and Collin, Katherine's kids, doing a play up on Newcastle. The school! Elsa's place.

"Wait," I interrupt Jamie. She looks as though she might chuck her stapler at me. "Was it a kid from the school?"

"Actually, it was Elsa Schultz' great-granddaughter."

It happens, more often than social services would like, that in a town as small as Santa Cruz, we know or know of the perpetrator and/or victim. That she's Elsa's great-grandkid makes me hurt all over. Jamie's demeanor has shifted from pissed off to mild concern. "Do you know this family, Leah?"

"No. Not personally. Katherine Middlebrook's kids went there and I saw Elsa a handful of times. It's just creepy. Sad." Already I know I'm going to refer the case to Katherine. Even though she knows Elsa, I don't think she knows Alyssa or Seth. Besides, she'll understand the culture of the school—what some would call a rich-hippy or tambourine-drumming fringe. That may be true, but Katherine's kids sure turned out great and have their heads on straighter than most young kids I encounter. "I'm guessing mandatory therapy for the family?"

Jamie nods. "Of course. Psych evals, supervised visits, you know the drill."

Yes I do. "I'll make a few calls. I've got someone in mind for the couple."

Katherine

Sure enough, my machine's red light is pulsating. If I'm lucky enough, it's a message from my regular clients. I hit the button. "You have two new messages. First message: 'Hi Katherine, it's Molly. I need to cancel tomorrow at 2:00. I'm off to see my daughter while she's on a layover in San Francisco; I take what I can get. But then, you know that already. Okay, I'm rambling, see you next week.' Next message: 'Katherine it's Leah. I didn't want to bother you at home. Well, actually, I did but promised myself I wouldn't bug you on your day off. Hope Mary's nausea is easing up. Give her a kiss for me. Anyway, I thought maybe you caught the paper this morning. I'm sure you know what I'm going to say next.'

I hit the delete button. I feel dizzy and a bit sweaty—probably another hot flash. I open the window even though it's only 62 degrees in here. Of course, I could be in Tahoe in the winter and if a hot flash hits, I'd want to strip down and roll around in the snow. I dial Leah. She picks up immediately.

"I knew you'd call after you read the paper," she says.

"I didn't even listen to your whole message. God, poor Elsa. I haven't seen her much except for the occasional wave across the church parking lot. The whole school community must be devastated." Carl and I schooled our children at West Side. It was quite an expense but worth it. Our children stayed young and protected through their childhood. They actually got to be children. "So, I'm guessing this is your case."

"Of course. What fun is my job without a little drama? Sorry, that was crass. I just thought it'd be good, you and me, working on a case together. Been a while."

"That's true."

"I hear some hesitation in your voice. Mom not doing well today?" Leah asks.

"That's part of it. I was just telling myself I needed to cut back. It's not like I'm full. Given the economy lately, people aren't exactly beating down the doors to pay over a hundred dollars an hour for private therapy." I can't bring myself to suddenly disclose my real hesitation. It's my private pain; a fact I've even concealed from Leah. "In this case though, I almost feel as though I owe it to Elsa and her family. She's given so much. It's just—"

"What's up? You afraid you can't be objective?"

"It's not that," I begin. "Just, Carl, well—"

"What'd Bob the Builder do today to make you crazy?" I hear Leah munching on her morning apple.

"He saw the article about the Buchanans in the paper and it really upset him. It's not as though I go blabbing about my clients to him, but I'm afraid his negative reaction could preclude me from ever sharing any feelings I'm having about the case. You know, it may contaminate how I perceive it and consequently, treat them." There's a pause. Leah's presumably taking in what I've said. I also know that Carl will worry about this bringing up the memory of Nicole's death.

"Well," she finally begins, "I'm sure that Seth and Alyssa are catching a lot of crap and judgment. Carl's reaction is probably nothing compared to what some are saying."

"I'm shocked," I say, taken aback. "You're actually defending Carl?"

Leah snickers, "Oh, come on. I love your old goat. He worships the ground you walk on. I just like to give him a hard time about his politics and tell him what is actually right—or left, in my case. I think that the town is going to have a lot of opinions about this case. It's going to be pretty high profile given that Seth's a local business owner and Alyssa's a former teacher at the school. Odds are you won't even be able to candidly talk about this case in your consultation group. At least you'll have me to confide in."

I hadn't even considered all this. I depend on my consultation group, a handful of other psychologists that I meet with monthly, to process cases. It's like an emotional dumping ground as well as a place to get feedback. Leah's right though—the minute I outline the Buchanan case, their identity will no longer remain anonymous, breaking the rules of client confidentiality.

"Why don't you fill me in on some of the details as I mull it over."

"Okay." I hear papers shuffle in the background. "All right, it looks like our hero father, Seth Buchanan, is thirty-two. He's being required to submit to weekly drug tests. He's been asked to leave the family home, at least temporarily. He's granted weekly-supervised visits with their surviving child. Elsa's been cleared to supervise those visits. That'll be interesting. And let's see what else...oh, he needs to attend an outpatient drug and alcohol treatment program."

I chew on this for a moment. "You said his parental rights are restricted."

"Mm-hmm."

"What about the mom's? They aren't pulling the surviving child and calling it a neglect case. She was at the drowning, too, wasn't she?"

"Well, it's messy, Katherine. The drowning occurred on Elsa's property. There were a lot of people present, and yes, ultimately the parents could both be charged criminally. If it was a pool and unfenced, hands down, they'd be liable. However, an unfenced pond doesn't have the same legal consequences. I think the D.A. will come down hard on dad because his blood tested positive for THC. Then again, this isn't Alabama; pot's practically legal here."

Sometimes the dismissal of marijuana as a drug that has psychological addiction really gets in the way of helping families that are riddled with this so called "non-addictive" drug.

"So, not only are they completely devastated by their daughter's death, but now dad has to worry about criminal charges. Plus, their older daughter could lose her father." I scribble down notes about the case as quickly as possible, circling the words: possible incarceration, break up of family. I'm already hooked.

"Your compassion never fails to amaze me. I say let him fry if he chose weed over his kid. Anyway, where you fit in is the mandated therapy piece. They've got to work on appropriate parenting skills, communication, recovery, grief, et cetera, et cetera. Here's the glitch—the wife, Alyssa, doesn't want to speak to Seth, let alone be in therapy with him week after week."

"Sometimes anger is an easier emotion to handle than despair," I say, all too familiar with this. As I consider the case, I take note of the mountain of demands placed on the Buchanans all at once. Resistance will be a major obstacle to overcome in therapy.

No one likes to be forced into confronting feelings. It can't be rushed. Across the top of the paper, I write down a couple of questions as Leah places me on hold for a moment: Am I up for this? After such a tragedy, can this family actually be reunited?

"I'm back. Sorry about that," Leah says.

"No problem. You've told me quite a bit about Seth. Tell me a little more about the surviving child and Alyssa."

"Their surviving daughter, Daisy, is five-years-old. She's been referred to Dr. Fowler, a child specialist in town. Christ, poor kid," Leah pauses. "Says here in the intake report that Kris couldn't get a word out of her during the interview."

"Scared? Too upset?" I ask.

"No, I mean, the kid won't talk. Period—to anyone. Hasn't uttered one word since the night her sister drowned."

Selectively mute. I haven't encountered that until now. "Post-traumatic stress disorder. Poor baby." This case is getting more complicated with each sentence Leah delivers.

"Yeah. As for mom, Alyssa is thirty-one. She used to teach kindergarten at West Side but has been a stay at home mom since Daisy was born. She is adamant about not having sessions with Seth in the room, but will see you alone. She mentioned that Elsa had given her your name a while back for couples work. Ironic."

"Maybe that'll be helpful in breaking through some of the initial resistance. We'll see."

"So you're taking the case?"

I fiddle with the jeweled chain on my reading glasses. The beauty of the beads mocks the ugly, pained words I've jotted down. "If you and I can support one another through this, I'll be fine. It's just one more case, really. We're a good team."

"You're the best, Katherine." I hear relief pour through her words.

"Don't be so sure of me. It's a lot of pressure."

I hang up and sink back in my chair. An old tape plays through my head, one that I had to learn to switch off in my early days of practice: What if I can't handle this? It doesn't matter that I hold certificates declaring my specialty in grief or that I've seen clients for nearly two decades. This is close to home.

I know that I am helpful to my clients. They tell me what relief they experience in having someone bear witness to their suffering. I've read volumes on parental grief. When Tory was at home, she'd look at the title of a book I'd be absorbed in on the couch and snicker, "Gee, Mom, some more light reading again?" Collin, using his knowledge of psychological language, diagnosed me as "death-fixated." I never told them that I was working on my own healing as well as educating myself about the issues of others. Like I said, losing Nicole was very hard on Carl and me. The right time to tell our children just never seemed to come around.

I look over at the clock and see that I've been gone much longer than my note to Mom said I would. A framed picture of Carl in my office catches my eye. "Carl, Carl. You'd be irate if you knew I'd just taken this case," I say to his smiling photo, a snapshot of him fishing down at the beach. It's no secret that therapists do their fair share of "pillow talk" with their spouses about clients. I never mention names and am careful about too much detail. But, it helps him understand why some nights I struggle to fall asleep or am in need of an hour-long bath with an extra glass of wine. I can't imagine not sharing this case with him, and yet, it's not possible.

Chapter 5

Alyssa

Peering out from Oma's yellow kitchen curtains, I watch a stream of cars head up Newcastle Lane. How can the world carry on? Parents take children to school; people fill up their cars with gas; ballet teachers teach little girls to point their toes, while I'm frozen in grief. Daisy, our dog Duke, and I have been staying with Oma since that night—nearly three weeks. Maybe we'll stay forever.

School was closed for a week after her drowning. The caution tape that circled the pond is now gone. Several families from the school feverishly constructed a wooden fence around the perimeter of the pond during the week's closure—the illusion of safety. I see familiar faces, now. Moms and dads glance up at our direction and grab their children's hands just a little too tight, probably thinking, 'Thank God that didn't happen to us.'

I see these intact families, know many of them personally, and am caught between feelings of utter rage and overwhelming gratitude...I'm a disaster. Casseroles lay stacked beside huge containers of soup and loaves of homemade bread in Oma's deep freeze. People love to feed the bereft.

Already there's talk of planting a memorial tree with a bench underneath to honor Nevaeh. Everything's moving too fast. It's like the quicker everyone can put this behind them, the sooner they can stop thinking about it.

Daisy plunks down beside me on the window bench as I continue to watch the school traffic. She shoves another blueberry muffin into her mouth. The child eats constantly but says nothing. "Is that good?" I ask, trying to get her to speak. She nods and extends her arm, offering me a bite. I take one and instantly feel the starchiness of it stick in my throat as though glue has been poured into my mouth. I can't fix this for Daisy. God, what a mess our life is.

There's a knock at the door. Oma answers it. I hear them chatting. It's my oldest friend, Gregory. He and I grew up two doors down from each other and practically lived in one another's yards and houses. We went to the same "hippy" school, West Side Arts, that Oma founded where knitting and gardening rank as important as history and literature. Even though we were raised virtually the same, Gregory and his brother Steven ran as fast as they could from their parents' simple life. Rather than hiding *Playboy* magazines under their beds in their teens, they collected *Soldier of Fortune*. Steven joined the Marines and Gregory works for the Santa Cruz police department.

Over the years, I thought he'd been too critical of Seth, judging him, warning me not to settle for a "pothead." I keep waiting for the "I told you so." Besides Oma, he's the only other person I trust.

I turn to see him give her a cordial kiss on the cheek. Oma was Gregory's kindergarten teacher and she adores him. "She's having another rough morning, dear," I hear Oma tell Gregory. "Seth will have his first supervised visit over here with Daisy tomorrow and of course, her counseling starts today. It's an awful mess. Maybe if you aren't busy, you can take her out during the visit; go down to the beach for a walk or something."

"Of course, Oma," Gregory replies in his confident police officer voice.

I'M RELIEVED TO turn away from the window. Daisy runs and hugs Gregory's legs. He kisses her head and tells her he wants to spend time with her mommy. Daisy smiles and skips silently over to Oma in the family room where Oma already has a storybook in hand.

Gregory hands me a bag spotted with delicious fat seeping through. "I brought you some croissants from The Farm. Chocolate." Usually, something from my favorite bakery in Aptos is my answer to nearly every crisis. Now everything is tasteless.

He wraps an arm around me and holds me tight. He smells the same way he always has, clean with a hint of Polo cologne. I love the familiarity.

"Thanks for coming over again," I say. He's been by every morning and night that he isn't working. I worry about how Jenny and the kids are reacting to him being away so much, but not enough to ask him to leave. Most days, I'm awful company. He works at rubbing the ache from my shoulders and head, only for it to return the next day. "You're going to get sick of me," I warn him.

"Been twenty-six years and it hasn't happened yet."

I smile and let his hands work the knots in my shoulders. I'm so tense today. It's the beginning of my mandated therapy. It's not the therapy that has me worked up, although I don't love the idea of being forced. It's that I'm going to see Seth. I haven't seen him since the funeral. Then again, I was so out of my mind that I can barely remember any details, other than seeing a hand painted urn that contained part of Nevaeh's ashes being lowered into the ground. Gregory was right; I shouldn't have stuck around for that.

I will not go to therapy as a couple. He lied to me again. Not only did he reek with pot when I asked him where Nevaeh was, but he also had the audacity to make up some lame excuse about looking for something in his car with Jeff. When I heard that his drug test came back positive, it was all I could do not to hunt him down and beat him with my fists. I believed him. I really believed him that night in the garage that he vowed to change, stay clean—God, what a fool. If I had a dollar for every time I've said that…and yet, when Gregory told me the D.A. was going for criminal charges, I thought it was the answer to my problems. Now all I can think about is bringing Daisy to see her father through prison bars and it sickens me. Nothing feels right.

I organize my life around Daisy's therapy appointments, check-ins from social services, plans for fleeing Oma's when supervised visits happen, and my own therapy. It all feels so pointless, except for getting Daisy the help she needs. When I wake from a nap or the occasional hour I do drift off at night, my first thought is Nevaeh's death. I'm back to day one, all over again, the pain so palpable that is slices through me.

Seth

I follow the landlord up the stairs. He breathes like we're climbing Everest. The chipped blue paint on the metal handrail reveals an avocado-green color beneath. He struggles with his fistful of keys, jiggling them until he finds the right one to unlock the door. He pulls open the caged-metal screen door as though he's about to let me into my cell.

"Damn keys," he says. "You'd a thought I'd coded them over the years but, ah, who has the time?"

I'm impatient with his chitchat. The door swings open and a mixture of mildew and cat piss assaults us. "Christ," he begins, "guess the last tenant had a cat or two." *Or twenty.* He throws open the window and says, "Here, this'll get some fresh air in."

The only way I can imagine the odor disappearing is if the place is stripped, gutted, and repainted. Watermarks, like mini crop circles, dot the ceiling and the old wooden floors are deeply scratched.

"So, as you can see, this is the kitchen, off the family room. Got your stove, refrigerator, and a sink. Sorry, no dishwasher. Guess you'll be using your hands." He laughs. I pump my fists, attempting to contain my impatience. I can't believe this rat hole is really going to be my place. "And back here, you got two bedrooms. One's bigger by a foot or two and the bathroom's in-between." Dank, smoky curtains hang from each bedroom window. The brown, linoleum bathroom floor looks as though the toilet has flooded it more than a dozen times; bubbles of water blisters surround it. I can't believe this is what $1,200.00 a month is going to get me. I can barely make that and the rent on our house (that ironically is sitting empty). First thing I'll do is rip those curtains down and scrub the hell out of the kitchen and bathroom before my social worker Leah comes for her inspection. I have to show her that I have a safe a place for Daisy, her own bedroom, and all that jazz. I peer through a bar lined window in my future bedroom at an alley below. I'm in prison.

"So, whattaya think?" asks Mr. Landlord.

I grab on to the bars and watch a bum take a piss on the street. "It's perfect. I'll take it."

Alyssa

I get to Katherine's first. Should I wait here in the car, stand by the door, or go on in? I look in the mirror and study the dark circles under my eyes. I grab a clip and pin up my hair, then rip it out and struggle to comb through my hair with my fingers. All I can think about is what Dr. Middlebrook already knows about us. She's got to be thinking what an absolute loser Seth is. I'm ashamed to admit that I ever married him.

I get out of the car and decide to walk down the driveway and introduce myself, when I hear Seth's truck pull up. I stare at him like I'm watching a monster in a nightmare, the one where I can't get away and my feet are stuck in mud. Everything about him sickens me; from the way his curly hair mounds on the top of his head to the way he blows smoke from his tight lips. I swear to God if he smokes around Daisy...

He slams his truck door and I jump. I grab each side of my wool sweater and tug it across my shoulders, forcing myself to take deep breaths. I can feel him approaching. I've never been away from him so long. If the circumstances were different, I'd be running into his arms. Now all I can do is try to make myself so small that I become invisible. Just as I'm about to knock, he grabs my arm.

"Don't touch me," I seethe, unable to recognize the voice that escapes me.

Seth retracts his arm as though he's been stung. "God 'Lyss, really? This is how it's going to be?"

How can I go from letting this man be inside me to loathing him in less than a month? "Don't talk to me. Let's just get this over with," I say, staring at Dr. Middlebrook's door.

"Look at me," he says in a low voice.

I lift my eyes, peering through my hair.

"It's still me. I lost her too."

I can feel my breathing stop and a lump form in my throat. "Don't do this."

As I wipe my tears, a woman, roughly my mother's age, opens the door. Her hair is pulled back in a loose knot and her face holds the compassion of sun on a foggy day. "I thought I heard some voices," she says. "I'm Katherine. Please, come in."

Katherine

The tension in the room is unparalleled to any I've experienced during the initial meeting of a couple. Right away, I'm drawn to Alyssa's and Seth's eyes. Yes, they are the windows to the soul, but it's more than that. Alyssa's are ablaze, full of anger and fear. However, the black rings beneath tell a different story, one of daily survival, like the eyes of Holocaust victims shown in documentaries. Seth's are wide and filled with worry. Streaked across the whites of his eyes are patterns of red veins laced like a fishermen's net, holding in a school of tears. Their visible pain strikes a familiar chord in me.

They continue to stand, watching me for direction. Alyssa continues to wipe her face and sniffle. Seth looks down at his feet, like a schoolboy in trouble. I sit down in my leather chair and say, "Please, take a seat anywhere you'd like."

Seth sits on the far left side of the couch. He turns as if to see whether or not Alyssa will sit beside him. She chooses one of the floral, high-backed chairs, farthest away from Seth. If I subtracted the tears and background knowledge of them, I'd see them as the poster couple for coastal California: tall, lean, bronzed. I pay someone nearly $100.00 every six weeks just to have a few streaks of Alyssa's golden blonde hair color to infuse into my gray. How deceiving looks are. The pain emanating from them is so intense that I excuse myself to crack a window. I'm sure my face is red with heat.

Returning to my chair, I struggle with how to start, then offer, "Seth, Alyssa, before we begin, I want to honor the pain and grief you must be experiencing over the death of your daughter Nevaeh. What a terrible thing for two parents to go through."

Alyssa's shoulders shake up and down as her tears give way to audible and pained sobs. Seth stares up at the ceiling, as though he can dam the tears from falling. I'm quiet for another minute or so, breathing in and out, centering myself in the midst of this emotional hurricane.

Alyssa breaks the silence with stuttered breath. "I still look for her. You know? I mean, I put Daisy to sleep and think to myself, where is Nevaeh? Is that crazy?"

"No," I begin, "that's not crazy at all. It's common for parents in the first few weeks after a child dies to search and wonder where the child is. You might even wait for her to toddle down the hall or see her in her bed."

Alyssa nods. Seth, however, is staring out the window, his brows knit together and his lips pressed tight. "Seth, what about you? Is this your experience?"

His face flushes and his stormy eyes stare at me intensely. "No, it's not, because I'm not home or anywhere remotely like home. I've been sleeping at my shop and I'm about to move into this…

this piece of crap apartment that I can't afford. So, no, I can't say I look for her, but I feel like a piece of me is missing. A hole's been ripped through my heart."

Alyssa clicks her tongue. Seth throws her an angry look.

"I just wish I could rewind time and—" he stops as his voice catches.

"And what, Seth?" I urge him.

"And bring her back. It's what you heard Alyssa and me fightin' about outside. I lost her too."

"Yes, Seth, you did. You lost a child, too," I reply. I remember a counselor pointing this out to me about Carl. Sometimes fathers are overlooked.

"Thank you!"

Since Seth is the designated "villain", I'm not surprised to hear that his grief is invalidated. All the same, I hope that I've offered him understanding. I check in with Alyssa. "How does all that sound to you, Alyssa?"

Alyssa's hands massage a wad of blue tissues from my coffee table. "Katherine, I'm afraid to say anything. If I do, I'm afraid I'll come unhinged. I really don't want to do that."

"Unhinged? Like, you might say something you'll regret? Strike him? Tell me what unhinged means for you."

"That I'll lose it. Scream at him!"

I look over at Seth. He shrugs. "I don't care. Lose it. Get it over with."

"That's not like me," Alyssa interjects. Seth scoffs but she ignores him. "Before this happened, I was pretty even-keeled. Now, I walk around either crying my head off or wanting to scream and hit my pillow."

"Sounds pretty normal to feel like doing all those things. I'm sure, Seth, that you are feeling some pretty intense feelings throughout the day, too." Seth nods. "Getting it all out is central to your healing. Holding back only aggravates what's going on inside you. I'm not saying it's okay to physically or emotionally assault one another, but it is important to be honest."

Seth and Alyssa look at one another as if asking for permission, then back at me. Alyssa inhales and straightens up in her chair. "Katherine, you don't understand. I can't do this week after week with him here because I don't want to see him anymore. Ever! *He's* the reason that I don't have my little girl anymore." Alyssa's voice raises an octave with each sentence. "*He's* the reason that our daughter Daisy won't speak anymore. *He's* the reason why I can't sleep, eat and why I can't decide if tomorrow is even worth living." She turns and faces Seth, now screaming, "You! You ruined our lives with your friends, your business, and your drugs being more important than your family! More important than watching your own child!"

The walls echo with her fury. I struggle with my own racing heart rate. The dam has broken and thousands of gallons of stored up water has just flooded the room. As frightening as someone's anger can be, I feel a sense of exhilaration in Alyssa's outcry. Seth, however, looks as though someone has taken a cast iron pan and hit him across the jaw.

"Seth, what's going on with you?" I ask.

He holds his arms up in surrender. "Is this what I get to look forward to every week? Hmm? To be ripped to shreds?" He turns away from me and catches Alyssa's eye. "Let me tell you something, Alyssa, you aren't the only one who thinks about killing herself. If it weren't for Daisy, I'd blow my brains out. Satisfied?"

Alyssa looks away from him. I decide to respond to his first question. "No, Seth, therapy is not about getting a lashing for what you did or didn't do. I want to hear what Alyssa and you are holding inside to gauge whether or not it's appropriate for the two of you to be in therapy together. At this point, I think it could be more damaging than healing for you two to be seen together."

Alyssa looks up at me, relief washing over her face. "So, are you saying we don't have to come?"

"No. I think at this point, a better course of treatment is for you two to come individually. We can work on the issues that child protective services has mandated: safety issues in parenting, addiction, co-dependency." I see them both roll their eyes but continue on. "More importantly, you will be able to de-escalate, share your grief privately, and not feel as though you have to defend yourself. Then, at a later time, we'll come together, the three of us, and see where we stand." Both nod their heads. Alyssa's shoulders drop a couple of inches.

"I do have one rule when I see couples separately: I do not keep secrets. That means if you begin to share something that you don't want the other to hear, I will stop you or ask that the three of us come together and discuss it. I hold very firm to this."

"What secrets could we possibly have? Our life is in the papers, written out all over the CPS reports. It's spilled out for everyone to see," Alyssa says sounding exasperated.

"It's very frustrating to feel that your privacy has been robbed from you," I offer.

"You have no idea," Seth whispers. I watch for Alyssa's reaction. Just as I supposed, her shoulders creep up and she shakes her head.

"Alyssa, you were adamant about Seth not being in sessions with you. Based on the limited information I've gathered today, it strikes me that even if child protective services hadn't asked Seth to leave your home, you may have?" I want to get Alyssa engaged in owning her feelings and have both of them disengage from blaming "the system" for the changes in their lives.

Alyssa opens her mouth to speak, then stops, as Seth and I await her response. "I guess so. Yes."

Seth's chin drops to his chest.

"Okay. Even so, I want you to avoid any big or hasty decisions over the next year. When you are grieving, you are more likely to be reactive and make poor decisions that you'll later regret. I'll be honest with you," I pause. Seth and Alyssa perk up and make eye contact with me. "The odds are not in your favor. There's an awful lot of blame that goes on when a child dies, whether the child died because of an accident or an illness. Just try and remember this day and my caution to you before you make any final decisions about your work, family, or marriage."

Seth and Alyssa remain quiet. I ask if they have any questions about therapy, find each of them an available weekly appointment, and have them sign a few required forms. Alyssa is starting to shuffle around for her keys. Seth checks his cell phone for missed calls.

"It feels like we're ready to end. But, before we go, I want to share what I've observed. I see two people in front of me who are suffering terribly. You are joined and connected in a way that no one else can imagine. Think about that for a moment." I stop and they both stare off, tearing up. "You hold more in common than you think. You both mentioned that at times, you feel so swallowed up in your grief that ending your life feels like the only viable option, that is, if it weren't for your love and obligation to Daisy. I just want to check in with you about how strong these feelings are about ending your life."

Seth taps the tips of his fingers together, as if revving up enough energy to let out more pain. "It's been tempting, especially at first. You know, I'm clean, for the first time in, well, since I can remember, and everything's really raw, really intense. I'm not used to having all these feelings whirling around."

"Mm-hmm. If you've numbed your feelings as a way of coping, this feels very different. As you put it, very raw," I agree with him.

Alyssa shakes her head and bites down on her upper lip.

"Sometimes it's all I can do to hold on but I know I can't hurt Daisy." Seth says.

I turn to Alyssa whose eyes are filled with fury. "Alyssa, how about you?" She looks straight at Seth. For a moment, I think she might extend her hand.

"It would devastate Daisy if you killed yourself. I think you've done enough," she scolds. She turns to me and continues, "I'm not going to kill myself, Katherine, if that's what you're worried about. I may want to die or numb out my feelings," a stab at Seth, "but my child comes first."

For the time being, I ignore her punches at Seth and try to find their common ground again. "So you both feel a sense of despondency and the thought has entered your mind to take your life. However, the part of you that is the responsible, loving parent, husband or wife says, 'No, I need to be there for my family.'"

They both answer with a quiet "yes".

"Should you ever find yourself in a place where that changes, you can always call my emergency pager, the county crisis line that I've written on your paper work, or 9-1-1. Okay?"

"Okay," they answer.

I stand and shake their hands, thanking them for coming. "Just remember, that while you may feel as though you *have* to come here, every act you take in life is a choice and today you *chose* to come here. I look forward to seeing you next week."

They exit, and I make my way over to my chair and collapse. I feel like I've just run the Wharf-to-Wharf race without my inhaler.

Alyssa

I walk up the steep driveway toward my car as quickly as I can. I hear Seth's footsteps behind me and then his hand is on my shoulder. "I'm gonna tell you something, and you're gonna listen without screaming at me or running off," he says.

"What?"

"I was not high the night our daughter drowned."

I have to restrain myself from wanting to strike out. "Shut up, Seth. Gregory told me that test was dirty."

"I swear to you I was not. I went up to my truck to get Nevaeh's blanket."

Just hearing the sound of her name and imagining her silky, pink blanket makes me weak. "Where is it then?"

His eyes look down at his empty hands. "I couldn't find it."

I turn and walk toward my car. Seth continues to follow me. "Leave me alone Seth. You heard Katherine. We could say or do things we'll regret. Now get away from me before I say anything else I may regret." I open the car door, throw in my purse, and struggle with the keys before I can pull out of the driveway.

"Alyssa, please wait!"

His words are distant, carried off with the cold, northern wind.

Chapter 6

Leah

I grab the Buchanan file, knocking the remains of my hummus and sprout sandwich onto my lap. Damn it. Working through lunch gives me a chance to review Katherine's initial impression of Seth and Alyssa before I make my visit to Seth's apartment. Scanning her notes, I see in bold letters, "NO COUPLES WORK— too angry." Hmm. She's the shrink. I'll have to get the nitty gritty over coffee tonight.

I check my watch, late as usual, grab my cell phone and pepper spray (don't leave home without it since that lunatic foster parent blew away one of the kids on my case load), and decide to walk to Seth's despite the cold gusts. Seth's new place is only a half dozen blocks or so from my office, which doesn't say much. Not that I don't love downtown, I do, with all its color, variety, and street musicians trying to make a buck. Give me quirky downtown over an enclosed, polished mall any day. I swear it's as if the '89 Loma Prieta quake hit only two years ago rather than nearly two decades. I'll be heading toward the town clock, strolling down the left hand side of the street, ready to swing into Bookshop Santa

Out of Breath

Cruz when I realize, duh, it's not here anymore. It was one of the many casualties of the quake. The "new store" is now on the other side of the street. The pan handling and homelessness remains constant, although these days there aren't the Vietnam Vets of the 70s—legs missing, rolling along in their wheelchairs, strumming guitars—type. It's more young kids. Angry kids. What's going on with our country that our kids are in the streets?

I carry a pocket full of change. Who am I to judge where they spend it. What's the saying, 'There but for the grace of God, go I.' I'm always one paycheck away from being unable to pay my rent, for Christ's sake.

Seth

I'm tearing through town to make it home before Leah Keller, my social worker, stops over for a visit. At 8:00 this morning, Cade from Freeline Surf Shop rang me at home. "You'd better come down and have a look at what someone sprayed across your windows," he said.

By 9:00, I had scrubbed off the remaining red paint where the word 'murderer' was splayed over the entire front window. Whoever did this also conveniently left the morning paper in front of the shop with the headline reading, *Local Business Owner Faces Criminal Charges in Death of Toddler*. The paper ran an old picture of me from my surf competition days. Cade clapped me on the back, assuring me it would all blow over.

I'm not so sure. As I light up a cigarette and throw back another cup of coffee, I catch my reflection in the rear view mirror. I look nothing like I did in the newspaper photo. It was taken eight years ago during a surf competition in Costa Rica. My eyes are filled with hope and my mouth is open—I can vaguely remember the punch line of the joke I was laughing at, something about an ice hole. I was *this* close from a major company offering sponsorship. I'd start the Big Wave Tour the following season, competing in amazing spots like Todos Santos, Mexico and Pico Alto, Peru. I had the world by the balls. Three weeks later, my dad was brutally killed in a drunk driving accident on Highway 17, the deadly mountain pass connecting Santa Cruz with the valley. Even in death, he was able to mess up my life. Like a vicious rip current grabbing another unsuspecting bastard, my dreams were swept out to sea. At only twenty-five years old, I stepped up and took over his surf shop. Every step of running his business felt as though I was walking in thigh-high water. I couldn't numb the feelings quick enough. A year later, along came Alyssa. Looking back, I see she was the best drug I'd ever found. I abused that, too.

I finally reach my apartment and sprint up the stairs. I have ten minutes to shower and rinse off the stink of these memories.

Leah

All I can think as I climb the stairs is, what a dump. Seth opens the door so quickly I nearly fall backwards. He's towel drying his hair all the while apologizing.

"You don't have to clean up for me." Of course, I know everyone feels like I'm their mother inspecting their room, looking for dust, cobwebs, and perhaps a joint tucked in their underwear drawer. All I really care about is if it's safe for his kid.

Seth stretches his arm out and sweeps it in front of him, "Welcome to my mansion." We both let out an uncomfortable chuckle. Even though I'm pretty sure this guy's a prick, I like that he can maintain a sense of humor given how upside down everything is.

"Daisy's room is on the left," he says, pointing. "I couldn't really afford much."

"A bed is fine," I reassure him. From what I can see, Seth has combed every garage sale in the county and turned trash into treasures. Hanging from the ceiling is a pink canopy that surrounds a wooden framed bed. It smells of fresh varnish. The dresser in the corner has a new coat of Barbie pink.

"Did you do all this?"

He nods, and looks down.

"Nice, Buchanan." He's put in 110%. "You design surfboards and furniture, huh?"

A timid smile spreads across his face. "Nah, I just kind of imagined what she'd like if she were here. Tried to make it different from the room she shared with her sister. She loves pink and is all into being a princess. Not a Disney princess, but a real one that live in castles." He walks over to the dresser and slides his hand across the top. "I sanded this thing down, along with the bed, over at my shop. Found 'em both at a garage sale. I want to paint some little flowers or something on the dresser when I have time. Get some pictures of the girls to put on top." Seth pauses, the words catching in his throat. "I, uh, I don't know how to get any though. I can't go into the house and Alyssa and I aren't really on speaking terms."

"Bring it up in therapy?"

"Well, Alyssa isn't in our sessions."

"I know. Talk to Katherine about it, she'll help you out with that."

The worry lines in his forehead relax. "Can I ask you something?"

"Sure."

"How long until Daisy gets overnight visits here? I miss her like crazy."

It's a question to which people want an exact answer and I'm usually stuck with an 'it depends' answer. Sometimes that response will wig a person out so badly that it gets us off to a delightful start. I sense that with Seth, this won't be the case. I pictured him as an asshole, superior attitude surfer with a huge chip on his shoulder. With him, all I feel is defeat. Maybe he needs encouragement to fight for what he has left.

I wander out to the family room, looking around at the yard sale coffee table and futon couch that holds the stains of other people's lives. I urge him to sit down beside me so I can explain my answer, surprised by the inch of compassion that's creeping inside me. "Seth, we kind of take things one step at a time. Securing housing and providing Daisy with a room and a bed is one step." I refer to my notes from a phone consult and am reminded that he's going to A.A. "Did you get a sponsor at A.A.?"

One of the requirements that Seth has to fulfill is to attend a drug and alcohol program. Standards are pretty loose within the county. As long as he can produce signatures from his meetings, a standard practice for those new to A.A., and meet with a sponsor who helps him through the 12-step method of recovery, then he's fulfilled this obligation.

Seth grabs a piece of paper from a stack on the coffee table. On it are several signatures of folks who attended the twelve meetings he's been to over the past three weeks along with the name and number of his sponsor, Rocco.

"Not bad, Buchanan."

He's beaming as though I've given him an "A" on a report card. "It's not terrible, the meetings I mean. I didn't know that a lot of addicts were normal people, you know, nurses, students, other business owners. Their stories are pretty grim, too."

I nod. "And your therapy? When's your next session?"

Seth retrieves his wallet from his back pocket and pulls out Katherine's business card; I recognize her lighthouse logo. "It's tonight at 5:00. One of my guys, Jeff, is closing up for me. The therapy is okay. Alyssa went off on me the first session, but then I kind of expected some of that. Katherine's cool. It's not like I really want anyone fishin' around in my head, but she doesn't treat me like I'm a scumbag. You know her?"

I have to be careful. I'm not going to blurt out that she's a close friend. On the other hand, nearly every social worker and therapist in this county has at least heard of one other. "Yeah, I know Katherine. I hear good things about her," I reply, dodging any further information. "So, I'll be in touch after I get a report from Katherine in a couple of weeks. I'll visit with Elsa and get feedback on how your visits with Daisy are going over there. In the meantime, keep your chin up, go to your meetings, and like they say at A.A., take it one day at a time."

Out of Breath

I get up and head for the door when Seth begins, "Hey, Leah can I ask you one more thing?"

"Sure. What's up?"

"The criminal charges, you think there's any chance they'll be dropped. I can't even deal with thinking about going to jail." He looks around the room and says, "I mean, this is pretty damn close."

A small pang of guilt ricochets inside over the crass remark I'd made earlier to Katherine. "I wish I had a crystal ball, Seth. You know, you tested positive for marijuana the night your daughter drowned. Some may draw the conclusion that you were negligent. Better that than getting caught with drugs on your person or testing positive for meth, though. Try to see this as a wake-up call."

He nods his head. I know he wants more; reassurance that everything is going to be fine. Even if the charges are dropped, things will be far from fine, given Alyssa's refusal to speak to him not to mention the grief that's going to be kicking his ass for who knows how long.

Seth

I wait to hear Leah's footsteps reach the last step, then slide down my door, collapsing from the fear that has mounted all day. I shove my t-shirt into my mouth so she can't hear my cries through the window. It's like I'm totally incapable of managing my emotions unless I'm sanding down a board or paddling out against heavy current. If I sit, even for a minute, I'm swallowed up with such sadness that it feels like I'm falling into a sinkhole. It's so damn painful. What I wouldn't give for just one hit of a joint or half a beer.

Last night, I was so on edge that I called Rocco and asked him to meet me at Betty's Burgers. I think over what he said last night, asking me if I knew why I got high.

"To relax, you know, unwind," I had said.

"Maybe, but I think that's really just a load of crap," Rocco challenged; his first generation Brooklyn-Italian, staccato accent breaking through.

"Everybody does something to chill out at the end of the day, have a drink, watch T.V., it's no different," I'd said defensively.

"If it's no different, then how'd you end up losing your family?"

I had wanted to walk out and tell him to mind his own goddamn business. Of course I didn't and I know he's right about me. There's no point in me going back to work today. I'm so wrung out. Things are slowing down anyway. It's not like I want to be around Jeff right now. It's tense between us. He doesn't get that I can't just have one beer or let him toke up in the back at the end of the day. What they said at A.A. about changing your circle of influence is impossible for me.

I wake up nearly four hours later. I had that same nightmare where I'm surfing over in Half Moon Bay. The swells are around twenty-five feet. I'm timing the waves—a perfect fifteen seconds in-between swells. I paddle out to the deep-water channel and get in the line up watching the horizon for a set. I start to paddle, generating speed when all of a sudden, I see Nevaeh out in the water on a little floating life raft. I can't fathom how she's gotten out here since Alyssa is up on Pillar Point, holding her camera to shoot. Nevaeh's positioned right where the wave is going to absolutely crush her. I scream her name, but the roar of the ocean carries my voice away. Just when the wave arcs and begins to curl down on top of her, I wake with my heart pounding, and drenched in sweat.

A siren blares through the window. The irony is cruel.

Chapter 7

Alyssa

My homework from Katherine this week is to walk Daisy over to her kindergarten class everyday—get used to interacting with people again, hear their questions like, 'How can I help?' and 'How's Daisy through all of this?' I force myself to shower and climb out of my sweat pants each morning, counting the minutes until I can jump back inside them and huddle by the fire with a cup of tea. The minutes tick off like years.

It's still so hard to open up with Katherine. I'm on hold, waiting to hear if Seth will face charges. I don't know what's worse, the thought of him not being held accountable for his actions or hearing that he'll spend time behind bars. Resurrecting Nevaeh is the only plausible relief. Some days Katherine offers me tea and I quietly sip it and stare out her window, watching for whales to spout. Katherine's good at being still. Just her presence is healing. Most moments, I am paralyzed by my worries over Daisy, fearing that we'll be trapped in this stuck place, obsessed with the "what ifs" of the night Nevaeh died.

Today, Katherine wants to talk about the upcoming holidays. Just hearing the word 'Christmas' is like anticipating an earthquake that will demolish my foundation. I huddle in the corner of her couch, gripping the flowered throw pillow, considering her question of how I'm feeling about the holiday season.

"I don't want to do anything. I have to, though."

"Why do you have to?" she asks.

I straighten up, slightly, replying, "For Daisy. I can't exactly cancel the holidays. And my social worker told me that Seth has been granted a full day visit with her on Christmas. I guess he's behaving well, or more likely, he's duped her like he did me."

Katherine cocks her head. This is always a sign that she's not quite in agreement with what I've said. "There's a lot in your answer that I want to address. First, you are right, you do need to do something with Daisy that is special. But there are ways you can do something for her that don't involve so much pain for you."

"Like what?" I ask.

"Well, what are your family's traditions?"

"Oh, the usual. We cut down a tree and decorate it. Oma already has the advent wreath up. Santa comes on Christmas morning then later on tons of family and friends gather at church then go back to Oma's to eat, exchange presents. You know, kind of what everyone does, I guess."

Katherine is quiet for a minute. "You mentioned that Oma has an advent wreath."

"Yes."

"The advent wreath commemorates the darkness of the season and our anticipation of Christ's birth which offers light. You know some of the clients I've worked with in the past have set up a memorial table for the person who has died. It's a place where photos and mementos can be displayed, honoring the dead and keeping the person present. It's a way of finding light in the darkness."

"I like that. I don't know if Oma and I are up for the whole tree thing, other than doing it for Daisy. This...this sounds meaningful." I'm already imagining the photo I want to use. Nevaeh is curled up on my chest, clutching her pink blanket, with her thumb falling out of her mouth. The picture's on my nightstand at the house. Luckily, Oma has a copy.

"You okay?"

"Yeah, just picturing an image of Nevaeh. I'm okay. Go on."

"Are you sure?"

I nod.

"Second, having a large group around on Christmas can either be comforting or completely exhausting, usually the latter. Talk with Oma and you two can decide what feels right. You need to honor your feelings. If that means telling people that you'll be spending a quiet Christmas alone, I'm sure they will understand."

She's so good at getting me to notice how I never pay attention to what I need. I want to reach out and hug her. "Sounds good."

"Finally, you mentioned that Seth has been granted visitation. What's your plan for coping with that?"

I sink back into the couch and rub my tired eyes. "Oh, Katherine, I have no idea. I know I don't want to be there."

"So, don't be there."

"What, just leave?"

"Is it possible for you to celebrate the evening before and early in the morning after Santa Claus comes. Then you can slip out and spend your day elsewhere—the movies, a walk, or perhaps stop by a friend's."

The ominous black cloud lifts. I don't have to stay. I know just where I'll go.

When I return to Oma's, she's pulling a fresh tray of cinnamon rolls out of the oven. The house swirls with the buttery, warm smell of my childhood at her house. I catch myself smiling, forgetting momentarily the nightmare that is my life. Daisy and I pull the gooey contents of a roll apart, chasing it with tall glasses of milk. Almost immediately I feel guilty over this simple pleasure.

"How about a nature walk, Daisy?" I ask as we napkin off our stickiness. She nods her head, bounds for the door, and slips on her boots.

Oma grins at me. "Good for you, dear. It's time to get out and enjoy the air of the season—clears the head, reminds us that God's still present even when we feel He's deserted us."

I offer a weak smile. I don't feel his presence. In fact, if anything, I'm nearly as angry at God as I am at Seth. How could he take my baby? I shove my wavering faith aside, grab my knitted cap, and head out with Daisy. "Oh, and Oma," I call out as I open the door, "while we're gone, could you get that picture of Nevaeh with her blankie that I framed for you?"

"Of course." She asks nothing of my request. I love that I never have to explain myself to her.

The silence of our walk is deafening. Daisy's usually so full of chatter, rattling off the details of her day in school; who cut in line at the swings, how the oatmeal at snack time was so delicious because of the maple syrup, or how she and Fiona got to hold the hand puppets during circle. Today, there's nothing but the sound of the wind moving through the trees and an occasional misplaced seagull.

"How about we gather some treasures for a special nature table, Daiz?" Throughout the year, we decorate a table at home and Oma's with plants, acorns, flowers and other objects that correspond with the season. This one will be for Nevaeh's altar.

Daisy lets go of my hand and scampers across Oma's property. She's shoving leaves, gnome hats (oak acorn tops), and eucalyptus acorns into her fleece pockets. She turns towards a maple tree that is still holding onto a few of its leaves. It's down near the pond. She heads over, then turns and looks at me, her eyes wide with the question, 'Is it okay for me to go there?'

"Go on, Daisy. I'm right behind you." The words escape me, causing goose bumps across my arms.

It's so unfair that the safest, most innocent spot of my childhood has been desecrated by the death of my child. It's like seeing a wrecking ball plow through 'It's A Small World' in Disneyland.

I can't get my head around it. I steady myself against an old oak that Gregory and I climbed as children. If I stare at it hard enough, I can make out the 'G' of his first initial. He didn't quite make it to the 'W' of his last name—Oma caught him and told him that he was giving the tree a wound that hurt like a deep cut.

Daisy tucks just one maple leaf in her pocket, then runs up and slips her hand into mine. We walk back up to the house after a long stroll around the horse stables. I alerted Oma of our purposeful walk before leaving. She's set evergreens from a pine tree out front on the nature table. It's ours to transform.

"Daisy, this is a little table we're going to decorate just for Nevaeh," I say with a quivering voice, trying to sound "normal."

She looks at me quizzically. I wish I could read her mind.

"You know how we put up the manger scene to remember baby Jesus? Well, this is a place where we can remember Nevaeh." From the back of the house, Oma joins us and hands me the photo of Nevaeh that I asked her for earlier. I place it amongst the evergreens. When I turn to see Daisy's reaction, I see her darting back to her room. "Daisy," I call out, "are you okay?"

Maybe this is too much for her. I run to the back of the house where the girls shared a room. Daisy is on top of her bed, reaching for a figurine on top of a shelf that Oma gave her last Christmas—a guardian angel. She carefully lifts the angel, slips down off the bed, paying me no heed, and runs back out to the living room. Next to Nevaeh's picture, Daisy places the angel. Then, as though nothing's happened, she pulls her treasures from her pocket and begins to scatter them around the angel and Nevaeh's picture.

Oma slips her arm around me and is wiping a tear from my cheek. "Children know how to grieve, Alyssa. It's we adults that have trouble."

Gregory

My shift is finally over, but the real work is ahead of me. Katherine's opened a late slot for me. I'm going to talk about Steven tonight if it kills me. He would have turned thirty-six this week. As teens, we would lie in our tent in the backyard and play a game we called, "When I get the hell out of here." I would start, with some cockamamie idea, like, 'When I'm outta here, I'm going to own a Ferrari." I'd feel all pumped up until Steven would say something like, 'When I'm outta here, I'm going to work in intelligence for the government and be one of those bad-ass sharp shooters.' I'd feel like a three year old with my thumb in my mouth. He didn't mean to level me. Steven was just that way—big ambitions, a hero, wanted to kill the bad guys. I haven't gotten my Ferrari yet, but Steven, well, he blasted plenty of those goddamn insurgents to hell.

I grab a Rolling Rock and peek in the boys' room. They're already asleep and it's only seven. Their arms hang off their beds near a litter of trucks and wooden blocks. I feel a presence behind me, and turn to see Jenny. Startled, I splash my beer on both of us.

"Sorry," I apologize, "you scared the hell out of me."

She sweeps a hand over the damp spots of her blouse. "Always ready for action, hmm?"

"What?" I'm irritated with her response. "No, I just—how were the boys tonight?"

"Fine. Just the usual 'When will Daddy be home? Please can we stay up so he can tuck us in?'"

"Not tonight Jenny," I say. I barely recognize who we've become. Jenny was all light and laughter, like the bright yellow paint that she painted our kitchen. Six years ago, after Alyssa called to tell me she'd just taken a home pregnancy test and it was positive, I remember doing two things: finding Jenny's number wedged in my Levi's and getting smashed until I passed out. Jenny helped me tuck away my fantasies of Alyssa with her perky personality and eagerness to please. All that light she had…it's become a shade of pale.

I push past Jenny and head for the bathroom. I need a quick shower before seeing Katherine. Actually, I could care less about how I smell for Katherine. I'm stopping by Alyssa's after my appointment.

"Greg," Jenny says as she sits on the bed and watches me undress, "I can't keep living the way we do. You're not home anymore. You're constantly over at Alyssa's while the boys and I are here, separate from you."

I throw my uniform onto the floor. Jenny will drop it off at the dry cleaners tomorrow. "I'm not going to Alyssa's." At least not right away, I lie. "I told you I'm seeing a shrink about my brother."

"And I'm glad you are. What about your medication? I don't see it in the cupboard."

"Not that it's any of your business, but I don't need that crap. I'll pull out of this in time."

"You've been saying that for a while...even before Steven's death."

"Jenny, we're not talking about this."

"That's the problem: you never want to talk about anything anymore. The truth is," she pauses and walks toward me, then leans against the doorframe, "I know you love our boys, but I'm not sure you're in love with me."

I wrap a towel around my waist, knotting it at the side. "What do you mean?"

Jenny takes a deep breath. This time she looks away, playing with the cosmetics lining the sink as she begins to speak. "I think it's best if we separate."

No tears this time, no hysteria over how we have to pull it together as a family. She's flat...resigned. It might be the free pass to do what I want, but it feels like I've been shot in the ribs, her demeanor is so cold. "Separate, as in divorce or separate as in see what happens?"

She sighs. "I've been talking with your mom about this the past six months and..."

"Whoa, wait a minute. You and my mom are discussing our separation? How quaint. And tell me, what did my mother say?" I don't know why I'm surprised or pissed off. Jenny and my mom talk nearly every day whether it's over the phone or in person.

Jenny's like the daughter my mother never had and my mom is the mother Jenny lost as a teen. Most guys dream of having their mothers and wives get along like family. For some reason, it makes me short of breath. Jenny props herself up on the bathroom granite counter.

"Oh Greg, please don't get like that. You know Lily is dear to me and I value her opinion. I guess I needed her permission, you know. I can't keep waiting for you to come around. I need to take care of myself…and the boys," she says as she dabs at her eyes.

I turn away, step into the shower and slam the glass door, causing it to shake. The hot water scalds my skin. I try to wash away the thoughts that fill my head—bad husband, absent father, distant son. No matter how hard I try, they continue to percolate through me, the words bouncing around like water bubbling in a pan.

I dry off and check my watch. I have twenty minutes until my appointment. Luckily, Katherine is about five minutes from here. Jenny comes back in the bathroom and touches my shoulder. I avoid her gaze, push past her, and grab a clean t-shirt from the dresser.

"Please Greg, talk with me." Her voice has resumed the rehearsed, calm tone.

"So since you have this all planned out, my mother and you, where exactly am I supposed to go with the mountains of money I make?" I ask as I loop my belt through my jeans.

"Your folks' condo in Rio Del Mar is available. No one's scheduled to use it until May or early June. Maybe by then you'll figure out what you need. I hope I'm part of that."

What I need. For starters, a vodka neat. Then how about more than three hours sleep. Really, I want to see what it's like to have my arms around Alyssa and not just to comfort her—to see how the curves of her body mold into mine the way I've imagined when I breathe in the smell of her hair. "Gee, I have a whole five months Jenny. I'll get right on that and let you know what I figure out." I grab my wallet, shove it into my back pocket, and head for the door. "I'm going to be late for my appointment. Don't wait up."

"Greg, please don't run off angry like this."

"How should I run off, Jenny? By the sound of things, I should pack my bags when I get home."

"That's not what I meant."

She's flustered. Good, let her stew.

"Don't worry," I begin as I open the door, "I'll be out of your hair by tomorrow."

Katherine

Walking up the stairs after my intense session with Greg, I accidentally drop my keys. I bend down to pick them up when it's as though someone has shoved me over. Luckily, I've landed on my backside rather than on my head. I put my head between my legs and breathe slowly. My heart pounds like I've been dancing all night rather than sitting and listening. I haven't had a dizzy spell like this since I was pregnant with Collin.

Scheduling someone after 7:00 is never a good idea these days with the lack of sleep I've been getting. Mom is up and around much more, but thankfully, she agreed to stay with us through the holidays. As much as it is a relief to me that she isn't alone, her presence demands my attention. I always feel "on." I'm up early, to bed late, and my mind is like a film, replaying each moment of the day.

Carl opens the door and the porch light floods the yard. "What are you doing out here? You okay?"

I quickly grab my keys and the file that has fallen to the ground. "Oh, you know me, a klutz at heart." I don't want to worry him needlessly. Carl offers a hand and I stand up, brushing leaves off my pants.

"Forget to turn the light on when you went down?" he asks.

"I suppose so."

"You okay?"

"I'm fine. How's Mom?" It's always my first question after I've been away.

Carl takes my arm and walks me inside. Suddenly, I feel like an old, sick woman being tended to by my son. I straighten up and gaze at my husband whose rugged look of weathered skin and graying temples still makes me swoon.

"She's fine. She turned in about fifteen minutes ago. She had a bit of a headache."

His words send adrenalin through me. "How bad was it? Do you think we should call her doctor?"

Carl gives me a hug and whispers, "It's probably just a headache. You're going to be sick yourself if you don't learn to relax."

The smell of his familiar shaving gel calms me down. "I know, you're right. I just keep waiting for the next sign. She's on borrowed time."

Carl sits me down, hands me a glass of Pinot Noir, and rubs my shoulders. I can't even form a sentence. Alyssa and Seth come to mind momentarily, how they aren't able to turn to one another for this kind of comfort. I let the thought drift away as Carl continues to knead away the ache.

"How was your session tonight? Awfully late wasn't it?"

"You're not going to make me talk about work while you rub my shoulders are you?"

"Sorry, I thought maybe you needed to vent."

I'm drunk from the way Carl is working my neck, or maybe I'm sipping my wine too quickly. "Oh, I probably do. I've got a couple of really hard cases." If he only knew… "This one, though, isn't so bad. Poor guy's a police officer and he's having trouble with anger on the job. His brother died over in Iraq recently. To top it off, his wife asked him to move out today."

"A policeman, huh? He show up in uniform?" Carl's tone has changed from one of concern to mildly playful.

"What?"

"I know how you love a man in uniform, Katherine," Carl teases.

I turn and see a wicked grin on his face. "Carl, don't be ridiculous. He's nearly twenty years younger than I am."

"Uh-oh, a young police officer. I better watch out."

I hit him with my throw pillow. "You are awful."

Carl wraps his arms around me, "Mrs. Middlebrook, you are under arrest for blushing. I'm going to have to take you to your room for being a bad girl."

"Shh, Carl, you're going to wake my mother."

"Wow, I haven't heard a girl say that in a long time."

I start to giggle as he leads me into our room. "Be gentle with me."

"Oh, I'm always gentle."

Chapter 8

Seth

Hearing that my court date was set to rule on criminal charges was not the Christmas present I was looking for. I spent last night combing through the men's department in Macy's at the Capitola Mall for something other than a t-shirt and jeans. The public defender, a sweaty, oversized giant of a man, said to get something conservative. He didn't tell me that conservative costs a fortune.

I'm sitting beside him, bound up in a white long sleeve shirt, blue tie and khaki slacks. I tug at my tie, trying to swallow. I swear someone has set the thermostat on eighty degrees. Sweat drips down my back. Greg and Alyssa's stares are like a laser pointed at me. Of course Greg showed up to "support her." When is he not around? He's like a wart that despite being burned off appears again and again.

No one is in my corner. I keep my mom out of the loop. God knows, she'd show up with liquor on her breath and make a scene when the judge decides to lock me up. The town sees me as a murderer. Despite Leah's prediction that the judge will throw the criminal charges out, I feel like a man already sentenced.

Out of Breath

We're rising as the judge enters. He asks us to take a seat. Words are falling from his mouth to which my attorney responds, "Yes, your honor," and "No your honor." They could be speaking Japanese and I still wouldn't understand or care. I can't hear them above the roar of anxiety in my head. I try to size up the man in the black robe before me. Does he have kids? What if his wife lost a baby? He'd want to have justice. Maybe his son's an addict and feels that "we" need to be taught a lesson. I turn to find Alyssa in the crowd, when I spot Leah in the back of the courtroom. She nods at me and offers a grin filled with sympathy. Maybe she cares, maybe she doesn't. I can't tell. Alyssa won't look at me. Her eyes are fixed on the judge as though she can incant her wishes to him.

The public defender nudges me with his chubby elbow. The judge is reading his decision. This is it, my last morning of freedom. I wonder how I'll see Daisy. Will Alyssa bring her to the jail? What if I'm transferred out of town? I know Oma will bring her for visits if I stay in the area, but she doesn't drive long distances. I bite at the cuticle around my finger.

"Mr. Buchanan," the judge begins, "according to the drug screening given the evening of Nevaeh Buchanan's death, you tested positive for THC. Having THC in your blood stream would not lead me to hand down a decision of criminal charges. However, since you were to be supervising your child on that evening and you tested positive for cannabis, I needed to consider this."

I'm toast.

"According to the police records, no drugs were found on your person. Now, while I believe that your behavior was reckless and irresponsible, I do not believe that it constitutes criminal charges. The sentence that life has served you is far crueler. For the time being, you are to remain in a separate residence from Alyssa and Daisy Buchanan, continue your counseling with Dr. Middlebrook, attend AA, and submit to weekly drug tests." He's still talking, but I'm checked out. I'm not going to jail. It's like popping up for air after hitting the bottom of the ocean. The news continues to wash over me, sending tears down my face. I don't even try to wipe them away.

I look back to catch Leah's eye just as Greg shoots up from his seat. He grabs Alyssa's hand and tugs her through the courtroom toward the door as though she were a child. Alyssa sobs all the way. I have a sick feeling that I've just escaped one sentence but been served another. She's lost to me.

Alyssa

All I want to do is sleep. Sleep away the shock of this day. Sleep away the sick feeling I have since I heard that Seth will go free for his crime. Free! Yet our baby is dead. I feel sick and want to stay under the covers, but I have to get up and go to Katherine's. As I pull on my thick, purple sweater, I hear my thoughts ping around my head, and a new thought spreads through me—I *want* to go to Katherine's. I can't get there fast enough.

I enter Katherine's office and fling my purse beside me on the couch. Katherine leans forward, waiting for me to begin. "Something's different about you. You seem less…mm, sad. Like you have energy for the first time since we've met."

"He got his verdict. He's free. No jail time."

Katherine nods. She seems to be sorting through her thoughts. "You finally have an answer. How do you feel about that?"

"Mixed up. But if I think about it, I feel like I've left that weird limbo place. Pissed. We've been on hold, waiting to see if he was going to jail for weeks. At least I know what's ahead of me."

"And that is?"

"Having to figure out how we share Daisy. Knowing he's around." I want to tell her all my thoughts. The ugly, dirty ones, but my fear of her judgment holds me back.

"What else, Alyssa? I hear something else in your voice."

It's like she's a mind reader. I take a big breath. "Okay, here it is: I think a part of me felt that Seth deserved to suffer. Like I am."

Out of Breath

"You don't think he's suffering?"

"Well, of course." I stop talking. "But still, he needs to pay for what happened."

Katherine has that "ah-hah" look about her. "So, beyond losing his baby, having to see Daisy only a few hours a week, being forced out of his house, and having his wife refuse to speak to him, he still deserves…what?"

I feel like I'm defending myself. "Whose side are you on?"

"I'm not on anyone's side. I just think it's a bit irrational though to say that he isn't paying for Nevaeh's death. He's paying dearly. Right now, I'm trying to help you understand your reactions, thoughts, and feelings about Seth not going to jail. Perhaps help you think about it as your loss as a couple rather than an individual loss."

She's stumped me again. The balloon of anger that I walked in has been hit with a blow dart. I'm left with its deflated, wrinkly image. "When will it finally dawn on me that she's really gone? She's never coming back, Katherine."

"No, she's not, Alyssa. I'm so sorry."

I don't know what else to say. I was sure I could rant and rave through my whole session. The energy is gone. Katherine does seem genuinely sorry. I see her tear up from time to time while she listens—this is one of those times.

"So we're back to you. I think that your anger at Seth and wanting some type of justice gave you another wall to hide behind. Now that you know he'll still be around, you have to deal with other feelings you've been keeping at bay," she says.

I don't want to deal anymore. I'm so tired.

"How is your support system? I know you have Oma. Who else is there for you?"

I almost blurt out Gregory's name, but I know how that will sound—like I'm jumping into another man's arms. That's not it at all. He's just so…understanding, present, attentive. All the things I wish Seth could be. "It's fine," I reply. "I have friends and a cousin I'm close with."

"Did you look into the parental bereavement group I mentioned?"

"I'm not ready for that Katherine. I don't want to share in a group. Way too scary."

"I understand."

Katherine

I do understand. It took me over five years before I could say out loud to a group, "I lost a child." However, losing a child isn't all that defines Alyssa. As our session continues, I want to move Alyssa to a deeper place of understanding herself. My gut tells me that even before their child died, Seth and Alyssa had bigger problems, including baggage they dragged into their relationship. What I find most curious is the absence of Alyssa's mother in her life. Not once has she mentioned her. I know she lives with her grandmother, Elsa, but where is her mother in all of this?

"Alyssa, when was it that you started to live with Elsa?"

"Umm, I guess probably in grade school." Alyssa begins to fiddle with a tassel on the throw pillow. "It was just easier. My mom was so busy. You know she taught at West Side Elementary, too." Her words can't get out fast enough. "It was really hard for her raising a kid alone. My dad died in a logging accident when I was just a baby. I guess we lived up in the mountains back then. I don't remember. She came down here to live by my grandmother. I loved being at Oma's though. There were always dozens of kids around, so it wasn't as though I suffered or anything."

"Alyssa," I interject.

She startles at my interruption. "Did I say something wrong or—" Her face is pained, betraying what she's just told me about her lack of suffering.

"No. You didn't say anything wrong." I pause. "I want you to check in with yourself for a minute. What's going on with your breathing?" Mine is shallow and tight.

Out of Breath

Alyssa shrugs. "I don't know, I guess it's kind of fast." She puts the pillow aside and shifts her position on the couch.

"Okay. Close your eyes if you would for just a minute. Put a hand on your chest and breathe deeply for a minute until everything slows down." I watch her comply with my directions. As she begins to slow her breathing, I see her neck and face flush and her nose begins to twitch. "You're doing great, Alyssa," I reassure her. "Now, you can open your eyes and I want you to repeat what you said a couple of minutes ago, 'It's not as though I suffered or anything.'"

Alyssa's eyes gently open and she parts her lips to speak, but only sobs escape. "I...I can't, Katherine."

"You can't. That's right. What can you say?"

She reaches for the tissue on my table. "That I don't really understand why my mother left me to live at Oma's. That my mother was gone...all the time, even when she wasn't teaching. I mean, I love my grandmother, but why—" her high voice cuts out.

"Why what?"

"Why didn't she want me? Why is she so far away now? Katherine, she didn't even come for the funeral. I mean I know Germany is a long ways away, but Nevaeh was her granddaughter."

I can see my mother at Nicole's funeral—black suit, black hat, black handbag; her hands shaking. Whether it was out of grief or withdrawals, I didn't know. Looking back, I suppose it was both. Nevertheless, I needed her there, regardless of our history.

"You needed to know she was there for you and she wasn't."

Alyssa nods. I want to hold her and tell her how sorry I am for her, but know this isn't appropriate. I need to let her experience her pain. "Can you make a statement about that?"

Through shuddered breath, Alyssa whispers, "I needed my mother and she wasn't there." The edge in her voice is gone, replaced with something new: vulnerability.

I MEET WITH Seth two days later. His past is a mystery to me. As the well-known Spanish philosopher George Santayana said, "Those who cannot remember the past are condemned to repeat it." Seth's past needs to be unearthed. I know his father is dead and the remarks that he makes about his mother are disparaging. With his criminal charges dropped, I think he'll be able to allow more thoughts and feelings to rise to the surface. However, he's also at great risk for relapse as the impact of memories and emotions surge through him.

"How is life going for you, Seth?" I ask.

"Everything's just...empty."

"Empty, how?"

"Meaningless. I go to work, come home, shower, go to a meeting. But, I'm...alone."

"You're connection to the people who matter the most to you has been broken."

"Exactly." Seth's demeanor changes—his eyes grow serious and he leans toward me. "I need to tell you something, Katherine. I know it was totally irresponsible of me to not watch Nevaeh, or Daisy for that matter, the night Nevaeh drowned. But, I'm telling you the God honest truth, I was not high."

So here we are, still dealing with denial. Back in my graduate school training, a wise professor told us to always go with the client's resistance. What good are we if they up and leave? And to remember that it takes trust and timing for the client to reveal truth. "Rather than defending yourself, Seth, I'm more interested in how things are going to be different in the future."

Seth sinks back into the couch and rolls his eyes. He's upset. I won't get into the addicts dance of "I didn't, I won't, I promise," so I change the subject, hoping his anger dissipates as we talk.

"You know, up until now, we've talked about how difficult life is adjusting to Nevaeh's death, worries about jail, addiction, missing Daisy, your discouragement over Alyssa's mistrust of you. I know this is very consuming. Yet, I don't feel that I really know you, your history, how you got to be the person you are today."

Seth raises his eyebrows. "Like, talking about when I was a kid and stuff?"

"Yes. You've mentioned your father's death and how your mom is relatively absent from your life. But, what about that?" Here's the landmine to where I want to lead him.

His posture tightens and he runs his fingers through his thick, brown hair. "Oh, Christ. I really hate to talk about my mother, Katherine. Alyssa, she's like the only one who hears me bitch about her."

"Okay, I understand it may be uncomfortable, but you do lots of things these days that are uncomfortable."

"And what does this have to do with what I'm going through now?" Seth replies, still sounding irritated.

I don't want to lecture him on the benefits of psychotherapy. I pause to think of the best way not to put him off. "Let's just say that a lot of who we are is shaped by how we were parented."

"I'm nothing like my parents if that's what you mean." *I hit a nerve.* "They didn't teach me anything. Hell, they barely parented me."

"Okay. So, when you were a little boy, growing up, and things in life were frightening or troubling, who kept you safe? Who did you go to with your fears?"

Seth scoffs, "Are you kidding me?"

He's dodging every bullet. Time for a story. "Seth, I was born into a family that was chaotic. My folks were very young when they met and they loved to drink. Unfortunately, they didn't slow down much when I came along and I became the little mommy of the house. I did most of the cooking and cleaning while my mom slept off her hangovers. My dad tried to hold a job, but he was better at being fired than hired." Seth listens with rapt attention. "After a few years of walking in their footsteps in my mid-teens, a teacher suggested I get help. I did and probably saved myself from going down the same path. Eventually, my mom got clean and still is today. My dad wasn't so lucky."

After a few seconds, Seth says, "No kidding."

I shake my head, "No kidding."

Seth

The only person I've ever told my life story to is Alyssa. We were naked in bed. She was pregnant with Daisy. I started crying after we made love. It was like making love to her brought out all this crap I'd been holding in. I was a little high, so things flowed easily. Telling Katherine, well, I could really use a cigarette at the very least.

"Where do I even begin? My mom, she's been a drinker my whole life. Loves her gin and tonics. God, that smell, to this day I can't smell gin without wanting to punch a wall. With the first drink she'd be kind of sweet, telling me how I'm her boy and how I'm nothing like my father, which really got me pissed. Back when I was little, he was my idol—knew all the right people, still hung out with the young surf crowd, toting me around like his little side kick. Then, after a couple more drinks, she'd be like, 'my life sucks.' I can see her cigarette hanging off her lip, the ashes dropping onto the linoleum, me being scared like a little baby that she was going to crack me across the face for something I did or didn't do. Hell, if I wasn't in trouble, she'd make somethin' up just to take out her aggressions." My hands are shaking. I shove them under my legs, hoping Katherine won't notice.

"What's going on inside you, Seth?'

"I'm...sorry, I'm shaking. God, I hate even thinking about me bein' a kid and putting up with all her crap."

"What specifically about that is so painful?"

I wring my hands, willing them to stop shaking. "What's so painful? What's so painful," I repeat, thinking. All at once, I can hear my mom's shrill voice screaming at me after I broke my arm skateboarding. The doctor bill was so much that she was going to have to ask my father for money. She'd had one too many drinks and hollered, "I wish you weren't born, you little bastard." Only, I'm not thinking this, I'm screaming the words in Katherine's office. I look up and Katherine is wide eyed, reaching her hand across the table to touch mine.

Out of Breath

"Seth, Seth. It's okay. You're here now, with me, and you're safe."

I'm trembling and my head is pounding. I feel Katherine's fingertips. They're soft, white, different, not like my mothers', full of calluses and yellow from nicotine. "I need a cigarette, Katherine."

"Sure, Seth. Please, take a break."

I walk out to her front yard and shake out a cigarette. With each inhalation, I feel my nerves settle a little more. Katherine's digging around into my past isn't something I signed up for. I look up at my truck and watch raindrops splash off the windshield. I could take off right now. I walk up the driveway, unlock the door and open it. One final long drag and I drop the butt into the rain soaked gutter. I pick up the soggy remains, toss it onto the floor of my truck, and head back down the driveway.

She's still sitting in the same position—legs crossed, file across her lap, pen hanging from the top of the file. She's not going to budge on this subject.

"You feel okay to continue?" she asks.

"As if I have a choice."

Katherine sets my file on the table between us, gets up, and sits down beside me. "Of course you have a choice, Seth. I'm not here to interrogate you. So many of your freedoms and choices feel as though they have been stolen from you. I don't want to rob you of your freedom of what you do or don't choose to share."

I sink back into the couch and feel tears sting my eyes. "It's just hard, Katherine. I've spent most of my life trying to not think about all this."

"Mm-hmm."

"I just...I wanted to be totally different from my parents and look at me! I'm an addict and I've been removed from my family—an absentee dad. It's no different than what my mom and dad did."

"I want to challenge your thinking on that. But first, tell me a little bit about your father."

I see my dad, his leathery face and hands, hair bleached out from the sun, dry as straw. I saw him smile only at certain times—after a good set, surfing down at the Hook or with a beer in his hand as he laughed with his friends. "He was a rock. Cold, solid, predictable."

"Was he affectionate with you or your mother?"

I scoff, "Hell no. I felt his hand only when it met my ass."

"And you? Are you affectionate with your girls?"

I think of Daisy and later Nevaeh and how they slept between Alyssa and me, our limbs tangled up, their sweet, milky breath, the best perfume I'd ever smelled. "I couldn't get enough of them. When I see Daisy now, she hardly leaves my lap or lets go of my hand."

"That sounds pretty different than what your father offered you," Katherine smiles.

"How about with Alyssa? Were you two openly affectionate?"

"Totally...well, we were at one point, anyway. It hurts so much to not have that...that touch all the time."

"I'm sure it does," she offers. "And you said that your mom has been drinking your whole life and still is."

I feel my spine stiffen. "Yup."

"You know, if you stay clean, Daisy will have little memory of your drug and alcohol abuse. I'm not saying that damage hasn't occurred. But, you have the remarkable opportunity of turning that around and at a time when she's still very young. You weren't given that option as a child. In fact, you're still dealing with it. See, you can't undo the past, but you can admit your failures to Alyssa and Daisy. It doesn't change the past but it offers healing—to all of you."

"I'm glad I didn't get in my truck and drive away earlier."

Katherine gets up from sitting beside me and sits back down in her chair. She offers a confused smile. "Would you really have left?"

"Naw, I guess not. How come you know all this and you barely know me and my family?"

"Training. But mostly, because I've lived it, Seth."

"That helps, you know. I thought you'd be kind of like a crabby old nun who looked down her nose at me for the hell I've put my family through."

"What if I told you that I see you as a remorseful young man who's still very much a wounded little boy inside?"

Her words hit the mark like an arrow striking a bull's eye. I shake my head and reply, "Yeah, well..."

As I drive back to the shop, the rain pelts against the windows and blends with my tears. I think of how I used to weave stories for the girls as I drove back and forth from work. It'd be quiet and I could really think clearly. First an image would come, then the words, sort of like a musician strumming chords then adding the lyrics. I open my mouth, talking to Nevaeh as though she's beside me, "Once upon a time, a little boy dreamt of a world where the giants were slain and there was nothing to fear..."

Chapter 9

Katherine

I've overbooked my schedule, cramming as many appointments as possible into the next three days. It's just so I can relax, get an entire week off between Christmas and New Years, and enjoy my children being home from college, I rationalize. Not being a quick learner from past mistakes, I plow through and ignore the nagging exhaustion and light-headedness that continues to plague me since the night I fell at my front porch. After the holidays I'll get things checked out.

Over the weekend, Carl and I cut down our Douglas fir up in the hills at our favorite Christmas tree farm, but have left it undecorated. Our children continue to decorate the tree each year. I thought their participation would wane during the early teen years when Collin felt it was "uncool" to do so, but he couldn't resist the opportunity to tell his sister how she hung the ornaments "wrong" and thus, had to step in.

Mom is doing so well that I have to pinch myself to remember that she has cancer...terminal cancer. After a bout of fatigue two weeks ago, her doctor ordered a blood transfusion. Now it's as though she has a new battery. She's reconnected with her knitting group from the Village Skein and is pumping out baby hats for orphans in Afghanistan with mach speed.

The lights downtown, Christmas carols echoing through the stores, and festive greetings contrast so deeply with the mood in my office. Like squeezing the toothpaste for one last drop, there's nothing like the holidays to eke out even more pain in my clients who are grieving a lost mother, father, sibling, and of course, a child.

Alyssa

On my way to the cemetery, I stop off and pick up a teddy bear and a small, plastic Christmas tree. Thank God the rain has lifted for a couple of days. The entire cemetery is bathed in decorations for the holiday—wreaths, shiny red ornaments, poinsettias, miniature trees, stuffed animals—as if this is a meadow of celebration rather than a field of death.

As I wander in between the head stones, I wonder what we would have bought Nevaeh for Christmas this year. Maybe Santa would bring an outfit for the dolly that Oma made her the previous year, or a new wagon that one of us could pull around the neighborhood or down the path to Hidden Beach. From my purse, I pull out the photo of Nevaeh that I'll show Katherine today. It was taken in our garden on the day we planted bulbs. Her tiny white teeth shine like crystals. I can't bear to think that her precious body has been reduced to ashes. I leave the tree and teddy bear behind, and with them, another piece of me.

Katherine

"Here are the pictures of my girls you asked me to bring," Alyssa says, handing me the photos. Alyssa is paler than usual today, her eyes puffy and red.

I take the photos. Nevaeh's photo is on top and I instantly feel a knot in my stomach. I always ask my bereaved to bring in photos of their loved ones who have died. Seeing Nevaeh's cherubic smile hits me hard. Carl and I took a few pictures of Nicole. Most people discouraged us, telling us it would only exacerbate the pain. They're wrong. I wish I'd taken rolls of film. Nevaeh is all Alyssa, only with curly hair. I wonder if it pains Alyssa to look in the mirror. Daisy's photo shows a wild, silly grin. She's the female version of Seth. And then I think, how painful it must be for her to look at Daisy's face, and in it, see her husband with whom she holds so much contempt.

Carl and I were never able to see whom Nicole resembled… at least, not until Tory was born eleven years later. I'll never forget the minute the doctors placed Tory in my arms. Carl and I gasped. The hospital staff chalked it up to emotional parents, but between him and me, we knew it was a combination of joy mixed with reactivated grief.

I try to steer Alyssa into talking about herself and Seth, or lack thereof, but she's ducking every question. Finally, I decide to take a back door approach and build up to it. "Alyssa, in our time together last session we talked about your mother's absence in your life and how you grew up without a father. Thinking this over, it seems to me that you had very few men in your life aside from your grandfather."

"I had uncles and cousins, but I saw them only a few times a year or on special holidays." She shrugs.

"Sometimes the image of who we want our life partner to be is based on the men in our lives—what they gave us, what we wish they'd given," I say, hoping to open up dialogue about her relationship with Seth.

"Maybe. I had a lot of terrible boyfriends before Seth. Not that he's a shining star now, anymore." The edge in her voice is back.

"How were they terrible?"

"Guys who were unfaithful and stuck on themselves. But then, I was pretty good at sowing my wild oats, as they say. It's not like I was Ms. Goodie-Two-Shoes. Back then I just wanted someone to hang out with. I didn't really think about any of those guys as a potential husband. I just wanted some fun."

"Fun?"

"You know," Alyssa said, her eyes averting my gaze.

"Alyssa, I'm not here to judge you. I just want to help you link some of your past behavior with decisions you made."

"I think if Oma knew half the stuff I did she'd be pretty upset and disappointed. She didn't raise me like that."

"Like how?"

Alyssa continues to look down at her hands, fiddling with a thread on her shirt. "She took me to church and told me to save myself for marriage. I kind of jumped ship pretty young on that one. I kept thinking that if I slept with a guy, he'd be committed to me; stick around for more than a few weeks."

"Sounds like that was a painful time."

"Yeah. I made a lot of stupid mistakes," she says. Alyssa pauses and stares out at the ocean.

I'm going to take a risk here. "And Seth…was he one of those mistakes?"

She rubs her temples and begins, "I don't know Katherine. Right now, yes, but at the time, I was so completely caught up in him, or at least the image of him. He was so popular, like a local celebrity, when I was growing up. We went to different high schools, but I'd heard his name. Later on, I read that he was about to turn pro in the surf world. Practically everyone had heard of Seth Buchanan and dozens of girls chased him; bedded down with him. When I saw him the first time down by the water and he noticed me, acknowledged me, asked me for my number, I was like, 'Oh my God.' I'd never been so crazed with a man."

"The man or his persona?"

"Everything." Alyssa's eyes grow wide and her whole body is animated as she describes falling in love with Seth. "Okay, from our first date out for dinner and a walk on the beach, and of course, amazing sex back at his place, we were inseparable. It's like I gave up my entire identity to become Seth's new girlfriend. It was so adolescent." Alyssa laughs an embarrassed laugh, her face turning pink, a pleasant change from the paleness of early on. "My grandmother was a little worried about me. I was away a lot and I kept promising I'd bring Seth over and introduce the two of them. I felt so guilty about staying over at his place so much." I notice Alyssa's expression turn serious. "And then as the weeks moved on, I had these...oh," she pauses and taps her forehead, "I can't think of what they're called." Her face falls into creases of worry.

"Second thoughts?"

"No, well, kind of. Red flags—things I worried about but looked the other way—like the drugs. I talked to a friend of mine, a guy who's like a brother to me, and he told me to dump Seth before I got hurt. I just kept telling myself he'd change if I hung in there."

"What other red flags, Alyssa? You mentioned you worried about more than one thing," I ask, worried that I'd not pressed either of them early enough in our therapy to see if domestic violence was an issue or not.

"Well, he has a temper, for sure."

My eyes widen with worry. Alyssa notices and immediately jumps in, waving her hand back and forth. "Oh, no, he never laid a hand on me, Katherine, or the girls for that matter. But when something bothered him or pissed him off, he could be...cruel."

"Can you give me an example?"

"Say hurtful things. Call me names, although that changed when the girls came along. Or, like this one time, God it seems so stupid now, he broke this CD of mine...it was so long ago, it doesn't matter." Alyssa tugs at the string on her shirt again and twists it around her finger. Her breathing grows shallow.

"It doesn't sound as though it doesn't matter if you brought it up."

Alyssa shakes her head as though trying to hold back the tears that are forming.

"Earlier, I said that we often build an image in our mind of who we want to be with based on our relationship to the men in our life. If I can be so candid, I get the impression that you and Seth sort of stumbled into one another's lives. Does it ever feel that way to you?"

"You know, it's like I had this tiny voice in my head saying, 'get out.' But then…" she pauses and takes a deep breath, "I got pregnant."

It's a big 'ah-hah' moment for me. "And yet, you have stayed together for six years. What has been the glue, the sticking point, aside from the children?"

Alyssa looks as though she wants to crawl out of her skin. "This is hard for me to talk about, Katherine. I don't like thinking about this."

"I know Alyssa. Most work in therapy is hard," I reply, unwilling to let her off the hook.

Alyssa tugs at the tissue box on the coffee table. "He's an amazing father when he's around, Katherine. You can't believe the transformation I saw when I told him I was pregnant. He started building Daisy a cradle the next day. He'd sing to my stomach. If I even lifted a sack of groceries, he'd freak, worried that it would hurt the baby. I don't know what he's told you—I mean, I know you can't say—but ever since Daisy was little, he would take her in his arms and rock her, whisper stories that he made up, lull her to sleep. He could be a children's writer. It's one of the things that kills me about all this, Daisy missing her daddy so much. I think she grieves him more than her baby sister." Her voice breaks. "One day, Daisy's life is like a storybook and the next, her sister is dead, and her father isn't allowed to live with her as though he's some kind of monster."

She's given me so much. It's tempting to pick apart the idealization of his fatherhood or the fact that she's now actually defending Seth to me. I hold back, going for the nugget in all of this and say, "So, he's not a monster?"

"No. No, he's really not." She quiets, seeming to ponder her own words.

It's clear to me that Alyssa fell in love with the fathering qualities in Seth. However, his frequent lack of judgment, particularly the night Nevaeh died, is the sticking point, the flaw that, up until now, seemed to overshadow his more redeeming qualities. I wasn't sure if Alyssa really knew Seth or loved him for who he was. I do wonder about the man Seth is becoming and if their marriage can be redefined as two people in love rather than parents who were virtual strangers, joined together through children. My work is to continue to get Alyssa past her rage and get them in therapy together—I think we are one step closer.

I'M HALF WAY through my client-marathon, and my adrenalin is keeping me fired up—well, that and an extra shot of espresso, which seems to be causing my heart to race a little faster than usual. Oh what I'd give to strip down out of my fitted suit and throw on my favorite sweats and a sweatshirt for the rest of the day. Not quite the professional look I've striven to emulate after the therapist who straightened out my life some years ago.

I spend evenings pounding out case notes, ignoring Carl's bids for my attention, and promising him and Mom that I'll make up for my absence during the holiday break.

Greg Wallace, my police officer client, has cancelled his session the hour before Seth's, leaving me ample time to get my thoughts together about Seth's session. I wonder if I pressed Greg too hard the week before about his brother's death. Sometimes too much disclosure results in retreat.

I open my door to greet Seth. His arms are extended, holding a giant poinsettia. The bright red leaves blend with the flush in his cheeks. "Merry Christmas," he offers, a bit shy.

"Seth, it's lovely. Let me put it on the coffee table where we can enjoy it." I offer Seth tea and he accepts this time. His demeanor is more relaxed than usual. Mine would be too if I had been worried about jail time. Leah called me as she left the courthouse to fill me in.

"You're different today," I say, as I sit down.

"It's a new day. They dropped the charges! I was as shocked as anyone. I thought I was toast, Katherine."

I smile, glad that something is going his way. "I'm sure that this is a huge relief."

"You have no idea."

"And I understand that you get a long visit with Daisy on Christmas day." As the words escape me, I realize that he may not know that Alyssa doesn't plan to be there. It's the first time in this case that the slippery slope of withholding information from one client feels like I'm colluding.

"Yeah, I'm psyched to see Daisy, but ah, I know Alyssa will be in her usual funk around me, avoiding me. I wish I could say I'm used to it, but I really miss her."

"I understand." We chit-chat for a few minutes and Seth talks about A.A. and how he's taking an inventory of mistakes he's made. He discloses that one of the more profound ones was rushing into his marriage with Alyssa. He's opened the door I was waiting for, and I race in.

"I was wondering about how you and Alyssa met?"

Light and longing dance in Seth's eyes—right off the bat I see how he pines for her. "It was a fluke, really. I'd been surfing all morning and I was walking up the stairs from the beach, and there she was, sitting on her cruiser. Her legs were tight and bronze and her hair was swept off to one side nearly touching her waist. I looked up at her said, 'Hey.' She smiled and said hello back. I asked her what her name was. She told me. I said, 'I'm Seth.' She said, 'Yeah, I know.'" Seth's face flushes.

"Sounds like you had immediate chemistry."

"Totally. We spent that night all over each other. But it wasn't like other times where I'd met some chick and bedded down with her for the night. I was like obsessed with her. I couldn't stand being apart. It's like God sent me an angel after my dad died."

"So you met her shortly after your father was killed?"

"Right after."

Falling in love when your life's been turned upside down—what a recipe for disaster. It goes in that category of 'don't make any major decisions the first year after a loved one has died.' Based on what Alyssa said, it explained some of the magnetism they had for one another.

"She opened something up in me. I can't explain it. Suddenly, all my feelings were pouring out of me like a dam had just busted open."

"Well, the timing of when you met may have had something to do with that, don't you think?"

Seth seemed to be thinking this over. "I guess. Later on, though, we fought like hell."

"Great passion can be like that—the opposite sides of the same coin. What were your fights mainly about?" I wonder if he'll cop to what Alyssa termed his tendency to be "cruel."

"I kind of closed off as time went on. Partied a lot. We fought about how much I used. Then after the girls were born, we got into it about how little I was around."

"So over time, you used drugs and partying as a way to avoid your feelings and being vulnerable?"

"You sound like my sponsor, Rocco."

It was good to hear that Seth was getting this from more than me.

"Why can't I let anybody in? I want to. With the girls, I could totally let loose—laugh, cry, act stupid. About the only time I can really be vulnerable is when Alyssa and I are…you know?"

"No."

"Sexual." Seth's face turns red again.

I find it curious that he's inhibited in talking about his sexuality. "It's embarrassing for you to talk about your sex life with me?"

"Well, kind of. You're like my mom's age so it's sort of weird."

Actually, I couldn't have wished for a better answer. I was hoping for a mother-son transference between the two of us, where Seth is able to view me as the good, idealized mother he's longed for. I know this will be short lived—I'll be on the flip side some day and in his eyes, be responsible for all of his calamities; it is the way of therapy.

"I understand, but I have a son who is just a handful of years younger than you and he and I have talked about sex," I say.

Seth looks as though I've told him that I scored hookers for my son. "Really!"

"Really. Remember, I'm not here to judge you and everything you say I hold confidential." I wait to see if this opens another door.

Seth stretches his legs out and a giggle escapes him. It's like being in the presence of a young adolescent boy. "Okay then. I guess you could say Alyssa and I have, or had, a pretty amazing sexual relationship. It was hard for us to keep our hands off each other. Even after Daisy was born. After Nevaeh, things sort of slowed down since she still slept between us." Seth pauses. His mind seems to linger over his last sentence. "I'd just get crazy emotional with Alyssa. I wouldn't say much, but half the time, I'd cry after or even during sex. Totally whacked, huh?"

"No, not at all. Being sexually intimate with someone can open us up."

"I just miss her so much. God. We had this fight the night before Nevaeh died. I was on one of my 'I won't get high, I promise,' weeks and of course, I came home stoned. She busted me and we got into it. Anyway, I was out 'working' in the garage and she came out there and we had this totally raw, intense sex, back like when we were dating. It's what we do to make things better."

"Hmm. Let me interrupt you for a minute. This is interesting. So, you two hadn't talked things over or resolved anything, but her approaching you ended up in a session of passionate sex. Am I hearing you right?"

"I know it's whacked."

I love his way with words. "Okay," I grin, "I wouldn't go that far. But it is similar to another pattern I see. Let me preface this with saying that I am not likening you to a batterer, someone who hits his wife. But, the cycle that you just described is quite similar to what happens in domestic violence amongst couples. There's tension, a blow up, and then promises to be better, followed by a honeymoon stage in which the couple tells themselves that everything will be fine."

"That's us alright." I'm quiet. I want Seth to chew on this. "So you're saying we had problems even before Nevaeh died."

"You tell me."

"I think I just did."

Autobiography in Five Short Chapters
Chapter Two

I walk down the same street.
There is a deep hole in the sidewalk.
I pretend I don't see it.
I fall in again.
I can't believe I am in the same place, but it isn't my fault.
It still takes a long time to get out.

—Portia Nelson

Chapter 10

Alyssa

Daisy rips open a shiny, green box—a gift from Oma. She pulls out her annual hand knitted sweater. This year's is black and red. She shoves her arms into it and slips it over her candy-cane decorated pajama top. She runs to the mirror in the entryway, silent, smiling, no words. I keep waiting for the therapy breakthrough I've been assured will happen.

I move through our quiet Christmas Eve like I'm sleepwalking. The candles lit in Oma's window throw off a soft, melancholic mood, mirroring mine. I glance at the grandfather clock in the living room, 8:30, willing the minutes to hurry up. I just want to go to bed and put this day behind me.

I help Oma collect the discarded wrapping paper and bows (she'll save them for another year) while Daisy opens up a board game I bought her. I give her my gifts tonight, knowing she'll be surrounded by mountains of presents when family members, friends, and of course, her dad comes over tomorrow. I'm sure this year the gifts will be overkill.

The doorbell rings and Oma and I exchange confused looks. I'm irritated—we're supposed to be left alone tonight. "I'll see who it is. Daisy, help Oma put those bows and paper into the closet."

I flick on the porch light and peer through the pained glass. My spirits instantly lift; it's Gregory with a gift bag in one hand and a Christmas floral arrangement in the other. I open the door. "What are you doing here?" I ask.

He leans over and kisses my cheek and says, "I wanted to bring over Daisy's gift and a little something for Oma."

Oma meets us at the entry way and she and Gregory give one another a hug. "Oh, Gregory, you're so thoughtful. Merry Christmas." She inhales the scent of the red carnations, then softens her tone and adds, " I'm so sorry to hear about you and Jenny. I'm keeping the two of you in my prayers."

"Thanks, Oma."

"That was sweet, Gregory." He plasters on his fake "holiday smile." "You look pretty miserable, too."

He shrugs. "It's quiet living alone without the boys. They're over at my folks tonight and then I get to pop over for a visit in the morning before they go to Jenny's parents. What can I say? It's too quiet everywhere."

Nevaeh's absence is so pronounced. By now, she'd be jumping at Gregory's feet, waiting to be swung around the room. Daisy enters, bringing with her a temporary relief and distraction from the pain Gregory and I hold. He lifts her up, comments on how pretty her sweater is, then hands her the gift he's brought. An odd mixture of relief and sadness fills me as I watch Daisy enjoy the evening despite Nevaeh and Seth's absences. Where is my family?

From the gift bag, Daisy pulls out a make-up kit filled with various colored nail polish and a mixture of fruit flavored lip-gloss. I throw him a glare and whisper "Gregory! No make-up or polish until at least junior high."

"Since when have I followed the rules," he grins, obviously satisfied with himself.

Out of Breath

Daisy wriggles out of his arms and runs over to the kitchen table with her make-up kit in hand. She pulls out a bottle of fire red nail polish, waves it in the air, and signals Oma to come put it on her nails.

"Just what I want my daughter to have, nails like a hooch."

"Oh, lighten up, it's Christmas," he says, nudging me in the ribs. "Speaking of which, you're still coming tomorrow, right?" After Katherine gave me "permission" to be away from Seth on Christmas day, I called Gregory to see what his plans were. Immediately he invited me over for Christmas day.

I grab a couple of beers from the fridge. "Absolutely. I don't want to be here, that's for sure." We clink our bottles together. "Cheers. You sure your folks don't mind?"

"Are you kidding, you know they love you. Besides, it'll be like old times when our families had Christmas parties together. Wasn't it the one time a year everyone rationalized getting schnockered?"

I smile, remembering the days. Life was so simple.

Daisy's gone to bed and Oma extinguishes the candles before a kiss goodnight. I watch her lumber down the hall. God, she's getting so old. Nevaeh's death has added a few aches and pains to her body. I nuzzle down in the sofa and lean into Gregory. The next thing I know, he's whispering, "Merry Christmas, sleepy head," into my ear. Two hours have passed. It's midnight—Christmas is here, despite Nevaeh's death.

"I can't believe I conked out like that," I apologize.

"You always have been a light-weight." Gregory shakes out the arm that held me, wiggling his fingers. "It was nice just to watch you sleep," he says. "You're so beautiful and looked peaceful for the first time in weeks."

Maybe it's the mood of the firelight or how relaxed I feel, but something stirs in me...unfamiliar and warm. The adolescent in me wants to punch him in the arm and tell him to be quiet, the way I did at a party in 8th grade when he told me I was a great kisser after a round of spin the bottle.

"It's late. You should probably get going."

"I suppose so," Gregory replies, getting up and stretching his arms. I follow him to the door. "See you in about ten hours or so?"

"Okey dokey." Why do I feel so weird?

Gregory leans in for what I think is a hug good-bye, but instead, his lips press softly on top of mine. I stiffen, taken aback by his kiss. When we part, he looks up, pointing to the mistletoe. "You don't like it when I break the rules," he says in a quiet voice, grinning.

"Right."

"Merry Christmas, Alyssa."

"Merry Christmas, Gregory." That night, I sleep deeper than I have in weeks. When I wake my first thought isn't the hell I'm living, but the memory of Gregory's kiss.

Seth

On my way over to see Daisy, I decide to pull over and buy a bouquet of flowers from a guy who's sitting on a folding chair on the side of the road. Gifts weren't something Alyssa and I exchanged so much; a hand knitted beanie from her, a pair of abalone earrings from me, that sort of thing. Money's been tight for so long. Then again, I think her giving outweighed mine two to one. I fork over a ten then grab another bunch for Oma, fishing for another ten bucks in my wallet.

The day stretches before me like I'm a kid on the way to the county fair—a whole day with Daisy. Each time the ache of Alyssa's distance from me resurfaces, I shake it off and try to focus on what is finally going in my direction.

As I pull up, I can make out several of my in-laws through the dining room window. Carolyn's clan is already here. Ricky and Trevor are outside, shooting their rubber-tipped bow and arrow, pretending they are knights in a forest. My eyes wander over to the pond. A pang of sadness shoots through my gut. I'd started building Nevaeh a bunk bed for her baby dolls back in early October—it still sits in the back room of my shop, unfinished.

I walk in with Daisy's gifts and the flowers—the buzz of conversation comes to a screeching halt. For an instant, I want to race back out to my car. Then I see Daisy rush towards me, clothed in a bright red Christmas skirt and black and red sweater, and that's all that matters. She smothers me in kisses and a gripping hug. She smells like chimney smoke, apple strudel, and cherry lip-gloss.

After I set her down, Oma is the only other one who approaches me. She folds me into her warm body, wishing me a Merry Christmas. I hand her one bunch of flowers. She thanks me and walks over to the kitchen to place them in a vase. My eyes scan the room for Alyssa, but I don't see her. Someone probably tipped her off when my truck pulled up. Daisy pulls me into the family room to show me what Santa's brought. A few of Alyssa's cousins nod and greet me with plastered on smiles. Carolyn says a few words, but they feel rehearsed. I'm not a welcome guest. I don't really care; I'm only here for my daughter.

Daisy rips open the package from me and her eyes dance with excitement. It's a new wetsuit. Her old one is two years old and a couple of inches too short. Booties and a hood are included for extra warmth. If I had things my way, we'd duck out right now and head out to the ocean. She grabs the wetsuit and points to the back of the house. "You gonna go try it on? Now?" She nods with a grin encompassing her whole face. "Okay," I say. God I miss her voice, but it's great to see her happy.

I slip into the kitchen, grab a mug from the cupboard, and pour myself a cup of coffee. Oma piles a mound of croissants and muffins onto a holiday plate. "So, everyone's acting pretty weird out there Oma," I say, leaning in to her.

Her joyful expression falls. "Seth, why don't you and I step outside for just a minute?" She wipes her hands on her poinsettia-decorated apron and leads me outside.

"What's up?"

Oma wrings her hands and says, "Oh, Seth it's not your presence so much, well, it is and it's not—"

I cut her off, "They all see me as a murderous addict. I don't care. I just want time with my daughter, wish Alyssa a Merry Christmas, and put the day behind me."

The worry in Oma's eyes deepens. "That's the thing dear. You see, Alyssa, she's not here."

I let the words sink in. As much as I didn't want a scene or deal with the tension, I looked forward to seeing her. Other than the day I saw her at court, I haven't been with her since that awful first session with Katherine. I miss her. I guess I shouldn't be surprised. She doesn't want to see me any other day, why should Christmas be any different. Whatever. "Where'd she go? Little cold for a day long walk on the beach," I say, hearing the edge in my voice.

Oma purses her lips—it's the look she gets when she hears someone blurt profanity or take God's name in vain. "She was invited to the Wallace's, dear."

"You mean, Greg's?" My face heats up and my temples start to pound.

"Yes. They're over at his folk's house. He and Jenny…they separated just before the holidays."

I want to drive my fist through a wall then go over there and ram it into Greg's stomach. My mind flashes to Nevaeh's funeral and how Greg stood by Alyssa's side, his arm around her waist, pulling her into his shoulder to comfort her. Then, at the courtroom, how he sat beside her and yanked her down the aisle and out the door to spare her any further torture from my presence. God damn him, to snake into her life when she's so vulnerable.

I can't respond to Oma's admission or who knows what will fly out of my mouth. "I'm going back inside to spend the day with my daughter," I say. Oma grabs hold of my arm.

"I'm so sorry, Seth. I told her it wasn't a good idea. Family is family, whatever the circumstance. I pray for the two of you every day, dear. I hope you know that." She looks as though she might cry my tears.

"I know, Oma. It's not your fault. This is my problem."
"There's nothing the Lord can't handle."
Maybe the Lord can handle this, but I have limits.

Alyssa

I step inside the Wallace's house and am thrown back in time—I'm seven years old and dashing inside to secretly watch the Power Rangers (television was taboo) with Gregory while his mother is tending her winter garden. I've kept in touch with the Wallaces over the years and bumped into them at school fundraisers or the flea market, but it's the first time in nearly ten years that I've gone back inside Gregory's childhood house.

Time stands still. In the corner, Mrs. Wallace's weathered piano is covered with a fine coat of dust and decorated with dried flowers, beeswax candles, and various pictures of the boys. There's one picture that grabs my attention—Gregory, Steven, and me on Halloween. Gregory and I are around seven and eight; Steven is ten. I'm dressed like a fairy and Gregory and Steven sport ninja costumes.

Lily and Gene, Gregory's parents, wrap me up in a warm, earthy hug. Even on Christmas, they smell of soil, mint, and something I catch a whiff of when I shop at Staff of Life...patchouli, perhaps.

"Alyssa, how are you coping these days?" Lily starts. Gregory's hand rubs up and down my back as he frowns at his mother's question. "What? I can't ask her how she is?" she snaps at Gregory.

Their bickering is comforting in a "coming home" sort of way. I think all they did was claw at each other once Gregory hit eleven. Poor Lily. "It's okay," I assure both of them. Gregory walks away and begins to rummage through the cabinet where the Wallaces keep their "special occasion" liquor (Gregory and I had lots of "special occasions" when we were teens). Lily takes my hand in hers as though I may snap in half. Suddenly, I'm a porcelain doll that everyone is afraid will break. I need a drink or two to get through this day. I eye Gregory who is pouring his dad and himself a Seven and Seven. He mouths, "Want one?" I nod my head up and down.

I want to bring up Steven; it's the elephant in the middle of the room. "This must be a difficult Christmas for you and Gene, also, what with Steven—"

Not even acknowledging my consolation, Lily breaks in, "Is Daisy with Elsa today?"

Okay, we're not talking about this. "Yes. And Seth is there too."

Lily nods a solemn nod and busies herself with the various pots on the stove. I'm sure that Gregory has filled his parents in on the arrangement between Seth and me. Lily wears this knowledge on her face like a newspaper headline. Gene joins us, a drink in hand. I wonder if everyone drank when we were kids. I always thought of my mother and her friends as health nuts, detesting anything alcoholic, dairy, or fattening. Maybe they had their secrets too.

"Alyssa, you're as lovely as ever," Gene smiles, ever the charmer. I wish he were my father. I used to fantasize about the qualities my father must have had—loving, kind, handy, and patient. I see how much of Gene's personality I borrowed to build the image of the ideal father; look what I chose for my kids.

We stand around in the kitchen, which still has 1980's blue and white linoleum, and mauve and grey colored "Blue Goose" design fixtures and potholders. Gene slips his hands into the giant potholders and pulls the tofurkey out of the oven, letting out a satisfied, "Ahh." Lily arranges homemade wheat rolls into a basket. My insides tumble with a mixture of joy, sadness, and jealousy as I step into this family's gathering. I stare out the window to shake off a wave of tears and see the old tree house. "Gregory, it's still there!" I call out.

"You know my folks, 'if it isn't broken, don't fix it.' The boys love to play on it as much as Steven, you, and I did." At the mention of "the boys" and Steven, the air in the room grows still. Lily and Gene exchange startled looks.

"Well, shall we?" Lily calls out, shaking us from our awkward silences. We each grab a dish and head for the dining room.

We eat a quiet dinner of yams (no butter), rolls, string beans, salad, and tofurkey. It's so vastly different from what Oma would fix, much to my mother's chagrin when I was young. Oma cooked two kinds of meat, ham and turkey, bucketfuls of mashed potatoes, plates spilling over with brown-sugared yams, and ten other dishes to add color to the meal. Each bite I take reminds me of how different my life is from just a year ago.

I survey Lily's face. Lines that threatened never to show now carve into her brow and wrap around her mouth. What she doesn't say speaks so loud. I know it's what people see when they ask me how I am and I give them what they want to hear… "I'm fine." Steven's vacant seat may as well have a spotlight on it; each of us keeps glancing at it, although no one says a word.

After a bottle of wine, the conversation flows more freely. Lily and Gene banter about their nursery and how much longer they can compete with a major chain store that threatens to wipe them out. We open a second bottle, and laughter replaces the aching silence as we tell stories from the past and enter the land of "remember when."

"Do you remember the time you two got caught with shaving cream all over yourselves? Not a stitch of clothing on, just gobs of it caked all over you?" Lily laughs, her eyes tearing up.

I nearly shoot wine out of my nose laughing when I feel Gregory's hand land on my knee under the table. "I think I had shaving cream in my ears for days," he laughs. He squeezes my knee and rubs it with his thumb. I know I've had a lot to drink but the buzz in my ears isn't from the wine. I look over at him and he simply smiles.

I help Lily with the dishes while Gregory and his father flip on a ball game in the family room. As we wash up the plates, talking about her winter garden, I think of the exercise in therapy that Katherine gave me to do over the holiday break: make a list of five things you are grateful for. Gregory gets added to my mental list for the void he's filling.

The Wallaces give me a purple, soft, alpaca scarf, hand-knit by Lily. I wrap it around my neck, feeling its embrace. I give them another candle to add to the dozens that dot shelves and countertops. I didn't have the energy to shop for much this year.

By 8:00, Gregory and I hug them good-bye and I promise to stop by more often, although the words are hollow intentions more than a promise. Gregory steers me out the front door with his hand in mine. The air is thick with chimney smoke—winter is here even though it's only 50 degrees.

Gregory opens his car door for me, but asks me to wait before I get in. He looks back toward the front door. His parents have gone inside. "I have something for you," he says as he reaches into his glove box.

"Gregory, we've said no presents since we had kids. That's a deal breaker," I say, wagging a finger at him.

"Be quiet," he says. "I think this year deserves an exception."

He hands me a tiny blue velvet jewelry box tied with a ribbon reading "Dell Williams", one of the last original jewelry shops in town. My hands shake as I untie the knot. Inside is a gold chain with a blue topaz dangling from it. I lift it up with my mouth hanging open. It's so "not me," but it's gorgeous...and expensive.

"Gregory," I begin to protest.

"It's your birthstone. Well, actually—"

"Our birthstone," I finish for him. Gregory and I were born a day apart, December 28th and 29th. "I don't even...I didn't get you anything—"

"Shhh," Gregory whispers, taking the chain from my hand and clasping it around my neck. I feel his breath on my neck as he says, "Think of it as an early birthday present." He turns me around to face him. "Beautiful. Perfect. Like you." Before I can say anything, he places a hand on my cheek and kisses me. The wine, the chimney smoke, the smell of Polo—it swoons me until I think my knees will buckle. I raise my hand and place it behind his head, pulling him into a kiss. Suddenly, nothing is familiar between us.

Chapter 11

Greg

I swing into my assigned parking space at the condo. Some asshole is a good three inches over the white line; leaves me barely enough space to open my door without scuffing it. In the past, I might have actually swung my door open and dinged the side in retaliation. Today, the irritation slips through me like the January winds blowing on shore.

Since Christmas day, my relationship with Alyssa has finally turned a corner. Long walks on the beach; afternoons with Alyssa, Daisy up on my shoulders giggling; secret kisses and touches between Alyssa and me when Daisy runs ahead to find a sand dollar or a piece of sea glass. I have no complaints. Okay, maybe two: I get even less time with my boys and Seth still exists in Alyssa and Daisy's life, even if it is in the form of supervised visits and phone calls.

Seth Buchanan. Each muscle along my back seems to spasm at the thought of him. That scumbag is like a giant wrecking ball. First, he slammed into Alyssa's life, stealing any hope I had of being with her. Then he robbed Nevaeh of her life, leaving Daisy, Alyssa, and me to sift through the rubble of her death. It's just a matter of time—Seth will slip up again. That'll start the divorce proceedings and Alyssa's permanent custody of Daisy. Then we can finally move forward as a family.

I toss my keys onto the counter and shuffle through the mail that Jenny forwards— just bills and junk mail. Living here hasn't turned out so bad. Thank God my folks refurbished it a few years back. The avocado green and hues of orange are replaced with a nautical theme of reds and blues scattered throughout the living room and bedrooms. Still, no matter how much I vacuum, a thin layer of sand coats the floor. It's a tradeoff; a wall of windows overlooking the Pacific Ocean trumps a few grains of sand in my sheets anytime.

The light of my answering machine is flashing red. I grab a beer and push the button. "Greg, it's Katherine Middlebrook. I have you down for 7:00 tonight. Just confirming our appointment. Looking forward to seeing you. Bye."

I've been ducking therapy like a truant kid avoiding the principal. Katherine's fine but I really think I've put Steven's death behind me and Jenny and I are a moot issue. I mentioned that my goddaughter was killed in our last session, although I didn't go into details or specifics. It feels too private. My partner, Bill, pointed out how different I've been—the old me, more in control, not flying off the handle. He's right. But it's not the therapy that's the cure; it's Alyssa. I finally have my prize.

I'm about to change out of my uniform when my cell phone vibrates. I flip it up and see that it's Alyssa. "Hey, I was just thinking about you," I say.

"Oh, I'm so glad you're home. You aren't in the middle of something are you?" She sounds worried and short of breath.

"What's wrong?"

"Oh no, nothing's wrong. I just…well, it's time for us to go. I've been packing up our stuff."

"Packing as in moving out of Oma's?"

"Yeah."

"Really? You want me to come pick you up?" I say, a little too eager.

"Could you? I need to go home…with Daisy, to our house."

It's been almost three months since Alyssa had me grab things out of the house for her. She swore she'd never go back—the pain was too intense without Nevaeh.

"Why now?"

"I need my own space, to sleep in my own bed. Daisy's therapist said it might help if she was in her own environment, although she's practically lived half her life at Oma's. It's not the same though. Her psychologist said that avoiding the environment where Nevaeh lived, not seeing her toys, clothes, all that stuff, will only prolong her grief and reluctance to talk." She sighs. I hear rustling in the background, the sound of things being shoved into a bag. "I just feel that it's time for me to move forward a little and I can't do that if I'm living here like a child."

My thoughts are racing. I want to run over, throw her stuff in my car, and help her move forward, too. I take a deep breath and steady my voice. "Whenever you're ready."

"I'm ready, tonight, Gregory. Sorry, I'm always asking you to drop everything, aren't I?"

Shoot, my appointment with Katherine. "No, no. I'm glad you asked. Let me jump in the shower and take care of a couple of things. I'll pick up some Chinese and be over in an hour or so."

"Thank you. You're awesome."

I can't shower fast enough.

Katherine

Mom decided to go home after Christmas, telling me that if she's not sick or helping in some tangible way, then she's in the way. I'm a bit lost. I didn't argue—I want her to hold on to her independence as long as possible. I just liked being able to check in on her throughout the day, pinching myself that she seems to be holding steady. With Collin and Tory back at college and Mom home, Carl and I have settled into our quiet rhythms again—quieter than usual.

It's this empty, noise-free time that leads me to our spare room where I keep my sewing machine, scrapbook materials, and our old photo albums. The albums eat up an entire wall. Carl jokes that when our grandchildren come along someday, he'll have to build me another room just to house the vast number of pictures.

I've labeled each album by year. Way in the back of a deeper shelf are the albums of Carl's and my dating years, marriage, and Nicole's baby book. The album, displaying baby elephants, giraffes, and teddy bears, has a thick layer of dust. It's been nearly a decade since I've opened it. As I look at the first page, tears instantly form. There she is: face scrunched, skin a bit too pale for a newborn. Below the picture is her name, Nicole Victoria Middlebrook. At the bottom, I've written the day of her birth, June 1, 1976 and the day of her death, December 7th, 1976. A mother should never have to write the date of her child's death.

I flip through the book, skipping over all of the "firsts" that were supposed to happen; first time she rolled over, first time sitting up, first time crawling. There were no firsts…only lasts. I have a few pictures of her life. Most were taken in the hospital. A couple of photos were taken outside on the hospital grounds. I begged the doctors for just a few minutes in the sun with her. I remember never being able to warm myself in the cold, sterile, pediatric wing at Oakland Children's Hospital.

I feel a deep connection to Alyssa and Seth. They had dreams for Nevaeh as surely as we did for Nicole—dreams of her dancing in pink tights and leotards, recitals, building sandcastles, proms, and a wedding someday. I guess those were my dreams, too. A tear drops on to the page beside Nicole's picture.

A headache forms at my temples and my heart flips around in my chest. I hear Carl round the corner. He ducks in and his smile drops as he sees my tears. He caresses my shoulders with his strong hands. I could melt and go to sleep in his arms. He squats down and asks, "What's going on?"

"Nothing. Just remembering," I say, as though it's a novelty. How do I explain that Nicole is always a living, breathing memory?

Out of Breath

"Why today?"

I shrug my shoulders, closing the album. I concoct a reason for my triggered pain. "I guess I think of her every year around this time. It was a dark January that year."

Carl nods. He's quiet. He helps me up and takes the album from my arms and places it back on the shelf, out of view, tucked away once again, then kisses me on the forehead.

"Mary call you today?" He asks. He seems eager to change the subject. I follow him out into the kitchen, noticing that the sun has set.

"Yes. Or rather, I called her twice." Carl pulls a couple of steaks from the refrigerator. Shoot. "Carl, I forgot to tell you that I'm meeting Leah after my last session tonight."

For all the independence and liberation of women that I promote, I'm still a 1950's wife at heart—dinner together, his shirts hand pressed, the house kept up by me and me alone. Call it a reaction to my childhood, but the predictability soothes me, filling in the gaping holes that my parents dug.

I get up on my tiptoes and kiss his cheek, rough from his 5:00 o-clock shadow. "No pouting now I left some pasta in the fridge. I should be home before 10:30. We'll sleep in tomorrow." His smile returns. If only therapy were this easy.

"Be safe," he says and pulls me into a tight embrace.

Back down in my office, I raise the thermostat. We never quite got the draft issue under control. But then again, my chill runs deeper tonight. I flip open Greg's chart to refresh my memory of where we left off. I've scribbled down the key issues to follow up on: anguish over brother's death, drinking more than usual, goddaughter recently deceased (no details-seems to be avoiding), marriage dissolving. Next to this, in bold letters, I've written: who is Greg's support system? With Greg, I seem to have more questions than answers. Greg is an aloof client who offers information, retreats, cancels, returns with honest answers and some vulnerability, only to cancel again. "Evasive," I write below my notes. "What next?"

The phone rings, interrupting my thoughts.

"Katherine Middlebrook."

"Oh, hey Katherine, it's Greg."

I look up at the office clock. He should be here within minutes. It's a cancellation call. "Hello Greg. Everything okay?"

"Yeah. Everything's great. Something came up though. A buddy of mine needs me to fill in for him tonight. I owe him, so...I know you'll need to bill me. I'll drop a check in the mail," he says in a hurried voice.

"Okay. Thank you for calling. I hope you're making some time for yourself and your needs," I say.

"I appreciate that. I'm taking care of myself. I'll call you for another appointment when I'm not so rushed."

"Okay. I'll look forward to it."

I hang up, shaking my head. I need to let him off the hook and tell him that perhaps he isn't ready for therapy, to come back in six months or so. One less case is fine with me. Frankly, I'm relieved that he cancelled. My head is somewhere else. How foolish to open myself up, sifting through those photos, before meeting with a client. Plus, my heart is doing that goofy thing where it's thumping in my chest. Carl's right, too much espresso. With our session cancelled, I could go upstairs and join Carl. What I really need is time out...not listening, giving, or remembering. I grab my oversized purse, slip my novel inside, and head over to Mr. Toots.

I spy one last table in the far corner of the tiny coffee shop. College-aged kids with books and laptops dot the tables. An older couple sits overlooking the water. They're engaged in a game of backgammon, peering intently at the board. Leah and I started meeting here years ago. We joke that we graduated from Margaritaville, which sits on the first floor, to second story Mr. Toots when we were called "Ma'am" by the snotty little hostess one Friday night. Tonight, a jazz pianist is promised to begin in an hour. I'm on my second *decaf*-latte when Leah walks in. She tosses her Indian cloth purse onto the table. Her cell phone, spare change, and a tampon tumble out.

I pick up the tampon, tossing it at her. "You still carry one of those around?"

"Every time I forget to grab one, Aunt Flow comes back for a visit. Between the hot flashes and mood swings, I feel like a teenager all over again, only my sexual tension's been replaced with crappy knees and bunions on my feet."

"I'm not the only one who feels like she's falling apart?"

"Hell no. God, my back hurts all the time, I can't sleep, and I need a damn fan on in the winter."

I feel reassured that my recent ailments are probably menopausal. Leah keeps fishing around for money in her purse. "Let me get this, Leah." I stand up to get her drink, pulling a five from my wallet. "When are you going to let some sugar momma into your life and let her pay your way?"

"Why do I need that when I have you?" Leah says, smirking. "Anyway, my love life, or lack thereof, is off the table. There is no one datable in this county."

Stew, the Jamaican UCSC student who works here most evenings, greets us. "My lovely ladies—the usual for Ms. Leah?"

"How she has a double espresso at night and sleeps is a wonder," I banter with him.

"It's how I keep myself ready and available for some young stud like you," Leah teases Stew with a wink.

He laughs, baring a sparkling smile that warms my insides. I leave him my five-dollar bill and sit back down at our table. Leah stares at me, quiet, unrelenting. "What? Do I have lipstick on my teeth again?" I ask.

"No. You look like hell, Katherine."

"Why thank you, Leah. I love you, too."

"No, seriously. What's going on? You're out with me on a Friday night; lover boy is home by himself and I know Mary's okay because I stopped by yesterday with a quiche and she looks better than you right now."

"You cooked?" I ask.

"Okay, I *bought* her quiche. Anyway, what gives?"

Where do I start? I sit back, trying to place the Credence Clear Water Revival song that's pumping through the speakers. "Just work. Tiring cases."

"The Buchanans fit into that category?" Leah whispers. Stew approaches with her hair curling coffee.

"You know, talking about them here, as caseworker and therapist, off the record…it's walking the line of being unethical," I add in a hushed tone.

Leah rolls her eyes. "Oh, Katherine. Quit being so high and mighty."

It would be the perfect segue way into telling her about Nicole. I fiddle around with the wooden stirring stick in my coffee. Somehow the words won't come out.

"Anyway," Leah continues, "who else can you talk to? Carl and your consultation group will figure out who your clients are the second you describe the case."

"I suppose so. I'm just afraid that what I tell you will contaminate your work with them and that's not appropriate."

"Look, no one is without their biases, least of all therapists and social workers. I just want to be there for you." Leah reaches out and squeezes my arm. "You look pretty down."

I'm touched by her tenderness. "A lot of conflicting feelings and thoughts are whirling around in me," I confess, but omit my personal issues. "I think I'm feeling a bit confused about how to help Seth and Alyssa come together in their session. Alyssa is so solid in her anger, but more than that, it feels as though she's not being totally up front with me. This is my intuition speaking, but I think she's holding out on me, not being honest about all that's going on with her. For instance, she recently admitted that she doesn't see Seth as a monster, and that he's actually a pretty good dad, and yet she remains completely closed to a session with him. Why?"

Leah sips her coffee, replying, "You wouldn't be irate with Carl if you asked him to watch Tory when she was little but instead, he went off, got high, and she drowned?"

No, but Carl was emotionally distant from me through Nicole's death…something that I've never really let go of. "If you're asking me if I would refuse to see him again, I can't be sure. It's hard to imagine shutting Carl out of my life." I'm anxious to steer the conversation back to my clients' lives. "You've met Seth. What's your impression of him?"

She leans back and crosses her arms. "You know, I thought I'd want to punch him in the mouth after reading his bio and all, but he surprised me. He's not the dead-beat I'd envisioned. He's stepping up."

I prejudged him too. And yet, denial is still an issue, given that he won't own up to being loaded the night Nevaeh drowned. "He's a lot more—"

"Tender," we both say at the same time.

"Yeah. So, that's what I'm struggling with, Leah. It's a horrible analogy, but I wish Alyssa wouldn't throw the baby out with the bath water."

Leah takes a swig of her coffee then shudders. "Oh Katherine, that was grim coming from you."

"I know, sorry. I'm not saying Seth is a saint, by any means, but there's something in him that resonates with me, feels familiar, you know. It's like he never got a chance to really get it together as a kid due to the neglect and alcoholism."

Leah raises her eyebrows. "Sounds like someone else's past. Kindred spirits I would say."

She's right. Sometimes in therapy as I listen to a client's history, our stories begin to line up, striking chords of familiarity that I swear are ringing out into the office. The alcoholic mother, emotionally absent father, the need to be self reliant— they were themes in my childhood, too. I want Seth to be successful and buck off the anchors of his past, just as I've had a chance to do.

"You're right," I confess, "we've got a common thread or two."

"I'd say it's more of a rug than a thread."

We chuckle. "It's hard, though, Leah, to watch Seth push so hard for more, like overnight visits, couples therapy, family sessions, while Alyssa pushes back with such...such intensity. What is she afraid of?"

"Maybe she's hiding something?" Leah says.

"Like what?"

"You're the shrink. Dig around."

"I don't like playing detective. It feels like I have an agenda," I say.

"What? Are you crazy?" She leans in, planting her elbows on the table. "You shrinks are master manipulators, orchestrating conversations to get what you want. I should know," Leah says, "I've had my fair share of head shrinking."

The jazz pianist arrives and warms up with a sultry, slow song, quiet enough that we can still hear one another talk. His tip jar, an empty goldfish bowl, is perched on the side of the piano, beckoning for spare change.

"All I'm saying is that sometimes people don't reveal things because they aren't ready yet."

"Well," Leah begins as she shrugs on her patchwork coat, "you better get a move on it because even before we had this conversation, I was going to recommend that Seth be granted overnight visits." We stand together, adjusting our jackets and purses. "Night Stew," Leah calls out.

"Good night my lovely ladies. See you again."

"You betcha baby," Leah chimes back as she drops several quarters into the pianists goldfish bowl.

As we stroll down the Esplanade toward the benches that line the seaside walkway, Leah gives my arm a big squeeze. "You remember that article I gave you a couple of years back?"

Leah's given me dozens of articles. It's impossible for me to pull just one and connect it to our conversation. "Want to give me a hint?"

She stops walking and stares straight at me. "The one about Compassion Fatigue."

Oh, that one. Well…I was in a slump a few years ago when I had a full case load, spent several weekends a year traveling to conferences as the keynote speaker, and trying to adjust to my son's age appropriate adolescent "push-away-from-Mom" time. Leah noticed that I was easily distracted, hypersensitive, acted more anxious than usual, and pointed out how often I characterized myself as ineffective with my clients.

A weak smile slips across my lips. "Yes, well, I guess we all experience that at times."

"Pft, burnout is practically a job requirement at CPS. But it's something in you…" she pauses, looking out at the dark ocean, "something different. Something getting you down? You're not hiding some mystery illness or anything?"

If it weren't for the darkness, she'd surely see my face flush. Carl wouldn't call Leah and tell her about my recent clumsiness at the door. "I don't know. We all have our aches and pains."

"How about dizziness, rapid pulse, insomnia?"

"Oh come on, Leah, I've been at this so long. I'm a bit far along in my career to be developing Compassion Fatigue." Suddenly the article is crystal clear, particularly the diagram laying out what contributes to Compassion Fatigue, including prolonged exposure to suffering, traumatic memories, and other life demands. I'm practically the poster child for the syndrome.

We find a bench and sit. "Come on, Kat, you know there isn't a statute of limitations on this sort of stuff. Just watch yourself. It's okay to put yourself first once in a while." She gives me a shove with her shoulder that holds the warmth of a deep hug.

A giggle escapes me. Sure, I'll put myself first right after I'm done caring for Mom, my clients, and our home. We sit together in silence watching the moonlight dance on the water.

Chapter 12

Alyssa

I'm going home. We're going home—well, two out of four of us are going home. It's a wild ride over. It's like I'm stuck on an amusement park ride in the dark. Gregory is close behind me in his cruiser. I find myself chattering non-stop at Daisy, reassuring her how wonderful it will be to see all her old toys, sleep in her bed, and play in her silk house. I try to read her expressions in the rear view mirror. All I see are two huge brown eyes staring back at me as though she and I are stuck on the same terrifying ride.

What is she thinking? It doesn't help to ask anymore. In fact, her therapist told me to stop with any feelings oriented question. These days, I'm worried about anything and everything that could mess her up even more. Because Daisy hasn't been introduced to reading or writing at our non-traditional school, communication on a chalk or white board is also out of the question. She signs a few words to me, such as hungry, tired, and I love you. When she signs 'I love you', it slices my heart wide open.

I see our rust colored house as we turn down the street. When I pull up into the driveway, I'm certain that the neighbors know I'm here by the loud pounding of my heart. I take a deep breath and exhale. "Okay, Daisy, here we are." Ready or not, here we come...

Daisy bounds out of the car like she's going to a birthday party. She races to the door; her doll clutched under her arm, and rapidly pushes and pulls on the door handle. "Wait a second, baby. Hold on. Let Mommy open the door." My keys jumble around in my palm from my unsteady grip. I finally get the door unlocked and she bolts inside, racing around like a new puppy. Greg's hand slips in mine. "That was strange," I say quietly.

"It's a big day for her, too."

"Yeah." We step inside and the smell of home hits me so hard that I nearly fall backwards. A combination of scents: wood floors, spiced candles that remain from autumn, the lavender scented laundry soap, the mustiness of an unaired house— it's "our smell" and yet it's oddly foreign. I'm shaking everywhere, completely unprepared for how difficult this moment is. Greg pulls me tight into his side and tells me it's okay, it's okay, it's okay.

Every room is layered with memories: the living room rocker where I nursed Nevaeh; the burnt orange couch where Seth and I took turns snuggling her while the other slept; the kitchen counter where Nevaeh babbled and pretended to cook while I stirred a pot of soup. It's like walking into one of my nightmares. Katherine warned me about how difficult this would be. I underestimated how it would hit me like a spray of bullets.

The tears come in waves. I slump into a chair at the kitchen table and try to pull myself together for the sake of Daisy. "Stay put, I'm going to see how she's doing," Gregory reassures me.

I nod. I hear him tell Daisy, with the measured insincerity that I too have mastered, how wonderful it is to be home. After catching my breath, I stagger through the hallway, passing photos that line the walls; photos of Seth surfing, mixed with collages of the girls, Seth, Oma, me—they're surreal, as though this is someone else's life.

I wander into my room. The hair on the back of my neck tingles. I smell him. Seth. Even though he's not here, slept here recently, or will ever sleep here again, he's still here. That mixture of resin, cigarette smoke, and the oils from his skin makes me want to vomit. I have a sudden urge to fling our wedding photo across the room, but again, I restrain myself for my surviving daughter. I'll change the sheets and throw out the old pillows to rid any trace of him.

Water. I need a glass of water. Turning to head back down the hall, I literally smack into Daisy, sending us both backwards and wide-eyed. "Oh, baby, I'm so sorry," I say, the words pouring out like water from a tap. "I was just going to get something to drink. Can I get you anything? Well, I guess water is all we have since we haven't been here for a while." I hear myself babbling on and think I've absolutely lost it.

Daisy takes my hand as though she wants to show me something, but she doesn't move. Her other hand beckons me to bend down closer to her.

"What is it Daisy? Are you hungry?" I make the sign for hunger.

She shakes her head back and forth so hard that her hair whips her cheeks. She clears her throat and opens her mouth. "Where's Daddy?" Her scratchy words cut through the thick air. I'm so stunned, I can't answer. Nearly three months and not one word, and these are her first, 'Where is Daddy?' Despite the sadness of her question, I can't help but burst into a smile.

Gregory comes in at the sound of her voice. We exchange deep looks of surprise. He mouths, 'She talked.'

"Oh, Daisy," I begin, "I...I don't know what to say. My God, it's so wonderful to hear your precious little voice." I bend down and kiss her cheeks, forehead, and ears as I wrap my arms around her little waist. "Daisy, Daisy, oh sweetie, this has got to be so confusing." I'm talking more to myself than her.

She pushes me back and looks at me with her newfound serious eyes. "He's not here?"

"No baby. He's not. Daddy doesn't live here anymore. Remember, Mommy told you he lives in an apartment down by the bookstore where we went for story time." Of course this doesn't make sense to a five-year-old. It barely makes sense to me and I'm thirty-one.

Daisy begins to cry...softly, like a kitten under a blanket. I hold her in my lap and rock her back and forth. "I'm sorry Daisy. This is hard. I know you miss your Daddy so much." It hits me that what I'm not talking about is Nevaeh's absence, too. I fill my lungs and say, "And your sister, too."

She nods her head and her quiet whimpers fill the room, echoing off the walls. I rock her back and forth, letting our tears drop onto her skinned knees. Gregory kisses the top of her head and says, "Why don't we show your mom what you set up in your room?"

I look up at him, puzzled but also relieved to interrupt what feels like my 100th nervous breakdown. Daisy gets off my lap and wipes her nose and face with her sleeve. I don't have the energy to get her a tissue. My parenting these days involves the bare bones of getting through a day.

She and Gregory walk hand-in-hand into Daisy and Nevaeh's room. At their little wooden table, she's set up dishes, cups, and a make believe pot of tea. I count the plates, one, two, three, four. "Sit down," she tells me. My eye catches Nevaeh's empty toddler bed as I slide into the tiny chair. Daisy begins to hand out our tea: wooden carved biscuits, felt grapes, cloth napkins. She pretends to take a bite of her biscuit, showing me to do the same. My imaginary biscuit has sprung to life and is wedged in my throat.

I swallow hard, staring at the two empty chairs. "Daisy, this is so sweet. Who are these places set for? Maybe Fiona or Uncle Gregory?"

She shakes her head, points to the chair next to her, and says, "This one is for Daddy." Next, she gestures to the empty chair beside me, and says, "This one is for Nevaeh. She can sit there when she comes back home."

When she comes back home. When she comes back home. The words ricochet in me like a gunshot. Oh my God, what do I say? 'Your sister's never coming home.' I look over at Gregory whose eyes have grown to the size of bowling balls. I gaze over at Daisy. She pours us more tea and takes a long, imaginary drink.

"What do you mean baby?" I ask, trying to steady my quivering voice.

"Nothing," she says abruptly. "It's just for my baby sister."

"Daisy," I start, trying to catch her eye, but fail as she places felt grapes onto Nevaeh's empty plate, "do you think Nevaeh is coming back? Because she's—"

"Drink your tea, Mommy," Daisy cuts in, sounding annoyed. "It's getting cold."

Even though Dr. Fowler, Daisy's therapist, told me that Daisy might have trouble with the permanency of Nevaeh's death, I shrugged the information off. My daughter would understand; she's bright beyond her years. I want to run to the phone and dial Dr. Fowler before I do any more damage.

Gregory leans over me and whispers, "Don't freak out. Just give her some time."

I nod and play with Daisy for another ten minutes then help her with bath time, spoon out some fried rice for her to eat, and slip her into my huge, empty bed. Before all of this...this shakedown of our predictable lives, the girls would start out the night in our bed and woke there too, sleeping only the wee hours of the morning away in their own rooms. Even then, I'd find them huddled beside each other like two purring kittens keeping one another warm.

With Daisy settled, Gregory and I reheat our Chinese food and take it into the family room where we both let out a huge sigh. "How you holding up?" he asks.

I chew my broccoli beef and think of how to answer him. "I can't believe she's talking again. I should be thrilled, but then when I saw the place she set for Nevaeh and Seth... she doesn't get it, *any* of it, does she?"

"It's a lot to take in. You handled it great." Gregory scoots close by me on the ground. I set my chopsticks on the coffee table and curl into his arms.

Out of Breath

"Did you see how serious she was when she was playing? Daisy was my wild child, the excited, bubbly, can't stay in her seat girl. She's so...somber."

"Alyssa, it won't be like this forever. I'm not a counselor, but you can't pretend to know what's going on in her head. Try and look at the positive—you're back home, she's talking, you two are moving one step forward." He takes my chin and turns me toward him, and kisses me. I smile and sigh. "That's more like it," he says.

"You think there's any beer in the fridge? Oh God, the fridge!" We both jump up. "It must be like a giant science project in there." I fling open the door, expecting the stench of rotten milk and thawed meat to blow me over. Instead, I'm looking inside a refrigerator that must belong to someone else. Everything is wiped down and sparkling clean like the day we moved in. A fresh box of baking soda sits beside a six-pack of Rolling Rock, a bottle of Pinot Noir, and an assortment of sparkling waters.

"Carolyn." I sigh. "It had to be her. She's the only person beside you that has keys to our house." This small act of kindness kicks off my emotions again.

We settle down in the family room. Gregory has grabbed some wood from out back and the fire crackles, throwing off delicious heat. "Did I really think that coming home was a better solution?"

"What are you talking about?"

I twirl my beer around in my hands. "Coming home to a big empty house, alone. Do you know that I've never lived alone a day in my life?"

"Well, yeah, I guess so. You have Daisy here, though." Gregory says.

"You know what I mean...it's not like Daisy can protect me at night." The thought sends a surge of anxiety through me. "I went from my grandmother's house to a family friend's place in Germany for a year, back to Oma's, then right into Seth's apartment."

"I guess I never thought about it that way," Gregory says, flinching at the word, 'Seth.'

I point to our empty bottles, "You want another?"

"Sure."

I return and sit on the rocking chair. The motion is soothing. "If Seth's work took him out of town, I always went over to Oma's. Now, here I am, a grown woman and I'm afraid to be alone. Some grown up." I chuckle, although it's a laugh filled with fear.

Gregory's quiet for a moment, then offers, "You know, I don't have to be in tomorrow until the afternoon shift. I could, you know, sleep on the couch if it would make you feel safer."

Yes, please. No, you can't. What are you saying? None of these words come out, but they bounce around inside my head like a game of pinball, competing for the answer. "It's a terrible couch, Gregory. We got it from a family at the school who took pity on our poverty. I can't put you through that." He looks wounded, rejected. I offer an alternative. "But then, I could sleep with Daisy in my bed and you could sleep in the girls' room. It's small, but if you slept on your side—"

"I'll be fine," he quickly replies.

I get up off the rocker and walk over to Gregory, running my hand down his cheek and kiss his lips. "Thank you, Gregory. You're way too good to us. I'll go make up your bed."

Greg

As I watch Alyssa walk down the hall, the way her hair sweeps across her sweater, the scent of roses that she leaves behind, I feel paralyzed. I don't want to screw this up. All night with Alyssa—this hasn't happened since we were kids.

I join her in Daisy's room. She's tucked a fresh set of flower pedaled sheets around the mattress. We're silent. Smiles pass between us. "I think I'll go take a shower," she whispers. I imagine slipping her clothes off, lathering up her body, kissing her in places that I've only dreamt.

"Okay," I say, my throat dry and tight.

"Thank you for staying here tonight," Alyssa says, kissing me again. I'm left alone with desire. Sleep is impossible, and yet my longing for Alyssa feels at odds with my surroundings: the hints of little girl innocence in every nook and cranny. I sweat despite the chill in the air. I hear someone toss and turn in the next room. She's that close to me.

At midnight, I decide to get up and get a cold glass of water to try to cool myself off. I peek in Alyssa's room just to watch her sleep.

"Gregory," she says in a soft voice as she sits up.

"I'm sorry, I didn't mean to scare you. I was just getting up to have a glass of water. Go back to sleep." She peels back the covers and slips her long legs out of bed. The nightlight coming from the hall shines just enough into her room that I see her hair spill across the front of her nightgown over her full breasts.

"I can't sleep either. Daisy's all over the bed."

"Ahh. You want something to drink?"

"Sure. I'm so thirsty. Must be the Chinese food."

We walk into the kitchen. Shadows from the eucalyptus trees dance across the halls. I can't quench my thirst no matter how much I drink. Alyssa leans into the countertop, offering a sensual outline of her waistline. I want to slip my hand around it, pull her to me, feel myself inside her.

"It's been a long time since we've had a sleepover," Alyssa says.

I nod, speechless.

"Remember how we joined our sleeping bags together in junior high?"

"Oh yeah...I forgot about that." Like hell. Forget Viagra, I had more than a four-hour erection that night. Right now. I could tell her right now that I'm crazy in love with her and have been all my life.

"I have some sleeping bags in the closet," she says, nodding her head towards the hallway.

"Okay." I'm barely breathing.

We're careful to make as little noise as possible as we retrieve the sleeping bags. One is blue the other is red. Alyssa begins to unzip hers and asks, "Why don't you put another log on the fire."

I get another log and toss it on top of the smoldering embers. Flames lick up around the fresh wood. Alyssa is bathed in golden light.

I take off my shirt, but stay inside my jeans as I slip into the sleeping bag. A self-consciousness I've never known around Alyssa sweeps over me—the extra few pounds I've put on since Christmas, the paunch of my stomach that I long to hide.

Alyssa crawls in beside me, adjusts her pillow, and props up on one arm to face me. We gaze at one another and listen to the crackle of the fire. I can't wait any longer. I reach forward, slowly, tuck her silky hair behind her ear, and kiss her long and deep.

Alyssa

We part lips for a brief moment. I stare into the eyes of the boy I've known my entire life. Suddenly he is no longer the boy who taught me to shoot a slingshot, but a man I want to touch, taste, and discover in a completely different way. Katherine is wrong—not every man I've been with sexually has been impulsive and rushed. We've built up to this moment for nearly two decades.

"I'm so tired of hurting," I say, looking into his steel blue eyes.

Gregory nods and slips a hand behind my head, pressing our bodies together. His hand travels down my neck. His fingers trace my shoulder, sending shivers down my spine. He reaches down and lifts my nightgown over my head and stares at my body. His gaze drifts to a scar on my left arm—a scar I got from a risky dare on the playground; a dare from Gregory. He cups his hand around my breast. My nipple hardens as he slips his tongue across. I shudder beneath his touch.

I play with the buttons on his pants, finally letting them open. Gregory's breath quickens as he slides off his jeans. We explore every inch of one another. Our lovemaking is tender, passionate, filled with tears of pleasure and tears of relief. We spend ourselves until both the fire within us and the flames in the fireplace are merely smoldering.

Out of Breath

It's cool in the room and we're ravished. Gregory stokes the fire then retrieves our leftover Chinese food and the bottle of wine. Sleep will come tomorrow. We feed one another, trying to subdue our laughter to avoid waking Daisy. I take Gregory's hand and look at each finger and knuckle—every inch of him is new. Could these really be the same hands that slapped my back during our games of freeze tag? I kiss each finger, noticing the white line around his left ring finger where his wedding band is missing.

"I think of Steven," I say, as I snuggle into his bare chest. I have an odd longing to tell Steven that Gregory and I are together. "I miss him. He was a wonderful brother to you."

Gregory's chest begins to shake. "I can't believe he's gone. They're together now, he and Nevaeh."

We smother our grief with our bodies, pushing the pain momentarily away. I didn't know how much I longed for contact, touch, and pleasure.

At dawn, I slip out of my bag, fold it up, and sneak into the shower. I reluctantly wash off the scent of our sex. It's foreign, wonderful, and medicinal. I throw on a fresh nightgown and crawl back into bed beside Daisy. She curls her body up against my side and calls out, "Mamma." I kiss her on the forehead, and she and I sleep.

I'm awakened to Gregory's voice of surprise echoing down the hallway. "Holy cow, I thought a dinosaur pounced on me." I look around the bed and see that Daisy is no longer there. She must have run down the hall to wrestle with Gregory. I use the opportunity to take my time getting out of bed. Outside my bedroom slider, I see that the weeds have choked the plants that Nevaeh and I planted back in October. Little green shoots at the edge of our planter box are starting to sprout; the tulips she and I planted the morning of her death. My newfound joy deflates like a helium balloon that's been pricked with a pin. I have the urge to run out and uproot the bulbs, not knowing how I'll stand the pain of watching them grow in day after day.

The dewy grass wets my feet. I pull my bathrobe tight to ward off shivers of cold, shivers of grief. I bend down and touch the top of one of the tulip shoots. Did her little hand touch this one? My nose is running now and I'm sure I look like a mad woman out here, barefoot, and blurry eyed. The sound of the sliding glass door draws my attention. Without turning, I say, "Remember when Nevaeh and I planted bulbs?" expecting Seth to be there.

"Mmm, no, not really."

Startled, I turn around. Of course it's Gregory and no he wouldn't remember. My head feels like a tumbler filled with jagged ice. Gregory looks at me with concerned eyes. "You okay?"

I stand up, sniffing. "Yeah, yeah. I was just remembering when Nevaeh and I planted these. I thought I told you was all," I say, covering my error.

Gregory walks over and rubs his thumb across my cheek. "A little dirt got on you."

"Thanks."

"We're going to get through this, Alyssa. It's just going to take a while." I nod, sure that he's right. He gives me a tight hug then leads me back inside. "I missed you next to me this morning," he says, grinning.

Before I can respond, Daisy runs into my room and jumps up on my bed. "What's for breakfast, Mommy? Pancakes? Waffles?" Oma has certainly spoiled her over the past few months.

"Daisy, your voice is a song to my heart." I grab her face and plant a giant kiss on her cheek. "Breakfast, huh? That's a great question. I think we'll have to grab a bagel or something."

"Let me run home and clean up and I'll take you out to breakfast. Then we'll head over to the grocery store," Gregory says as he picks Daisy up and holds her on his side.

I stare at them a long while…Daisy who is so dark skinned, dark haired, with eyes the color of midnight; she could never pass for Gregory's and mine. Seth runs thick through her blood.

"Thanks, but I think I need some time alone with Daisy."

Disappointment washes over his face.

"You've done so much for us. And thanks for staying and keeping us safe last night," I add, trying to measure my tone for

Out of Breath

Daisy. I squeeze his arm; electricity runs through me. A secret grin passes between Gregory and me. "Daisy and I will head over to The Bagelry before we go get groceries at Staff of Life. It'll be good for us." Daisy flashes a giant grin. Going out for bagels and hot chocolate on Saturday mornings was another routine that vanished after Nevaeh's death.

"I understand. Call me later though?" He leans in and kisses Daisy on the cheek and says, "Bye kiddo." He tussles her hair, and continues, "Good to hear you talk again." He kisses my cheek and whispers into my ear, "Last night was amazing." His voice is seductive and his breath is moist.

I feel myself blush as I tell Daisy to go get dressed. "Don't start what you can't finish, Gregory."

Gregory looks around. He must be checking to see that Daisy's out of sight, then kisses me so hard and deep that our teeth touch. We part; I want more. "Believe me, I plan to finish what I've started," he says.

A nervous giggle escapes me. When I survey his face, it's as serious as stone.

ON THE WAY to the market, scenes from last night flash through my mind. There is a tenderness to Gregory that I knew existed under the surface. His sarcasm, stoicism, biting wit, they all fell away like a shell, letting me see his soft inner core. My face feels hot when I recall the way he looked at my body…naked…his hands and tongue dancing across me. I wonder if we are truly a couple now; lovers. Of course we are, but I can't be "out" with our relationship. I can barely go outside without tripping over someone who knows Seth. It would crush Seth if he found out I was having an affair. Or is it an affair I'm having? Affair sounds so dirty, adulterous, and secretive. Regardless, I'm not ready to deal with Seth's reaction.

"Mommy, look what I made on my MagnaDoodle!" shouts Daisy. She startles me out of my thoughts. Having Daisy chatter with me breathes relief into my veins. Her endless stream of conversation distracts me from the anxiety that screams through me about going out in public. I haven't grocery shopped or even run any errands since moving in with Oma. And I pick a Saturday, of course. Half of Santa Cruz is circling the block looking for parking at Staff of Life.

Katherine said that re-entering society would be one of the toughest parts of resuming "normal" life. The confusion, the difficulty of making decisions, and feelings of anxiety are unwelcomed companions as I peruse the aisles. She couldn't be more right. Looking at the bulk bins that hold flour, raisins, whole grain rice, my head begins to buzz. I'm crippled with indecisiveness. Daisy seems oblivious. I've given her a honey stick to keep her busy.

I'm half way through the store, on a quest for sliced bread (surely I can manage sliced bread) when a woman with long, fire-red fingernails and the sallow skin of a smoker nearly races down the aisle toward me. "Alyssa Buchanan," she announces, "It's so good to see you." She grabs me and pulls me into her. She smells of bourbon and Marlboro's, an odd contrast to the bulgur-wheat smell of the store. "And hello to you little one," she cants, tickling Daisy under the chin with one of her red nails. She cradles my arm, petting it like I'm a cat. "And how is Seth holding up? Poor darling."

First off, I have no clue who this woman is, although her smell is vaguely familiar. Second, how dare she ask how Seth is! If she knows us or even reads the papers then surely she's aware that Seth nearly went to jail over Nevaeh's death. I begin to answer but she's talking over me, "Of course it's been a terrible adjustment for everyone I'm sure. What with all of his court dates and supervised visits, Jeff hardly has a minute to spare covering the shop for Seth. I hardly ever see poor Jeffrey."

At the mention of "poor Jeffrey", everything clicks—this is Jeff's crazy, alcoholic mother. Of course she's sympathizing with "poor Seth and Jeff." Over the years, she's bailed Jeff out of the county jail more times than I can count; her big excuse: boys will be boys. I have the urge to slap her across the face. Instead, I retract my arm, and silently count to ten before I tell her to go to hell. "Got to go. You take care now," she says, leaving me slack-jawed in isle four.

I grab my bread and half a dozen or so items and race to the checkout stand. Breathing as though I'm in labor, the freshness of my daughter's death washes over me. I can't do this. I turn up the radio on the way home, attempting to drown out the panic inside me. Daisy sings along to the Beach Boys. I glance in the rear view mirror, expecting Nevaeh to be beside her sister with her blankie in one hand and her thumb in her mouth. Her blankie! When I returned home yesterday, it was the one thing I was sure I'd come across. Seth's story of going off to look for Nevaeh's blanket was such a smokescreen for getting high. I'm sure it's in the piles of dress up-clothes and baby blankets.

My skin is wet with perspiration. "Daisy, did you happen to see Nevaeh's blanket in your room when we got home yesterday?"

She says no in between the lyrics of "California Girls."

Finding her blanket will be like finding a piece of Nevaeh. I pull up to the house, grab my small bag of groceries, and usher Daisy to hurry up. I throw the groceries onto the kitchen counter and race down the hallway into the girls' room. My pulse quickens as I upend each toy and toss every item of clothing that's strewn across the floor. I dig through the dress up box, coming up empty handed. Ripping off my sweater that is soaked with sweat, I throw open the closet doors, forcefully shoving back bag after bag of outgrown baby clothes, teething rings, and unused diapers.

I hear Daisy's voice call out in a quivering tone asking, "Mommy, what are you doing?"

"It's got to be here. I know it's got to be here somewhere."

"Mommy, what are you doing to our room? Stop!"

"I need to find Nevaeh's blanket, Daisy! I have to find it."

"Mommy—STOP!" Daisy shrieks at the top of her lungs.

I stop. Sweat drips down the side of my face. I turn to see my daughter wild with fear. I shove aside a patch of clothes and stuffed animals and pull her into my lap. She falls into tears. We've been home a little under twenty-four hours and she's cried twice;

good job, Alyssa. "I'm sorry if I scared you. I'm sorry. baby. I just miss Nevaeh so much."

Daisy continues to cry. Then, from her tears I hear the most horrifying words. "I'm sorry, Mommy. I'm sorry."

I take her chin and hold it in my hands, asking, "What? What do you mean you're sorry?"

"I'm sorry, Mommy. I didn't watch Nevaeh. I'm sorry."

My daughter assumes she's responsible. Oh my God. "Daisy, no, it's not your fault." She won't look at me. "Daisy, look at Mamma. Listen to me, it-is-not-your-fault. Understand?"

Daisy still won't look at me. I place my head down, looking up at her from our laps. "Daisy, I want to hear you say, "It's not my fault."

"It's not my fault," she says, compliantly, but with no emotion.

"Louder Daisy. Say it like you mean it! It's not my fault!"

She repeats it a little louder.

"Louder, Daisy!"

"It's not my fault! I miss Nevaeh, Mommy. I want her to come back," she cries out.

She's said it...in words. Finally. "I know baby. I want her back too."

We sit on the bedroom floor holding each other for nearly an hour, until Daisy drifts off to sleep. The milk and yogurt I bought has probably soured, but I could care less. All her weeks of silence, who knew all that was inside? Now it's pouring out like a river. I pick her up and carry her to my bed and cradle her like a baby into my body. If I could rewind time...if we only stayed home from the festival, if Seth had only kept an eye on the girls...if I could go back to the way things were. But where would Gregory fit in? Back to being just a friend? I'm too exhausted to ruminate on what could have, should have, or might never have been. Sleep is the only reprieve.

Chapter 13

Seth

I get my first unsupervised visit with Daisy today. It's been four months since my daughter and I have had a "normal" outing together. Oma's been great, not hovering, pretending to read while she "watches" us at her house or on the playground, but it's not the same. It's like I'm a predator rather than a dad playing with his kid. Enough is enough. I hope the next motion from the courts allows me to move back home, although I can't imagine Alyssa will be thrilled with that— too bad, it's my home too. It seems that Alyssa's bitterness and complete avoidance of me has lessened lately. It's got to be the therapy. It's like Katherine's always been in my life. How did I do my life without her and Rocco's support?

I've got a cooler filled with Odwallas, hummus, sesame chips, and apples. If I'm going to do this right, I sure as hell am going to play by Alyssa's strict nutrition rules. Over the phone, I tell Daisy that we are going to take a walk around the one-mile redwood loop at Henry Cowell's State Park. I remember the last time we were there: Daisy was four, all eyes, and sprinting over the pine needled path. Nevaeh was barely one. We took turns holding her, pointing out banana slugs, and snatching leaves from her mouth.

If I could just get Alyssa alone and go over the details of the night Nevaeh died. I need to clarify what really happened. I understand that she didn't believe me initially, what with Gregory at her side, feeding her huge doses of poison. Katherine says I should save any real conversation with Alyssa for her office, but that session, well, it feels like the dangling carrot.

I've practiced my plea to Alyssa out loud so many times that it's like a prayer. I rehearse it again in the car on the way over to pick up Daisy. *'Alyssa, I know what it looked like the night Nevaeh drowned. I should have watched her. You know I'd take her place if I could and give you back our baby. But I can't. I wasn't high that night, 'Lyss, you've got to believe me. I said what I meant in the garage the night before the fair, that I'd never use again, that I'd get help. I've been clean ever since. Please find a way to forgive me and let me be the dad and husband I'm becoming. I love you, I miss you, and I want our family back.'*

My hands tremble as I grip the steering wheel. Rocco helped me write my "speech" during one of our meetings. I put it on an index card and keep it tucked under my CD visor.

I wind up Oma's road to pick up my daughter. Sounds of the schoolyard pour in through the car windows. Nevaeh should be at the parent-toddler group today with Alyssa. I roll up the window to block the sound of children's laughter. Oma is by the door, shaking out her kitchen rug. She's got her usual get-up on: a broomstick skirt, draped blouse, and an apron stretched around her thick waist. I smell the pastry she's baking from yards away.

I greet her with a kiss on the cheek. "Hey Oma. Smells great as usual."

"Oh, thank you dear. What brings you up this way?" She wipes her hands on the front of her apron and looks at me completely puzzled. "Just in the area?"

"No, I'm here to pick up Daisy for the afternoon," I say, craning my neck to spot Alyssa and Daisy inside.

"Oh dear," she says, throwing her hands to her mouth as though a big secret is about to escape.

I pull my small day planner out of my pocket, consulting it. "I got the date right. Did Alyssa forget?"

Oma wrings her hands. "I...I can't believe she neglected to tell you...to call you."

My back instantly twists into a knot. What now? "What's going' on, Oma? Something you need to tell me?" I steady my voice, although every part of me wants to raise my voice in frustration.

"Seth, they moved back home."

"Home as in our home, home?"

Oma nods.

I pace back and forth across her front yard that's lined with daffodils and crocuses. "When did this happen?" I hear how curt I sound, chastising myself for taking this out on Oma.

"Friday."

"Friday as in four days ago? Why did Alyssa hide her plans from me when she dropped Daisy off at the park last week for my supervised visit?"

"I don't know, dear. It came as a surprise to me, too. I'm so sorry. I assumed she told you. But there's something else, Seth. Why don't you come have a seat with me over here," Oma continues, pointing to a wooden bench that I put together for her a few years back. I sit down and brace myself. "It's about Daisy," she says.

I jump up, ready to race over to the house. "What? What's wrong with Daisy?"

Oma grabs my hand and pulls me to sit down again. "Nothing, dear, nothing. It's good news. She's speaking again, Seth. Daisy has her voice."

I want to be thrilled but I feel robbed, like I missed her birth. "I'm missing so much."

Oma's wrinkles crinkle up around her eyes and mouth. This whole thing has aged her more than ever. She places an arm around my shoulder and leans in close. "Do you know what her first words were?"

"I'm afraid to ask," I reply, looking out at the playground where two children are spinning in circles on the tire swing. Daisy will never get to do that with Nevaeh.

"She said, 'Where's Daddy.'" Her voice cracks.

"She said that?"

"Mm-hmm. You know how much she loves you Seth and so do I. You're like a grandson to me. We all make mistakes. This one, well, it was a big one. But there's nothing that God doesn't forgive, so I must forgive you too. Alyssa, she'll come around. I pray for your family every morning and night. Don't you worry. Now," she says as she claps the top of my hand, "you go on and get Daisy for your visit. I'm so happy for you two to have this day." Her eyes twinkle like stars in the midnight sky. "I'll call Alyssa to tell her you're on your way."

My head is caught in a tornado of emotions. Oma's faith and belief in her God and in me are almost painful. I never know what to do with mercy, forgiveness, and kindness; a good thrashing, well that's familiar.

ON MY WAY over, I realize that it's been nearly four months since I've been in my neighborhood, on my street, or let alone inside our house. Rocco told me to stay away while I worked through my early recovery. Relapse prevention was nearly all we talked about. If I saw our house, vacant, imagined my daughters running across the lawn, well, Rocco's right, I would have needed a drink just to get me back to my rat hole apartment.

Walking up the driveway, I instinctively reach for my keys to let myself in, but stop. Should I knock at my own front door? I've lost where I belong. I knock on the bright red door. Alyssa said she loved a red door. I painted it without even consulting the landlord, figuring the place could use some attention. Daisy was just a baby.

On the other side of the door, I hear the sweetest sound I've heard in weeks, "Daddy! Daddy's here, Mommy! Daddy's here!"

She throws open the door and jumps into my arms. She smells like sunshine.

"Let me hear you say my name again," I say, as my heart threatens to burst.

"Daddy!" she says again, leaning back, showing me a wide grin, revealing another lost tooth...that I missed. It's only been a week since I've seen her but I swear she's grown and changed. She's losing her preschool chubby cheeks and is lean and long. "Are you staying now? Can we make popcorn tonight and you can tell me a story before we go to bed?"

I'm having a mountaintop to the depth of the valley moment. I want to tell her yes; at the very least, promise that I'll be moving home soon, but I can't. "Not tonight, Daisy, but I have a special afternoon planned for us." I swallow my own tears and disappointment.

"But I miss you. I want you to come home," Daisy says, her joyful expression collapsing.

I hold her tight and rock her little body. "I do, too Daisy. I do too. Soon, baby. Soon."

Alyssa appears from the hallway. I wonder if she's been looming in the hall, eavesdropping. Her hair is pulled back into a loose ponytail, showing the full beauty of her face—strong cheekbones and ocean blue eyes. Her jeans and tiny t-shirt show off her teen-like figure. I want to reach out and touch her. Her eyes tell me to stay where I am.

"Honey, let your dad come in so you two can get ready for your visit," she says, prying Daisy from my arms. I don't like being referred to as 'your dad.' It has a "my baby's daddy" feel to it, like I'm not part of them...separate, removed.

"Hi 'Lyss," I say, somberly.

"Seth."

I shove my hands into my pockets, trying to conceal my anxiety.

"Come in," she says, expressionless, and walks over to the kitchen table. "Daisy and I made these to add to your picnic."

She hands me a basket with a blue handkerchief lying over the top. I pull the cloth back and see her special blueberry-sunflower seed muffins, breathing in the familiar aroma. "You didn't have to do that, Alyssa."

"It was Daisy's idea," she says with a measured tone. She turns to Daisy. "Go and get your sweater, honey." Daisy runs down the hall toward her room.

As Alyssa turns, the afternoon sunlight catches the sparkle of a necklace I don't recognize. I strain to see it—a single blue topaz, her birthstone. Pretty fancy for Alyssa. Maybe it's something Oma gave her for her birthday (a birthday that I actually remembered this year with a mailed card and sent flowers...daisies).

Alyssa is oddly aloof today. Not raging, not irritated, just strangely disconnected; like life is moving on just fine without me. "So, how is it being back home? I guess I thought you might have called and let me know." I'm trying hard to not sound combative.

A genuine look of surprise washes over her. "Oh, gosh Seth. I'm so sorry. I should have called you. It's been so hectic." Her face is flushed and she wipes her hand across her forehead. We both look around the house as if to say, 'she's really not here.'

Guilt, my familiar companion, rips through me. Of course it's been hectic. Maybe that explains her strange demeanor. I need a reality check that I used to live here. Everything is just as it was and nothing at all the same. A stream of beer bottles line the garden window. Alyssa drinks, but not that heavy...at least, I'm hoping that's not her way of coping. I thought maybe I'd left them there to be tossed into the recycling can back in October, but it's not my brand...Rolling Rock. A memory of Greg at a family BBQ last summer flashes through my brain: he's laughing as he tosses back a Rolling Rock while turning the steaks. I feel my neck seize up with tension.

"Must be lonely?" I hedge, sizing up her reaction. She looks away and shrugs. "Oh, uh, you mind if I grab a few things from our room?" I ask. "I could use some more of my clothes; sweatshirts, thermals, and stuff."

"Sure, go ahead. I'll grab you a bag."

I start down the hallway and will myself to not look at the pictures lining the walls. I need to make it out of here in one piece but I'm starting to splinter. Walking into our room, the sweet smell of Alyssa's lavender perfume and rose-infused cosmetics stir in the air. Something seems to be missing, though. I can't place my finger on it. I rummage through my drawers, grabbing a sweater here and a thermal there. Every morning when I'd dress for work, I'd look up from my dresser to catch a glimpse of the picture of us taken on our wedding day. I'm holding her in my arms and the coastal breeze is blowing her hair like a veil. I peek my head up—it's not there. I look around the room to see where it's been moved, but it's gone. In fact, every picture of me, the one of me surfing down in Costa Rica, the picture of Daisy, Nevaeh, and me on Father's Day last summer, they're all gone! It's *me* who's missing from the room.

Daisy bounds into the room and rattles me out of my stupor. "I'm all ready, Daddy."

I'm so dizzy. "What? Oh, yeah, come on, let's go." I take her hand and rush down the hallway. I pass Alyssa, unable to look at her. "I'll have her home by supper," I say, as I strain to conceal the fear and anger that are twisting my gut. I shove my clothes under my arm. Daisy skips out to my truck.

Alyssa reaches for me and grabs my shoulder. The heat of her hand, her missing touch, it burns of unspoken confessions. "Here. Don't you need this?" She holds out a paper bag for my clothes. I look at her hand on my shoulder then up at her eyes. They're the eyes of the guilty. "I know this is hard Seth—"

"Don't," I say and shrug her hand off. I won't take her pity.

DAISY SEEMS TO be oblivious to Alyssa's and my cold encounter. What she hasn't said in months, she's now making up for. Her voice is like a songbird that fills the car with sweet melodies. I shake my head at the clashing emotions that bounce around. All through our walk in the damp, mossy redwoods, I struggle to stay present and savor this time with my daughter. The beer bottles, the missing photos, Greg's face, they cloud my vision like I'm under murky water.

Daisy fills her pockets with pine needles, leaves, and acorns. "Here," she says, holding out a handful of her collection, "you can put these out on the table at your house. That way, you'll have decorations like Mommy and I do at our house. I mean," she giggles nervously, "ack, you know what I mean."

I bend down on one knee and fold her into me. "I know this is confusing, Daisy. Things will get better," I tell her, hoping I'm right.

She begins to twirl a strand of her hair around her pointer finger. "When can I come see your house and sleep in my bed that you made?"

"I hope soon baby." How do I explain to her that people like Leah make those decisions for me? I can't. I barely understand all this myself. My cell phone goes off. I didn't know I'd get reception under the blanket of trees. I recognize the number—it's Leah. "Hang on a second, baby, I need to take this call." Daisy nods and scampers down the path. If only I had her resiliency. I flip my phone open. "Hello"

"Seth, it's Leah."

"I was just thinking about you," I say.

"No wonder my ears were ringing. All good thoughts I'm sure," she banters.

"Of course. What else would I be thinking?"

"Alright, enough kissing up. I have good news. Starting this Friday, you get Daisy overnight one night a weekend. If things continue to go well with counseling, Daisy's therapist thinks she's ready, and your drug tests stay clean, looks like you'll be back home in a couple of months."

I'm speechless. Daisy is waving at me from a wooden bench that she's walking across.

"Seth, did I lose you?" Leah asks.

"No, uh, sorry. I'm…stunned. You'd have to know the kind of day I've had. This is great Leah. I'm actually with Daisy now up at Henry Cowell's. Can I tell her?"

"Of course. Now go have fun with your kid. I'll call Alyssa after we hang up and sort out all the details. Give me a call tomorrow afternoon, 'kay?"

"You bet. And thanks Leah."

"Don't thank me. You're the one doing all the work."

She's right. I am doing the work. I haven't missed an A.A. meeting, I pay my bills, I've been clean for nearly four months, and I'm like an open book in counseling. I have earned this. For the first time in my life, I'm actually proud of myself. I run to catch up to Daisy and call out, "Guess who's coming to stay the night in her new princess bed this weekend?"

She screeches so loud that I'm sure a ranger is going to come running. We spend the rest of our visit making plans for hot chocolate, popcorn, and storytelling as we munch on Alyssa's muffins and the stuff I've brought. As dusk settles in, we pack up, climb in my truck, and head back to town. Daisy tells me all about the tea parties she has with Alyssa and how they're cleaning out the weeds from the garden after school. It all sounds so normal, so every day. I want that normal, every day life back. Then again, I'm not sure I ever had it to begin with. I hope it's not too late to start now.

Daisy's been quiet for a few minutes—her afternoon rhythm of crashing right before dinner; something that Alyssa had to teach me about parenting. She perks up as we near our neighborhood. "When are you moving back home, Daddy?"

"I don't know Daiz. It depends on a bunch of things."

"What things?"

My sobriety, Katherine and Leah's recommendations, my work in counseling, and Alyssa's mindset—these are the things I want to lay out, but don't dare. Katherine and Leah pounded into me the inappropriateness of discussing any of this with Daisy. So, instead, I answer, "Grown up things," and pat the top of her head in hopes that she can accept my answer.

Her face is wrinkled up like she's thinking about something. "What's up, Daiz'?"

"I wish you were home. Sometimes I feel a little scared at night. I sleep with Mommy most of the time."

We round the corner to our subdivision. Blossoms are beginning to unfold on the plum trees that riddle the sidewalks with purple stains in the summer. "Why are you scared, baby?"

"Cause you're not there. And I hate the dark. Nevaeh hated the dark too. That's why we liked to sleep together."

I can picture it like yesterday, the two of them in Daisy's single bed all squished together, their hair weaved into a tangle of brown and blonde. Pangs of guilt stab at me. "You miss Nevaeh, huh?"

"Yeah. Mommy cries a lot. I try and make her better, but she even cries when she thinks I'm asleep next to her."

Thinking of Alyssa weeping, alone…it's awful. I want to be beside her, comforting her, holding her.

Daisy begins again, "That's why Mommy has Uncle Gregory come for sleepovers so we're not so scared and sad. He makes us laugh and takes us to the beach a lot."

Daisy keeps on talking but I'm deaf to it. I feel my foot slack off the gas pedal as I coast down our road toward the house. Uncle Gregory is sleeping over. Oh my God. First my little girl drowns and now that son of a bitch is sleeping with my wife.

"Daddy, are you listening," Daisy asks, shaking my arm that feels numb. "I said that tomorrow we're going to go down to Castle Beach and fly Uncle Gregory's big box kite. Isn't that neat?"

I will my lips to speak. "Yeah, ah, wow Daisy, that will be something." I can taste bile in my mouth. Every word she speaks feels like I'm standing on railroad tracks with my laces tied to it as a steam engine barrels toward me.

I pull up to the front of the house and slam my truck door harder than I should. She's oblivious and takes my hand as we walk up the concrete walkway. My mind begins to form disturbing images of Greg's hands pawing at Alyssa in places that are solely reserved for me. Worse yet, she's reciprocating, taking him into her arms, her body, her...

Alyssa opens the door. Her hair is damp from showering. The first thing my eyes wander to is that necklace—of course, it's got to be from him. She used to go on about how they were so close that they were like siblings, born practically on the same day. Some brother he is!

"You're back. How was your walk and your picnic?" she asks us.

Fire shoots from my eyes. She steps away from me then looks down at Daisy who hands her the picnic basket.

"Here Mommy. We ate everything. It was so much fun. And guess what? I get to spend the night at Daddy's this weekend! I'm going to go pack my backpack right now." She zips down the hallway leaving the two of us. Alyssa dodges my eyes like a flashlight shining in her eyes.

"So, you wanna come in or something? What's going on?" Her voice is peppered with anxiety.

"I take it Leah called you while we were out," I say, following her a bit too close, as she wanders into the kitchen to put away the basket.

"Yes." She shakes out crumbs from the cloth that held our muffins. "I thought you'd be thrilled."

"Oh, you thought I'd be thrilled, hah?" I move in close, trapping her in between my body and the corner of the kitchen. I can smell her fear.

"Seth, what's going on? Back off. You're freaking me out."

I don't move a muscle, other than the ones that are twitching and firing. "What's going on? I'm pretty sure you have a good idea of what's going on Alyssa," I snarl. "I think you're the one who's thrilled that Daisy will be away overnight with me." I place my lips near her ear. "That way, while she's away at my place, you can screw Uncle Gregory in our bed without her getting in the way."

Alyssa slumps to the floor, sobs catching in her throat.

"Daisy, I'll pick you up for our sleepover," I call out as I dash for the door. "Love you." I can't wait for her reply.

On my way to the liquor store, Daisy's words crash over me like I'm being slammed by a monster wave. Out in the ocean when that wall of water comes down on you, you're slammed beneath the surface. The first thing you have to tell yourself is, 'stay calm.' Not an easy thing to do when you've been driven down, deep under water, and you hope the thrashing ends so you can swim to the surface. Today's not one of those days—I thought I was so close to the surface but it's far above me. I'm caught inside in between two monster waves: my child's death and my wife's affair. Once during a competition, I was held down for three waves and my surfboard "tombstoned"—the board pointed straight up, perpendicular to the wave, with me at the bottom of my extended leash. I was *out of breath* and thought, 'this is it...I'm gonna die.' When I popped up, the exhilaration of actually being alive was unreal, although I was far from being out of trouble, working hard to make it ashore. Today, I can't seem to catch my breath.

Once inside the apartment, I crack open one beer after another. The neighbors pound on the wall, screaming at me to turn down the stereo. To hell with 'em. They didn't just find out that someone else is bangin' their wife.

I pick up a plate, smash it against our shared wall, then another, and another, until my fury brings up every ounce of alcohol I chugged. I spew into the sink. The next hour is spent puking into the toilet.

Morning light pours into the window. The crash of the metal garbage dumpsters floods the room. I roll over on the futon and try to recall the evening before. My head feels as though a baseball bat has bashed it in. I never had hangovers before; of course, I wasn't so much a hard drinker. Pot didn't really give me hangovers. I grab my watch off the coffee table. There's no way I'm in any shape to open the shop in an hour. I dial Jeff. A girl's voice, one I don't recognize, answers the phone in a throaty, sleepy voice. "Put Jeff on the phone," I bark.

"Dude, it's like 8:00. What the hell?" He says.

"I hope she's not somebody's wife or girlfriend."

"What the hell's your problem? Last time I checked you're my boss, not my priest."

I sift through newspapers and empty beer bottles to find my cigarettes. I light one up and take a drag. "Just shut up and listen, okay. Somethin' went down with Alyssa last night. I need you to open the shop. I don't know if I'll be in today or tomorrow."

"Sorry, man, it's just early, I'm kind of hung—" Jeff starts.

"Whatever. Just open the shop. I'll call you later."

It looks like a tsunami has hit my apartment—broken glass, cigarette butts, and empty beer bottles litter the floor. Daisy's innocent words, 'sometimes Uncle Gregory has sleepovers,' replay over and over in my mind. I barely make it to the bathroom as I bend over and toss up everything in me. I throw water on my face and brush my teeth—twice. I get a whiff of my shirt, the stench of sweat and booze; I need a shower. I soap up and let scorching water beat down on my shoulders as my mind wanders to dark places. This little love affair between Gregory and my wife—*my* wife—it didn't happen overnight. I'm sure it's been building for a while. And Alyssa, she's like a vault. She doesn't talk about private stuff, except with Gregory. Hold it! What about Katherine? She's got to be talking about the details of her life with Katherine. I towel off and throw on some clean clothes. How long has Katherine sat across from me giving me that sweet look of concern, all the while knowing my wife is screwing some other guy? I grab a beer bottle from the edge of the sink and smash it against the mold-infested shower wall.

I overturn cushions and pillows looking for my keys. When they don't turn up, I run down the stairs and see that I've left them in the ignition. I smack my forehead. Unbelievable, the truck's still here. I jam the car in reverse and slam into the garbage dumpster.

"Son of a bitch!" I scream, and throw my head on the steering wheel and bang the sides with my fist. My cell phone sits in the cup holder, just to the right of my periphery. I flip it open; I've missed three calls from Rocco. Crap. We had a meeting last night. I've never blown him off.

A rap on my window startles me. Great, it's probably a cop. I look up and see Rocco's crinkled face. He's grimacing, holding out a carton of orange juice, a bag full of bagels, and a bottle of Vitamin B. I open my door and get out like a dog that's made a mess on the carpet.

"Come on, let's go clean house," he croaks.

I tag along behind him, my tail between my legs. We step inside and the stench of stale beer, puke, and cigarettes brings back another wave of nausea.

"Impressive. What'd she do now?" Rocco asks, walking around as he surveys the damage that is my living room.

"Who says it has to do with her?"

Rocco limps in and shoves a discarded t-shirt off the futon and sits down with a groan. "Seth, I been at this a while. I know what sets a man off...what sets me off anyway. The fact that you could stay clean when your kid drowned, well, I told ya, that's somethin'. This," he shrugs, 'well, only a broad could set a man off like this." He chuckles and shakes his head. "You wanna tell me about it, or what?"

I take a deep breath and begin. Over the next hour, Rocco helps me sweep up broken dishes, toss out bottles, and wipe down the kitchen and bathroom. He listens with little interruption as I blubber through the details of Greg banging Alyssa while Katherine turns a blind eye.

"When do you see that Katherine again?" Rocco asks.

"In a couple of days."

"Well, you won't know if Katherine kept her mouth shut unless you ask her," he says matter-of-factly.

"Like she'll be honest."

"You know what we say in the program to talk like that. HALT. Your hungry, angry, lonely, and tired. You gotta suit up and show up and stop dwelling in all this."

I roll my eyes.

"Guess your sobriety date just got changed," he adds for extra measure.

Out of Breath

Great, I'm a failure at recovery, too. As if reading my mind, Rocco nuzzles up so close to me that it's as close to cuddling with an overweight, Italian man I ever want to get. "Hey, if you don't think I've relapsed before, you're nuts. 90% of us do, okay." He raises his dandruff-ruffled eyebrows for effect. "You dwell in your misery, you know that. That'll be the reason you drink, light up, snort somethin' up your nose, shove a pill down your throat, shoot somethin' into your vein. Got it?"

I nod. Something inside me relaxes. I didn't know that. Maybe I'm not such a piece of crap. "I just…I can't believe Alyssa and…" I can't finish. "And I miss Daisy so much. And my baby girl."

My throat balls up and I can't speak. Before I know it, my jaw quivers and my shoulders shake, releasing tears. Rocco pulls me into his flannel, grey shirt, then into his warm barreled chest and rocks me, stroking the back of my hair, whispering, "Let the tears go, Seth. Give this to God. Let him carry this for you. It's too big. Let him carry this."

I've never been held by a man.

Chapter 14

Katherine

The kids will be home in a little over two weeks for spring break. Wasn't it just Christmas? In childhood, time crept by; nowadays, I feel like I'm lapping the track at a NASCAR event. I've been knee deep in spring cleaning, ripping apart closets, planting flowers, and touching up dings on the walls. Carl affectionately refers to this as my "manic mode." As I swift the corners of the ceilings, sweat forms on my brow. Carl touches my arm. "Slow down, babe. You do know that the royal family isn't coming. The children will enjoy their time at home whether cobwebs line the ceilings or not."

I know he means well, but I can't stop myself; cleaning is my therapy. Mom called earlier and asked me to go with her to the doctor's; they need to discuss her latest lab work. Doctor's don't call a patient in to tell them all is well.

I jump in the shower and allow the warm water to cleanse away the dirt, fatigue, and worry. This afternoon is a full line-up of clients; most curious of all is Greg who called out of the blue. It's been a month since I've seen him. The urgency in his voice has me wondering.

Out of Breath

We meet and immediately I recognize a freshness about Greg that envelops him, replacing the angst and aloofness that enveloped him in the early winter. Ironically, his first announcement is that he and Jenny are in midst of divorce proceedings. Even couples that have horrible disdain for one another usually display a certain amount of emotion. Gregory shows only relief. I ask him how it's going with his children now that he's moved out.

"We see one another as often as my schedule allows. Jenny's real easy-going about letting me come and go. Shouldn't be any trouble after the divorce is finalized." Greg wiggles his foot that is crossed over his knee. His whole being pulses with energy.

"Is there any consistency about the days they are able to see you? Children thrive when there's rhythm and predictability to their days."

"Well, my schedule changes, so…" His voice trails off. I pick up on a hint of discomfort.

"How are they adjusting to your place?"

Greg squirms in his seat. "We keep our visits limited to parks, baseball games, stuff like that. I figure they're most comfortable in their home."

"Their home?"

"You know, where all their stuff is."

I want him to hear how removed he sounds. It's just not clicking. Seth enters my mind and the huge strides he's taking to help Daisy adjust: the room he custom designed for her, the thoughtful picnic he planned. Like Leah said, he's far from the dead-beat dad that we pre-judged him to be.

"So, Greg, you called me after weeks of not seeing one another. I wonder what brings you in today." I sit up straight, taking note of how annoyed and preoccupied I am.

"Actually, I wanted to thank you for the few times I did see you and how you helped me sort out what I really needed." Greg leans back in his chair with the same air of content that walked in the door.

I'm puzzled. I didn't do anything to help him sort out his issues, particularly not in a handful of sessions. "How so?"

"Well, talking about Steven, Jenny, all that, I feel relieved… better. But truthfully, I've met someone else and things are going great," he says, stretching his arms above his head and placing his hands behind his head.

"Ahh," I sigh. So, this explains his mood; nothing like the euphoria of infatuation and passion as a source of distraction from underlying pain.

"What?" he asks. "Do I sense disapproval?" His tone is sarcastic.

"Disapproval, no; concern, yes. You've had two major losses: the death of your brother and your marriage. I always worry when major decisions are made in the midst of such great losses."

Greg shakes his head at me. "My marriage has been over for a long time, Katherine. It's not like I woke up one day and it was finished. It's been building…trust me."

"That may be true, but without time to process that loss and what went wrong, you may repeat the same mistakes in your next relationship; particularly if you've just met this woman."

"No, no, no. No risk of that. That's where you're wrong." Greg leans forward. "She's not a new woman."

"Oh." Great, he's been having an affair and not telling me.

"No, it's not what you think. We've known each other our whole lives, since pre-school. Our parents always thought we'd end up together."

"So what happened? Why didn't you?"

Greg's face contorts with familiar anger. "She got pregnant by some dick-wad and tried to make a go of it. What a joke this guy is."

"So she's divorced," I say, offering him the benefit of the doubt.

"Soon. I've loved her my whole life, Katherine. Nothing's going to mess it up this time." Something about the intensity in his glare causes me to shiver. "She's in this huge mess right now. Remember

I told you about a friend I had whose daughter died? That's her anyway…"

As Greg continues to talk, my breath grows shallow. *Please God, I pray, tell me this is a coincidence. He can't possibly be talking about Alyssa.*

"…When we're together, I'm like a different person. I'm totally open and have nothing to hide. She grew up with Steven and me, knows my parents are total fruit loops, you know what I mean?"

"Mm-hmm," is all I can muster.

"To be with her this way, it's just totally amazing. I can give her everything that she and her other daughter deserve—stability, safety, security."

"She has a little girl other than the one who died?" I ask. I'm on a fishing expedition; my counseling skills have just flown out the window.

"Yeah, Daisy. She's five and thinks I hung the moon for her."

If the floor could just open up and swallow me now. I don't know how much longer I can play dumb, pretending I don't know this mystery woman. I take a deep breath. "Greg, does this child, Daisy, know that the two of you are…well, intimate?" It's a gamble I'm taking to press for more information purely for my benefit and the sake of Seth and Alyssa. The boundaries are getting fuzzier by the minute.

"No, we've played that down. We kind of sneak around when she's asleep or at her father's apartment," Greg says with a smile that turns my stomach.

How quaint. My clients are having an affair right under my nose. I have an overwhelming urge to reach out and smack the grin off of Greg's face. What is the matter with me? I shift in my seat and struggle to maintain eye contact. "And the father? He knows of your, what shall I call it, affair?" *Careful.*

"Seth? Beats me. Truthfully Katherine," he says and leans in close to me like he's got a secret he's dying to share, "I can't wait until the son of a bitch knows I'm sleeping with his wife."

The blow hits me hard. Hearing the way in which Greg delights in Seth's misery is agonizing. How in the world am I going to face Seth? Or Alyssa? This is privileged information told to me in confidence by another client. I cannot break confidentiality.

"Oh God, that bastard'll come unhinged." Greg laughs a sadistic laugh. "Their whole marriage he's been suspicious of us. He practically threw her in my arms after Nevaeh drowned."

Here I've been cheering Seth on, hoping for his and Alyssa's reunification; talk about having my own agenda and being off the mark. "You seem to have an incredible amount of disdain for her husband. Can you talk about that?"

"He's a druggie, Katherine, a textbook, pothead surfer who runs around like he's seventeen. You want to hear the real kicker?" *How do I make him stop?* "I was the arresting officer the night Nevaeh died."

Everything is upside down. My neck cramps and my pulse soars. If I could only rewind time and never have let any of these three into my life. Greg is practically manic.

"The satisfaction I had dragging his ass down to the station—it will never be matched. I told her he was bad news all along. Alyssa's always had a thirst for the wounded."

I cock my head, taking a stab at him.

"What, you're saying I'm no different?" His face is flush.

"I didn't say that. You said she's always had a thirst for the wounded. She married a wounded man and is now having an affair with a man who has left his wife, is grieving the death of his brother, and is struggling with anger issues."

For a minute I think he might jump out of his seat and throw a punch at me as his fists ball up in his lap. "I'm different Katherine and a lot of that is behind me. Give me a break."

I need this session to end. "So, what is it you want from me today?" I want to tell him to get the hell out of my office and out of the Buchanans' lives.

"I don't need anything, Katherine. You see, I got my prize. I just thought you should know why I don't need your help anymore, tell you thanks, and say good-bye."

Out of Breath

His words, 'I got my prize' hang thick in the air. He has completely objectified Alyssa. I'd heard of other therapists caught in a triangle of clients who played with each other's lives. I counted myself lucky to have escaped. This is a catastrophe.

It's customary for me to extend my services to a client should future problems arise. After Greg pays for his session, I merely thank him and bid him good-bye. When I hear his cruiser pull out of my driveway, I fall into my chair and weep. I weep for Alyssa who is using an affair as a distraction from her grief. I weep for Seth and his tireless efforts to become new, unshackled from his past, and the husband and father he so desperately wants to become. "How do I fix this?" I call out into the quiet of the room. Leah was right; the privacy of this case is dangerous and isolating. Even though my training pounded into me that I'm not responsible for the solution, I can't help but feel that I've somehow failed my clients.

At the end of the day, when I've nothing left to give, I meet my mother at her doctor's office. The loud ticking of the clock; the calendar sponsored by Pfizer; the slippery feel of my silver beaded bracelet: these are all things that help distract me as I hear the doctor utter the words, "Your cancer is spreading, Mary." My mother listens with rapt attention. I catch every fifth word or so—metastasize…liver enzymes…full body scan. A whooshing sound fills my ears; I may faint.

"I wish we had better news, Mary. After the scan, we'll know more. Doris will help you schedule your appointment." Dr. McGuire offers a soft touch to her arm. My mother returns a faint smile.

"I'm sure you'll figure something out, Kent." She's known Dr. McGuire since he was little Kent McGuire who was on my second cousin's little league team.

"I wish all my patients had your optimism and fight, Mary," he says on the way out. "Good to see you, Katherine. I'll be talking with you soon."

We're all being so polite; so appropriate. I want to scream. Instead, I nod and lift my hand to say good-bye, but my legs have turned to Jell-O. I slump into the vinyl chair beside the examination table.

"Oh, Katie," my mother starts, "don't write me off yet," she says with a scold.

If this isn't denial, I don't know what is. Between my clients' crazy lives, my exhaustion, and this, I don't know how I'm functioning. "Mother," I begin, giving her a stern stare, "enough of the 'it's all going to be fine,' routine. This is serious. I'm scared and I'm entitled to my feelings. I don't know if I believe some miracle cure will wipe out your cancer. I'm a realist, Mom."

The protective, paper shield beneath her crinkles as she slides off the table. She squeezes my shoulder—her version of a comforting hug. It should be the other way around; I should be comforting her, and yet, it feels good to have someone at my side. "I've never asked you to be anything but who you are. I'm sorry you're frightened, Katie."

I keep my head tucked into her side. "You keep telling me that everything is going to be fine, that everything will work out. When you do that, I just feel crazy. Kind of like how when I was little and saw Daddy beating you up and the next day we'd all sit around the breakfast table eating pancakes, asking each other to pass the syrup."

Mom takes a big breath and sits down in a chair beside me. Her gown slips off her shoulder revealing her bony clavicle. "I haven't always been the most honest parent; certainly not one to openly talk about myself, my *feelings*." She accentuates the word feelings like she's discussing an STD. "When your father would come home empty-handed, drunk, and the electricity would be shut off again, I just had to tune that out and plow through. Otherwise, I'd wither up and die of shame. I'm not a quitter Katie and I don't lick my wounds. What I endured made me strong."

"I understand that your optimism and strength were coping mechanisms."

She frowns at me. "Now you're talking to me like I'm one of your clients."

"Sorry. I'm just trying to understand and make sense of all this," I say while I stand, smooth my skirt and slip into "good-daughter" mode.

My mother slips her gown off. Her underpants sag and the cups of her bra gape. She slips on her blouse and says, "You don't have to agree with me, understand me, or believe in miracles. But I won't go down without a fight and it would mean a great deal if you'd be beside me cheering me on."

I stand humbled. My mother doesn't need me to confront her denial. Nor is she truly capable of comforting me the way I wish she could. However, I know she loves me and wants me by her side. This, for now, is enough. I hug her and she shudders just a bit.

"Absolutely." I look at her just in time to see a lone tear fall from her eye.

"Enough of this. Aren't you taking me to Gayle's for lunch?"

At Gayle's, Capitola's finest eatery and bakery, we grab "our" place—a handcrafted mosaic table with a French blue china pattern. The air of the restaurant is filled with fresh baked bread and delicious pastries. I never make it out of here without a big black and white checkered bag filled with thousands of calories. Our sandwiches and iced teas arrive. I shake a sugar packet and watch the crystals sink to the bottom of my glass.

"I took on a new case this year, Mom; parents who lost a child." The words tumble out so fast that I shock myself.

Her sandwich at her lips, my mother stops, replaces her sandwich on the plate, then picks up her napkin and dabs the corners of her mouth. "You don't usually talk about your work with me." Her words are filled with wonder.

"I know. I can't help but think of you and how much our relationship changed and deepened when Carl and I lost Nicole." I'm asking for support that she may not be able to offer.

My mother nods knowingly. "Are you sure this is wise; seeing this family? For all the work you do with the mind and emotions, I've always wondered why you've kept so quiet about Nicole."

"Me too." I gaze out at the other patrons who are dining out on the patio. A group of women are huddled together, laughing, sipping bottled water. I haven't been doing enough of that. "I tell my patients that over time, their grief becomes less raw and consuming. I know that's true; it was with Dad. But losing a child...I don't know, I wonder if one ever really fully recovers."

"Are you asking me or telling me?" my mother questions.

"Neither. I'm just talking out loud."

"I'm glad you're talking about her." My mother reaches across the table and touches my hand. This time there's more than a lone tear. I wonder who they're for— Nicole, me, her uncertain future, or perhaps all three; I know not to ask. Once again, I've underestimated the depth of my mother's emotions.

AFTER I DROP off my mother, I run a couple of errands, then drag my weary self through the door. I'm met with the amazing scents of prosciutto, cream sauce, and garlic. Carl walks toward me with a giant grin, sporting an apron that reads, 'Kiss the Cook.' "Just a little something I saw on Rachel Ray this week," he says, lips puckered as he awaits his kiss.

I look around half expecting a caterer to make a mad dash out the door. "Since when did you start watching Rachel Ray?"

"I have to do something while my woman's away all the time. Come, taste this." He spoons some of the white sauce into my mouth.

"Oh, Carl, it's delicious; so much for a low calorie day. What brings this on?"

He pours a glass of pinot grigio, scrunches up his nose, and hands it to me. "You've been a little grumpy."

Out of Breath

I feel a bit defensive, but know he's right. "I've had a lot on my mind." I let him pull me into an embrace; something else I've been too preoccupied to enjoy. "Just when I think that men are scum on the bottom of my shoe you go and redeem your gender."

"Yikes—some guy's in trouble," he banters as he lets go and starts to prepare the salad.

"If you only knew. Enough of that." Oh God, I do have some of my mother in me. "I don't even want to think about my clients and the chaos they create for themselves."

"That's more like it." He sets the avocado aside and pulls me in tight again. "You know I don't like to share you much. You've been so distant. I miss you."

Carl's love is like a warm, heavy blanket—comforting, sometimes too heavy, but warm, and soothing. I have been distant. I think back to the morning that Carl tossed the paper at me that headlined the Buchanan's tragedy. Was it then that I began to push him away? That was part of it. Revisiting Nicole's death, the distance that it placed between us, our silence, how Carl got so very quiet…all of these old, stashed away memories play fresh in my mind. I need to bring this up…but maybe not tonight.

After our amazing meal, we tear at each other's clothes like two hungry teenagers. Afterwards, as I rest in his arms and play with the gray hairs on his chest, I vow never to shut him out again.

"How was lunch with your mom today?" Carl asks and reaches for his glass of wine.

I don't want the mood to end, but that seems unavoidable. Why can't time just freeze? "Her cancer's back."

Carl raises up on one arm and nearly spills his wine. "Why didn't you tell me earlier, Babe?"

"I didn't want to ruin the wonderful dinner you were preparing. And, I needed time to be with you…normal time, not talking about crisis." He strokes my hair. I'm safe.

"Let's move her back in," Carl says. He needs to fix this.

"Eventually. She's hardly admitting that she's sick; you know how she is."

We remain quiet for what feels like hours. I wonder how he hasn't drifted off to sleep. I get up and slip on my nightshirt. Carl pulls on his boxers and a T-shirt. "There's something else, Carl." I look at the clock; it's nearly 11:00 and we both have early mornings. I consider retracting my statement or making something up.

"You've fallen in love with one of your patients and he's twenty years younger." Playful Carl has returned. I'm actually relieved; the seriousness was dragging me down again. I nudge him in the ribs. "Sorry," he chuckles, "couldn't resist. What's going on?"

How much can I really say? I'm full to the brim and about to spill over the edges. "It's messy. I just need you to know that I'm involved in a really tough case."

He looks at me bewildered. I usually offer up more details. Rather than beg for more, he kisses me softly and says, "I don't pretend to understand how you keep it all straight; your cases, our life, your worries over your mother. I'd lose my mind. But I can see that something is getting to you. You have a full plate. Remember to take care of you, too. I love you and need you too much for anything to happen."

"Okay, it's not just work."

Carl sits up and leans against our headboard. The lines in his forehead deepen. "This have something to do with you looking at her pictures the other day?"

That he doesn't say Nicole's name irritates me, but I let it go. "Sort of." I sit myself up beside him. On the walls, shadows dance from the candlelight. "Do you think about Nicole, Carl?"

"All the time."

"Really? You never mention it."

"I don't want to upset you."

We're the proverbial couple who remains silent lest one upset the other. "I'm sorry if I gave you that message when we were younger. I'd love to hear you talk about her, what you felt then, and how you feel today. It would make her real again; know what I mean?"

Out of Breath

He nods his head. We ignore the clock and spend the next hour talking about Nicole. Suddenly she's with us again…the daughter we lost, the daughter we've found. When our eyelids grow heavy, I fall asleep in his arms; something I haven't done since we were newlyweds.

Chapter 15

Alyssa

I'm curled up in my rocker pretending to be a grown up. I have a new book (well, new to me), a cup of peppermint tea, and our lab nestled against my feet. If someone were to peek through the blinds, they might comment on how content I look as I turn each page and occasionally reach over for a sip of my tea. On the inside, I'm a mess. My heart is keeping pace with a runner who's on a steep incline. I have to reread each paragraph just to make sense of the words on the page; words that should be translating into coherent sentences, paragraphs, ideas—they don't.

Oma met Daisy after school to spend some time together to bake, nibble, and visit. Time with Oma is really important to Daisy; my life was filled with special "Oma moments." Then, Daisy called after their baking session asking to spend the night. She misses living there. I know part of me does. It's never lonely there and the warm scents of bread, pastry, and roasting chicken seem to linger in the walls and stick to the forty-year-old yellow drapes. Plus, when Daisy's there, she doesn't have to contend with my wild mood swings: crying one minute, throwing her in the car for a trip to the beach the next.

Out of Breath

It's so tense between Seth and me since he found out about my relationship with Gregory. He won't even come to the door to get Daisy; he calls from his cell phone and lets me know he's in the driveway. Maybe I'd react the same if I knew he was sleeping with someone else. Just the thought punches me in the gut. I shut my book and toss it onto the coffee table. Duke stirs, giving me a look of annoyance for waking him.

I walk into the kitchen to dial Seth, but replace the phone… again. What can I say? Sorry. No, I'm not sorry. Sorry you're upset? Nothing fits. I slump down on the kitchen floor, as memories bite at me: my chaotic past with Seth; long, lazy days cuddling with Nevaeh; Daisy and Nevaeh playing dress-up in my old clothes; the fire in Gregory's eyes when he holds me.

My heart is more than racing now; it's about to jump out of my chest and wiggle across the floor. I check my pulse—it's too fast to be normal. What if I'm having a heart attack? No one in our family has heart disease though. This doesn't make sense. Sweat drips down my back. I rip off my sweater. Duke gets up and paces around me. His tail stops wagging as my tears splash near his feet. I look up at the kitchen clock. One more hour until Gregory is off. I go to the kitchen sink and splash water on my face, hoping that it will penetrate the blazing heat I'm throwing off. I can't wait. I need to call him right now. I dial his cell number; he picks up immediately.

"Gregory," I pant.

"What's the matter?"

"I don't know. I …I can't seem to catch my breath and my hearts racing. I feel dizzy." I can hear my own voice escalate like I'm getting higher and higher up in a hot air balloon. "I'm scared, Gregory."

"I'll be right there. I'm just up the road cruising the cliffs."

I wish I could calm myself down, and tell him, 'No, no, don't be silly. I'll be fine.' Instead, I whimper, "Hurry."

Within minutes, Gregory's keys jingle outside the door as he lets himself in. He rushes toward me. I gasp when I see him in his uniform, gun hitched to his side. It throws me back to the night Nevaeh died. He unsnaps his duty-belt and lays it on the kitchen counter. "Come here," he says as he draws me in to him. I sob into his well-padded chest, feeling the scratchiness of his shirt on my face. "What's going on, Alyssa?"

I shake my head. "I don't know. I let Daisy stay at Oma's and I told myself I'd be okay." I point to the family room, continuing, "I was reading but the words were just a jumble. I was trying to deal with being alone. I guess I'm not very good at it." I don't say all the other things I think and feel, like how Seth has been racing through my thoughts nearly every day since he stormed out of here. Or, how I feel like I've just broken what was left of his heart.

"Come on, let's get you a few things to leave at my place. This way, you can just come over and stay or wait for me to get home. You need to get yourself out of this environment," he says looking around at my shattered world.

I obey, head down, nose sniffling, as I follow him into my room. I mechanically toss underwear, shirts, my comfy sweats, and a pair of jeans into a bag. Maybe he's right—I need to think about living somewhere else. The thought is too big, like trying to swallow a fist-sized jawbreaker.

I climb in beside Gregory in his cruiser. I wonder if he can read my frantic thoughts and memories; they're so huge that they must be visible like cartoon thought-bubbles over my head. Last time I was in this seat, my child was being rushed to the E.R. It was a drizzly, miserable evening, the type of moisture that gets into your bones. Tonight, the weather is similar, like I'm caught in a horrific déjà vu. My earlier memories are now replaced with different, equally awful ones.

Gregory hits his wipers then fiddles with his police radio. I recall Seth in the back of the squad car that night while Gregory and I stood outside. I remember Gregory telling me that he'd be taking Seth down to the station. Seth's face was bruised and bloody. How in the world did that happen? I find that the memories come like trickling water, accumulating, leaving me with a flood of questions.

Out of Breath

"How did Seth get so banged up the night Nevaeh died?" I ask.

Gregory looks at me as though I've just asked him how the latest alien abduction investigation is going. "What? That's a little out of the blue."

"I know. I was just thinking...kind of like having a flashback to that night. He was a mess."

Gregory shakes his head as though trying to rattle a memory loose. "I...uh, I don't remember. Something about he and Jeff getting into it. I don't know."

I turn away and stare out the window. My breath fogs the glass. Jeff? That doesn't make sense. "Are you sure? He's the closest thing Seth has to a brother. Why would they get into a fight that night?"

Gregory stares straight ahead at the wet road. "Beats me. Since when did either of them behave like adults?"

"Well, it's not like they're tweakers or something." My face is hot and I feel irritation creep up into my temples.

Gregory looks at me from the corner of his eye. "You're kidding me, right? You think Jeff and Mr. Wonderful stick to stuff benign as pot. Get a grip, Alyssa. Who knows what else was floating around in Jeff's system? Seth's lucky I caught him on a good night."

I click my tongue against the roof of my mouth in disgust. "Gregory, he didn't shoot heroine or freebase. You wouldn't have caught him with anything else in his blood. I should know."

Gregory screeches the car to a halt in the middle of the street then pulls off the side of the road. "Oh really? You would know? What the hell is going on with you tonight? First, you call me because you are freaking out at home. Can I remind you that you are alone because you're scumbag of a husband let your daughter wander off and drown? Now you're defending him? You should know," he repeats. "You didn't even know how much of a problem he really had!" he screams.

I'm pressed up against the passenger door. I want to jump out and run home. "Take me home."

"What?!"

"Stop screaming at me and take me home."

Gregory jams the car into park and punches the ceiling of the car. I haven't seen him this angry since we were kids and the neighborhood bully grabbed me by the throat during a game of freeze tag. Gregory punched him so hard that he knocked one of the kids' teeth out. He takes a deep breath. "What do you want from me? You've said yourself you should have never married the guy. Now you're playing all this crap down?"

"You know, I've been in a very dark place the past several months. I've said and done a lot of things that I can't be held responsible for," I say as I cower in my corner in the car.

"Oh, so you're saying that you didn't mean what you said? That he is the man of your dreams?" The veins in Gregory's neck look as though they're about to burst. "What else have you done and said that you don't mean, huh? Maybe sleeping with me? Telling me that I'm the answer to your prayers? Is that something you can't be held accountable for either? I'm no shrink, but it sure looks like you're trying to pick a fight with me and I just don't get why I'm the bad guy. All I ever do is swoop in to your rescue and pick you up off the ground when you can't deal. But hey, I'm not your saint of a husband." Gregory throws open his door, slams it shut, and walks around to the back of his squad car.

The vibration of his anger rings through me. I break down in sobs of confusion. After a few minutes, I remind myself that this is my best friend who's standing out in the rain. I've hurt him. I creep out and walk to his side, placing an arm on his shoulder. He shrugs it off.

"Gregory, I'm sorry. I'm just...you know. This is me, Alyssa. Don't push me away." I slide my hand in between his crossed arms.

"What do you want from me?" He asks again, his voice back to its normal pitch.

"I don't know. But I don't want this," referring to his outrage.

Greg

I turn to face Alyssa. She takes my hands in hers. They're soft and tiny, like a doll's. Her hair is sticking to her neck and face. Even when she pisses me off, I want to grab her and never let her go. "I do know what I want. But, until you're sure what you want and believe, I can't keep doing this...this, whatever it is we're doing because it's screwing with my head too much. Some days, it feels like you're with me...totally with me...mine. Other days, I don't know where you go, but it scares me."

I've envisioned my confession of how long I've loved Alyssa nearly my whole life. I pictured it on our honeymoon, us naked, entwined, lying in bed. I never dreamt it would be through glassy eyes as I lean against my squad car in the rain. "Alyssa," I begin as I place my hands on her waist, "I've wanted you...this way," I squeeze her, "for as long as I can remember."

Her eyes throw me a look of surprise. She never really knew?

"I never had the guts to tell you when we were growing up. I was always the brother you didn't have. So, I pushed my feelings aside." Her brow is furrowed with confusion. "Then, when you came back from Germany, I'd hoped that time and distance would sort of kindle something, but—"

"I met Seth. Oh, Gregory," she breaks in, staring down at our feet. "I didn't know. Really." She puts a hand up to her forehead. "This is a bit much to take in. I mean, maybe if you and I had—"

"Alyssa, I love you," I whisper, wanting to interrupt any second-guessing she might have. I grab her hands tight, begging her to love me back. "I've loved you my whole life. Frankly, I can't imagine life meaning much without you in it. So, don't ask me to be sympathetic about Seth and what he did or didn't do. I want you—all of you—and I don't like to share. You know that by now."

"Take me home," she says. The words hit me like a bullet. I nod, drop her hands, and make my way to the car door. "No," she calls out and takes hold of me. I'm in her arms and she's pressing her body tight into mine. Her lips cover my mouth and our breath is short and filled with sighs and whimpers. "Take me home," she repeats as we break apart. This time I understand.

Alyssa

The endless crash of the waves mimics the roar of our passion. It tumbles through us and throws my doubts onto the sand like a weathered piece of sea glass. Naked in one another's arms, relief and exhaustion spread through me. Sleep comes swiftly after two nights of anxious wakefulness.

I moan and turn over, confused. It's morning. Gregory nudges my shoulder and strokes my arm, calling out, "Alyssa, it's okay. Wake up. I'm here." The view of the ocean pours in through the blinds. I take a deep breath and wipe away the tears that have bled into my waking thoughts.

"I was having the worst dream."

Gregory wears a worried expression. "I know. You okay?"

I sit up and reach for my shirt that is tangled in a mound of our clothes. I shiver. The fire died hours ago and Gregory always forgets to turn on the heater. I stand, pulling my arms across my body. "I just need to wash up." My head is clouded with unsettled images of my dream…my breast, a baby, a looming figure. I turn on the shower and let the hot water thaw my bones, willing myself to tuck away the recurring hum in my ears and erratic pulse. Then it dawns on me: I have an early appointment with Katherine.

"Gregory," I call as I stick my head out from the sailboat print shower curtain. "What time is it?"

"A little after 9:00," he hollers back. Crap! My appointment is in less than an hour. I lather up, shampoo, and search for conditioner. No conditioner? Greg pokes his head into the bathroom holding a cup of coffee. His smile fades as he sees me toweling off in a hurry. "I thought I'd join you…help you get to the places you can't reach."

"I'm sorry." I lean over and give him a quick kiss. I take the cup of coffee and sip it. It's not sweet enough. "I have my therapy appointment. I totally forgot. I'll come back after? We can go for a walk or something? Hang out before you go to work?"

"Sure, I'll be here."

He follows me out to the living room. I rummage through the bag I packed last night and grab my jeans and a sweatshirt—there's no time for me to drive across town and get something else. After a quick embrace, I set the coffee, cold and untouched, down on the counter and race out the door. I look around for my car. My car! Oh, this morning is growing more frantic by the minute. I turn to run back inside and Gregory stands at the door with the keys to his truck in hand.

"I think you might need these," he says with a smug grin.

"Thanks. I'll be careful."

"Don't park too close to anyone. Oh, and we're getting you a cell phone today; time to join the 21st century. I need to keep you safe."

I'm in too much of a hurry to argue. I offer a weak, "Uh, okay. I guess." I run to his truck and call out over my shoulder, "And grab me some oatmeal and honey conditioner from the health food store." I can just imagine him rolling his eyes.

Greg

Back inside, it looks like a small tornado has ripped through the condo. Traces of Alyssa are everywhere: Her panties strung over the arm of the recliner, her toothbrush next to mine, an assortment of clothes scattered across the family room. I remember what it was like to have sleepovers when we were young. For an entire day, the scent of my room would take on that girly, sweet, flowery-scent, wiping away the usual dank smell of socks. Today, I want to freeze time and bottle her scent to carry with me.

I grab her cup from the coffee table, take it out to the balcony, and watch the morning surf. The swells are huge and the crash of the waves startles me the first time I hear it without the buffer of the windows. I replay the evening like a movie: my confession to Alyssa, her change of heart, an amazing night of sex…sex like I imagined it would be with her. Another enormous set rolls in, crashing into the shore, sending walkers running up the sand to avoid getting their shoes wet. That's when I feel it, like the nip of a sand flea at my leg on a warm summer afternoon, the bite of worry that eats at my heart…she never said 'I love you' back—not after I professed my feelings out by the car; not after I repeated it when I was inside her, our bodies completely one; not after I whispered it as we dozed off to sleep. 'I want you,' 'I need you,' but never, 'I love you.' In time…I know she loves me; she's just overwhelmed.

I toss the lukewarm coffee onto the ice plant covered hillside below. I can't get Seth's image out of my brain. Alyssa threw 'I love you's' at him like a rich man tosses pennies onto the sidewalk. What I wouldn't give to be a fly on the wall at her therapy session.

Katherine

I can't relax. I've tried soft music, herbal tea, even an Advil, but I'm completely uncentered as I wait for Alyssa. She cancelled our last couple of meetings saying that she'd come down with something. *An affair? Lovesick?* This is awful; pretending to know nothing about her affair is ridiculous. To be true to yourself and honest with your clients is one of the cornerstones of therapy and now I have to behave completely inauthentic.

I greet her and search her face for clues…something that I've missed: a guilty look, new hairstyle, something. She's more disheveled than usual; not that I care how my clients dress, but with Alyssa, her presence and self-care are a barometer of how she feels. At first, she lived in sweat pants and oversized sweaters. Lately, she's shed that husk.

"Everything okay?" I ask.

"Oh," she says as she pulls her damp hair into a knot behind her head, "yeah, I was doing some stuff around the house today and I didn't have time to change."

Out of Breath

"Stuff" before 9:00 in the morning. Okay, I'll give her that. It might be my imagination, but she's avoiding eye contact. "I see. So, where do you want to begin today?"

Alyssa takes a deep breath. Maybe a confession is coming. It's like I'm trapped in a story and want the page to read faster. "Actually, it's about Seth." Okay, not exactly what I had in mind, but we'll see where this goes.

"What about him?" I ask. Alyssa shifts and fiddles with her fingers. I look at her hands and notice that her wedding band is missing.

"Well, now that it's been a while and I don't feel all spaced out and quite as foggy inside, I have a lot of questions about the night Nevaeh died, but I can't seem to get them answered."

"What kinds of questions," I ask, intrigued with where this is going.

"Mmm, like, where exactly he was when she drowned. He sticks to this…this stupid cover story of looking for her blanket in his truck, but I wonder…" she trails as she stares out into space for a moment. "I wonder if it's actually possible, you know? Maybe he really was." She shakes her head as though wanting to toss out the thought. "Also, why was he all beat up and bloodied later on that night? Those sort of things."

I hear her words, but I'm no longer present. It's happening… the blur of her words, questions, and stories colliding with Greg's rendition. Greg told me that he was the arresting officer the night of his goddaughter's death and I know from what he shared early in treatment that anger on the job is frequently an issue. I jot down notes to myself about the intersection of these facts.

"I'm sorry, Alyssa, I'm a little distracted. I just need to write some notes to myself. Could you go back to where you were wondering about Seth and how he looked beat up on night of Nevaeh's death."

Her face scrunches. "It looked like he'd been in a fight. His face was bleeding and his eye was swollen. How the hell did that happen?"

I have to "play-dumb" and feel sick about it. "Seth was arrested that night. Any chance of police brutality?" As the words fall out of my mouth, I can barely stand myself. I'm sure my eyes give me away.

Alyssa flushes and drops the hair clip she was fiddling with. "Oh, no…you see, the officer, well, he's a friend of the family which made it sort of comforting but, you know, weird. He was on call that night and heard the 9-1-1 call go out, so he raced up to Oma's place." Alyssa's face is pained. Her voice softens. "He stayed with me at the hospital and then went back looking for Seth. He knows Seth's history…it's… complicated."

I'll bet. I always feel like the more words a client uses in an explanation, the more damning they are. "So this friend who arrested Seth, what is his name so we can speak about him in first person?" I watch again for signs of recognition. It's painful. Alyssa looks like she wants to scream and run out of here. She fiddles in her purse for something, pulls out a chap stick, applies it, and then reaches for a tissue.

"Gregory. Greg actually. I've been calling him Gregory since we were little kids."

"So you've known him a long time?"

"Uh-huh," she answers, her voice going up an octave. "Since we were preschoolers."

"And Seth and Greg, do they have a friendship as well?" I internally wince at my leading question; Leah's right, I am manipulative.

"Oh…no. They, uh, they don't get along too well. Anyway, getting back to what I was saying, I just have these questions and other thoughts about Seth."

She's quick to change the subject about Greg, but I'm curious. If she's involved in an affair that Greg describes as amazing, then why the sudden surge of wondering about Seth, unless…

"What other thoughts, Alyssa?"

Her eyes spill tears like a creek overflowing its banks. "How much Daisy misses him. Even silly things like how he's missing out on the tulips that are up in the yard…ones that Nevaeh helped me plant. He took her picture in the backyard that morning before he went to work, before…" she cuts off as deep sobs catch in her throat. Alyssa hasn't broken down in a while.

"Before her drowning," I finish. Alyssa nods. "That's not a silly thing to get choked up over. You said earlier that you feel like your head is emerging from a fog. When that happens to someone who is grieving, I find that they often have new and different thoughts and feelings about the person who has died or other critical people in their lives—often they're surprising and unexpected." I'm practically begging her to think about Seth and the remorse he has.

"It's everything, Katherine. Maybe my chemistry is off."

"Tell me about that."

"Sometimes I'm short of breath, my pulse races, I…I'm dizzy. I feel like I'm having a heart attack is what it feels like," she says, her eyes widening with fear.

I consider that we share similar symptoms. However, I refrain from saying this. Maybe this case is getting to me more than I think. "Have you consulted your physician?"

"Naturopath," she corrects me. "Yeah, on the phone anyway. She says that given the stress I'm under, it's expected. She gave me a new herbal remedy to try."

I think about her symptoms; mine are a nuisance, but they don't cause me to worry all that much. "You know, what you're describing sounds a lot like anxiety. When anxiety floods us, sometimes a person will experience a panic attack. Have you experienced one before?"

"I'm not sure."

"You would know; they're hard to miss. It will indeed feel like you are having a heart attack, only the physical sensations of an accelerated pulse, shortness of breath, and such are driven by anxiety rather than a malfunction of the heart. In my experience, a person experiencing panic attacks may have some sort of intrusive thought, feeling, or conflict that has been suppressed. When the body and mind can no longer cope with the conflict, then physical symptoms develop."

Alyssa nods and places a hand on her chest.

"In other words," I continue, practically drawing a line from point A to point B for her, "if a person denies that certain feelings exist or has an intense aversion or even guilt about an issue, the body responds. Does that make sense?"

"Yes," she whispers.

I've given her my "sermon on the mount" about anxiety and panic disorder, and all she can say is, 'Yes.' This is one of those moments in therapy where I want to rip out my hair and speed along someone else's process. *All in time, Katherine. All in time.*

"What's coming up for you?" I ask, hoping that I can disguise my irritation at Alyssa's avoidance.

"I...I need to think about all that." She pauses and seems to drift off somewhere in her mind. Worry spreads over her face like a mask. "Do you ever think this stuff ever spills into our dreams?"

I perk up. "Yes, of course. Is there a particular dream that you want to share?"

Alyssa folds her legs up underneath her. She looks so young and vulnerable right now, like she's about to share a scary dream with her mommy. My empathy returns and I'm finally where I need to be in this session: present.

"Yeah, I had this dream this morning, I guess, right before I woke up. It went on forever, like I'd been dreaming for hours." She looks down as though consulting her dream journal. "This one...it was so bizarre. I was at some party. It was dark. I can't really place where I was, only that I've never been there before. I'm sitting down watching everyone talk, drink, eat, when suddenly someone places a baby in my arms—a newborn—and I instinctively know that I'm supposed to nurse this baby." Alyssa's hands whirl around with great animation. Her breath grows shorter with each sentence. "So, I look down and I am completely naked from the waist up and my breasts are just...just *huge*, engorged with milk and this newborn is rooting for my nipple. I hold her up to my left breast and feel the surge you get when a let down happens. You know what I mean?" Alyssa checks in. I nod, enraptured by her dream.

"So I'm nursing this unknown baby like it's the most natural thing in the world, when I look down and see that it's Nevaeh! The hair she had as a newborn, dark like Seth's—not a trace of blonde like she had as a toddler, and yet," Alyssa's voice tightens, "I know that she's going to be taken from me. As that thought goes through my head, a stranger," she pauses, as though willing the dream sequence to come back to her, "uh…a man, walks up to me and says, 'You'd better get on with that because she has to go,' and then walks away."

"So, I'm totally wigging out and when I look back down, my other breast is leaking milk all over me and on Nevaeh. So, I take her off my left breast and switch her to the right and she's just gulping it in, too fast in fact, just…just drowning in my milk, making all those sucking and nursing noises that babies make and I think, oh my God, she's going to be sick; I need to take her off; it's too much; I need to burp her. So I stop nursing her and as I do, she lets out this huge wail. Right then, she's ripped from my arms, and I wake up drenched and covered in sweat! Oh, God, Katherine, it was terrible." Alyssa throws her hands over her face.

It's as if Alyssa and I have been running sprints down the beach. We are equally breathless. I clear my throat and lean forward. "You're pretty shaken up, Alyssa." For that matter, so am I. I reach across and squeeze her hand. "There are some very important messages from your subconscious that I think you are meant to hear."

Alyssa looks up in surprise. "What are you talking about?"

"Well, I want you to go back to the part where that voice of authority comes up to you and tells you that you'd better hurry up and get on with it because she has to go. Is there anyone in your life who you think that would represent?"

"I…I have no clue, Katherine."

"No one in the past who warned you that things aren't going the way they should or that you might have made poor choices."

"Oh..." Alyssa replies, mulling over my question. "Well, maybe one friend."

"And he or she warned you...told you that things might not turn out right?"

"Yeah."

She's connecting those dots, but not saying it out loud. "You also said that the baby was nursing, gulping your milk so fast, the way newborns often do. You stated something after that. Do you recall what you said?"

Alyssa stares at me as though she's just seen a ghost walk into the room. "I said... she was... drowning in my milk. And then that person came and snatched my baby, Katherine." Alyssa stops and horror creeps over her face. "Oh God, Katherine, *I* drowned my baby...I did it too."

I say nothing. I want her to work this through.

"I was there that night. I should have watched her more closely. I could have kept her in the kitchen with me, but I wanted the girls out of my hair," she cries. "I did it. As much as Seth was irresponsible, I had a hand in her death—me!" She pounds her chest with her fists.

I slide next to Alyssa on the couch. I don't want her to completely decompensate; that isn't what I'm after. In a hushed voice, I say, "Alyssa, is it possible that nobody killed your baby, but rather, this was a horrible accident? And now, two parents are grappling with the same sense of guilt, self blame, and grief as they scramble to make sense of their loss?" Oh, how I wish they were together in this session.

Alyssa tears one Kleenex after another out of the box, blows her nose, and wads them up into a ball. "It's been so easy to blame Seth for all of it. I even," she pauses and shakes her head, "I can't believe I'm telling you this, but, I secretly wanted him to fail at his sobriety. Now I think he's probably in better shape than I am. This is crazy!"

"What's crazy?"

"All of this. Me!"

Out of Breath

Despite her new revelations, I'm amazed at how Alyssa is keeping one central ingredient out of this recipe: her affair. Yes, she owns up to her feelings of failing Nevaeh by not keeping her close, knowing that Seth had a record of being undependable. Certainly, it seems that her fury at Seth is calming down. Maybe we are closer to a joint session than I'd thought before today. I sit back in my seat and ponder where to go with our remaining time. Alyssa looks exhausted; I don't want to press her anymore. I decide to go somewhere safe. "Tell me about Nevaeh; what she was like; what she meant to you."

Her face softens and she relaxes a bit into the couch. "She was mine, Katherine. I've never admitted this to anyone, but I had this feeling from day one that when Daisy was born, she was Seth's... his looks, the way he can act so aloof, his energy, you name it. Then along came Nevaeh," she whispers in the voice of a woman telling a love story. "From the moment I saw her delicate little features, blue eyes, and later her feather-blonde hair, I knew she was mine. Mine. I thanked God. It sounds terrible, I know, but she was so attached to me that she'd cry when Seth would want to hold her; I sort of...liked that. That's sick, isn't it?"

It's a question that I don't need to address. Nevaeh met a need in Alyssa, appropriate or not, that was healing; and then she was ripped away. When Nicole was born, I toyed with holding off my master's program just to enjoy the few precious years that she was new. It was liberating during my pregnancy to think that I'd get to spend all my time at home, or at the park with her. Instead, I spent six months in the hospital anticipating her death.

"I used to say she was a piece of heaven."

I nod and wait for her to continue, knowing there must be more.

"Do you know how we chose her name?" Alyssa asks.

"No, it's so unusual. Tell me."

Alyssa points to my desk. "Grab a pen and a piece of paper."

I get up and retrieve the items, intrigued.

"Write her name down and then write it backwards."

I pick up the pen and in capitals write her name forwards, N-E-V-A-E-H, then spell it backwards: H-E-A-V-E-N. I look up at Alyssa. Goosebumps travel up and down my arms.

"I know," Alyssa says, shaking her head. "I'm not very religious or even superstitious, but God, Katherine, I gave her that name to tell her that she was my gift from the heavens and then she was yanked away from me. Yanked back up to heaven." Alyssa covers her face with her hands.

"Oh, Alyssa. It's such a beautiful, thoughtful name. No one and nothing can take away that bond you have with Nevaeh, not even death."

"Do you think that her death is God's way of punishing me, Katherine? Punishing me for not living how I should've in the past? I'm talking crazy, help me."

I wondered when Alyssa would address the spiritual aspects of her loss. Uncommon is the person who doesn't bring God, his faithfulness, absence, or his wrath into the room. After Nicole died, I was so angry at God that I stopped praying, going to church, and even contemplated abandoning my faith altogether. It took nearly ten years for me to return to my old parish. My pastor never stopped calling or visiting over the years. I wonder if I ever thanked him, or just saw it as part of his job. "Punishing you? Is that your perception of God?"

"No. I don't know," Alyssa answers shaking her head. "I've strayed so far. I went to church with Oma all my life. I was baptized as a baby and went with Oma to church until I was a teen, but I don't know what I really believe. How can God be loving and caring and then let babies die?"

"Sure. The image of a loving, caring God who allows horrors on earth such as war or the death of innocent children is hard to reconcile."

"Yeah," she says, but her mind seems elsewhere. "Do you know that Seth and I were trying to get pregnant right around the time that Nevaeh died?"

"I didn't know that."

"When the social worker came out with the doctor to tell us that she was really gone, one of my first thoughts was, 'Oh God, what if I'm pregnant.' My second thought was, 'What if I'm not.'"

"Either way that compounded your grief. Can you see that?"

Alyssa sniffles and wipes her eyes. "Yeah, I guess so. My life is such a mess." She stares at me intensely and continues, "When will it end?"

That's a good question. How about ten years. No, twenty. I'm sorry, thirty? "It doesn't go away, but it does change." There's a secret bond we share. I'm tempted to disclose Nicole's death, but it would take away from her own experience.

"Alyssa, I wonder how you feel about having a session with Seth next month?" Her posture grows rigid and she fidgets with the string of her sweatshirt. "I'm sensing that a lot of your anger toward him has simmered down. I think it's important that the two of you talk in a safe setting. There is so much that he needs to hear about your grief and so much you need to hear about his."

"I guess so. I'm scared though."

"Scared of what."

"Just…stuff. Feelings. How he'll be around me and how I'll be around him. What we'll talk about." Fear creeps into her eyes.

Convincing Seth that a session with his wife is necessary, the wife who is now involved in another relationship, but it won't be easy. I'm picking up subtle clues from Alyssa that I'm not hearing her whole story. It's not just the blatant concealing of her affair, but I sense a longing for Seth that I've never heard. This would be such a positive sign of her forgiving Seth and redirecting all the anger she had at him. If only there wasn't this little mess called Greg.

Chapter 16

Seth

I'm completely swamped at work. Jeff and I are sorting through the winter wetsuits, marking down the prices for the approaching Memorial Day sale. Boxes packed full of spring wetsuits and lighter weight suits line the entire back wall of the shop. I've fallen way behind in getting the summer merchandise pushed to the front—brand name bikinis, board shorts, and this year's T-shirts sporting our logo. It all should've been out weeks ago. I'm overwhelmed. I'd kill for something to take the edge off. As soon as that thought enters my mind, so does a mountain of guilt. Old habits die hard.

I can't push out the intrusive thoughts of my wife sleeping with Greg. Aside from Rocco, I've kept it all bottled up...another old, bad habit. I can't face Jeff with this news; it's too damn humiliating.

"Damn it, it's already 1:30!" I haven't had a thing to eat all day. "I gotta grab a sandwich before I see my shrink. Start digging into a few of those boxes and make sure everything in them matches up with the statement. I'll be back to close up." I fish around for my lighter. The nicotine keeps me in motion.

I'm calling Katherine on her crap today. The pressure in my temples builds as I drive across town. So much for not keeping secrets. What a crock.

Katherine

When I open my door to let Seth in, his stoned-face expression and radiating fury nearly blow me over. He follows me and throws himself into a chair. He knows. She must have told him.

"Can I get you a glass of water or some tea?" I ripple of unease goes through me.

"No, nothing."

He's visibly upset. I sit across from him and ask him what's going on, sure that it's about Alyssa and Greg's affair.

"I learned something from A.A. this week; a slogan they borrow from Einstein," he starts.

"Oh?"

"Something like, 'doing the same thing over and over again and expecting different results, it's the definition of insanity'."

I swear his nostrils flare like an angry bull. "That sounds right," I say, steadying my voice. "How does that fit for you?"

"Mm, that's the question isn't it," he says with a hint of sarcasm. He leans forward and rests his elbows on his thighs as he glares at me. "I figure I've been comin' to therapy here for, oh, what, about five and a half months or so, kept my nose clean so to speak, been working the steps, showing up for my parenting classes. That should set me right on course to get my family back, don't you think, *Katherine*?"

The way he just spoke my name, well, it's as if I were a four-letter word. This isn't simply generalized anger; it's directed at me. "You've been doing great work, Seth. I'm very pleased with how committed you are to your recovery." I leave out, 'And how you're striving to get your family back.' Somehow, I'm worried this will really set him off today.

"Uh-huh. That's great. I guess what I'd really like to know, though, is how I'm supposed to trust you or any other woman when you and my wife are keeping secrets from me?" His voice thunders through my office. "That's right," he pauses and stands up, screaming down at me, "I know about Alyssa and Greg. How long have you known, Katherine? How many times have you sat across from me, listening to me pour my heart out when you know Alyssa wants nothing to do with me?"

I'm sure he can hear the pounding of my heart as it races to an aerobic rate. The room feels askew. I can't reveal what I know. Alyssa hasn't told me of her affair, only Greg has. I scramble for an answer. "Seth, Alyssa and I have not discussed this. I am true to my word. If she were to reveal this to me, I would immediately request a joint session and have her talk about it in your presence. Now please sit down. You're frightening me."

"Oh, give me a frickin' break Katherine," he exclaims, then drops down onto the couch and pounds the cushion beside him.

"I'm serious and you need to de-escalate and let me speak." I straighten up, imagining a shield of protection surrounding me; it's an old technique I learned in my first internship, to let the daggers of another's anger bounce off an imaginary shield.

Seth bolts upward. I immediately cower—so much for my shield. "Jesus, Katherine, I'm not going to hurt you." He walks away toward the expansive window and stands there with his back to me. His fingers are interlaced as he grips the back of his head. I hear him start to whimper.

"She's lying…to you…her therapist. I totally thought you were in on this. I've been freaking out."

I take a big breath. "Come back over here, Seth. Come on, come sit down." The lion has turned into a hurt kitten.

"I'm sorry. I'm sorry. God, I'm so sorry I scared you," he begs. "I just thought…"

Out of Breath

"Yes, well, in the future, please ask rather than accuse." I feel like I'm talking to my son, but then, this has been a relationship filled with transference.

"So she's never really talked about this?"

"You know I can't discuss what we do or don't discuss in therapy, but I can assure you that I am not keeping a secret for Alyssa." Well...sort of.

"You're her shrink! Why hide it from you? Isn't that why we're here, because we've screwed up and made a mess of our lives? To top it off, she's with a guy that she's been calling her best friend forever."

I let him vent. Eventually, he runs out of steam, his language grows less colorful, and his voice steadies. "You must feel so betrayed." I can finally say something completely honest.

"You have no idea," he says. "It could have been any guy in Santa Cruz County, but it has to be Greg? The history we all have, the time he's spent at my house, with my children. Who knows how long this has been going on? The guy's married...with two kids. Kids who are alive! Son of a bitch." He slumps into the couch.

"Tell me more," I say, dabbing at the sweat that lines my forehead.

"It's crazy. He's everywhere in my memory: my babies' births, their birthday parties, holidays, even on the night..." Seth stops, barely able to speak, "...even on the night Nevaeh died he was there. He took Alyssa away that night. I...I was so scared. I was supposed to be watching her and then suddenly everyone was screaming. Next thing I knew, Nevaeh was being dragged out of the pond and my wife was wailing in Greg's arms. I couldn't deal. I ran off and hid."

"You hid? What do you mean? Where?"

"Out on campus. I just needed to be alone, by myself, with nobody around, no crying, no accusations, but I didn't know, I didn't know, Katherine."

Seth is re-experiencing that night's events and his trauma is right at the surface. "Seth, I want you to take a deep breath. You're here right now and you are safe. I want you to hear me. You are here in my office, and no one is after you to tell you that you are in trouble. See if you can steady your breathing."

Seth complies after taking deep breaths for several minutes. His eyes are shut and he makes no attempt to wipe away the tears. "I was up in the tree house. It's where the girls used to play. I must have stayed up there for hours. I knew that Greg would come looking for me eventually."

Dear Lord, Carl built that tree house. "Why? Why Greg?"

His eyes remain closed as though he's watching a movie in his head. "He's always had it in for me. I knew he'd want to pin her death on me...draw conclusions."

"I'm not following you. What do you mean? Is it because he knew of your drug history?"

Seth's eyes fly open. He wipes his face with his sleeve. "Katherine, I told you this before and I know you didn't believe me then. I have no reason to lie, so hear me out. I was not high that night."

His words send a shiver through me. "But your drug test—"

"Less than twenty-four hours before her death I was high, so..."

"So the test couldn't discern the last time you used. You would have had THC in your bloodstream." I stare at Seth. In his eyes I see truth.

"Where were you then?"

He closes his eyes for a moment, inhales, then opens them back up and begins, "It was a long day. Alyssa was up early with the girls, trying to get them ready to go over to Elsa's and set up for the Harvest Fair. I was already in the truck having a smoke and my coffee when Daisy and Nevaeh climbed in to give me a hug good-bye. We got into a tickle fight, and Nevaeh was squirming around my truck, jumping up and down on the seats." Seth has a faraway look. "Later on at the fair, Alyssa said she'd looked everywhere for Nevaeh's blanket and couldn't find it. I remembered she'd had it in my truck that morning. Later, when the girls and I were down on the playground, Jeff said he needed a smoke, so I asked Daisy to keep an eye on her sister while I went up to the truck with Jeff to try and find her blanket. I had a cigarette while Jeff grabbed his pipe."

"Marijuana?"

"Yup."

"So naturally Alyssa assumed you'd gotten high, too."

"Leaving Daisy to watch Nevaeh is a mistake I will live with the rest of my life. But I swear on my dead child's life that I did not get high."

"And the blanket?"

"I never found it. I still can't. It's part of why Alyssa doesn't believe me," Seth says, looking deflated.

It's a big hole in his story, but for whatever reason, I'm not hung up on the absence of the blanket. He has no reason to reinvent his story; he's already lost everything. "So you told her about this?"

He nods and recaps the argument they had in front of my office before their first session. "If I could just find it."

I've heard a lot of cover-up stories over my years as a therapist. Sometimes in couple's therapy, I hear the most ugly excuses for unfaithfulness; excuses that carry a tone of outright smugness. I wish Leah were here to listen to this. She'd hear the despair in Seth's voice.

"This is such a different story than the one I've held in my head. Your state of mind and why she was out of your sight. Why didn't you try and tell me again sooner?"

Seth shakes his head. When he looks up, his gaze focuses on something behind me. I turn and see him stare at a photo of my children when they were toddlers. It's a picture of them in our sandbox—Collin is funneling sand on top of Tory's head; Tory is completely enraptured with her brother with no trace of irritation. Seth looks back at me. "Does it matter, Katherine? It doesn't change anything, really. She's still dead and Alyssa is involved with someone else."

"It does and it doesn't change things. On the one hand, Alyssa deserves to hear this and you certainly should be given the opportunity to explain yourself again now that her anger has calmed down. On the other hand, we're talking about the ability to trust you, forgiveness. Not easy stuff, even without a drug history." I pause to gather my thoughts. "I guess what I'm saying is even if you find that blanket, the real issue is whether or not Alyssa can forgive you and trust your word."

Seth lets out a puff of air.

"I want to schedule a session for the two of you." Seth begins to protest but I go on. "I can't keep listening to you both, knowing about this affair. You have to address this."

Seth rolls his eyes. "Never in a million years did I think she'd cheat on me. I thought she loved me like I love her."

"People make poor choices when they're distraught." Like cocoon their feelings, work too much, push their spouses away so that there's no invitation to talk…so many stupid things.

"We'll take this one step at a time, Seth."

"Yeah, one step at a time."

I know I'm playing the hand of God, moving my clients around like pieces on a chessboard. Yet, when I took this case back in November, I agreed to take Seth and Alyssa as a family. That means I need to get them in here, together. I may have made an enormous clinical error in allowing separate sessions. Even though they were filled with fear, rage, and blame, perhaps I set the stage for Alyssa's secrecy.

With Seth gone but the ghost of him present, I pound out a report to Leah summarizing the last few sessions with Seth and Alyssa. Along with it, I place a recommendation for joint sessions to begin next month. I'm also requesting a collaborative meeting between social services, Daisy's therapist Dr. Fowler, and myself to discuss family reunification. I don't know how Seth or Alyssa will react once they're given the "all-clear" to live in the same house. I hope they will consider Daisy's needs above their own.

I hit the fax button and send my report off to Leah. I hear Carl's car pull up and relief washes over me. He is my life, my present, and my sustenance. This will all be over soon. In just days, the kids will be home and the house will be filled with the music of voices, CD's from their collections, and friends from high school. Mom will stay to catch up with her grandkids. It might be their last year together.

My cell phone vibrates over on my desk. I see that it's Leah. "That was awfully quick."

"I could say the same," she returns. "So, your report is early. Usually I'm thrilled to get them two days late. What gives?"

"I think it's time to move this case along. Plus, Tory and Collin are coming home and I don't want any reports lingering over my head." A lie. She'll know.

"Mm-hm. That's quite a change," she says. I can hear her sifting through my report. "You wanna cut the crap or do I have to keep at you for more details?"

Busted. "I had a very productive couple of sessions with Seth and Alyssa. Also, I believe that the circumstances surrounding Nevaeh's death are different than we originally thought."

"Like how?"

"You know that drug tests can be misleading. Seth says he wasn't high that night; that the evening before he was, so it showed up in the chem panel."

Leah's silence roars over the phone line.

"He told me that Nevaeh had lost her blanket. He thought it might be in his truck. It was a terrible decision on his part, but he says he asked Daisy to watch Nevaeh. You know what happened from there."

More quiet from Leah.

"You don't believe him," I say.

"Why did he tell you this now?" Leah's no putz. She's street smart as well as job smart. I knew this wouldn't go over well.

"He tried to tell me before, but I thought it was denial. But after working with him week after week, I sense that he's telling the truth. I'm not underestimating his need for treatment. He still needs to work on a mound of issues in therapy and stick with his recovery plan. I just think that the reason he left Nevaeh unattended paints a different picture of his judgment and state of mind on the night of Nevaeh's death."

Leah is silent again. I swear I can hear her thinking…it's like a dull hum. "It's not adding up. You're holding out on me. I can feel it."

That Alyssa's having an affair with a man who wants to possess her, who also drinks, and has a history of violent outbursts. "I can't, Leah. I just can't tell you all the details. You'll have to trust me on this one. It's my clinical opinion that we move forward with joint sessions and that Seth be allowed to move home; he poses no threat to his wife or child." I hear her shuffle more papers around then the scribble of her pen.

"He's never missed an appointment with you, right?"

"Right."

Her pen is tapping in the background. "Still going to meetings; showing up with signatures?"

"Yes."

"Okay, I'm going to have to trust you on this one, Katherine. Don't make me look like a jack-ass."

"Leah…"

"I know, I do that all by myself. That joke is growing as old as my saggy rear end. I'll arrange a meeting with Dr. Fowler for us. If she concurs that this is in the best interest for Daisy, Seth will get to go home by early June. Alyssa may not like it, but it is where the man lives. They'll have to keep seeing you, of course."

"Of course."

"If they can't figure it out, we did our job; family court will have to settle the rest. God help 'em. See you in on Saturday."

God help them indeed.

Autobiography in Five Short Chapters
Chapter Three

I walk down the same street.
There is a deep hole in the sidewalk.
I see it is there.
My eyes are open. I know where I am.
It is my fault. I get out immediately.

—Portia Nelson

Chapter 17

Alyssa

Another monthly "anniversary" of Nevaeh's death has come and gone; another month marking our family's death. I hate how windy it is down by the beach. It rips through my hand-knit sweater; I should've brought my coat. Seth's Carhartt coat is the one I really want, but it's not in our closet anymore. There's not a surfer in sight; too choppy. Only a handful of walkers are out. It's almost too quiet.

As I walk past the patch of green grass alongside the cliffs where Seth and I were married, my session with Katherine haunts me. Going over Nevaeh's drowning wrung me out. Katherine was so different this session. I can't put my finger on it, but her questions seemed…well, leading. When she asked, 'Why are you so adamant that Seth didn't go to retrieve Nevaeh's blanket? Is it possible that he was doing that?' she got me thinking and wondering if he was telling the truth. Maybe he was looking for her blanket. Would it change things if that were true?

I practically bump into a woman walking her Saint Bernard. We both gasp and apologize. It's too cold to keep walking. I sit down on a bench, one of the dozens that line West Cliff Drive that memorialize a loved one who has died. I'd like to do this for Nevaeh—have a bench with her name on it. I could come and sit with her, eat a bagel, sip my tea, and tell her all about our lives.

Leah's telephone call, telling me that Seth will be allowed to return home by summer, has me nutted up. He's entitled, but surely he won't come back. Not now. Maybe I have done the very thing that Katherine warned against: making a hasty decision in the first year of grief. I'm like the white caps of the waves, unsettled and edgy.

I return to an empty house for a warm shower. Seth gets Daisy tonight. By the time I'm ready to cook myself something for dinner, the familiar acceleration of my pulse is revving. I feed the dog, leave him plenty of water, kiss him goodbye, and head for Gregory's. I know I need to tell him about Katherine and Leah's recommendations for Seth to return home, but he's going to flip. He'll want me to move in permanently. I can't do that to Daisy; she's blind to what's going on with us…I think.

Gregory's on his second drink when I arrive. I can tell by the way he tickles me a little too hard and kisses me so rough that my chin stings from his razor stubble. It's not the Gregory I know. Those nights when he's had more than a few drinks and we're in bed, it doesn't feel like making love, it feels like sex. He holds me down with such force that I have to remind myself that I'm okay… it's him, it's just a weird thing he likes, I guess…something to help him decompress.

I fumble around in the kitchen to look for something to fix us for dinner. I settle on baked potatoes, salad, and steaks that have thawed. I tear up the Romaine lettuce and toss it into the salad spinner as Gregory wanders in from the patio and wraps his arms around my waist. The alcohol on his breath is toxic. I wriggle out of his grip under the guise of retrieving a tomato.

"Not so fast," he says, grinding me into his body.

"Gregory, stop. The steaks are going to burn on the grill."

"Let 'em," he slurs.

I duck under his arms and walk out to the patio to check the steaks. "Stop. And you've had too much to drink. Go have a glass of water."

He follows me out to the patio, popping open a fresh beer. "What, you afraid I won't be able to get it up for you tonight?"

"What? No. Shut up, Gregory." Disgust seeps from my pores like the liquor from his. "I need to talk to you about something. Stop being so creepy." I close the lid to the barbeque, go inside, and sit on the edge of the couch. Gregory sets his beer down on the glass coffee table. I watch the moisture pool around the bottom. How do I get the words out? "It's about Daisy and Seth, and social services."

"They finally wise up?" He asks, rubbing his hand over my thigh.

I shake my head and push his hand away. Maybe I should wait until he's a little more sober. The longer I wait, though, the more it feels like I'm on a rollercoaster that is stuck at the top and I'm anticipating a huge drop. "No, I mean, that's not it. My social worker thinks that Seth will probably be allowed to come home next month." I shiver with each word.

Gregory bolts out of his seat. Suddenly I'm a child in trouble. "She said what?"

And the ride has begun. "I know, I know, I'm shocked too. I thought this would be a much longer process or different. I don't know what to think." If I keep talking, maybe I won't hyperventilate. Gregory's eyes burn a hole into me.

"What do you mean you don't know what to think?" He leans in so close that I can feel the heat of his anger. "The hell he's coming home! Just because he's jumped through some court mandated hoops of A.A. meetings, parenting classes, and a few stupid therapy sessions—"

"They're not stupid," I say, feeling defensive of Katherine.

"Excuse me? Are you saying that he's become Father of the Year now and is entitled to—"

"Entitled to what?" I interject, standing up.

"To...to...to just waltz back into his family? God damn liberals down at child protective services," Gregory says, grabbing his beer.

"It's possible that he wasn't actually high the night Nevaeh died, you know," I say, hardly recognizing my childlike voice.

"What? What are you talking about? Where is all of this coming from? I tested him myself." Spit is flying from his mouth he's so outraged. I want to look away but I won't let him intimidate me. Our eyes are locked in an ugly stare sown. "You know," he says, poking his index finger uncomfortably hard against my breastbone, "it's beginning to sound an awful lot like you're defending him. Maybe you *want* him back home. Did you talk to him recently?" Gregory lunges for my purse and begins rummaging through it.

"What the hell are you doing?" I holler, attempting to pull my purse out from his grip. Gregory swings the other way, pushes a button on my phone, and scrolls through my recent calls. "Oh, so because you set up my phone you're entitled to know who I talk to and when. Give me that!" I shout.

He presses the phone up to his ear. In the silence of those few moments, I hear Seth's voice echo into the room. "Hello. Alyssa? Hello?" Gregory slams the phone shut and hurls it onto the couch.

"So how long has this been going on?" he screams.

"I don't think it's any of your damn business when or if I talk to Seth. He *is* still my husband." I seize my purse from the couch and grab my phone. "I'm leaving. You're drunk and acting like an ass." I start for the door, but Gregory jerks me by the arm.

"Wait a minute, come back here. We're not done yet." He continues to tighten his grip on my arm. Fear filled tears spill down my cheeks. "Exactly when did you and Seth begin to have little chats on the phone? Or are you doing something else besides talking?"

"Shut up, Gregory before you say something you're going to regret," I squeak.

"Me, regret something? No, I think that's your problem. I think you live with regret every day of your life," he sneers, shaking my arm so hard that it jars my entire body. "Regret over Seth, regret over letting him father your children, regret over Nevaeh's death. And now, maybe there's regret over something new. Hmm? Regret over me. Tell me, Alyssa, are you actually thinking of giving this guy a second chance? Are you?"

I want to say "no" but the words aren't there. In that split second that I consider his question, I realize I have no answer.

"Oh my God. You are! Son of a bitch." Gregory lets me go and I begin to shake uncontrollably. He walks to the kitchen, pours vodka into a tumbler, and sucks down the liquid before I can even move an inch.

"I'm outta here. You're scaring me. I want to talk to you about this but not when you're—" my words are cut short as Gregory draws his arm back and hurls his glass at the fireplace behind me. Shards of glass surround my feet. I'm gulping mounds of air but I can't catch my breath. "Oh my God. Oh my God." I run for the door.

"No, Alyssa, stop. Damn it. Stop! I didn't mean to…Please, Alyssa."

I stare straight ahead, fumbling for my keys. I'm sure I'll feel a blow to the head or the grip of his hand on my shoulder any second. I stumble to the car; my hands can barely get the key in the ignition. I back my car out and screech out of the parking lot. I barrel across town, not knowing where I'm going or what to do. My head is spinning, my pulse is out of control, and the car is getting harder and harder to navigate. I'm within five minutes of Oma's, when I pull over into the parking lot of a small surf shop and try to breathe the way Katherine taught me—in for four counts, hold for four counts, out for four counts. It's not working. I'm having a heart attack.

I fumble with the buttons on my cell phone and push in the most familiar number.

"This is Seth."

"Seth," I pant.

"Alyssa, what's wrong? You called a few minutes ago but hung up. Where are you?"

"I'm on Mission by the school…across the street. I think I need to go to the hospital."

"Don't move. I'll be right there."

I stare at the blue mural of ocean creatures painted on the wall of the elementary school. I count them over and over again, one anemone, two crabs, three jellyfish; I'm losing my mind. I know that it will take Seth nearly twenty minutes to get from 41st Avenue over to Mission. The minutes tick by way too slow. I finally see his truck pull up. He opens my door and sweeps me into his truck.

Seth

Alyssa's a mess. She's pale and quivering from head to toe. I pull her head onto my lap and stroke her hair, telling her everything will be fine. Is this what it takes to touch my wife…to have her by me…another brush with death?

"Seth, I think I'm having a heart attack," she cries.

"Shhh, you're going to be okay. The doctor's gonna find out what's wrong and take care of you. Just close your eyes." I lay my hand on her clammy cheek. God, please don't let anything happen to her. Her hand comes up toward mine. I think she's going to brush it off of her face, but instead, she laces our fingers together. Her touch surges through my whole body.

At the hospital, the triage nurse collects our information. The E.R. nurse ushers Alyssa into a room, asks her to slip into a gown, and says she'll be back to get her history and take her vitals. Alyssa looks like a child in an oversized nightie. I have the urge to crawl in bed beside her and whisper that I'll never leave her side.

The nurse is back and begins her litany of questions: history of asthma, heart trouble, recent illnesses? No, no, no. She listens to her heart and checks her blood pressure, then tells her the doctor will be in soon. The lack of urgency catches me off guard. What the hell is going on? I follow the nurse out into the hallway. "Hey," I call out, "she's just going to have to sit there and wait. What's going on?"

The nurse's smile dips into a look of irritation. "The doctor will be in as quickly as possible. It won't be long, hardly anyone's here. It's your lucky day," she says and her smile returns. I make a quick phone call to Oma, letting her know the situation. Daisy's already at her house…looks like my overnight visit with her will have to wait.

I return to Alyssa's room. She reaches out and grabs my hand. "I'm scared. Seth. What if something happens to me? What will Daisy do?"

"Let's not go down that road." I squeeze and kiss the back of her hand, willing everything to be fine. The doctor pokes his head in. He's clasping a clipboard that holds Alyssa's information. Placing his reading glasses on, he reads over her paperwork, and then looks up to greet us.

"Hello, I'm Dr. Petrolli." He leans over Alyssa and shakes my hand then places a hand on Alyssa's shoulder. He's a short, balding, Italian man who resembles Super Mario. His moustache moves up and down when he talks. "What's happening with you today?" he asks Alyssa.

"I don't know. I think it's my heart. I can't get my pulse under control and I'm short of breath." Each sentence is a struggle.

The doctor nods and jots down some notes. He places the clipboard down on the counter and begins the examination; his stethoscope slides around from her back to her chest. "Big breath. Good." He looks up at me and asks, "Any history of early heart disease, blood pressure problems in the family?"

I shrug my shoulders and immediately feel like an idiot. I should know the answers. I look at Alyssa who shakes her head, "no."

Dr. Petrolli nods again, feels around the base of Alyssa's neck and asks her to say, "Ah," as he peers inside with a little light. "Been under any unusual amount of stress? Recent changes?"

Out of Breath

Alyssa and I look at one another like deer caught in the headlights. Our delayed response has the doctor scanning both our faces for an answer. "Yeah. We, uh," I begin, not knowing where to begin, "we're separated right now. And, uh, our baby girl, she died this past year," I manage to get out although not without my throat clamping shut. Alyssa tightens her hold on my hand.

Dr. Petrolli inhales and his eyes widen. "I'm so sorry." He cocks his head; recognition washes over his face; there's only one hospital in town. "I remember," he whispers, giving Alyssa's hand a squeeze, looking only at her. Of course he wouldn't recognize me; I wasn't here that night. I was too busy being a coward.

I worry that this connection will put Alyssa into a deeper tailspin, but she simply closes her eyes, blinking away tear after tear. "Yeah, that's us."

Dr. Petrolli sits down next to Alyssa. The mood of the moment is so tender that all my fear comes flooding down my face. He smiles at me and tells me to sit down. "Alyssa, I'm going to run some tests to see how your heart is functioning. We'll draw some blood, make sure there isn't an infection bringing about your symptoms." He pauses and leans a little closer to her. I wish Alyssa had a father who offered her as much care as this doctor has in these few moments; or a husband, for that matter. It's how I want to be, now. "Here's my thought—and this is without knowing what's going on internally—but based on your history and what I know of you, I have a feeling that your symptoms are brought on by anxiety. Sometimes the body takes over when the mind is on overload."

Alyssa listens raptly and replies, "My therapist said that she thought I might be having panic attacks. She told me to see my doctor, but I...I didn't think it would happen again."

Dr. Petrolli stands. "I'm glad to hear you're seeing a therapist. Sounds like you're on the right track. Let's run these tests and I'll be back to go over them later." He turns to me and places a firm hand on my shoulder. "Just sit tight and stay by her side."

"I will." I will.

Alyssa is hooked up to various wires and machines and blood is drawn from her vein. I let go of her hand only when I'm in the way of the nurse. Dr. Petrolli's words seem to have calmed her down a little. Already her color has returned and the trembling has been reduced to an occasional shiver. I ask for another blanket. A nurse brings in a freshly heated one. I wrap it around her, tuck the sides in tight, and kiss her forehead. Her skin is salty and familiar.

I'm not sure where to tread. The last time we had any real conversation face to face, outside of arrangements for Daisy, was our nasty exchange about her and Greg. Where is Greg, anyway? He's everywhere, usually. In fact, why did she call me tonight? Even if he were working, he'd drop everything for Alyssa. Dr. Petrolli's question about being under any unusual stress comes to mind. Maybe there's more going on than Alyssa is letting on…again.

"You can go if you have things to do, Seth," Alyssa offers, breaking through my swirling thoughts.

"I don't have anything to do. I'm fine. I was just thinking."

"Yeah. About what?"

I want to distract her from her worry and not kick up her anxiety. I search for a favorite memory. "You remember the time when you and I were first goin' out and we went camping up in Manchester?" I say with a small smile.

"Oh my God, remember the rain?" she says, her worry lines smoothing, looking like herself for the first time in nearly a year.

"And then the ranger came, telling us we should probably pack it up." A small laugh escapes and Alyssa giggles. I put my hand on her cheek. "It's okay for us to laugh, huh? I mean, we can think about stuff and it's okay to think it's funny…to laugh once in a while?"

"Yeah, I think so," she says, as our laughter turns to tears. We've never had this intimate of a connection since Nevaeh died. Something inside has told me it will never be okay to be happy again…that I deserve only misery. Rocco and Katherine have been up one side and down the other on this, but I didn't get it. Now I think what I need is Alyssa's permission…permission and hopefully, one day, her forgiveness.

We spend the next couple of hours tiptoeing around our past. It feels like I'm on ice skates and am slipping around the rink hoping not to crash as I steer clear of any recollections of the girls. I've held Alyssa's hand for nearly two hours—probably the longest ever.

Finally, Dr. Petrolli returns. His face is turned up in a gentle smile. "I think you're going to make it, kiddo," he says, placing a loving hand on Alyssa's foot. "All your tests look great. No indications of heart trouble or infection. So," he continues, in a more serious tone, "it's as I suspected. I think you are experiencing panic attacks, which make you feel as though you are having a heart attack. Your heart rate increases, you feel short of breath, shaky, your thoughts race. Sound familiar?"

"Yes, all of it. Oh, I'm so embarrassed."

"Embarrassed?" He shakes his head as if to scold her. "No, no. Concerned is more appropriate. I want to give you some medication—"

"Ah, I don't like medication," Alyssa interrupts.

"Okay. You don't have to like it. But, if this happens again, you don't want to come running back here, right?"

"Right."

"So, I want you to have it on hand. This way, if you experience what you did earlier today, this will combat your symptoms to some degree. How are you feeling right now?"

Alyssa shrugs. "Better, but not perfect."

"Okay, I'm going to have the nurse give you an injection. It's pretty standard for folks who wind up in the E.R. for a panic attack. It's going to make you pretty sleepy, so you'll be taking her home and watching over her?" he asks, looking at me.

"Sure," I turn to Alyssa, as if asking for permission. She nods and squeezes my hand.

"Okay. Follow up with your doctor and your therapist. There's a good deal of treatment outside of medication for this as well. It was nice to see you again, Alyssa. Seth," he adds, and shakes my hand once again. "Look after yourselves and again, I'm sorry for your loss."

The injection doesn't make her a little sleepy; it totally knocks Alyssa out. The closest thing to medication she ever uses is Arnica, a plant extract used for bruising or pain. Even through intense back labor with both babies, Alyssa refused anything medicinal. How did things get so crazy? Our life this past year has been a series of one blow after the other. I guess it started long before Nevaeh's death—I'd been delivering significant doses of stress all through our marriage.

Back home, I help her get into our bed and watch her sleep. It's like watching Sleeping Beauty.

Alyssa

I float in and out. Hazy memories, like a thick fog, seep in and out of my mind: the crash of Gregory's drink, the anger in his face, the E.R. doctor's description of panic attacks, Seth's hand in mine—this one blows the fog away and has me sitting up in bed.

I must have heard him come in. He's beside me with a cup of soup and some juice. It's dark like midnight. "What time is it? Where's Daisy?" I can hear the slur of my words; this drug has me stoned.

"It's about 11:30. Daisy's fine. I called Oma from the hospital when I knew everything was okay."

"You did?" Oh my God, he took care of everything.

"I did," he says, smiling. "Oma will bring her over tomorrow."

I sip the juice he hands me. It feels so good on my throat. "You're still here," I whisper.

"Someone needed to keep an eye on you…unless, there's someone else you want me to call."

That nameless someone else being Gregory, of course. "No. Stay," I say, patting the mattress for him to sit down. He sits beside me on "his" side. Seeing him next to me, it's like he never left. "I must have really freaked you out."

Seth raises his eyebrows. "That happen before?"

I nod. "Katherine told me I was probably having anxiety attacks. I just didn't know they could get that bad. I really thought I was dying."

"I believe you. And yeah, you scared the crap out of me." A yawn escapes him and he offers an apology.

"I'm sorry. You're tired. This has been such a long day for you. Go and get some rest. I'll be fine." I really want to say, 'Stay here, don't leave…I'm sorry.'

"I'm fine. I'm used to late nights with my meetings and all." He stands. The weight of his body leaving the bed hurts. "I'm gonna grab a pillow and the comforter off Daisy's bed and sleep on the couch. I'll check on you in a bit."

"No, you don't have to do that. I mean—I don't want to put you out." Come back.

"You're not putting me out," he says. The look in his eyes holds so many words that neither of us will say.

I can't fight the medication stupor that is returning. As I drift off, I'm comforted by the familiar sounds of dishes clanging, the running of water, and Duke's collar jingling.

Seth

I check on Alyssa and see that she's asleep. I need a shower, but don't want to disturb her. I really don't want to use the kids' bathroom. All I can see in that tub is my two girls with mounds of bubbles piled on their heads. God, they loved to play in the bathtub forever…until their fingers were like raisins. I flick on the light. Alyssa painted little fairies along the top of their bathroom wall. I close the lid to the toilet, sit down, and put my head in my hands. Crying comes as easy now as my anger used to; it's nearly out of control lately. Katherine says I've stored enough tears in my life to cry for a year.

I wish Alyssa were in here with me; we could wash away some of the pain. I wanted to lay down next to her tonight and tell her I still want her, need her, love her, but I just can't figure out what the hell's going on. She started calling me here and there a few weeks back with nonsense questions about Daisy's and my visits. Each time she called, we talked a few more minutes. I was less tense with each call. Then tonight—what the hell? I want to ask what brought all this on. Something tells me things aren't as great with precious Gregory. God, just the thought of him and Alyssa together, here, it makes me want to hurl a piece of furniture through the wall. Rocco told me to run it off…run like I'm pounding out all the fear, anger, and crazy jealousy. I haven't been this fit since I was twenty-one.

When I'm done with my shower, I tiptoe into our room and manage to open a drawer and pull out a T-shirt and some shorts without causing Alyssa to stir. Duke waits for me by the couch. His tail thumps the floor so hard that I tell him to shush. I spread out Daisy's comforter when I hear a ring tone that I don't recognize. After looking around, I notice it's coming from inside her purse. "Hello," I whisper into the phone. The line goes dead. I close the phone and look at the screen for a name and can't help but smile…Gregory. He heard my voice; ah, the secret delight of another's misfortune.

"Seth," Alyssa calls out.

I run into our room. "Yeah."

"Did someone call?"

I consider telling her that Gregory called to gauge her reaction. No, that's my ugly old self. Instead, I say the truth, "Yeah, but they hung up." It is the truth…

"Oh."

"Go back to sleep," I say, and turn out the hall light.

"Seth," she calls out before I make it down the hallway. I walk back to the door and look in. She sits up and grabs her hair and tosses it in front. It fans across her chest and stomach. I take a big breath…I shouldn't be having sexual thoughts when she's so distraught. "Thanks again. I know things are weird and messed up right now."

I'm on her mind. That's enough right now. "I'm just glad you're okay. Get some rest. I'll see you in the morning." I start down the hall but decide to make a detour. I wander into the girls' bedroom, close the door, and turn on the light. The emptiness is like a black hole; I worry I'll be swallowed up. On the windowsill is a picture of the four of us taken down at Hidden Beach on the Fourth of July. Daisy's on my shoulders and Nevaeh is in Alyssa's arms—the way it always was. Alyssa held onto her so tight and in a moment, she was swept away.

I can't really blame her for hating me over the past several months. Maybe if I'd left her in charge of the girls down at the beach and one of them drowned, I'd be the one casting blame. I don't know. Katherine is working hard with me in therapy on stopping the blame; quit blaming my mother for the way I turned out; quit blaming my dad's death for me winding up with his business. Perhaps Katherine's doing the same with Alyssa.

I look at Nevaeh's picture before I switch off the light and whisper, "Tell me little one, can Mommy and I beat the odds?"

Autobiography in Five Short Chapters
Chapter Four

I walk down the same street.
There is a deep hole in the sidewalk.
I walk around it.

—Portia Nelson

Chapter 18

Katherine

This isn't supposed to happen. The children are home for two weeks of spring break and my mother has been hospitalized twice since her blood transfusion. I needed this break to regroup, enjoy my kids, and savor time with my mother. Instead, I'm here inside the hospital, bidding hello to the nurses who have become familiar faces.

My mother is transforming into a paper-thin image of herself. A morphine pump hooked to her arm delivers pain relief and rest. No matter how many layers I wear inside this icebox hospital, I can't get warm.

"Katie," my mother calls out in a hoarse whisper.

I jump from my seat, setting aside my knitting project—a scarf that I intend to give her in the fall. I doubt she'll ever see the scarf or the fall. "What do you need, Mom?"

She struggles to sit up and groans as she shifts positions. "I need you to help me go to the bathroom."

"Okay." I put my hands under her arms. My mother winces. Every touch is too hard. Her bones ache. I ease her over to the commode beside the bed. Her skin sags like an elephant hide. I've bathed her a handful of times over the past several weeks and watched the lifelong twenty pounds she vowed to lose disappear.

When she's finished, I wipe her, pull up the adult diaper, (she'd told me six months ago she'd rather die than use these) and steady her back to bed. As she settles herself, a muffled cry escapes her. I've seen my mother cry only a handful of times; I'm not asking her to be strong as she dies, but it tears my heart out to watch how vulnerable she really is.

"Are you in pain, Mom? I can ring for the—"

My mother's boney hand grips mine. I look into her horror-filled eyes, as though an intruder were walking into the room. "I'm dying, aren't I, Katie?"

My mother has never uttered these words before. Death is a forbidden subject. All through her cancer, she's made plans for the future, including a trip to Cancun next December with her grandchildren, Carl, and me. Her denial has driven me nuts; and here I am, finally hearing her acceptance and I want to tuck it under the bed.

Mom's eyes widen at the lack of my response. "I don't want to die," she says through her tears.

"Yes, Mom, you are." I feel my shoulders begin to shake as overwhelming sadness spreads. I lean on her bed and put my face beside hers. I need my mommy right now and she's dying. I'm trying really hard to be an adult. "I don't want you to die, either." We remain cheek to cheek for what feels like hours. Finally, I stand up, reach over to her morphine pump, and depress the button. Mom's body sinks into the mattress, her lips part, and she dozes off again. I don't know if she needed the pain relief, but I did.

BACK HOME, I try to keep pace with my children who've taken up every inch of space.

"Mom, have you seen my bathing suit? I left it hanging in the shower last night. Collin probably threw it in the hamper all wet," Tory screams down the hallway.

Out of Breath

"I wrung it out and it's hanging on the line outside, Tory," I call out while I fold what feels like my 99th load of laundry in a week. Didn't the kids just come home a few days ago? Was this what life was like a mere year ago? I'm about to collapse.

"Brittany called to say that everyone's meeting at the harbor at 1:00. I can drop you off if she can drive you back. I have an afternoon meeting around that time. Then I'll need to go by the hospital to check on Grandma." Today's my big meeting with Dr. Fowler and Leah; just one more thing to pile on top of this day.

"Mom, I'll be back around 5:00. I'll stop in and see Grandma on the way home," Collin shouts from the opposite end of the house.

"Okay, don't forget to give yourself plenty of time to get ready for Dad's party tonight. I want everyone ready to go by 7:00." Oh, yes, and it's Carl's 60th birthday party tonight…a surprise I planned nearly a year ago complete with friends and distant relatives flying in from out of state; not quite something I could cancel at the last minute.

I turn my voice the other direction toward Tory once again. "I want you showered and ready by 6:00; I know how you operate."

"Okay," she hollers over the stereo blaring Keith Urban; at least they've outgrown the hip-hop phase.

I reheat my coffee that sits untouched on the counter. The cream looks stagnant. Oh well. Piles of laundry, iPods, scattered hairclips, and CDs clutter every inch of our house. Cleaning up in the midst of the kids' return is like herding cats. I'm too tired to care.

The phone rings just as I sit down. I don't even make an effort to pick it up since every call is now for one of the kids. I didn't realize that Carl and I had so easily made the quiet adjustment to a kid-free home. I had envisioned pining for them—an empty nester that searched for her children in the faces of others. I do think of them daily when they are gone and love having them home, of course, but this year has been packed with challenging cases, my mother's illness, and the nagging feeling that I'm not quite myself...out of energy, easily fatigued, more edgy than usual. I don't have time to pine for them.

"Mom," Tory calls out, "it's Auntie Leah. She wants to know if you're making her dress fancy for Daddy's party." She giggles.

A smile spreads across my face. Ah, the familiar banter of Leah. She's the closest person on my side that the kids have had for an aunt. Leah never forgets their birthdays (and knows exactly what to get them), gossips with Tory about girls who choose boys over friendship, and trash talks with Collin. The kids look at her as the "cool aunt" who can keep a secret but who will steer them the right way.

I pick up the phone and answer Leah's question. "You wear whatever keeps your little hinny comfortable. Save your stockings and fine skirts for Holy Week." Already, I feel lighter.

"Oh Christ, Katherine, Holy Week again? How many days do we have to go to church?"

"Oh, about five or six," I laugh. She complains, but never misses the tradition.

"Super. And there's nothing little about my hinny."

"Oh, Leah, we love you just the same."

Tory snickers on the other line. "Okay, Tory, hang up. I need to talk shop with your auntie."

"So when does our week-of-holiness kick off, anyway?" Leah asks before we venture into the real reason for her call.

"This coming Monday. You call to remind me about the meeting regarding Seth and Alyssa today?"

"Just checking in. I know you've been tugged a thousand directions with the kids home and Mary stuck in the hospital. How's she doing today anyway?"

My smile fades. "I called earlier. She didn't answer, so I assume she was sleeping. I'll stop by after our meeting."

"You hear anything from Seth or Alyssa this week?"

"No, not a word." My regular attending clients know that I'm taking two weeks off. I included a voice mail stating this, just in case a new or returning client called. And who should call, not only once, but three times, emphasizing the urgency of his calls, but Greg Wallace. I'll call him back after my break; I'm too irritated to be bothered with him.

"Okay, after our meeting, no more work—promise!" Leah commands.

"I know."

"I just might even tell you about a date I have lined up for next week if you're good."

"What? Leah, you can't leave me hanging like that."

"Oops, I've got another call I've got to take. See ya tonight, sugar."

Something in the universe is definitely shifting. Leah has sworn off dating or relationships for years. She's had plenty of women interested and Santa Cruz, a gay-friendly community, offers her a plethora of choices. A few years back, a child advocacy attorney who was strong, young, lovely, and unsure of her sexual orientation broke Leah's heart. Leah joked that she could not only turn off men, but women, too. Her laughter disguises a deep pain. I hope she's ready to let some of the ice melt that's surrounding her heart.

Greg

I'm driving south on Highway 1 to a job interview in Seaside. When the job opening posted down at the station, I read over the description a dozen times; it's my dream job. It'll get me off the streets and out of this communist town. My sergeant pulled me aside and assured me that the job was practically mine. I'm not an idiot: working for the D.A.'s office will get me out of his hair. I'll make a hell of a lot more money and with child support coming due, I'll need every penny. I'm not sure if I'm running toward or away from something, but I can't stay still.

Alyssa won't return my calls. I can't keep from replaying that day over and over in my head when I "lost it." What did Alyssa think, though, that I would help her work through her feelings like a shrink? Right! She can't just slip in that she's thinking of getting back together with Seth and act like I'm going to be supportive and hand her over to Seth.

I reach for a Tums in the glove box that sits beside my handgun; something I'm supposed to have in the trunk when I'm off duty. Stupid law…I'm a cop for Christ's sake. I haven't been able to keep the acid under control since that day. When I'd finally sobered up, somewhere around 11:00 or so that night, I hightailed it over to her place. She needed to hear me out. I wish I'd driven drunk and ran my truck up a telephone pole rather than to have seen Seth's truck in the driveway. I even dialed her phone. I can't believe she ran to him. Son of a bitch.

A family of three is flying kites on one of the sand dunes beside the highway—that should be us. Everything had come together. What the hell happened? I'd booked a hotel room at the Embassy for Alyssa, Daisy, and me to stay this weekend after my interview. Daisy could swim in the heated, indoor pool; we'd enjoy happy hour, later head over to Dennis the Menace Park in Monterey. I even set up a meeting with a local realtor to look at condos in the area. We needed to start fresh, get away from Santa Cruz…too much history.

I miss my exit. Damn it. I gotta push all this aside before my interview. It's a skill I've mastered through years of pushing things back, back, back. The day before Alyssa ran out in hysteria, I was the first officer to arrive at a gruesome accident…a drunk driver hit an electrical pole and a live wire landed on their car.

I couldn't do anything…*don't hear their screams*…I couldn't do anything. *Don't see their screaming faces. Don't see Alyssa's pained, worried face. Don't see Seth's car in the driveway. Don't see her tears—don't see it, don't feel it…don't.*

Alyssa

Not speaking to Gregory is forcing me to be a "big girl." I'm on my second week of being alone with Daisy at night. The first two nights were spent wide-eyed with wild bouts of anxiety. I willed myself not to use the medication, fearing dependence, but ultimately had to break a tablet in half and use it. By the third night, after reading in bed for over an hour, I slept for six. Within a week, all I needed was to read a chapter of a chick-lit book that Carolyn leant me and I was out for the night.

It's been good for me, being alone. I shop, cook, sing out loud, tend the garden, weep…lots of weeping, and write. I've filled up pages of my journal. It's like all the bottled up questions that I never dared to ask are free to be answered.

The newest thing: Seth calls every day, 10:02 on the dot, two minutes after he flicks on the lights and turns on his cash register at his shop. We've talked about the weather, how his business is finally recovering from the bad press he received, what Daisy did the night before…everything except our feelings and how intimate we were on the night of my panic attack. Today, I want it to be different. To pass the time, I clean out cluttered cupboards, wipe down the counters, and fill garbage bags with clothes I'll never wear—anything to pass the time before he calls.

Finally, at 10:00, I sit in the kitchen, willing the phone to ring. At 10:30, I feel sick inside. I make a cup of peppermint tea. By 11:00, I'm pissed. At 11:30, I'm frantic. Daisy's going to Oma's for lunch and a walk at the beach. That leaves me an afternoon to brood. I grab my purse; I need to get out. Just as I storm out the door, the phone rings. I consider letting the machine pick up. Finally, on the third ring, I dash back inside and pick up.

"Hello."

"Alyssa. God, sorry. You wouldn't believe the morning I had. I ran an ad in the *Good Times* for a sale on summer wear and I'm swamped."

I'm so relieved that he wasn't avoiding me that I whimper.

"Are you okay? What's going on?"

"Nothing. It's just one of those days, you know?"

Seth is quiet for a minute. "Hang on, let me go into the back. Jeff," he calls out, "I'll be back in five. Sorry," he continues, "yeah, I know."

"Do you have more good days than bad now?" I ask. I want him to let me in.

"Not so much. Sometimes it's a good day and then I think of her…see her sweet face."

The conversation stops. The only sounds are an occasional sniffle. This pain is unbearable.

"Thanks again for taking care of me when I was such a mess." I say, changing the subject.

"You don't have to thank me."

"No, really, you could have got in trouble staying over given the court's order."

"Oh, come on, Daisy wasn't there. Elsa could've testified to that. I'm so sick of people treating us like criminals."

Us. It's the first time he's said "us" in ages.

"It'll be good to have that session with Katherine soon, don't you think?" I ask.

"We'll see." Something changes in his voice. "I think you still have a lot that you need to sort out, Alyssa."

His tone is paternal; I want to hang up. Of course, he's right. I just didn't want to hear that. "I know. I know you're hurt, Seth." The words hang in between our lines with no response.

"I don't think I can talk like this over the phone, 'Lyss."

"I'm sorry. You're right. There's so much I want to say. So many things I want to ask you. It's hard to wait," I hear the words rush from my mouth unable to stop them. "I'm just…I want you to know that Daisy and I really miss you. And that," I swallow hard, "that I still love you, Seth."

"I need to hang up, Alyssa. This is—"

"Seth, wait, just tell me—"

"Alyssa, I have a store full of customers. I can't do this. I'll wait for Katherine's call about our appointment time. I'll call you tomorrow."

He doesn't wait for my good-bye. He didn't say, "I love you, too." Now I sit…alone…with my thoughts. I slide down to the cold, kitchen floor. I'm a little girl again. I want to throw a tantrum, pound every pillow in the house, and scream at the top of my lungs. But I don't.

I remain, frozen, on the floor until the sunlight stops pouring through the windows and I know afternoon is here. I'm spent and need a shower. I round the corner of the bathroom and peer into the mirror, catching my reflection—the face of a liar, a betrayer, and an adulteress looks back at me. Everything I've eaten today comes surging up my throat. I throw up.

As I fumble for the mouthwash in the medicine chest, Seth's scissors tumble into the sink, clanking. I read somewhere that dozens of American women grieving their deceased loved ones from the terrorist attacks of September 11th cut off their hair…that it's connected to an ancient ritual of grieving. I pick up Seth's scissors and pull my hair down in front of me. For nearly twenty years, my long, blonde hair has been my defining look. I slice through a handful of it, and then feverishly chop away at the rest of my hair. Segment after six-inch segment crumples into the sink, the ground, around my feet like a weeping willow losing its leaves.

I drop the scissors and survey what I've done. It needs a little evening out along the edges, but it sits nicely on my shoulders. I dust off the bits of hair, strip my clothes, shower, and throw on my nightgown. Before crawling into bed, I call Oma and tell her I need a night to myself; she doesn't question me; she understands my darkness.

Hours later, I wake to the sound of Duke barking for his dinner. I crawl out of bed, feed him, and pick up the phone once more; this time I dial Katherine. I know she's not in, but I leave her a message. "Katherine, it's Alyssa. I have to see you before our joint session. I have some things that…that I haven't been honest with you about. Please call me when you can. I need to be up front with you…about everything."

Katherine

If I were in Hawaii, I'd be sipping exotic drinks, working on my tan (what little tan I can achieve), and enjoying late-night strolls with

Carl; the vacation he's been after me to take. Instead, I'm slowly creeping down into my office (thanks to a lingering hangover from Carl's party) to check my voice mails. While I'm at it, I may as well jot a few notes in Seth and Alyssa's file. Dr. Fowler concurred—it's time for Seth to go home.

Leah's roast of Carl still rings in my mind, causing me to break out in giggles in between note taking. Although the planning of his party was yet another thing on my long list of "to-do's", the evening was a welcome distraction from the mountains of stress. Surrounded by forty of our family and friends, minus my mother, of course, I danced, drank, and momentarily forgot that I'm fifty-one, have a dying mother, and am immersed in a convoluted, mess of a case.

I check my messages and am hit with the rush of Alyssa's words and how she "needs to be up front with me about everything." So, she's finally ready to confess and I get to be the priest. Hmm. It would only take a minute to return her call. I could even squeeze her in for a session when Carl goes out for his annual round of golf in Half Moon Bay at the Ritz with his college buddies. I pick up the phone, start to dial her number, then stop and replace the phone. Carl told me before the party that I actually looked like myself. He said I've been distant. In good faith, I don't want to break my promise to my family about bracketing this time just for them and myself. I save Alyssa's message, climb the stairs up to the house, and reheat my coffee.

Seth

I pace my apartment as I wait for the distinct thump of Rocco's limp up the stairs. After Alyssa's phone call, I've gone through a pack of cigarettes in less than three hours. I can't rush back into things with her. I don't even know what's going on with her and Greg and am too angry to ask. All I've wanted to do for the past several months is to move back in with my family, start over, straighten things out, and live clean and sober. But it's like she's playing head games with me— push, pull, push, pull. And how about the, "I love you" she threw at me? Of course I love her, but Jesus, I can't push stuff under the rug...not anymore.

Rocco's rap jolts me out of my ruminations. He gives me a once over and surveys my apartment. "Jesus, Mary, Joseph," Rocco says, "that wife of yours is gonna be the death of you yet." He limps into my living room, swipes the ashtray that's overflowing, dumps it in the trash under the sink, and sets a pot of coffee to brew. I rant about my recent conversation with Alyssa. Rocco shakes his head and every once in a while throws in an, "Mm-hmm" or an, "Oh, I see." He picks up the clothing I've tossed around in a fit of anger and replaces it on hangers in my room. Me, I follow him around like an enraged adolescent, taking a clean shirt from him and shoving it over my head.

"She said, 'I love you.' Who says that after cheating on her husband and not even coming clean about it? Huh?"

Rocco pauses and takes a long, slow sip of coffee, breathing in the aroma. "You done? With your tantrum, I mean." He cocks his head and throws me a crooked smile.

I'd like to punch that expression off his face, but it's not really him that I'm pissed at. Rocco's become the father I never had. I don't know how to behave like a real son, to take advice. "Yeah, I guess," I say, sitting down next to him.

"Well, here's how I see it," he starts. "She's confused, but she's being truthful. She does love you. Granted, she made a mistake in hooking up with that piece a' crap cop, but maybe she realizes that she goofed. We don't think straight when we're grievin' do we?" He looks around my apartment, then he scoots over and leans in real close, so close that his Grecian formula makes my eyes water. "And maybe," he whispers, "just maybe, part of Alyssa had this little affair to get at you; a little bit a spite." Rocco's eyebrows arch as he awaits my response.

"Hmm," I say, although not totally convinced.

"It's not rocket science, son. She probably doesn't know how to undo the mess she's made. Know anything about that?" He pauses, but I'm still not biting. "Remember what I told you about runnin' around with your old surfer playmates and how that would screw with your sobriety?" he asks, taking another long sip of coffee.

I leap to my feet. "She *slept* with someone else. How can that even compare? Are you f-ing kidding me?"

Rocco stands. "You know what, this isn't about Alyssa. This is about you. Your pride," he says, getting in my face, then pecks me in the chest with his arthritic-index finger. "That's what's in the way. Your ego is bruised. Another man got in your bed."

We stare each other down. I clench my fist and let go as I bounce forward on my feet. Rocco's breath gets shorter as the seconds pass—I think we're going to go at it. Finally, he jerks his head away, takes a step away, and moves toward the window. "Pff," he says with disgust. "Trouble is, you and I need to talk about the next step you're about to work on; perfect timing, the way I see it."

"How can you say that and just discount what I just said. I don't give a crap about the next step. My wife is completely screwing with my head!"

As if I said nothing, Rocco continues, "You know, this next step, it's a bit like getting a root canal, digging up stuff from your past, takin' a look at it, seeing how you might have pissed people off, hurt 'em. In the end though, the wound stops festering, life's less painful, and it gives you and the other person a chance to heal and move forward."

We lock eyes again. "You gotta give this one to God, Seth. It's out of your hands. What can you do? What do we say in the program? Can you control others?"

"No. I can only work on me." I pull at my hair with both hands.

"Yes. Good to know you're actually listening. Now sit down, shut up, and listen to my story."

"Like I have a choice." I drop to the futon.

Rocco ignores me. "My sister was a single parent, making squat as a waitress, had four kids to feed. I'd show up, out of work, broke, having pissed every penny away. She'd clear the heaps of laundry off the couch for me to sleep on until I got my act together."

"Sounds nice."

"Oh yeah. It was so nice that you know how I paid her back?" Rocco looks past me as he rubs his grey whiskers. "I ripped her off. Cleaned her out, and not just once. She was part of the dance, too. Enabling—you know the jargon by now. The point of the story is that she was the first person that my conscience hit me with. Bam," he exclaims, slamming his palm down on the kitchen counter, "like a bullet to the brain the guilt was so bad. My sponsor didn't let me wallow in it though. He had me sit down, write a letter, detailing every way I ever hurt her. It was a long letter. She didn't write back right away. I sent her checks. Paid her back a little at a time—part of making my amends. Little by little she began to trust me I suppose. After a year or so, she called and asked me to lunch." Rocco pauses and retrieves his wallet from the back pocket of his jeans. "Let me show you a picture I carry around with me."

The photo is black and white, weathered, and torn around the corners. It's a snapshot of a young boy and a girl, cheek to cheek. The date in the corner reads 1952. "That you?" I ask, taking the picture. I can make out the resemblance if I squint; liquor and cigarettes have taken their toll on a man who looked like an Italian James Dean.

"That's me," he replies, with a sigh. "I know. I had dames lined up back then."

"No kidding?"

Rocco raises his eyebrows. "My sister died last year." The mood in the room shifts as he takes the picture back and replaces it in his wallet. "Cancer. I carry that picture around to remind me that I only got to be the brother I was supposed to be for the last fifteen years of her life. I couldn't change the past, but I did get to make things better." Rocco sits down and peers at me. "You know why I told you that story?"

I think for a minute. "I guess so." A familiar ripple of discomfort rolls through me; the same feeling I get when Katherine hits me with similar revelations.

"Alyssa didn't exactly walk into Greg's arms all by herself, did she?" He's quiet, awaiting a response I won't give him. "So what we're gonna do is spend tonight and probably a few more looking at what you did when you were drinking and getting high with Jeff and your other playmates. Get you to see how you were really pushing Alyssa away. 'Cause ya did," he continues, catching my averted eyes. "Didn't you? Push her away?"

I shove off the futon, walk to the window, and stare through the bars at a homeless man who's digging through the trash looking for cans. Katherine brought up the issue of my pushing Alyssa away, but I danced around it, dodging her questions. This time, I feel like a lion trapped in a cage.

"I hit a nerve, Seth?" Rocco asks.

"I didn't make my wife sleep with someone else," I answer through clenched teeth, keeping my back to him.

"No, but let me ask you this." He joins me at the window. "Before Nevaeh died, who'd Alyssa spend her time with when you weren't around?"

I turn and meet his eyes. "What?"

"You know, who'd she go shopping with, to the park? Who were her girlfriends?"

"Alyssa isn't like that. She's kind of a…I don't know, a loner, I suppose, other than hanging out with—" I stop abruptly. Rocco looks at me with a 'see I told you' look. "I told her that I didn't like her spending so much time with him."

"So whad' you do about it?"

I want to swipe the grin off his face. "What did you want me to do, police her?"

"Hmm, interesting choice of words."

I roll my eyes and head for the fridge.

"Why'd she have so much time on her hands? Where were you?"

I crack open a Diet Coke. "At work. I needed my down time. Part of my down time involves surfing and that's also good for my business." My voice quivers. Inside, the knots are building in my stomach and my temple is throbbing. *Crap. Get a hold of yourself, Seth.*

"Was getting high good for your business, too?"

"God, why do you got such a hard on for me today?"

Rocco scoffs and turns for the door.

I pound the counter. Rocco doesn't even flinch. He's right. I know he's right. He heads for the door, and turns the knob to leave. "Wait!" I shout. "Just...come back and sit down. Okay?"

He turns and looks me up and down then shakes his head. "Okay. Then order up some pizza." He pauses and points his finger at me. "And the good stuff, not that take-n-bake crap you got out here with the cardboard crust, 'cause we just got started. It's gonna be a hell of a long night. I swear, Seth, if I didn't love you, I'd keep walking out that door. I'm gettin' too damn old for this."

Chapter 19

Alyssa

Daisy's been out in the back yard for an eternity. She's spent nearly half of her spring break with Oma, a couple of days with Seth, and the rest with me. It's awful for me having to split up her time between Seth's and home. More and more, I consider the damage it will do to her not having Seth back home.

I meander out into the backyard to see what project she's taken on. Yesterday, she helped me water the new seedlings that are poking through the ground. Prior to Nevaeh's death, the two girls were nearly inseparable when Daisy was home from school. Nevaeh toddled behind her, a perpetual shadow, imitating Daisy's movement, echoing her every word in her toddler-speak. I wonder if Daisy's lonely. I don't want to ask for fear that I'll upset her. Jesus, I'm doing exactly what some people have done that to me—avoided checking in for fear that I'll fall apart. I need to check in with her.

I pick up an open bottle of bubbles wondering where the lid is. I'm sure it's buried amidst the ankle-high weeds. The purple wand bobs around begging me to use it. I squeeze my fingers into the narrow bottle, withdraw the wand, bring it to my lips, draw in a deep breath, and blow out. As I watch the iridescent bubbles float down to the ground, I realize that this is the first deep breath I've taken in months.

Daisy is busy with a box of sidewalk chalk. I squat beside her to check out the square house she's drawn, complete with a smoking chimney, grass on the sides, and a long path leading up to the front door. The guests inside are ants.

"Whatcha' doing Daiz'?"

She doesn't look up. Her tongue sticks out as she grabs a brown piece of chalk and presses down hard onto the sidewalk making the shape of a tree trunk. "I'm making a tree for the ants so they have shade."

"Oh. I see you've built a house for them, too." The ants are pacing inside, circling their enclosure, bumping up against the sides of their "house", unable to cross the line that Daisy has drawn. "Looks like they can't get out."

"Yup," Daisy answers, non-pulsed. "They won't. Ms. Samantha says that ants won't cross a chalk line." She lifts her head and looks at me as she sets down her chalk. "See, it's their home." She points and continues, "That's the mommy, that's the daddy, and those are all their babies. They all live there and nobody leaves." She gets up, walks away, and takes a long drink of her apple juice. Clearly, nobody was crossing any lines in the ant family.

I walk over and kiss the top of her sun-warmed head. "It's a wonderful house, Daisy." And then, I take a stab at doing what I need to. "You okay out here by yourself? Do you feel lonely?" Without Nevaeh, I omit.

"I'm not alone. You're here." She looks up and smiles. It's an unconvincing smile, though. I give her a hug and then walk inside to check if Katherine has returned my call; the timing would be wonderful. No, still no message.

I head into the garage to change the laundry loads and retrieve Daisy's Easter basket. Our garage rafters and shelves are crammed with accumulated holiday decorations, ill-fitting clothes, miscellaneous surfing equipment, and boxes of pictures and knickknacks that Seth and I brought into our marriage. Of course, as time goes on, I'm learning that we brought more than just knickknacks—we brought crates full of personal history.

As I rummage through boxes, I stumble across my old photo albums. I pick one out of the box. It's covered in dust and the edges are yellowed. 1980 is scrawled on the front in my mother's handwriting. The cover makes a crackling sound as I open it and a picture of Gregory and I stares back at me. Gregory is eight and I'm seven. His eyes are bright and serious. In one hand, he holds a drawn sword, in the other, a shield. His mouth is open-wide, revealing spaces where crooked teeth would later grow. I'm beside him, his princess, with golden hair, a yellow, flowing gown, and a sparkling tiara on my head. My head is turned; I'm staring at him with a broad smile, my hand positioned in front of my mouth as though I'm stifling a giggle. Had Gregory always wanted to be my knight in shining armor?

The door that leads from the house to the garage slams shut. Daisy calls out my name. I wave a hand from between the mounds of boxes. She walks over and peers over my shoulder, placing her little hand on me. "Who are they?" she asks.

"That's me and Uncle Gregory when we were kids."

"It is?" She squats down beside me and holds the album up close. Her face scrunches up as though she's searching for some resemblance. "You look like Nevaeh, only older." My stomach lurches. I put my hand on top of hers. She's right, of course. "Yeah, we look alike."

"I miss Nevaeh," Daisy sighs and twirls her fingers into her hair.

She's talking about Nevaeh all on her own! I take her free hand and kiss it. "I know you do, baby."

"I miss Uncle Gregory, too When can he and the boys come over and play?"

Just like that, she's onto the next thought. 'No,' I want to tell her, 'let's talk about Nevaeh all day long.' Then I'm reminded of

Dr. Fowler's explanation of childhood grief—they can only take on bits of pain a little at a time.

I struggle to switch gears and address her question about Gregory. "I don't know when we'll see them, honey. Gregory's pretty busy these days." I don't tell her that we're not speaking, that I'm afraid of his anger, yet missing him all the same. Another tinge of pain swirls inside. I think about Gregory so many times throughout the day. Outside of the months I spent in Germany, I've never gone so long without speaking to him; even then, we wrote weekly. Every time I pick up the phone to return his calls, the image or his angry face stops me. The more I think about the past few months with him, the more I see how unpredictable he is. Even as kids, I could never really forecast his moods. As a friend, it was easy to dismiss, as a lover, not so much. Recently, I'd assumed that his marriage problems were from his hidden feelings for me. Now, it dawns on me that Gregory's anger, mood swings, and drinking were the bigger issues in their separation; I was simply the catalyst.

She looks at the picture once more, then, with a serious look, glances up at me. "I liked your hair better long."

"Did you?" I touch my hair. "Maybe I'll grow it out again."

The doorbell rings and Daisy jumps up and starts for the door. "Hang on a minute," I call out, trying to get my balance as I stand up and toss the photo album back in the box. "What did I say about answering the door without me?"

"I know. I just want to look out the window. Maybe it's Daddy!"

That would be nice. Maybe. It's not, though. The brown-suited UPS guy is at the door holding a large package. Right away, I notice the Deutschland postmark—a package from my mother. Great, just what I need, an intrusion from my mother. Daisy flits around the room, running in circles.

"Open it! Open it!" she screams with excitement.

At key times during the year, my mother barges her way into our lives: Christmas, Easter, and birthdays. I slit open the tape with scissors and fold back the sides of the box. Daisy reaches in and pulls out bars of European chocolate. "Can I have some now? Please! Please!" She bobs up and down like she's on a pogo-tick. "Mommy, I promise I'll eat lots of carrots later." She's five and she's already got me figured out. I'm too weak to argue. I hand her one of the bars, warning her to have just half; she'll be bouncing off the walls within half an hour.

Digging through the package, I see that there's a gift bag for me along with a card attached. I contemplate tossing the card directly into the garbage. I've never understood how my mother could abandon me when I was just seventeen by moving to Germany and think that an occasional letter, gift, or phone call will somehow fill in the gaping holes she left. These gifts and letters, tokens of her "love" merely fuel my anger and disgust.

I pull the contents out and struggle to read the label; like my tolerance for her antics, my German is fading with time. There are several packets of bath salts, my favorite rose-scented lotion (that I can never afford), and a tube of an herbal remedy for anxiety; Oma must have let information slip through. I decide that I'll need all three to get me prepared for joining Oma at one of the Holy Week services. I've dodged going to church, let alone Holy Week, for years with the excuse of busy schedules, naps, early bed times, and the routines of the children. I owe it to Oma this year, given all she's done. Oma's convinced that hearing God's word and being around the "community of faith" is just what I need. We'll see. I keep wondering where God has been in all of this.

By four o'clock, Daisy is spent from her sugar crash and is asleep on my bed. It's the perfect time to slip into the tub. I open one of the packets of bath salts and sprinkle them into the steaming water. The room fills with lavender; I feel an initial sense of calm. On top of the towel on the side of the tub is my mother's letter. Maybe sliding into the water will ease my nerves enough to open it. I slip into the water, shivering from the near-scalding water. I close my eyes and I breathe in the aromatic steam.

The letter may as well have a red flashing light and a screaming alarm, because I can't keep my attention from drifting to it. May as well get this over with.

Dearest Alyssa-

I know I should have written when your precious one was taken back in October. I left several messages, but alas, you never called. I was so bereft that I couldn't find the words to write. Never did I imagine that my own child would suffer as you. I'm sorry, Alyssa, that I'm not the mother you deserved. I know that Oma has given you what I couldn't. For that I will always be grateful. I can't go back in time, but if I could, I'd like to believe I would do things differently. Losing your father when I was so very young…it did something to me. It's difficult to explain, other than a part of me died with him. Can you imagine?

No, I can't imagine Seth being snuffed from our life like my father was. Yes, I know, a part of me died with Nevaeh, too. But why is she talking about her grief!

I don't know how you are coping with the loss of Nevaeh. Perhaps you are very busy with Daisy and the school. Probably, you are doing better than I would.

I sit up in the tub and have the urge to wad up her letter and send it sailing into the trash.

I just want you to know how sorry I am and that I think of you often. Happy Easter. Give Oma, Daisy, and Seth my love. I hope you can come to Germany and see us one day. Perhaps it's not too late?

Blessings,
Mom

I torture myself by reading her letter over and over again until the bath water is cool. *Probably you are doing much better than I would.* How could she possibly know given that she conveniently stays a continent away! And that bit about my dad's death…well, it would be nice if she had shared how heartbreaking that was for her, rather than my assumption that I was merely a hideous reminder of what she'd lost. Then it hits me…Daisy never hears me talk about missing Seth.

I towel off, rip the letter into tiny pieces, and flush them. I slip on a skirt and lightweight sweater for church, lay down beside my sleeping child, and whisper, "I'm sorry, Daisy, for this crazy year. I do miss Daddy. I miss Nevaeh. I miss our family."

I EASE INTO church hoping to go unnoticed, but am spotted by a group of Oma's friends. Their perfumed hugs and "I'm sorry's" linger on me like a thick scarf. Public appearances have been getting a little easier; however, this one is not. Finally, I find Oma in the sea of people and ask her to find a pew and sit down; I need to blend in and disappear. I fumble with the church bulletin, feigning interest in upcoming events. The air is thick with incense and paraffin as the altar boys make their way toward the front. Behind them, in a flowing white robe and a gold sash, is Pastor Mic. Oma told me that he replaced Father Kelly a year and a half ago, shortly after we christened Nevaeh. His face is kind, young, and almost familiar, like the saints captured in stained glass throughout the California missions.

We stand and begin to sing a familiar hymn. I hum the tune amidst the barrage of vibrato church voices. My eyes burn from the mixture of smells and smoke. I dab at them and Oma and Daisy throw me a concerned look.

I wave my hand in front of my face and whisper to Oma, "It's just the incense. I'm fine." I'm so tired of everyone handling me cautiously, like a breakable ornament.

Maybe I should call Gregory when I get home today. I owe him the opportunity to explain himself and apologize in person. His messages are a repeat string of apologies. Ugh, I'm so distracted in here. What am I doing at church when I could be walled up at home in my jammies?

The minister signals us to rise once again. A member of the congregation walks forward for the reading of the Old Testament.

Out of Breath

She tells us to join along by following the leaflet in our bulletin. I turn to the appropriate page. It's an excerpt from Exodus, familiar to even the "unchurched"— the Ten Commandments.

"You shall have no other Gods before me," she says, leading us. "You shall not make for yourself a carved image—any likeness of anything that is in heaven above or that is in the earth beneath, or that is in the water under the earth. You shall not take the name of the Lord in vain."

I feign interest and fumble with a button on my sweater that has come loose. I look up at the stained glass window depicting Jesus with his crown of thorns. The predicted rain has moved in and streaks the windows; blood drips down Jesus' face.

"Talk Mommy," Daisy says, squeezing my hand. "You're supposed to read the words."

I smile and nod, joining in, "Honor your father and mother." My face flushes. I look at bloody Jesus who is also now crying. "You shall not murder." A pounding sensation mounts at my temples and I sway. "You shall not commit adultery." Like colored jagged glass trapped in a kaleidoscope, everything swirls and tumbles before me and inside. My hands are so sweaty that Daisy lets go to wipe off her hand. I can't stay here. I've got to get out of here but I'm trapped in the middle. Oh God, not here in church; I can't have a panic attack here. The flutter of a thousand humming birds fills my chest.

I tell Daisy to stay with Oma. I scrunch past her and Oma, ignoring their puzzled looks and questions of, "Where are you going?" Just as I'm near the end of the pew and can make my escape, my heel catches on the kneeling bench, sending me flying into the aisle and onto my knees. Gasps and collective breaths of sympathy rise with me as I run toward the doors to the annex. I don't slow down until I've pushed open the outer glass doors and stammer toward the crowded parking lot that's being doused with steady drops of rain.

Katherine

Out of the corner of my eye, I see a shorthaired, blonde woman fall in the aisle. Is it...? It can't be. Leah and I turn to one another with looks of surprise. "Is that—" Leah begins.

"I'll be back in a minute," I whisper to her. Leah attempts to stop me. "Not a word, Leah," I say, peering at her. I sneak past Carl, Collin, and Tory who are equally confused. Carl mouths, 'Where are you going.' I tell him I need a tissue and fake a sniffle.

I look around the annex, but only see a couple of teenagers who've managed to slink out before their parents notice. Holding my jacket over my head, I make my way outside, scanning the parking lot and grounds of the church. On the side of the church, tucked under the eaves, I see her, face covered, although her sobs cannot be stifled.

"Excuse me," I begin, unsure if it is Alyssa, "I just wanted to see if you were okay. You seem upset."

She turns and I'm momentarily startled; at least half the length of Alyssa's hair is gone. "It is you," I say.

"Katherine," she replies, equally stunned, "what are you doing here?"

"I—this is where my family and I attend."

"You go to church with my grandmother?"

"Technically, although I don't see her all that much. What's going on?"

Alyssa hiccups, and has difficulty speaking, like a child running to her mother after a terrible fall. I place my arm around her and she falls into me. The trembling in her body ripples through me. "Take a deep breath. Let's head inside to one of the Sunday school rooms and get out of this rain."

We walk together, my arm holding her pressed to my side. If I let go, it feels like she'll merge with the puddles. I find a vacant room and flick on a light. I help Alyssa with her coat, throwing it onto the tightly woven blue carpet. Alyssa rocks back and forth in her chair, curled up in the fetal position.

"What happened in there tonight?" I ask.

"I...I've done some terrible things, Katherine," she starts. "I've wanted to talk to you so badly this week." I start to interrupt with an explanation as to why I haven't returned her call, or perhaps at this point, an apology, but she cuts in. "No," she interjects and holds up a hand. "I know that your kids are home and you need a break. It's just been a really, really crappy time." I nod. "I haven't been honest with you; but then, I guess you know that because you see Seth."

And Greg. "I'd like to hear what you have to say."

"I'm having an affair," she cries, unwilling to look at me. "An affair. Me! I've committed adultery, Katherine. I did exactly what you warned against. I was just so angry with Seth. And my friend...he was there. He cared, I think, although I'm not even sure of that."

I'm relieved to hear her confusion; maybe Greg's dark side is showing. "It's been difficult to pretend that I didn't know," I say with honesty.

"I'm so sorry. I've put everyone in such an awkward place," Alyssa says, wringing her hands. "I may as well be a murderer, too. I didn't watch her, Katherine. I should have watched her more closely and none of this, none of this, would have happened."

So, we're back to this, again. I need to get Alyssa to move away from this thought process. "Does that make Seth a murderer, too?"

"What?" she says, finally meeting my eyes. "He didn't do it intentionally."

"So what makes you different?"

"I don't know. I've screwed everything up. God, Katherine, look at my life! What do I do?"

I know she's broken and it's exactly where she needs to be. I sit with her, holding one of her cold, fragile hands, and remember when I broke. It was in a meeting with my parental bereavement support group. Five years had passed. Carl brought up the idea of getting pregnant. I lost my mind. All of my pain and fear of losing not only

Nicole, but also another child, jumped to the surface. It was the beginning of my healing; and then I tucked the residual pain away.

I take a deep breath. "Alyssa, you don't do anything with this gut-wrenching pain." Alyssa wipes her eyes and focuses on my words. "The affair, your relationship with Seth, those are things that can be worked on; handled. Your grief, though, has in many ways been kept at bay by the distraction of your affair. It fed you and served a purpose. However, it may not be working so well anymore?"

"How can you tell?"

"I know because I lost a child, too." There, I said it.

Alyssa's lips part and she lets out a small gasp. "When? Why didn't you tell me?"

I cock my head. "You know, there's a fine line between disclosing personal information to a client for your own gain or for the benefit of the client. In this case, I felt it was too distracting… until now. Forgiving yourself is a very difficult thing. It will be harder than letting go of this affair, forgiving Seth, and healing from Nevaeh's death. I punished myself a long time; so long that I nearly split up my marriage. To be honest, Nicole's death is still something we don't talk much about…it's like it's taboo. I hope for your sake that it can be different for you. It's not easy to bear this nearly thirty years later."

In our silence, I can see the hamster wheel in Alyssa's head turning. "I'm sorry."

"Thank you. Me too." I pause. "So, back to you. There's a lot going on?"

"Yeah," she says, exhaling. "Lots. I got this letter from my mom, too, today."

"Mm. Do you want to talk about that?" I ask.

Alyssa clenches her teeth and lets out a groan. "How come she can turn me upside down so fast?"

"Mothers can be that way."

"I want to be different. I want to be the good mommy—the fun, caring, staying home and baking mommy. I don't want to become my mother," Alyssa pleads.

"You love Daisy very much and I see you putting her needs before yours. You are a good mommy." My eye catches an image of the Virgin Mary and baby Jesus. Why do we women hold ourselves to such a lofty standard?

"Am I really when I invited another man into my life?"

"That doesn't make you a bad parent, although there can be consequences. You have some decisions to make." I squeeze her hand and stand up. "You okay?"

She nods and sniffles.

"I'll see you in a few days. We'll talk more then. It's good for you to process some of this before we meet together with Seth."

"I guess so. You know, we talk almost every day now; chit-chat, though, not this kind of stuff."

Another surprise. "Sounds like you're both wanting more contact." I smile, pleased with what's happening between the two of them. "Well, I'm going to head back inside. Is Elsa here?"

"Yes, probably worried to death and searching all over for me."

We head for the door, back toward the church. Alyssa stops and touches my arm. "Hey, I just want to thank you for this and for telling me about your daughter. I would have never guessed—you always seem so strong; so together."

If she only knew…"Alyssa, you're stronger than you give yourself credit."

Alyssa

Back at my grandmother's, Oma's tiptoeing around as though Nevaeh's death just occurred. She doesn't know about Gregory and me; I hope. I let her think it's simply my grief…it *is* grief, just on so many levels now.

Daisy and I settle into Oma's rocker. I feel ashamed for my anger at my mother; not because I'm not entitled to it, but because I was given the best mother a woman could ever want in the form of a grandparent.

"Tell me a story," Daisy says.

"Oh, I'm not much of a story teller. That's Daddy's job."

"I know, but Daddy's not here." Oma stops putting the dishes away in the kitchen and stares over at me. Her look of pity and sadness rips through me. She wipes her hands down her apron and moves toward us.

"Tell her about the time you and I made jam for Christmas gifts and we forgot to add the right amount of sugar. Oh, my, what a gift that was," Oma laughs.

She's saved me again. Daisy gets her story and I get to relive a wonderful memory that I'd tucked deep inside. By 11:00, my arms are weary from holding my sleeping child. I told Oma that Daisy and I would like to stay a couple of days; I'll get Duke in the morning. I carry Daisy down the hall to her home away from home. Just as I'm about to step out, she whispers, "Mommy, when's Daddy coming home?"

"Soon, baby. Soon."

I never make that call to Gregory. Another day passes with this great silence between us. There's only one place I want to be, and so I climb inside my daughter's bed and listen to the rhythm of her heart.

Chapter 20

Seth

By 3:00, I've finished sanding the last of it. I run my hand along the smooth edges of the board. Beads of sweat mix with my tears. Rocco sits on a stool in the corner. We're quiet. There are no words. I hand Rocco a mask. He refuses. I slip mine on as I apply a thin coat of protection to keep the board from weathering. It'll never meet the waves of the ocean, but it needs to stay strong.

Another hour passes. Rocco's slipped into the kitchenette of my shop and is brewing a third pot of toe-curling coffee. By 6:00, I've stuffed everything into my backpack that I need. We wrap the board in a packing blanket and place it in the truck bed. The bright, blue day mocks my pain; I wished for fog. The drive across town is quiet and still. I tap out my cigarette when we arrive. It's important that I'm here first. Katherine warned me that the shock could be overwhelming to Alyssa, but I want to make a statement…hopefully redeem myself. I want to turn her world upside down like she's done to mine. I don't want to hurt her, all right, maybe a little, but she needs to see with her own eyes that

I wasn't lying. I loved my baby. I had good intentions. I lacked judgment. In the end, did it have to cost me everyone I love?

"It's over here," I say to Rocco, pointing. He should've gone home at midnight; he wouldn't hear of it. I stop and lay down my backpack. I grab the mallet inside, take hold of the miniature surfboard, and slam it into the moist earth in front of Nevaeh's headstone, tapping it into place. I will myself to not look at the dates etched into the stone marker. It's still too startling to see her birth and death dates—they're too close together.

Jeff called just days ago to tell me that he found something weird in his old workbag, a bag that held tools and a change of clothes. Amidst his things was a woman's robe...pink—Nevaeh's blankie. Somehow it wound up inside his bag. I figure Nevaeh must have dropped it behind the seat and it slipped into his bag the morning of her death. While I was being arrested for presumably sneaking off to get high, Jeff grabbed the bag from my truck; drugs were amongst the other miscellaneous items in the bag. He tossed it to the back of his closet where it remained until he got a flat in the driveway the other day. He told me he'd searched everywhere for it and finally remembered tossing it in his closet. Please, God, let this be the catalyst that moves Alyssa from doubt to belief...from disbelief to trust.

I withdraw the sash from the robe and tie it around the surfboard. It looks like a present. I return to my backpack and pull out a photo of the four of us, a small nail, and tap the photo and sash into place.

"Happy 2nd Birthday, Nevaeh. Wherever you are, know that Daddy loves you...misses you...everyday. I wish you were still here. I'm sorry. I love you, baby." I drop to my knees and hear the quiet steps of Rocco as he walks back to the truck.

Alyssa

Preparing for my child's birthday should be fun and exciting. There's the party planning (a fairy or princess theme), hand-made invitation, streamers, the cake, homemade, of course. Last year when Nevaeh turned one, I invited a handful of moms and their babies from our parent-toddler group to meet Daisy, Nevaeh, and I at the neighborhood park for fresh apple cider and carrot cake; Seth had to work.

This year, the planning is different. How do I commemorate my dead baby's birthday? She celebrated just one. The leading up to it has been much worse than the actual day. The week leading up, I've gone in and out of bouts of anxiety, quiet contemplation, crazy crying sessions, and bursts of manic energy. The only thing that calmed me down was the mindless work of dusting baseboards, light fixtures, and sucking up dust bunnies from under the furniture.

I've promised Daisy that I'll take her to visit her sister's grave. I'm not sure if this was her idea or one prompted by her therapist. The permanency of Nevaeh's death is settling in for Daisy as time passes. She tells me that she talks to her sister who's up in heaven. When I peek in her room, I don't see a place setting set for Nevaeh anymore. How she'll make sense of part of her sister's ashes buried under the ground, I'm not sure. I focus up toward heaven rather on the cold earth below. Nevertheless, I'll bring her. Not today. Today is for me.

After dropping Daisy off at Oma's, I drive downtown to purchase a bunch of chrysanthemums. One year when I was a child, we had a teacher in training from Japan who stayed with us. In the center of our table was a giant vase of mums. With a shocked look, Kumiko told us that this flower is reserved for the dead in Japan, purchased to bring to the cemetery. Since then, I've equated mums with death.

I wish Seth and I were going up to the cemetery together today. I'd like it if we were together every day, but today especially. I wonder if he's made it up to Nevaeh's grave yet. He'll probably go after work. By the time I arrive at the cemetery, I'm totally wrung out. I feel like someone has taken a vice grip and is slowly cranking it around my skull. Of all the times I could cry, the tears won't come. Is it possible that I've run dry? I grab the flowers and suddenly feel foolish, alone, and unsure of what to do. Can't someone lead me through this, like Katherine?

When I think back to her funeral, the memory is cloudy, as though I'd been sedated like the night of my panic attack. Shock; I know that now. If I could just recall the details more clearly, it would be something else to hold on to of my baby. I remember my cousin Caroline read a poem about a new angel in heaven. If I could give a piece of advice to those who haven't lost a child it would be this: don't tell us we have a new angel in heaven. We want our children here, not in another galaxy as some sort of celestial being. I think someone from the church sang *Amazing Grace*. Daisy had clutched my hand so tight during the service that my fingers went numb. Dead hands. Dead baby. Then the ashes we buried. I couldn't put all of her in the ground. I begged to hold on to a piece of her. Buried deep in my closet is a tiny urn that contains a handful of her ashes; I've yet to look at it.

As I continue to weave through the headstones, stalling, unwilling to take the shortest path, my mind rewinds the internal tape of her funeral. I was so livid with Seth. When he hugged Daisy I wanted to rip her out of his arms. So often over the past seven months, I've replayed our interactions: the moment we saw her body, freezing and soaked; the looks we exchanged when he was in the back of Gregory's patrol car; the screaming match we had outside of Katherine's front door. In some ways it feels like years ago, and in other ways, like yesterday. The one lingering conversation that continues to bounce around inside me is when Seth told me, adamantly, that he did not get high that night; that he'd gone off to find her blankie.

I'm within twenty yards or so of Nevaeh's gravesite, when something sticking out of the ground catches my eye. I squint and blink—a surfboard? Here? I drop the flowers and pick up speed and nearly trip over my black, broomstick skirt. I grab the top of the board to steady myself as my eyes survey it from top to bottom. A picture of the four of us is secured by a pink…oh my God! Oh my God! I finger the silky fabric. It's the sash of my robe—a part of Nevaeh's blankie. I rip it from the board and hold it to my nose, willing there to be something of her scent, but it's gone; only the smell of fresh turpentine is there. The ground feels like it's shifting and I fall to my knees. He was…he was telling the truth. It can't be! But what about…? I don't have time for "what abouts" and "what ifs" anymore.

I run back and get the flowers and put them in the vase that is dug into the ground. "Nevaeh, for your birthday, Mommy's going to try and figure out this mess." I kiss her photo that's nailed to the surfboard, whisper I love you, and then race back to my car. The traffic gives me time to think about what to say. The more I drive, the angrier I get; pissed that he didn't have the decency to call me and tell me, 'Guess what, I found her blanket.' He had to nail a piece of it beside her grave?

I burst into his customer-filled shop with the sash in my hand. I blaze behind the counter where Seth is showing a customer a bar of surf wax and shove the sash into his face. "Where the hell did you get this?" I scream.

Seth

I apologize to my customer, grab Alyssa by the wrist, pull her toward the back, and pass Jeff, telling him to go up front for me. When we're out of earshot, I stare down at Alyssa, and say, "What the hell are you doing? I don't need any more bad publicity." I let go of her wrist and she rubs it. I fling open the back door and signal her to follow me out; only the dumpsters and Jeff's and my trucks are around for this conversation.

Alyssa shoots her hand into my face, clutching the sash of Nevaeh's blankie. "Where did you find this? Are you trying to push me over the edge?"

"Push you over the edge?" I want to rip my hair out of my head. "I've been trying to tell you for months that I was looking for her blanket that night in my truck." I'm just getting started, like an engine revving its motor. "You wanna talk about being pushed over the edge, try having your spouse screw around on you after your baby's just died. Hah? How about that? Then when her new boyfriend starts showing his true colors, she starts crying her heart out, pleading for help when panic sets in. So don't talk to me about getting pushed over the edge, Alyssa. I've been so far over the edge for so long now that I don't know if I'll ever get back up!" My face is on fire. I want to drive my fist through the concrete wall. I grab the sash from her hand and continue, "I told you from the beginning, back in October, that I wasn't going to get high again, *ever*…and I didn't. The minute Greg took over the investigation *he* tainted it."

Alyssa opens her mouth to speak, but I won't let her. It's my turn to open the floodgates that've been damned the past half a year. "That's right, he told me that if I didn't cooperate, go down to the station, and keep my mouth shut to you that he'd dirty up my test even more…make it look like I'd done meth, or worse." Alyssa's eyes begin to fill with tears. "Oh, don't get all dewy-eyed and surprised. You know he's done some crappy things over the years and this wasn't the first. He may have had some suspicions, Alyssa, but he didn't go by the book. And that "fight" between Jeff and me—"

"Gregory," Alyssa winces, raising her hand to her mouth. "It was Gregory who did that to you?"

She's finally getting it. "When I asked Daisy to keep an eye on Nevaeh, I was searching for her blanket. I didn't have my proof until Jeff came across it in his workbag that was missing. I was going to wait and show you in our session with Katherine, but Christ, I feel like you've been playing head games. You don't want to speak to me, you have an affair, then, bam, overnight, you're calling me for help and we're talking every day on the phone like…like, nothing ever happened! I can't pretend, 'Lyss. I'm upside down. I can't figure you out." I lean against the wall and grab my cigarettes from my shirt pocket, light up, and take a deep drag.

"I…don't even know what to say," Alyssa says, with defeat in her voice. All the anger that raced in with her seems to have flown out the back door. "I'm so sorry."

I shake my head and scoff. "What do you want from me, Alyssa? You want me to tell you that I forgive you? That it's okay? That I understand? Well, I don't. You don't even know the hell I've been through the past six, seven months. Doin' my recovery, trying to make heads or tails out of Nevaeh's death, missing Daisy, you, wanting to kill myself half the time." I finger the pink sash. "I probably shouldn't have done that today. My sponsor warned me that—"

"Your sponsor?" she interrupts.

"Yeah. I go to meetings, meet with my sponsor, the whole A.A. deal."

"There's so much I don't know."

I take a final drag of my cigarette and stub it out on the ground. "Look, I know that this," I rant, shaking the blanket sash from her hand, "doesn't absolve me but you need to consider that I'm telling the truth. I may have been a jack-ass of a husband at times when I was loaded, and I'll sure as hell never forgive myself for not watching Nevaeh, but for the last time, I'm telling you, I was clean that night. I wouldn't have traded my baby for any kind of score. Not ever!"

"But the drug test?"

"Remember the night before?" The last time I was high. The last time I made love to her. The last time we were a family of four. She nods. "There ya go. My test would be dirty for at least a week." I feel like my head's going to explode. "Look, you think this over. I need to go back inside and help Jeff. I'll see you at Katherine's on Thursday. Sorry if I rattled you. I needed you to see the truth." I toss the sash back at her.

"I'm sorry too."

I open the door and slam it behind me, leaving Alyssa alone amidst the garbage bins. I'm halfway through the store when it's like a giant wave throws me down and sweeps me back out. Jeff signals me for help up front. "Give me five," I tell him. I turn around, hoping she hasn't left, and swing open the door. She's still there, stroking the sash, sniffling, wiping tears from her face.

I reach for her shoulders, push her gently against the wall, and press my lips firmly onto hers. She drops her purse and her hands dance in my hair. I feel like a lovesick teenager, moaning and sighing as we cling to one another. When we break apart, I feel her trembling.

"I know. Shhh, I know. I should have done this differently," I apologize.

"It's me who should be saying I'm sorry. God, I miss her, Seth. I just want to touch her one more time."

I run my hand through her cropped hair. I was so angry earlier that I hadn't noticed she cut it.

"I know. I cut it all off. I'm a mess," she cries.

"It's fine. You're beautiful." I kiss her again, hold her face in my hands and stare into her eyes. "I miss her too." We hold one another, rocking back and forth—this is what I've wanted all along, the comfort of my wife. I want to freeze time. "I'll bring you her blanket on Thursday. You should have it." She nods and offers a faint smile. "I really need to go." I stroke her damp cheek and kiss her again. She tastes like roses.

Katherine

There's a draft in the house, one that isn't from cold weather or single windowpanes. It's a chill that's swirling inside me, whispering of death, one that feels familiar…frightening. On the Monday after the children returned to their universities, my mother's oncologist called me to suggest hospice care. I thought I could do it; I thought I was enough. My pride has fallen; I need help. Carl looks as lost as I do while the hospice social worker interviews us. I keep one eye on the clock; my session is less than thirty minutes from now. Death never behaves.

My mother drifts in and out of consciousness in the next room. A hospital bed was delivered early in the day. Collin's room has been transformed from a trophy case to a hospital wing. Carl and I never do intense sorrow well together. You'd think that with all my training, I'd know how to pull us together, process our feelings, and be able to voice my needs. No, we hide in our mutual corners showing the uglier sides of ourselves—pettiness, frustration, and irritability—we are human.

The sideshow to this circus in my mind is my session with Seth and Alyssa, now just a couple of days away. I pray that my mother can hold on long enough for me to see this case through. Then, I can hand it off to someone else. I may need to take an extended leave when she passes.

Five minutes until the hour, I interrupt our hospice interview, apologizing for needing to leave. She knows I have clients this afternoon and offers me a sympathetic nod. Carl blows out a deep sigh like a steamship; I know what he won't say, 'Cancel your damn session.' I excuse myself and walk down to my office, willing the pain and heaviness in my chest to go away…a new symptom to add to the barrage of others.

With a sense of dread, I wait for Greg's footsteps to crunch down the pebbled path to my office. I plug in my tea cozy and light a vanilla scented candle that Tory bought me. Over the spring break, Greg called me almost a dozen times. Each message, his voice grew increasingly agitated. Discomfort, in my opinion, does not require immediate attention. However, his anger management issues do have me on high alert. I grab my pepper spray from my purse and slip it into my pocket.

I look over Greg's file, once again marveling at how intertwined his and the Buchannan cases are. Holding secrets has drained me and stretched my memory as to which client disclosed specific information and who did not. Seeing Greg always left me depleted of energy in a way that only a few clients had over the course of my professional life. He feels like a nervous, caged tiger waiting to pounce.

At ten past the hour, I double-check my appointment book to be sure that I have our day and time right; given my own mental status, it wouldn't surprise me if I made an error. No, it's today. I peek out from the blue, laced curtains that Mom sewed me years ago; still no sign of Gregory's truck or squad car. At half past the hour, I give up, and enjoy the sweep of relief.

Greg

I have a last ditch effort. I've bought three containers of tulips—white, purple, and pink. Alyssa loves the tulips she and Nevaeh planted. She says they symbolize life, death, and rebirth. I hope my offering will signify the same—our life, the death of the past, and a new start. I figure she's heading over to the cemetery after dropping Daisy by Oma's for school. It will take her a good hour, hour and a half, round trip. That gives me time to go over to her place, slip inside, and place them on the table with my card.

Technically it's not breaking and entering, even though I'm not a wanted guest at this point; I do have a key. I let myself in. Duke gives a bark or two but wags his tail when he sees me and comes over for a scratch on the head. It's been weeks now since I've been here; it feels like months. Just a couple months back, it had begun to feel like home. Unbelievable. I place the tulip pots on the center of the table and into the plastic holder, slip a card that reads: *Missing Nevaeh, missing Daisy, missing you. To new beginnings— Gregory.* If this doesn't get to her, I don't know what will.

As I'm about to head out, the phone rings. I give Duke another pat and open the door to leave when a familiar voice comes over the answering machine.

"Alyssa, good morning. This is Katherine. Thinking of you on this day. I wanted to ask you and Seth if we could push our appointment up by one hour to 5:00 rather than 4:00 on Thursday. Sorry to inconvenience you, but I have a nurse stopping by to check on my mother. Looking forward to seeing you both; it's been a long time coming."

Katherine! What the hell? And why is she talking about therapy with Seth and Alyssa? I lose my bearings, like a passenger aboard a stormy ship. Katherine is their therapist? She sat across from me all these months as I poured my heart out all the while she's seeing Alyssa and Seth? She knows about our affair but she's looking forward to seeing *them...together*? She knew! Oh my God, she's encouraging their relationship. It all makes sense—Alyssa's avoidance, her not returning my calls.

"Son of a bitch!" I shout, hearing my words echo down the empty hallway. I grab the tulips from the table and slam the door behind me.

Chapter 21

Alyssa

The day is really here: our session together with Katherine. This could be a new beginning for Seth and me. Maybe there's a way back together. Daisy joins me for my recent daily walks on the beach; part of my panic attack therapy. We walk nearly an hour, hand in hand. It's like she senses the importance of this day too, because she flits around, chasing the gulls and sandpipers like a dog off her leash. If there's any blessing in the tornado that's ripped through our lives, it's the strength of Daisy's and my relationship. I no longer see her as the distant, aloof daughter. Rather, I see her as the sweet child she is; complex, loyal, and deeply attached to her family. I tried so hard to shape her into who I wanted her to be and in the meantime, missed who she is.

As much as I want to trust Seth, I worry that the change in him is temporary. What if he starts using again? I know life is filled with "what ifs", but this is a big one that will impact Daisy and me. Oma says that's the definition of faith; believing without seeing; that God is at work in us.

Seth says he'll share things with me in our session, information about his recovery, realizations that he's come to via A.A., and in therapy. Even without the words, I see a new man. His eyes are bright and clear, filled with a longing to make things right.

I'm not the only one, I'm sure, who is dealing with trust issues. I'd be naïve to think that forgiveness is immediate. My affair with Gregory has deeply hurt Seth. My drug of choice was an affair.

Seth

I grab my Camels and toss them onto the passenger seat of my truck. I've been cutting back steadily for two weeks, down to three a day. Even though it seems like everyone at A.A. is a chain smoker, Rocco reamed me for this one last addiction. The thought of Daisy hugging me and not coming away with the smoky after effects keeps me motivated. Today, I could really use a pack and a half just to get me to the session.

Nevaeh's blanket rests across my lap. It's like a talisman—proof that she existed. Rocco and I stayed up half the night rehearsing my, "How I Shredded My Marriage" speech. I need to get through it, own my share of responsibility in how I pushed Alyssa aside, not giving my family top priority, let her hear that I'm not dodging responsibility any more. There's nothing that I can compare recovery except the terror of meeting a twenty-five foot wall of water and surrendering to its power. When I try to master it, I only get sucked under and spit out onto shore…or worse.

I pull up to Katherine's. Alyssa's beat up car is already in the drive—déjà vu. I blow out a big breath. Kissing her the other day didn't fix it all, but it was the fix I needed to get me where I am.

Greg

I jump into my squad car. I have just under an hour to take care of things, plenty of time to bust up the nice little reunion at

Katherine's office. I flip on my scanner and pray for a quiet evening. It's my last shift before moving down to Seaside.

Katherine

I've been "off" all day. Never mind that I shattered my favorite mug that Mom bought from Carmel over ten years ago, or that I cut my finger while picking up the pieces. And even though Mom's been perkier than usual, talkative even, I know better than to trust that. It's a warning sign: the dying often has a last, sudden burst of energy before death. All of this has caused my heart rate to be all over the place: beating steady, rushing off like I'm in a race, back to steady. It's got me quite unnerved. I've waited months for Seth and Alyssa's session to come. The hospice nurse is reading beside Mom's bed. Everything is in place. I need clarity. Sadly, all I can think is: I'm so tired.

Alyssa

I'm waiting for Seth in the driveway, this time with hope. As I eye my wedding ring that I slipped back on this week, I hear the familiar hum of his engine coming up Katherine's hill. My whole body tingles. He jumps down from his truck holding Nevaeh's blanket. I run and grab the blanket, pressing it to my face while his arms wrap around me tighter, tighter, tighter.

"I wish I'd believed you," I whisper. He smells new, like fresh rain, clean and pure.

"I wish a lot of things. Come on, let's go in."

When we walk in to Katherine's office with Nevaeh's blanket clasped in between our hands, Katherine looks at us with wonder. "Is that...that's the blanket, isn't it?" she asks.

I look up at Seth who is beaming. He nods without saying a word.

Katherine smiles, showing us to the couch. Seth and I sit down side-by-side, hand-in-hand. Her smile widens. "You both have worked hard for this day. What a difference between today and that stormy day in November. There was so much tension back then that it hurt."

Seth squeezes my hand. I start, "I told him about what happened at church the other night. How I ran out and you were there." Katherine acknowledges me. I suppose she's wondering if I told him everything and so I go on. "I hope you don't mind, but I told him about you…how you also lost a baby."

She remains quiet. Seth interjects, "I'm sorry, Katherine. I never gave you credit for knowing how ripped up I've been. Now I know you get it."

"I get it. But grief is different for everyone. I had time to prepare; your loss was sudden," I say, bringing the focus back to them.

"Even so," Seth says, "she was your baby."

"Yes, she was. Thank you. So, where to start? I know privately, you both shared with me a number of things you wanted to bring to this meeting. Who would like to begin?"

I open my mouth to say that I'll go first, but am caught off guard by the screeching of tires right outside Katherine's window. The three of us jerk our heads toward the window when the door bursts open. It's Gregory.

"Gregory!" I gasp. "What are you doing here?" He's in his uniform, gun at his side and is completely wild eyed, worse than the night he threw his glass against the wall. We're all on our feet. Seth shoves me behind him.

"I don't know what the hell you're doing here, but this isn't any of your damn business," Seth shouts.

Greg takes a few steps forward. "That so? I don't think you're in any position to be calling the shots around here."

"Greg," Katherine says in a shaky voice. "Nice to see you again."

"Again?" Seth and I say simultaneously.

"I'll bet, Katherine," he sneers, rubbing his thumb across his knuckled fist.

My head ping-pongs back and forth from Katherine to Gregory. "You two know one another?" I settle on Katherine for an answer. Her mouth is shut but her eyes are screaming with fear.

Gregory takes another couple of steps, this time closer to Katherine. "Go ahead, Katherine, tell Seth and Alyssa how we know each other. Tell 'em how I've been coming here all these months. I bet you've fed Alyssa a load of crap about how she should stay away from me." With every word, Gregory's voice escalates; this is feeling oddly familiar, only he's not holding a glass this time. This time, his hand is moving closer and closer to his gun.

Katherine pushes her hair off her forehead, which is glistening with sweat. "Greg, I'm able to see you at another time, but I must ask you to respect this hour I have with Seth and Alyssa."

"Respect!" he shouts. "Oh that's rich, Katherine. How can I respect any of you—a pack of liars! Fakes!" He moves his hand to his holster.

I grab Seth's arm, shaking it, as if to tell him, 'do something.' I slip around the other side of the couch. Seth is grabbing at me to stay behind him. "Gregory, please, talk to me," I plead, moving within inches of him. All this time I've been avoiding him. Now I feel personally responsible for his rage. I've got to diffuse this ticking bomb. "Sit down and we can all talk about this…together. Please!" I grab his arm that's inching up to his holster.

"*Don't touch me,*" he seethes, his eyes remaining fixed on Seth and Katherine. "Tell them, Katherine…tell them how I spilled my guts about my brother, my marriage, my lover," he spits, staring at Seth with vindication. "All the while you were working on getting this douche bag back together with her," he barks into the air, grabbing my arm and shaking me, and screams, "You little whore!" He shoves me over to the couch.

I feel like I'm going to vomit. He's going to kill us, all three of us. Oh my God, Daisy. I've got to save us for Daisy.

"You're going to have to answer for your behavior, Katherine," Gregory shouts.

"I never," Katherine gasps, "I never broke your confidentiality. I promise. Please, sit down like Alyssa said. Let's talk."

I watch Katherine taking in gulps of air. I look back at Gregory. He grabs his gun from his holster and holds it out pointing at Katherine. "Gregory, no!" I scream.

Autobiography in Five Short Chapters
Chapter Five

I walk down another street.

—Portia Nelson

Chapter 22

Alyssa

The E.R. waiting room is oddly quiet. Every other patient has some sort of surfing or skateboard accident—everyone except Katherine. Seth and I are slumped in a corner waiting for Katherine's husband Carl to arrive. I'll never be able to shake off the dread of this hospital—this just adds to the many bad associations. Back in October when Gregory and I followed the ambulance over, I remember how it ripped me apart to be pushed out of the room, my daughter separated from me, hearing the frenzy of the emergency room staff as they tried to bring her back. The dark wooded front desk, the painting of the hibiscus flower on the wall, the piercing beep of machines intended to save lives; they're all horrific reminders that she couldn't be saved.

"I knew just by the way the doctor looked at me, that she didn't make it…that they couldn't bring her back," I say.

Seth looks at me, puzzled, and then acknowledgement washes over him. A look of anguish blankets his face. "I'm so sorry I wasn't there for you. So, so sorry."

I nod and let him comfort me; it's so overdue.

The slider doors whiz open and a frazzled, gray-haired man rushes in scanning the room. "I'm looking for my wife, Katherine Middlebrook," he says to the admissions personnel.

She tells him she'll buzz him in. We stand and I make eye contact with Katherine's husband. "Are you the couple who called me?" He's winded and his eyes dance with fear.

"We are," I answer. "You must be Carl." Thankfully, I'd remembered his name from Katherine's reference to him in a therapy session, and found his number in her cell phone contacts.

"Yes, thank you." He places a warm hold on my shoulder. His eyes tell me how deeply in love he is with Katherine and how frightened he is...I know this fear. "You two can go. Thanks so much for staying." He reaches for the doorknob.

"We'll be right here," Seth returns. Carl looks at him, perplexed, then leaves us behind.

I lay down across Seth's lap. The hard chairs are getting to me and I've been sleepless the last few days leading up to what was to be our "big session." Carl looked out of his mind. I know from what Katherine told me about losing Nicole that she and Carl have been together forever. To be married longer than to have not...it's hard to imagine the type of bond they have. Lying here on Seth's lap, I want that feeling, that familiarity, that security.

Within a couple of hours, more and more people are streaming in with lacerations, limps, and coughs. Seth and I tell the woman at the admitting desk that we're walking over to the solarium; it's a less sterile environment where plants and flowers supply a garden-like atmosphere. We find a wooden bench inside the solarium and collapse. Even though we're in the midst of another crisis, although completely different, we need to say what we didn't get to say at Katherine's.

"I hope we can get to where they are," I say.

"Who?" Seth asks, looking around.

"Carl and Katherine. You know, older, wiser, forgiving." He's quiet. I feel a tinge of fear. "I never talked to Katherine about

Gregory, you know," I begin, feeling a jolt of anxiety take off like a spark surging through me. I'm really going to talk about this.

"I figured. Now I get it...how she knew but couldn't say how she knew. What a frickin' mess. He was her client, too," Seth says, referring to Gregory.

"How did she keep it all straight?"

Seth shakes his head. His posture is rigid; we're moving into difficult territory. I take his hand. He doesn't grip it back. "Seth," I say, looking up at his eyes. He avoids eye contact at first, then relents. "I was faithful to you before Nevaeh died...even after until recently...after Christmas—"

He holds up his other hand. "Spare me all the details. I know...I know you didn't...have anything going on before. I'm not an idiot, though. He's been trying to split us up since day one. He's been in love with you forever. How did you not see that? It used to drive me nuts!"

"Sorry." It's my new favorite word. "I do see that now, although it's not love, Seth. He wanted to own me...possess me." I have felt that since childhood—Gregory was insanely jealous when anyone came before him. "I'm sorry that I let him in."

He nods and stays quiet for a while, then gets up and paces in front of the lush, green ferns. "I've learned a lot over these past few months, Alyssa. I know I wasn't a saint. Forgiveness is a process, though. It's going to take time...for both of us I guess."

It's like I'm talking to a stranger in some ways. I think I've never known the man under the mask. He's even more beautiful now. Gone is the tough exterior of intimidation that announces to the world: Don't cross me. I stand and take his hands like a couple before a minister. Our rings meet with a metal ting as he squeezes my hand this time, then brings it up to his lips and kisses the back of my hand.

Seth

The fog feels like it's seeping through the windows. Alyssa's shivering. I make my way out to the parking lot to get a blanket from my truck, hoping I can dig around and find a spare cigarette under the seat—I need one more to get through the night. As I'm jogging through the parking lot, I recognize a woman running toward the main hospital doors; it's Leah. After reaching Carl back at Katherine's office, Carl had instructed me to call Leah, Katherine's dearest friend. Hearing this was another head scratcher for me. Talk about six degrees of separation.

"Leah," I call out.

She spins around, her wild, long, grey hair flying in the opposite direction. "Oh, Seth. How's Katherine?" she pants; worry painted across her forehead.

"I don't know yet. Carl's in with her." I point over to the solarium and continue, "Alyssa and I are waiting in there, checking in periodically."

Leah rubs her hands across her face; she's crying. I'm taken aback. "You were there, huh?" she asks.

"Yeah."

"You'll have to fill me in later. I want to get in there," she says, turning to go inside the hospital. "Katherine was right about you all along," she calls out over her shoulder. "You're a good guy, Seth."

I'm stunned once again. This night is filled with one surprise after another. I can only think of a handful of times that someone told me I was "good." Daisy told me I was a good storyteller. An old lover used to tell me I was good in bed. No one's ever commented about me, my character, being good. Rocco said I'd be in for more than just self-examination and making amends to others. He said I'll need to learn to love and accept myself, mistakes, failures, and all, or I'll never stay clean. I replay Leah's words over and over, trying them on like a new pair of shoes, '…you're a good guy, Seth.'—They're a little uncomfortable, but over time, they'll feel all right.

I grab the blanket, forget about the cigarette, and head back up. With every step I take toward the hospital, I tell myself that now's the time to fill Alyssa in on some of my thoughts…new understandings. I feel more anxious than I did the first night we went out. She's lying down on the bench and looks like an angel. I don't want to startle her. I gently lay the blanket over her that I retrieved from the car. She shifts and lets out a sigh. An hour later, I'm still walking around with my hands in my pockets, willing her to wake up—I can't take the waiting.

"I dozed off. Sorry," she apologizes, sitting up sometime after 10:00. "How's Katherine?"

"They don't know, or at least they aren't saying."

"You want to get some coffee?"

"No, I'm kind of coffeed out," I say. "You think you're awake enough to hear me out?"

"Sure, I'm fine. Here, sit down. You must be exhausted."

"No, not really. My adrenalin's keeping me going." That's an understatement. I sit beside Alyssa and take a big breath. Time for "the speech."

"I know I checked out of our marriage a long time ago. Maybe even checked out of life. I never said what was on my mind and if I didn't agree with you on something, I'd snap or just blow you off. Part of my work in therapy and with Rocco is keeping a journal of my feelings, what sets me off, what hurts. I'm learning to "tune in" Katherine says."

"I had no idea you even saw that in yourself," Alyssa says, her voice filled with awe.

"Well, I didn't. It took…" the unspoken that needs to be spoken… "…this disaster to snap me out of it. I wish it could have been something else other than our daughter's death." I shudder. "I hate saying that, but Katherine says it's important to say it, 'her death', rather than dancing around, avoiding the words."

"I know," she says. "She tells me the same thing."

"I'm gonna be working on this stuff, recovery, not hiding my feelings, for a while. Forever. You know that, right? I'm going to fall down, disappoint you, and be an ass once in a while, but I'm working hard to be different…better. Good. A good man."

"You already are, Seth...better...and you've always been a good man, just lost...like me. I've spent so much time worrying about not turning into my mother that I nearly lost myself and our family in the process. It's going to take a lot of work to rebuild our relationship but we can try, can't we?"

I stand up and shove my hands in my pockets, unable to look directly at her as I form my next sentence. "There's one condition, 'Lyss. Whatever happens with Gregory, charges or not, your friendship with him is over. No more Uncle Gregory, no keys to the house, no visits during holidays or any days. It's over." This is it...this is the first test.

She nods, blinking away a tear...for who I'm unsure. "It's over," she says and reaches for my hand.

Alyssa

It's amazing to hear Seth speak with so much depth. Prior to having Daisy, other than talking about surf conditions, the girls, or telling a story to them, I've never heard him talk that much period. I'd like to think that Katherine would be proud of us right now. She has to be okay. She needs to hear how our session went; the one she prepared us for, but one that we led all on our own.

Katherine

Out of the corner of my eye, a very young doctor, young enough to be my son, is talking. I hear my name. I blink, trying to get everything into focus, then bring my hand up to rub my eye when I realize that tubes and wires are connected to my arms and chest. I know I'm in the hospital, but I can't figure out why or how I got here.

"Hello," I call out, hearing my voice resemble the croak of a frog.

"Katherine," the doctor calls out. "She's alert. Let's get a read on her vitals." He's calling out orders, sounding very serious, but kind.

Out of Breath

I squint, trying to make out the time on the clock that's in the hallway—3:00. Is it afternoon or morning? It's impossible to tell in here with no windows and artificial light. I want to pull out all these tubes and wires and get out of here. I spent enough time in hospitals with Nicole to last a lifetime.

The young, clean-shaven doctor is by my side along with a nurse who looks like she could be in music videos. Thirty years ago, I can't recall hospital personnel looking so soap-opera perfect. "How are you feeling?" asks the chisel-faced, young doc.

"Confused. Tired."

"I'm Dr. Stone."

"Hello, Dr. Stone."

"Do you remember how you got here?"

He's quizzing me. "Carl?" It's my best guess.

"Actually," he starts, correcting me as he looks into my eyes with a bright, little light, "you arrived by ambulance." He points to the ceiling with a dot of light. "Look up. Good. Any of that sound familiar?"

Ambulance? No. I shake my head.

"The medic says that you collapsed during a therapy session that was about to start. A couple was with you and an officer barged in during your session...another patient of yours."

A session. I was in a session with Seth and Alyssa. Greg came in. There was a gun. I start to pat my body down, looking for evidence of a gunshot. "I'm okay?" I ask. "Did you remove the bullet?"

Beautiful Dr. Stone offers a weak smile. "No bullets today, I'm afraid. We're still waiting for some of your tests to come back, but it looks as though we're dealing with some irregularities in your heart. It's quite common that these go undiagnosed until there's a problem. We need to find out what's causing it and how we can treat it, okay?"

"Okay," I answer, feeling about three years old, waiting for the doctor to hand me a lollypop. "Your sister and husband are here and would like to say 'hello.'"

Sister? Heart trouble? What about the gun? Suddenly, I sit up, practically fainting and setting off all sorts of bells. "Dr. Stone," I shout, although it's more like a loud whisper. He comes back in, asks me to lie back down, and turns off the various beeps and adjusts some of the leads. "Was anyone else brought in for a gunshot wound tonight? The couple I was seeing?" My heart races as I consider the possibilities. I remember Greg brandishing his gun, pointing it at me, and Alyssa screaming. If anyone would take a bullet for me, it would be Seth.

"We haven't had anyone brought in for a gunshot tonight. If someone was shot, it's possible that they were air lifted to Valley Medical."

"Can you please check for me? I'm worried that one of my clients may have been injured tonight."

"I'll see what I can do. You need to look out for yourself right now. Sit back and rest. I'll bring your family in."

I can't rest, wondering if Seth or Alyssa, or both of them are injured…or worse. The curtain opens and in walks Leah and Carl. "Look who's awake? My little sister," Leah teases.

Carl rushes over to me, tears pouring down his face. "Katherine. Oh, I'm so glad you're all right. I'm so sorry I wasn't home. Bastard."

I'm still a little foggy about what happened to me and why I'm here. All I care about is finding out if Seth and Alyssa are okay. "Were there any shots fired? Is everyone okay? How are Seth and Alyssa?"

Carl and Leah shake their heads and Leah answers, "Okay, Kath, time to focus, here. You are in the hospital and need to worry about yourself. Everyone's fine. No shots were fired."

Carl throws Leah a look. "And you know this, how?"

Leah shoots him a stare, ignoring his question and continues, "That reminds me," Leah says, turning to Carl, "we need to update them after we catch up with Mother Teresa here."

I ignore her sarcastic dig. "Update who? Oh heavens, Carl, you didn't call the kids did you? Don't tell me they're here?"

Out of Breath

"No, Katherine, your clients; Seth, Alyssa."

My eyes lock with Leah, scorning her for breaking their confidentiality. She reads my non-verbal scold and replies, "It's a little late for a breach in confidentiality. They're the ones who called Carl, met him in the lobby, told him about what happened tonight."

I breathe. "Oh. Wait, they're here?"

"They want to be sure you're okay. They've been here all night waiting," Leah says proudly.

"No kidding?"

"No kidding."

I reach for Leah's arm with the hand that isn't gripped by Carl's. We lace fingers. I can finally think about myself. "Am I really okay, you guys? Don't hide anything from me."

"Us? And experience your wrath," Leah toys.

Carl squeezes my hand. "You're fine. They think you've had an undiagnosed heart problem probably for years. The doctor said it's unusual that you weren't experiencing any symptoms given how you collapsed. The stress of today, or I guess I should say, yesterday, aggravated things, but I told them you've been feeling fine."

I look away, ashamed.

"Katherine. I'm right, aren't I? You've been feeling fine?" Carl asks with an edge to his voice.

I shrug. "There's been...things...stuff I've been noticing." Carl drops my hand, rolls his eyes, and shakes his head.

"Jesus, Katherine, so I was right that night down at Mr. Toots. Only it's a little more than Compassion Fatigue. When were you going to look into that? What kinds of things?"

I feel like a child who's in trouble. "Dizziness, shortness of breath sometimes, feeling scatter brained. I've had a lot going on this year with Mom," I pause and look at Leah, "and other stuff at work." Then, like a punch to the gut, I realize we're all here and my mother's at home! "Mom! Who's watching Mom?"

Leah crouches beside me, pulling up a chair. "Relax, tiger. I took care of it. I stayed with her until a Hospice volunteer could make it over. She was asleep when I left and seemed okay. Now, see, this is just the thing the doctor wants you to stop doing, putting the whole world before you. Christ, even in the hospital, you're trying to orchestrate everyone's life and make sure they're okay."

Her words sting and I fold.

"Oh God, now don't go crying. Come on Carl, let's give her a hug and make her better."

I laugh through my tears. What would I do without these two? Carl holds me, kissing me gently on the cheek, whispering, "I love you. You're going to be okay. Shh."

"I'm tired. I think I'm going to shut my eyes a bit."

"Atta girl. Come on, Carl; let's let her get some rest. God knows we'll be here until next summer. We'll see you in a bit, sugar." Leah kisses my forehead and Carl gives me another kiss on the cheek.

Leah

We leave Katherine's room, but Carl stops me before we walk out into the lobby to try to find Seth and Alyssa. "I should've noticed she wasn't herself. Why didn't I see?" He's still blubbering.

"Oh, come on you big baby. She's going to be fine. She has to be. Who would hold us all together and keep saving the world?"

"I'm serious, Leah. Why didn't I notice?"

Carl looks about eighty years old from worry. "I know. This scared the crap out of me too. But you heard the doctor; he doesn't think it's anything serious. Maybe it's a wakeup call for Katherine. Time for her to look at herself for once."

"That bastard is going to pay, Leah. Why'd he go after Katherine, anyway? What the hell happened? You seem to know more than you're letting on."

Since all bets are off and everyone's confidentiality is a moot point, I begin to spell things out for Carl. I tell him about Seth and Alyssa's separation, the affair I finally put together between Greg and Alyssa, and the fact that Greg didn't know that he, Seth, and Alyssa shared the same therapist. "He thought Katherine was colluding…it was crazy keeping it all straight; the worst of cases. Don't worry about it though. That's over now."

"What? How? I mean, how do you know?"

"It's a small town, Carl. I got a friend down at the Sherriff's office. I called while I was waiting for the hospice worker to show. He told me that one of the medics back at your place recognized Greg before he ducked out amidst all the chaos. The Sherriff's office sent out an APB on him."

"And they got him?"

I pause, imagining the scene, and shudder. "Not exactly."

Carl's face flushes. "He fled?"

I put my hand on his shoulder and squeeze it. "They sent a couple guys over to arrest him. When they got there, his gun cleaning kit was on the coffee table." I pause to see if Carl gets it. He continues to look confused, so I start to spell it out. "He made it look like an accident."

Carl shakes his head. "I'm not following you, Leah."

"He shot himself, Carl. Made it look like an accident, like he was cleaning his gun. It's not uncommon. It's a way of protecting his family."

"Jesus Christ."

"Yeah." I think about how this is going to really shake up Katherine and Alyssa. "I'll notify Seth and Alyssa tomorrow. We'll see how Katherine's doing in the morning before I say anything. God knows she'll be poking around, figuring out what happened on her own if I don't tell her soon."

"Thanks, Leah…for being there for Katherine. For us. I don't tell you that often enough."

"No, you don't, but then again, I say a lot to piss you off." I chuckle and slug Carl in the shoulder. That's all I need is Carl getting more emotional with me; I'm a hair away from bawling my eyes out as it is. "Hey," I start, shaking back the tears, "you do know what brought Seth and Alyssa in, don't you." Carl shakes his head. "Their baby died."

All the color drains from Carl's face. I've said nothing of the drowning. I feel like that's up to the Buchanans; they're entitled to some measure of privacy. "What's up, Carl? You look like you've seen a ghost."

"Their baby died? And she agreed to see them?" He says, sinking back against the wall.

"Yeah, so?"

Carl searches my face like he's looking for something. "You don't know, do you? All these years as friends and she never told you?"

Now I'm confused. "Never told me what?"

"About us. About Nicole."

"Who's Nicole?"

"Our baby. The baby we lost."

My brain's just been shaken like a game of Boggle and the letters aren't quite settling into place. Here I've been involved in the daily life of Katherine and Carl Middlebrook, attended every stinkin' birthday for their children the last umpteen years, and spilled my guts about every corner of my heart to Katherine, and she has this little gem that she's never shared. Christ! Carl spends the next few minutes catching me up.

The piece of the puzzle that's missing: painful, intrusive memories. "She should've told me. I would have never asked her to take this case. In all these years, this has been lurking in her thoughts as she's dodged case after case where a baby's died. I should've put it together. That explains the extra stress she felt. Hell, it was messy enough even without that." I wonder if she ever told the Buchanans. "This is a lot to take in."

Carl squeezes my shoulder. "Go home and get some rest. I'll call you in the morning."

"Maybe I will. I'm pretty bushed. Give Katherine a kiss for me and tell her I'm gonna kick her in the ass for keeping such a big secret from me."

Carl smiles and we open the doors to the lobby. "Let me walk you out."

I roll my eyes. "Seriously, Carl. I'm fine."

Out of Breath

It's nearly 4:00 in the morning. We walk, silent, through the empty, quiet hallways of the hospital. Once outside, my eyes fix on the solarium where Alyssa and Seth have been holding vigil all night. They're not so different from Carl and Katherine, knowing another level of unthinkable grief. A tattered, Mexican blanket covers them as they sleep. I look at Carl and we both give a nod and head toward the door.

I try not to startle them as we enter. Alyssa sits up and nudges Seth awake.

"Sorry. Didn't mean to wake you guys," I apologize.

"No, no, don't be sorry. How's Katherine?" Seth asks.

We squat beside them. Carl groans.

"She's doing well," Carl begins. "Her collapsing was most likely due to an undiagnosed heart condition—cardiac dysrhythmia. Her heart essentially gets out of rhythm. It's treatable with medication."

Both Alyssa and Seth breathe a sigh of relief.

"In a way, it's a wake up call for Katherine. Maybe she'll learn to slow down and not chase so many rabbits at once," I jump in, unsure that Katherine's capable of anything that doesn't involve a dozen things pulling at her at once.

Alyssa hugs herself and directs her attention to Carl. "Katherine has been like an angel to us over the past several months." Alyssa grabs hold of Seth's hand and squeezes it as they exchange a private moment. "I don't know if you know, maybe Leah's filled you in, but we're the couple who lost a child last Halloween night."

Carl looks at me with a bewildered expression, as if to say, "*This* is who they are?"

"Our baby drowned up at the school."

Carl sways and looks like he might fall over. Maybe the toll of this night is catching up to him.

"I uh…" he looks back and forth between Seth and Alyssa, then over at me, "I read about it. I'm so sorry." He withdraws a handkerchief and pats his head. His emotional reaction has me whirling.

"Come on, old man, let's get you home," I say.

"Just a minute. I'm fine," he says sternly. "Tell me, what was... what was your daughter's name?"

"Nevaeh," Seth and Alyssa say in unison.

"Nevaeh. It's beautiful. How did you come up with that name?"

Alyssa's breath catches and Seth gives her a one-armed squeeze. "It's heaven spelled backwards."

Carl tears up. I've never seen him cry; tonight he can't stop.

"We lost a baby, too, Katherine and I. I guess she may have told you."

"She did," Alyssa says. "Nicole, right?" Alyssa's voice soft as silk.

"Yes. Nicole."

This moment is so private. I feel like an intruder. I grab Carl's hand, feeling the rough calluses from fence building and "Katherine-to-do-lists."

"I'm sorry for your loss, too. Katherine says it gets better, but it never quite goes away," Alyssa says.

"She's right," he answers, pushing himself up with a grunt. He shakes his head. "She's right." Carl extends his hand to shake Seth's, but is pulled into a deep hug, instead. Carl chuckles and awkward chuckle.

As they break, I am pulled in to Seth's chest as Alyssa drapes her arms around Carl. It's an outright love fest and I need to get out of here before my eyes start to water.

"Thank you again for calling me and staying here all night. That was really something," Carl says.

We say good-night again and head back out to the early morning.

"You all right, old man?"

Carl nods. "Yeah. I'm okay."

"You looked like you saw a ghost when they told you who they were." I pause and search Carl's face for an answer. He shakes his head and blows his nose. "You wanna talk about it?"

He scoffs. "I didn't know. I didn't realize it was them; the couple I read about in the paper way back when Katherine probably took the case."

He's figuring out why this case took a toll on Katherine. Shoot, so am I.

"It explains so much," Carl says. "The dizzy spells, sleepless nights, moodiness like I'd never seen. I didn't know. I would have listened. I could have been there for her like I should have back then."

I turn Carl to face me and plant a giant kiss on his lips. He jumps back like I've electrocuted him. "Don't get excited! You're not quite my type." I pause and we giggle. "Oh, Carl, it's taken you a few years, but you're getting it!"

We arrive at my jalopy of a car. The creak of the rusty door spills into the quiet of the night. "Go on, now. I'll see you after I catch up on my beauty sleep."

Alyssa

Daisy starts school in just a few hours. Thank God Oma's here for us…again. She said she's been praying for Katherine all night. What's between Oma and God seems to be working: more than one of her prayers seems to have been answered.

I'm finally feeling the effects of the last twenty-four hours. My muscles ache and I need some serious sleep. I wonder where Seth and I will go from here.

"I guess we should go get my car up at Katherine's, huh?" I ask, as we head for Seth's truck in the hospital parking lot.

"We can do that later. Let's go home."

Home.

Like a teenager, I slide beside him and curl into his side, feeling the weight of his arm around me. More than once I nod off. The house is cold and quiet. Duke greets us, wagging his tail, his collar jingling as he lumbers towards us. I flick on the light and see that there's something on the table. It's a basket, a note, and a vase of daisies. Seth walks over beside me and we read the note together.

Dearest Seth and Alyssa-

I knew it might be late when you finally made it home, so Daisy and I made you some muffins to nibble on. Sleep in. I'll take Daisy to school and walk her home to my house for lunch...later if you need. Remember the words of our Lord in the book of 2 Corinthians, the old has gone, the new has come.

Gute Nacht-
Oma

She knew Seth would come home.

We say nothing and turn out the light. Seth takes my hand and leads me down the hallway as if it was any other night in our life together. We walk past the pictures lining the hallway that describe an early chapter of our life; one of innocence and ignorance; a life that portrayed the façade of happiness but was riddled with emptiness and confusion. Yet, it was a life with two children rather than one. I don't want to look back, and so I look forward to what is beginning, what is new.

When I wake, tangled up in Seth whose warmth takes the deep chill off my bones, I whisper a word of thanks to God. I slip from the bed. Seth moans, turns over, and continues to sleep. I part the curtain and look up toward heaven. It's always in these first hours of waking that I feel a direct line to Nevaeh, as though the world, still quiet, stands still for the communication of souls. "You had a hand in this, didn't you, little one?" I whisper.

Oma is right, the old is past. I'm ready to go forward holding Nevaeh in my heart. I pray that God forgives my infidelity and that in time, so does Seth. I pray that our marriage can be restored... actually, be different, better, full of life. And I whisper, for the first time, a prayer of thanks...for the short moments I had with Nevaeh. Every one of them is precious and each a gift. I know now that Nevaeh and Daisy have taught me more about love and forgiveness than I ever thought possible, that I've merely tapped the abundance of grace that exists.

Seth stirs and reaches for me. I close the curtain and climb back into bed. I've finally found rest. The new has come.

Epilogue Five Years Later

Alyssa

Seth and Daisy are side by side, zipping up the back of their wetsuits at the water's edge. Already at ten, Daisy stands just below Seth's shoulder, the two of them like long, thin seals with legs. I never quite know what goes on inside her. In her, I can see the familiar storms that used to brew in Seth. With enough space and hugs, she shares her feelings, but only in spurts. She is fiercely protective and nurturing of little children, saying that she's going to be a preschool teacher when she grows up. She's done four consecutive years of junior lifeguard training. Watching her in the water, I never quite relax. Dr. Fowler, who she continues to see periodically, says that Daisy meets her fears head on every time she dives into the water; that children are wise and resilient.

A few feet away from me, Skye chases after a sandpiper. His little feet leave deep footprints along the shore. I resist the urge to shout out, "Be careful!" Skye was our surprise after nearly three years of worry that I could never love another child or enjoy a breath without the fear of death ripping him or her from my life. Oma says that God sent Skye to us for a lesson in faith. After his first birthday, I was completely unprepared for the rush of grief that temporarily swallowed me. Trips to the beach, walks through the park, not to mention, attending the Harvest Fair, were all terrifying events, as if the Grim Reaper lurked amongst each event, waiting to snatch my baby. I worried over Seth's sobriety. I guess I wasn't the only one worrying about that; Seth went to nightly meetings in October.

Behind me on the dry sand is my team that led me from the darkness of "that year"— Oma, Carolyn, a handful of other relatives, some old friends, some new from my parental bereavement group, and Katherine and Leah. Katherine saw us through our second year of recovery after taking a few months off to grieve her mother's death and evaluate her hectic schedule.

Today marks five years since Nevaeh died. Over the summer, we decided it was time to scatter the remainder of her ashes this fall. Natural Bridges State Beach seemed like the best place to commemorate her life given that the monarch butterflies are making their return to huddle in the eucalyptus trees in the grove above. Their beauty always captivated Nevaeh; we called them little fairies.

After the mess of Seth's and my separation and the courts involvement in our lives, Seth never actually moved back to our home; too much history. Instead, the two of us found a small cottage on the east side. The day the moving truck arrived to load what we would take with us, I awoke early and unsettled. I was ready to leave, that I was sure. Too much pain and confusion wallpapered the house. But I would miss the reminders of Nevaeh's short life with us. I could still see her in every inch of the house. If I closed my eyes, I could hear her little feet patting down the hardwood floors.

Before I packed up the final box with cleaning supplies, I grabbed a shovel I'd left out in the garage, slipped out into the backyard, and dug in the dry, summer dirt. I knew it was a risk to disrupt them at this stage, but I wasn't going to leave those tulip bulbs buried. They were one of the last tangible things I had left of Nevaeh and they were coming with me.

Early in my therapy, Katherine had let me borrow a handful of bereavement books. I remember reading in one how death opened the door to new life. I had thrown the book across the room. Now, I was beginning to understand. Just four months after moving into our place in La Selva Beach, Seth's mother died of cirrhosis. When we went to clean out her place, we found a long letter of regret addressed to him. In her absence, something inside of Seth was set free, like a caged bird taking flight. In a session with Katherine shortly thereafter, Katherine asked us a simple question: What would you attempt to do if you knew you could not fail? Without hesitation, Seth said, "I'd want to work with kids who were like me…lost, alone, heading for addiction. I see myself taking them on surf trips, hanging out with them, kind a like taking them in and offering a safe house."

"So what's stopping you?" Katherine had asked.

Within a year, Seth had pitched the idea to numerous surf shops, community groups, churches, and charitable clubs, asking for their financial and practical support. Together we opened a non-profit surf company dedicated to wayward kids; we call it *Bailing Out*. A well-known owner of a successful surf shop became our primary financial supporter. He donates supplies and money for plane tickets for the kids. Seth wishes he could sell his business and devote all his time to *Bailing Out*, but the reality of bills keeps him straining to find that 25th hour in the day. I have fallen in love with my husband in a way I never thought possible as I watch the pain and passion of his life transform hopeless, angry, and emotionally abandoned kids into role models and leaders.

I am now the mother to many. Our door and kitchen remain open. Teaching turned out to be my calling, but not in the classroom. Instead, it's done in our living room, around our huge oak kitchen table, on plane rides down to Costa Rica, or over a campfire down on the beach.

It took nearly five years, but we finally found our breath.

Katherine

Like a proud parent on graduation day, I watch Seth and Alyssa and their two children as they prepare to scatter Nevaeh's ashes. Leah and I pass tissues back and forth to one another; Carl looks on with a faraway look. We visited Nicole's grave this morning…it felt like the right thing to do. We frequently go to the cemetery now. Alyssa and Seth tell me that I led them through the hardest time in their lives. The truth is, they woke me up from my slumber of hidden grief.

The three of us were mutually shocked and derailed by Greg's suicide. I'd never lost a client due to a suicide. I scrambled to find clues, signs, a mistaken diagnosis. When it comes down to it, I'm like the surviving spouse, friend, or loved one, echoing the sentiment, "I had no idea he was this despondent." His battle with depression was masked with his rage—the elusive client with deep wounds. Under all that rage was a sad, defeated young man. He left no letter, unanswered questions will plague us. Alyssa took his death particularly hard. Self-blame is part of the puzzle for most bereaved by suicide; it was huge for Alyssa. Her guilt would have swallowed her had she not plugged into a suicide bereavement support group. That and Seth's newly acquired gift of listening without judgment shored her up.

When Mom died just days after I collapsed, it finalized my decision to take a break from counseling. I thought I'd get bored. I didn't. I thought I'd be under stimulated. I wasn't. I think I'd been burning out for several years, sacrificing my happiness and health while placing everyone's needs above my own. It's as if I'd been lugging a giant backpack filled with the pain of hundreds. It made me strong, but I was ready to delegate the load to others. Now I feel like the monarchs that flitter overhead: light and carefree.

Seth

Daisy and I paddle out for about thirty yards or so. We're silent. We get beyond the sets where the water is still as glass.

"You doin' okay, Daiz?"

She nods her head and offers a weak smile. I look behind us to see our tribe who are here for this moment. The chorus of birds and sea lions makes me smile. Bobbing up and down on my board, I pull out the bag of ashes and along with it, a thin strip of Nevaeh's blanket. It's taken me the past five years to forgive myself for not being present for my family. I don't know about forgiving myself for not watching Nevaeh. It is my recurring prayer that my guilt not rip me apart and that over time I can release the shame like a bag of ash. I'm humble enough to know that I'm one drink or joint away from screwing things up again. Humility is new, but it's growing on me.

I think back to the nights that the girls were little. They'd be dressed in their matching flannel pajamas, Daisy begging for a story, Nevaeh bouncing up and down on my knee as though she couldn't contain her excitement. The memory of her is growing faint. Seventeen months is all that I had her. I barely remembered the sound of her voice until Skye was born. Hell if he didn't have the same speech pattern, dropping his "l's" and "r's". I about fell apart the first time he started talking.

What I do remember is the way her kisses left my face wet; how tiny her fingers were wrapped around one of mine; the way she liked to rub noses with me before nodding off to sleep. Maybe I remember more than I thought; it still stings…remembering.

"Ready?" I ask Daisy.

"Yup."

I pour the ashes out of the Ziploc bag into my hand. The silkiness of the blanket contrasts with the powdery-pebbly mixture of ash. I squeeze them, then toss them into the air. Some bits hit the ocean quickly, like pebbles in a lake, while others drift with the breeze. Daisy removes the gardenia leis that she, Oma, and Alyssa strung. One by one, she tosses them into the sea.

"You're my girl, Daisy," I say, grabbing her hand.

"I know, Daddy."

It's our code…our way of saying 'I love you.'

Alyssa

People dab at their eyes. Oma holds my hand and gives it a tight squeeze. I adjust Skye on my hip and watch his smiling eyes. I feel Gregory's absence in a deep way today. I do miss him. Not in the way that we ended up, but in the way we began. I don't think he meant for things to get so out of control. Losing his friendship was hard enough; losing him entirely is brutal. He was like family. I wish I could go back and change the direction of our friendship. Maybe he'd still be alive. Then again, I'm learning that those left behind by a suicide death always replay the day, the week, the year before the suicide, second guessing every conversation, thinking, 'I could have prevented this.' It's a fallacy, but one I continue to wrestle with. Two losses in the space of a year was grueling; Gregory was so alone.

Skye grabs my face the way he does when he wants my immediate attention. "What they doing, Mommy?" If we thought our other two were precocious, Skye knocked them out of the park. At eighteen-months-old, he was speaking in full sentences, filling any moment of silence with the song of his voice.

"They're letting Nevaeh's ashes go."

He cocks his head. Even though we've explained what this day would entail, we know a two-year-old can't quite grasp that he had a sister who died a few years back, let alone, whose ashes are being scattered. A fluffy cloud billows overhead. I point to it and say, "Look, there she goes," as though she's being carried away on a cloud.

"Who?"

"Baby Nevaeh," I answer.

"Where she going?" he asks, mouth parted, as he squints up at the cloud.

"There," I point.

"I don' see her."

"See way, way up in those clouds where that puffy one is? Above that is heaven and that's where Nevaeh is. She'll always be our little baby in the heavens." My throat constricts and tears sting my cheeks.

Skye's face brightens. "Oh, yeah, I fink I see her now. Dere she is. Dere's baby Nevaeh."

Nevaeh will forever remain my piece of heaven who toddled at my side with her blond mound of curls bobbing as she bounced along. I can't believe that she'd be six and a half now. The memories of her are growing foggier; something that makes my heart hurt almost as much as losing her to death. I've recently started watching our home movies of Daisy and her. Sometimes Seth will join me. Other times, he says it pushes him too far to the edge, wanting to numb the pain. I don't know if either of us has moved past the guilt of not watching her that night. We're great at extending forgiveness to one another, but not so much for ourselves. Katherine says that time is the greatest healer, to trust the process. She'd know.

That first year with Katherine was bitter sweet; I've grown in so many ways. Learning to try to forgive my mother is one of them. Now when she writes, I write back. When she calls, I'm less apt to make an excuse and hang up after talking for only five minutes. She's promised to come out every year, but has yet to come. I see now that she's limited. I'm learning to mother myself and allow the love of other wonderful women in my life to be like caulking that fills the cracks.

I put Skye down. The feeling returns to my arms. "Look, here comes Daddy and Daisy." They walk up on shore, dripping wet, with their boards under their arms.

"Hey buddy," Daisy says, squeezing her waist-long brown hair onto the top of Skye's blond bob. He laughs and protests by slapping her thigh. They're siblings all right. Daisy peels off her wetsuit and wraps a towel around her waist. "I'll race you up the hill to the monarch trail. Bet you can't beat me," she teases.

Skye's bright blue eyes widen and he purses his lips. "Oh yes I can," he says with his brow knit and teeth clenched as he tears up the hill, kicking sand behind him.

Seth unzips his wetsuit and lets the top half hang down, revealing his bare chest—he's still the sexy twenty-something surfer I saw coming up the beach stairs, even though he's approaching forty. He pulls me into him, kisses the top of my head, then reaches down to finger the necklace he gave me after Skye's birth: a silver figurine of a mother embracing her three children. I kiss him. "Thank you."

"For what?"

"Just...thank you."

We follow the crowd up the paved path. Bits of conversation spill into the autumn breeze. We join one another again in silence on the monarch trail where we stand in awe of the thousands of butterflies that have gathered to roost until spring.

About the Author:

Susan Salluce, MA, CT, holds a Master's Degree in Counseling Psychology and is a Certified Thanatologist—a death, dying, and bereavement specialist. With a passion for writing, impacting the bereaved, and having experienced her own sense of compassion fatigue, she wrote *Out of Breath*.

Susan continues to contribute to the field of bereavement through her writing, consultant work, and her work with Friends for Survival, a non-profit dedicated to those affected by a suicide death. She is currently at work on a parenting book based on her blog and a chic-lit book due out by 2013.

When Susan is not working on her novels, you can find her either in the foothills of the Sierra Nevada's or on the beaches of Aptos, Ca. What she truly calls home is anywhere she is with her amazing, loyal, and fun children, Kellen and Marina, and with her best friend/husband of twenty-three years, John.

Please visit her website at: http://www.sipnsharewithsusan.com and on Facebook at: https://www.facebook.com/pages/Susan-Salluce/154860991268296

Author photo by Bob Thomas, www.TheImageArtCompany.com